THE YANDILLI TRILOGY

Rodney Hall was born in England in 1935. He was taken to Australia as a schoolboy. Having left school at sixteen he began supplementing his daytime earnings by occasional work as an actor and as a baroque recorder player. He resumed his formal education at thirty-three at Queensland University. He has three daughters and lives with his wife on the coast of New South Wales.

Rodney Hall's work has been published in Australia since 1962. He has written two biographies, eleven collections of poetry and six novels. *The Grisly Wife* won Australia's premier literary prize, the Miles Franklin Award, in 1994 and *Captivity Captive* won the Victorian Premier's Prize for fiction in 1988.

by the same author

JUST RELATIONS
KISSES OF THE ENEMY

RODNEY HALL

The Yandilli Trilogy

faber and faber
LONDON · BOSTON

This paperback edition first published in Great Britain
in 1994 by Faber and Faber Limited
3 Queen Square London WC1N 3AU

Captivity Captive first published in Great Britain
in 1988 by Faber and Faber Limited
The Second Bridegroom first published in Great Britain
in 1991 by Faber and Faber Limited
The Grisly Wife first published in Great Britain
in 1993 by Faber and Faber Limited

Phototypeset by Intype, London
Printed in England by Clays Ltd, St Ives plc

A CIP record for this book
is available from the British Library

ISBN 0-571-17416-7

2 4 6 8 10 9 7 5 3 1

FOR MY MOTHER

with gratitude for
that irreplaceable gift, a happy childhood,
and for taking the courageous step in 1949
– as a widow with three children and
neither money nor prospects –
of returning to Australia

Contents

ACKNOWLEDGEMENTS

I am grateful to my dear wife Bet and my daughters Imogen, Delia and Cressida, who all helped me and enriched my life during the writing of this trilogy.

My editors in Australia, the USA and the UK contributed valuable advice and encouragement for each separate volume – Pat Strachan, Hilary McPhee, Robert McCrum, John Glusman and Judith Lukin.

I am indebted to John Stinson, Ian McCalman, and Suzanne Rickard. Also to Hall Caine and Wesley Stacey.

Without my wonderful agent, Elaine Markson,
I might still be in the wilderness.

Laymen often ask men of learning
why Adam did not first cover his mouth,
the part that had eaten the apple,
rather than his loins.

WILLIAM LANGLAND
Piers Ploughman

The Second Bridegroom

I must face the fact that you will have forgotten who I am. So if you have the patience I shall tell you. And for my part, of course, I must at last get to know you too.

I am near-sighted. My impressions of you have been those of a man who sees no details at a distance. I am given little enough to go on at the best of times. I see a blurred world of large simple shapes; as with my first view of the new land we reached at the end of our voyage south from Sydney. Looking back on it, I try to guess how this wilderness might have appeared to you.

Let me call the scene to mind. Sunshine blazes across a sea so amazing calm we hold our breath. We are in an untouched place. Stunned by sheer light – by the glare of bleached sand and the brilliant sea breaking as a white crust – I peer into the water but I don't like to mention what I think I see down there. Surely those with long sight could not fail to notice? The water is clear as air. We all look. No one speaks. Yet I would swear I can make out a sunken ship, a brig like our own or a barque. Squinting to get it more definite, I see masts and spars. Also a hull wedged among undersea rocks. Who has been here before us? What hopes are already drowned? Wind ruffles the light and the wreck is gone. Still no one speaks. They look. And I look. I glimpse a mast again and a crow's-nest. Yet they are the ones who can see – and I only think I can see. But how vivid this ocean is, with a lick of satin parallel to the coast a quarter of a mile out, like a wake and yet too broad to be left by any vessel: it is as if our whole future had already come, swept past, and gone before we even arrived. Meanwhile the past has been scuttled. A slight swell lifts that sleek ribbon and passes beneath without breaking it, like a muscle under skin. A minute later, when the swell reaches us, riding here at anchor, we rise to its gentle authority. We also subside.

This movement is not sudden enough to rock the body still fettered to my own.

The bosun had him dragged up from the squalor belowdecks and me with him, as if there was no difference between us. I am a disgusting object from living in filth and cramming my head with torments. As for him, he is not at all disgusting though he lies lifeless. Waxy white, you would think him more handsome than ever.

Can you put yourself in my place? The carcase was unstrung, a boneless weight flopping on the other end of my manacle. Such was the climax of our time spent locked together. Even after deckhands had dragged him out into the open and let him drop, he tugged me violently.

Fraternity rose to the slight swell with the grace of flight, her masts rocked, her idle rigging slattered. The dazzle of that peace kept us all in check. The livestock in the hold fell silent as well – listening, I suppose, to make what sense they could of the journey's end. I fancied I could hear their committee breathing. Now and again, to keep their balance, hoofs clomped down there, unseen.

As for the place itself, a rocky headland tilted and righted. The utter wild and untouched look of our new home sent a thrill through me so I felt outrage that I would soon be dead.

Two ospreys (I knew this by the way they flew) floated above and scattered reckless cackles on the air. We were close enough to shore to hear the anxious prattle of small birds among the bushes as alarm spread beneath those great shadows sweeping from one hooked arm of the cove to the other.

But the shadow fallen on me was the Master's shadow. I did not look up. I only looked at that dead fellow whose head lolled so near mine I could see it shocking clear: we were still linked by a chafed wrist and awkward arm, his being out of joint dragged at mine. But as for the fellow's breeches and naked feet, these were far enough away to belong to a man still full of life.

I confess to you that I did not care to look too long at that head.

Here in a beautiful haven, I thought, my living body is soon to be thrown overboard with his dead one. He will weight me down and drown me. Or if he don't the Master is sure to put a bullet through my skull. That is how it goes with the law. What is the difference between a corpse with a bullet hole and a corpse without? The law is for one part of mankind to explain how its oppression of the other is for the good of all. Law is a kind of algebra, in which unknown quantities are given names as simple as X and Y.

You must be aware that being near-sighted often goes along with being bookish, in my case an actual apprenticeship to a printer. Enough to say, for the moment, that I was familiar with Mr Hogarth's simple tale of rewards for diligence and that I might have hoped to end up wearing a Lord Mayor's chain of office in my old age. I was clever and quick. But such comfortable daydreams pass away, as this present dream will pass. My purpose is not to complain against fate. You will be surprised, but my purpose is to be frank. Put simply, I cannot afford to live in my past so I beg to inhabit your present.

I admitted killing Gabriel.

So now, the Master said, you owe me fifteen shillings for this man. And he let this fact settle before turning aside. Why should I waste another fourpence on powder and shot to be rid of you? he added.

I stared out at the shimmering sea, that vague dazzle, also at the empty sky. I knew then that I had not been shot.

The quartermaster came to unlock the manacle. When it would not open they fetched a carpenter. He brought his axe and at one blow buried it deep in the deck. Gabriel's hand flew off and slithered jumpy under the rail to flap into the scuppers. His body convulsed. I dare say there is little point in describing what a severed wrist looks like, budding undriven blood as dark as resin.

He shall have a Christian burial on land, the Master ordered, that way at least he'll be good for manure. They threw a length of sailcloth over Gabriel Dean's face and left him with me.

Does it surprise you to be told that the life of a felon has much in common with the life of a soldier, being spent largely in the boredom of waiting? There we were. We had reached paradise. The silver glitter of water buoyed us up – a company of twenty, as I now saw, ten assigned convicts, a master, a mistress of course, a quartermaster, boat crew and paid labour – all but one of those on deck gazing this way at the new land, or that way out to the horizon's perfect straightedge, where dark sea met a milky sky. We waited. What we were waiting for no one told us. Direct overhead the blue deepened, perfect and empty. The headland cupped us in lush vegetation. Forest trees stepped right to the dunes at the back of a sandy beach. We waited. The sun swung vertical above. A white ruff along the sand marked the end of our voyage. Half a dozen large birds flapped away from a lagoon. They were in no hurry. They had considered the threat for some hours. As they swept overhead I recognized them: pelicans. We waited. The sun sloped in from the west, netted by treetops calling with owlish cries, lingering on the drowsy air.

Our memories have plenty in common with short-sight, don't you think?

The point was that there we floated, raiders, with no idea we were being watched.

I lived instant by instant, expecting to be punished. Beyond question this punishment would have fallen to my lot had my crime come to light at any other time. We all knew we had arrived at a new beginning. We shared a sense of destiny. With everyone afraid that the future might be founded on false hope I warranted only such attention as could be spared a minor irritation.

Still the sunken ship wavered under the water. Still nobody said a word about it. The day drew on and itself began to sink away.

I never fathomed the Master's reason for keeping us aboard until the last light. Only then, at the time when we felt most like the marauders we were and most at risk, did he order us ashore. The men looked terrified. They knew that no sooner were we marooned on this shadowy land than the sun would set and leave us helpless. We would be wholly without light unless we chose to offer ourselves as targets by lighting lamps and building a fire. So when the pinnace's keel ran against the sand not one among my brothers in servitude cared to be first into the warm sea.

What did I have to lose? I slipped over the gunwale.

I looked back. The ship could be seen but nothing of what was happening aboard until, by a small moving blob of amber, I knew the Mistress had left her sickbed to negotiate the rope ladder. She hung there against the dark hull. The current, turning *Fraternity* and the boat with it, showed me the Master's black shape reaching up to steady his wife. Did she need rescuing? He must have his arms full. Were they swaying together, staggering as the smooth swell lifted their boat; were they preoccupied with keeping their balance even on that silky sinking sea? One cow began to moo from inside the hold, sounding like a muffled herald's horn. So my moment was offered me. A gift. In the still evening anything seemed possible. Dusky golden light stood in the air. Even the little waves slapped the beach softly. I waded ahead alone, stepping up the sandy slope, aware that others would soon follow but alert to the fact that I heard no sound of them churning the shallows. Was it worth the risk of a spear in the chest or a shot in the back to keep on going, to make a run for it? Most likely I would be hunted down and dragged back by the hair, flogged and starved.

To tell you the truth, these horrors touched me only as a cold spot settling in the small of my back. My chance would last no more than a few seconds. I was out of the water and still walking. I clutched the dangling manacle in my hand and ran. I ran until a dapple of shadows confused my vision. I plunged among tall smooth tree trunks and undergrowth.

While still able to see, I must run and run and keep running.

But this proved impossible. Between death and death the best I could do was stumble and lurch. I had to clamber over logs and force my way through thickets. I plunged into a freshwater lagoon as brown as tea. Driven by knowledge of what I had done back there, letting out my fear in grunts and sobs, I was also driven to escape the revulsion I felt at the creature I had become. This was a sickness of the conscience. Reason could not help. So the choice was made for me, I accepted the chaos offered. No wonder those others did not follow: they saw the same thing. Yes, they shouted of course. But not until nightfall did I hear these shouts and by then they were mere memories, ghost shouts heard as much in the blood as in the ear.

Graft had been paid for me. Such was the knowledge I carried in among the networks of insect wings and scuttering claws. I did not know what death meant; but I did know what it meant to have been paid for, to have a grubby finger forced in my mouth feeling round my teeth, to have my feet and hands valued and my trade cited like a dog's dam. Add to this that back there in Sydney I knew one thing my new master could not have known – so craven was I, so schooled as a brute, that I wanted him to buy me. I primped to appear a desirable object.

Reason brought me to this.

Then came the chance to be free of reason itself. In the beauty of evening, ospreys gliding above, the massed confusion of the unknown taking the form of a forest offered me, on arrival here, a death cleansed of humiliation. The chaos rushed to meet me and dodge me.

Big animals fled crashing ahead through the bush as I went, leaping away, fanning out, uttering no cries but thumping the earth at every bound of terror. Parrots, catching the fear, wheeled as a screaming skein of crimson and royal blue. I escaped west towards the fading light, a confusion of fear widening in circles around me, news of my stumblings already known miles inland. While panic triggered panic those shapes remaining quite still escaped my notice. Some I might have even brushed against without recognizing them as human. Slender and dark like young tree trunks, daubed with mud and leaves, as I was later to see, they had painted each other with living earth and the fugitive design of shadows in this place. Just as the fleeing animals fled in silence, the still were still in silence.

I lay on the earth and heard the silence thunder in my blood. I dug at the soil to bury my misery but found it hard under a mulch of rotting twigs and strips of bark. I could still just see but could not go on. This was where my pride had delivered me. I looked up at the first stars beyond the crown of trees until I felt the starlight crawl on my skin.

Ants seethed all over me. Tearing my clothes, I thrashed around to be rid of them, using my last moments to blunder a few yards further into oblivion.

The last light, having ebbed away, brought me to a halt. Each minute the cloisterish dark damped and suffocated me more, till nothing but that dark was left, the infinite dark of our turning planet. I should confess, although I believe in the Bible, I accept no church. So I suppose you could never call me a religious man – and this might have had some bearing on my troubles from the start. Yet that instant of recognizing darkness for space filled me with terrified joy.

Even if the Master caught me in the morning I had won at least this for myself.

And I was the man who had brought darkness to Gabriel Dean on the previous night. Remote as that crime already seemed, this is how near it was still. I had planned the murder. It was no accident. Once he was asleep I set about my task with the only weapon to hand, because he was strong and I was weak. Could it also have been because he was beautiful and I was ugly? Certainly his arrogance showed up my humility. Beware the humble.

So darkness was in me as well as around me.

The climate in these parts being mild, I found the night crisp but not too cold for sleeping rough. I scooped all the dead leaves in reach for coverings. I planned to head inland, away from the rising sun, to put as much distance as possible between me and the coast, making the least possible noise while I was about it. This much was commonsense, meanwhile I must sleep.

In fact hunger kept me awake, the knot in my bowels, the brief dribble of burning piss. My brain, taking charge of the spirit's fascination, began to tackle the task of carving the chaos into bite sized meanings.

Even I had learned certain things about New South Wales from accounts written by various hands and from the talk among my fellow convicts. So my brain set to work on the noises presented me: the chirrups and scratchings being animal; rustles and whispers vegetable; the rising sea's rhythmical thud mineral. Further, my education helped me frame a more exact catalogue: the scratching might be small quadrupeds, possibly of a kind with rats or squirrels; chirrups, being by far the most general and continuous of the animal sounds, signified insects mating; similarly I heard large leaves being moved by the breeze, tree trunks leaning against one another to utter occasional lovers' moans, grasses whispering. Meanwhile, overriding everything, was the treetops' remote agitation. This was what kept me awake when I desperately needed rest.

At the time I did not recognize the symptoms as symptoms. Let me not appear to claim any awareness whatsoever. I had no idea I was being laid hold of by the rational world of my upbringing to battle against the allure of a thing without form. I thought I was doing well. I took pride in being self-taught. I was an idiot.

Once, from the direction of the sea, I heard men cry out in the distance. Animal, I said, and trembled.

Growing cold I diverted myself with a brief sermon on cultivating feathers for warmth and passed from the example of God's common chicken in winter to His albatross skimming above freezing wastes of an Antarctic ocean, thence to the proof of a down quilt. Again a man's cry. Had this one sounded closer, or had the breeze slackened? It made me shiver.

Speaking of ghosts: lying there on my mat of brittle sticks, I did not feel Gabriel's body twist and shudder again as it had when I was in the act of murdering him, though this was a nightmare I made ready to endure. My fear was not fear of his survival or the violence of his revenge but fear of flinching, lest I dislodge the mound of dead leaves I had heaped on me to keep my misery warm.

Rumour had it that the Master's name was Mr Atholl. I saw several fellows put themselves forward when he was picking his men, from which I deduced that he had a reputation. But there was little chance for me to form an opinion. What shall I say? He looked like any other man of substance. He spoke clear in an educated accent. He had definitely never been a ticket-of-leaver, his smell was all wrong. He appeared strong in body and a browbeater. Chained together between-decks, we agreed that the ship must be his own. And this was spoken of as the most exceptional thing about him. Beyond doubt he had a grant of land to go to. One of the sailors told us the crew were to stay and become the Master's shepherds when we reached land; there was a butcher, he told us, and the carpenter who would build the house was also an axeman. Plain that Mr Atholl intended to set himself up and stay. Plain that he intended us to stay too.

Everybody had opinions about the wife – most things I could not repeat. The fact was, we agreed, that the Master was right to be firm and not waste too much time listening to a woman's grievances. What would be our long term fate if he petted her overmuch or indulged her? That's what we asked in the knowing way of gossips who know nothing. We agreed she would only come into her own when her husband was installed on his acres and she, like the cattle, might be big with young.

I do remember something Mr Atholl told us while we lined up at the barracks back there in Sydney – he promised we would help establish a new kind of settlement, and that we would bless the day. We saw he had bought the latest line in farm machinery when we lugged his plough and reaper aboard, stowed his chests of tools and seed, before we were manacled in pairs.

You can chain him and me, Gabriel Dean offered holding his wrist ready, I'll keep the runt in order.

That was me. And that was the beginning.

Three days may not seem long to a person in a cabin with a bunk, blankets, water to drink and water to wash in, but we spent it shut away from the light, shitting where we sat (I am outspoken because I believe you have the same scorn for the feeble niceties of language), brawling over the food they threw at us, guzzling from a drink can, scrambling for rank against rivals. Some men knew others from being in prison together. A few had even arrived on the same transport and could be picked because they dared say so little, knowing too much. Some, like me, had been in the colony less than a week and knew nobody.

The common wisdom was that transportation might be stopped at any time, that when a new Governor was appointed he would bring the system to an end, and that ours had been the last shipment. I do not know what truth there was in the story but it branded us: as if we stole some right from older hands, as if we made special claims on the future by worming our way into history. So from the first we were treated with particular cruelty.

My dreams of the past – and we all dreamed of our losses – had skies of torn paper and little boxes filled with hopelessness. The present was something haphazard. We lived for the future. Any piracy, any theft, any evil would be made all right by the future: isn't this the truth of our colonial philosophy? I am sure you have thought about it yourself. From the Governor down to his scullery maid we became Australians, a race with one foot in the air, caught stepping forward.

The bigger this great island is supposed to be, the more it appeals to our gambling vice.

Since we were infants at our parents' knee hadn't we heard tales of fabulous lands being discovered and explored? Did we not follow the adventures of Sinbad as if we ourselves were the ones to be caught and carried by the giant roc to its nest? Tales, all tales. And tales tell a hidden truth as well as the things they seem to say.

Here in New South Wales one thing we do know is that this will be the last foreign shore, the last unknown land, the only adventure to yield none of our desires: no gold, no cities. Even the trees are strange to us and the animals are those useless freaks the whole world hears of, egg-laying flying reptiles, fantasies of Nature. Instead of taking us forward, what we see takes us back to the beginnings of time. The real and the fabulous have not yet gone their separate ways. There is nothing to prevent our fables taking root here. And we have brought plenty of them with us. One of these fables, as you shall see, had a part to play in my downfall.

I want to confess to you and to share my thoughts.

No wonder book knowledge is a good deal feared. We who have it are cursed for tying others to the past. They look down on us too, as knowing only what is already known. But is our future so different from what our past has been? And does lack of knowledge make a person bold? Here, a man like Mr Atholl may set out in his 90-ton ship, go where he pleases, stop in paradise and say: As I read the map, this bay is mine. And take it just as it is, without tales, whole in its beauty, never tainted by our sort of knowing.

You may wonder why I say such things. Let me add that in my own way I am a word man also. Many felons are handy at crafts; though who besides a printer enters into a trade with words? So I am set apart, halfway like the Master. But I do not keep my knowledge to myself. This may be why the others hate me. I am hated the moment I open my mouth and the words escape me. My workman's lilt is little help; if anything it brands me as a traitor to the comfortable sort of ignorance. The Master set the seal on their resentment when he said: I shall one day be glad of a printer and there might not be another happen my way.

So Gabriel Dean came to promise he would keep the runt in order.

There is a quality of cruelty that goes with beauty; and not by chance. The beautiful are well aware they can do as they please. Even their victims will forgive them because they answer our deepest need. In them we recognize an ideal. Have you thought about this? They flatter us with their friendship. A man's wife may be excited by him if she sees he has the loyalty of a beautiful friend, his own meagre portion glowing in the radiance of the other. And isn't this a fact anyway? Surely it is true that, without making any effort to be like them, some glimmer of the style they have from Nature rubs off on us?

Just as I was the last to be chosen for Mr Atholl's household, Dean was the first. The Master remarked: He'll sire a pretty race built like Vikings. How much more strength the Master showed later when he turned his back on my crime, as if speaking about any lag, with the words: So now you owe me fifteen shillings for this man.

I have come to believe that Mr Atholl knew he and I were shackled to the same bond of words, words to be broken out of before the new kingdom could find its airy regions among the clutter of old misfitting uses. That's the best way I can put it. I hope I make sense. And although he had more use for Gabriel Dean than he would ever have for me, we shared another bond, as you shall learn, in our fatal ambition to be loved by one woman. Yet we were always opposites. He was a horse man and I have never even learned to ride.

So, the Master put up a fence because he feared his herds might cheat him of power by running away. Just as his little herd of human beasts, with their starved souls, might be more ready filled than himself by such gifts as the land offers.

When you put all this together you will see that maybe I did not bolt out of fear that he would punish me for Gabriel Dean's death but for fear the Master wanted to possess my soul.

That first night of my escape, as I lay shivering in a sweat of terror, the ocean booming like a cannon, I thought of the *Fraternity* and how she must be tossing at anchor. I could picture the panic on board while they made ready to take her out to sea, beating against the wind, to ride at a safe distance from the rocks. This put me in mind of the crew and cargo. Who was still aboard? Could any of the livestock have been ferried to land yet? And what if the weather obliged the ship to stand offshore for another week? Wouldn't this be the saving of me? As for *Fraternity*'s human livestock, the one thing I wondered was whether they had yet buried the corpse of the only beautiful man among them. And with what words. The words interested me as always. Ah, there it was again: I will take heed to my ways that I offend not in my tongue – I will keep my mouth as it were with a bridle – how does it go? – something about the ungodly – in my sight I held my tongue and spake nothing – I kept silence, yea, even from good words – yes, that's right – but it is pain and grief to me – my heart was hot within me – and while I was thus musing the fire kindled and at last I spake with my tongue – Lord, let me know mine end and the number of my days, that I may be certified how long I have to live.

Do you know the Psalms? If so, you will see that I had this part of the service by heart ever since I set the type myself for our congregation's prayer sheet. My job was to check the spelling and correct the proof as well, and take it round to the vicar.

Of course I remembered the Master's promise that Gabriel Dean would be buried on land. But would it be the Christian service as usual (The snares of death compassed me round about, and the pains of Hell got hold upon me) or was he bold enough to let the ocean do the talking and simply shovel in some soil while listening to the solemn drum of a swell against the cliffs?

I shivered, and thought these things to stop myself shivering.

What sort of burial would he offer me when his men came upon my body torn by snags and dead of hunger? Such were the questions I put as I lay among queer plants, my teeth chattering, hearing around me the movement of animals which ought not to be tied to the name animal. There were no answers.

When I could, I made a beginning: I promised not to try reading the messages I heard and smelled and touched, tasted and saw. I would respect them as having no use. None of them would be the same tomorrow. Nor were they the same yesterday. Each moment is the present: it sounds and smells and tastes only of itself.

I was in a fever and brainsick. Often at the source of courage lies something pitiful. Perhaps I had the fever from Gabriel. He fell ill on the day we set sail, the day he fixed me with a glittering stare and held his wrist against mine, inviting the trooper to chain us together. Was it that I dared not move, or was I indifferent? A curious flutter in the blood as I relive the moment (let me, above all, be truthful with you) suggests that I had been less passive than I thought. Might it not be that I so mistook his motive as to be proud he chose me?

Once we were fastened together by the manacle the character of this device became clear. The clasps fixed around my wrist and his were joined by a short iron bar with only three chain links at either end. When he raised his arm I must perforce raise mine at least some of the way. When I wished to raise my arm he had the opportunity of forcing his down to prevent me. By a mercy the clasp was somewhat loose on my wrist, though cutting tight into his, otherwise I think he would sure have broke my arm, so violent did he twist it to keep me, as he said, up to the mark. Even before we left the quay at Sydney he pressed against me so I could feel the strength coursing through him. And when I tried watching the swooping seagulls he fixed me with a scowl until I met his eyes. He smiled then, and I knew what to expect.

No sooner had we stumbled into the steerage of *Fraternity*, hearing cattle protest under the floor, than he used the iron bar of the manacle and felled me with a terrible blow. Then I was hoisted to my feet and cursed for a clumsy fool.

So began the tortures. Had his energies not been sapped by illness I doubt I would have lived. With each assault he delivered a homily against idle ways. The preacher's tone of these good offices afforded the company such amusement that a deckhand was sent to ask were we Frenchies and begging for a taste of the cat?

Do you begin to see what kind of life I faced? The blood dried on my cheek and my hand was caked with blood. Gabriel Dean invited me to throw my whole weight against his arm. Yet I could not shift it. For a moment I comforted myself that this victory should appease him.

What is the point? he snarled.

Why were we not Frenchies? one asks, looking back. Why were we in this miserable hole instead of out on the streets and burning our Bastille? By what right of Nature was it not myself but Mr Atholl who seized a thousand acres of virgin land with the assurance of doing the crown a service?

The manacle had FJ stamped on it. The blacksmith who forged it wished to be known by his workmanship. I had to carry it with me when I escaped, of course, clutching the bar in the hand fettered to it or else have it bang painfully against my leg as I ran.

I clutched it long after I had fallen among the tangled bushes and burrowed into my bed of dead leaves.

You must imagine me, on that day, once I felt safely clear, lying low, seeing nothing, alert to the sound and smell of the wild. I confess that I prayed: Only let me come upon water in the morning, Lord, and I shall not complain. This was the last time I prayed to the God of our childhood, the stone dragon at Kirk Braddon, and the first prayer of mine He ever answered.

Just as I will end my life here in the newest British colony, I was born in the oldest, the Isle of Man. Not until my father's time were we out from under the heel of the Earl of Derby, styled King of Man.

Think of it. Jesus Christ himself might not have scorned such a title.

Mere words, you may say. Did the dragon need a title to strike fear in the hearts of our folk? Well, as to the matter of words, I am the one who knows. The law – I mentioned this in my previous letter – is for one part of mankind to explain how its oppression of the other is for the good of all. England and Scotland wrangled over the Isle of Man. Scotland and Ireland wrangled. And then Denmark and England. Finally, between England and Ireland, it came down to science: was the island (being midway between them) hung off the English coast or the Irish coast? Lawyers got busy and came up with a proof as good as any. They brought serpents and toads from Cumberland and set them free. When these creatures flourished and began infesting the island the law accepted this as proof of British sovereignty . . . the fact being well-known that neither kind of vermin can survive on Irish soil.

It all comes down to soil in the end. And we know our own, which will someday be ours entire.

What was it that I heard as I lay on the ground under my heap of shifting leaves? Tiny things. I believe it to be true that those of us with imperfect eyes have keen ears and keen noses. I heard crawlings and slitherings among the roots. Sounds you might have missed. I was still sobbing and gone in the knees while the jungle crowded over me. The muddle of terror, without let or way, was as bewildering as that world of leaves. Yet listening to the tiny sounds, I found my panic began to give place to calm. I could neither see anything nor do anything. I must accept what the world sent me. Serene now, I reviewed such facts as I knew: that the denizens of the Antipodes were flying squirrels, hopping fawns, insect sticks with the wingspan of a hawk, scorpions able to stand upon two legs and bite their victims as well as sting them to death, owls with horns, and water badgers half-bird half-animal. The lags on our transport talked about huge herons without wings which could kill a man with a blow of the leg, snakes spitting poison darts, giant ants and man-eating spiders. I thought of our Manx dragon at home, our four-horned rams and tailless cats. So what would an Englishman choose to fear if that were the coast he had just landed on for the first time? These were the fears of foreigners. No doubt our folk were monsters too, of a sort, with a language which we kept to ourselves and no other nation could make head nor tail of. My father never spoke a word of English, not even to curse the Earls of Derby.

So I lay and shivered. Wind rushed sudden among unseen trees to sound like gusts of approaching rain.

I will never be found, I thought, I am in the most secret place on earth. Perhaps no human foot has ever trodden here. Perhaps no poet has attempted to tell of its real monsters. Yet the night noises, apart from that rising wind, were tender. Cheepings came to me from every direction so that I thought of them as a web of fairy bells. I listened, as enchanted as a child.

I heard a man.

So this was the true monster. My heart had no doubt of the matter. He trod cautious. Twigs cracked under his feet like they had under mine. But he had control and stepped with care. There was no terror in him as he came. Only in me. His long pauses were proof that he was listening. He listened as hard as I did. But perhaps he had good sight and this would count against him: his ears less sharp than mine. I could not hear him breathing, only his feet nearby. Nor did he curse under his breath the way I had while I ran in panic to escape the Master's hirelings. He stopped. He came on again. Yet I was right: I could never be found. Might he trip over me? No – a chance like that would offend against Nature and the natural disorder. I had control of myself. Then I heard him away to my left. And again farther off. What if it was some other large beast of prey? Some meat eater pausing not to listen but to scent the air? This I had not thought of while I lay so calm of a sudden. The joke is that, once he was gone, he took with him my feeling of being safe.

Did I sleep? I do not know.

Towards the middle of the night an unearthly light crept into the bush. Lying there gazing at the treetops I was astonished to find that what I had taken for a dense umbrella of leaves showed itself as frail lace. Close by my face, where I could focus, starlike growths sprouted around me, and glowing fungus. Even the plenteous dead leaves matted on the forest floor each had its own shape when brought up close, its honed edge, pointed and curved. They were like lily leaves afloat on the dark planet. A spider hung silvered in her web. And a radiant veil of harmless insects flew past stretching and retracting.

I tried to recapture my fear in the name of commonsense. I, who at the best of times could see nothing sharp beyond reach of my hand with its dangling manacle, peered into the night for signs of movement among the trees. I was expecting a threat which moved. It never crossed my mind that there might be danger in what stood still. You could scarce blame me; don't we all picture the hunter running or stalking or pouncing? Hunters who stood fixed, doing nothing, were no possible threat because they had not yet been imagined. So, although I suffered a feeling of being watched, I remained too ignorant to care. And this saved my life.

Before dawn I dropped off several times. Better than the previous night aboard ship when I had no sleep whatsoever. So I woke refreshed, the sun about to rise behind me. If the lacy moonlight had given me back a lovely world, those few moments before I staggered to my feet and shook enough terror back into my head to drive me on showed me a glimpse of heaven.

Some few birds had already woken. They talked more than sang. Their messages were disagreeable, the most persistent being bantam-squawks. A mouse, I could plainly see its furry shape, scuttered among leaves still warm with my warmth. The surrounding scene resembled a tangle of grey wool, perhaps a witless weaving. Mocking me from right above my head came a terrifying cackle. I leapt to my feet, drenched with fear. I stared up, able to make out nothing other than branches and foliage spread against a sky pale as whey. The sound did not come a second time.

The truth was that since there was enough light for me to see by, there was also enough for the Master who hunted me. I listened. Other bird-cries happened like stones knocking together, accidental. The light strengthened. Then the first songbird, high above, opened his throat and gave out penetrating notes strange as the man I once heard sing alto in the *Messiah*.

Do I surprise you? I want to surprise you.

At this signal a great tree branched into fire! The forked trunk, still solid with night, tapered up as bough-shaped tongues of flame. The breath of happiness caressed me, smelling of the sea. Parrots swooped among glowing sprigs.

The day was already my enemy. I knew I ought to escape yet I could not deny myself the simple marvel of this burst of rosy light as it steadied and strengthened to brilliant gold and the whole top of the tree shone like a hood of jewels. Hints of blue swept through the air above. Even at risk of being noticed I watched until the marvel faded. A firming wind set the forest in motion. I was caught in a mesh of sound, netted by slishings and patterings.

I looked around. Morning had come. It might be my last morning and I knew this. One could see quite well. The dense tangle of dead and living plants wove a single messy tapestry which hung right before my nose. There seemed no foreground or perspective, just a simple up and down without any way through.

Away behind me a cow lowed mournful notes of warning. There could never be an instant's doubt as to my direction. Not only must I keep the risen sun behind me but I must escape the constant ocean's muffled bass drum.

When fear took hold it was more desperate than ever. I ran, stumbling, up to my ankles and sometimes up to my knees in the mat of fallen branches, peering at vague threats, betrayed by the great hubbub I made as I went. But how else could I go? This was a country where stealth was an art that must be learned. Hopeless to bother with it now. So whatever blundering speed I could manage must give me a better chance than ginger care. You know how it is in a forest: as you run, the nearby trees sweep past you, a bow wave arcing around on either side, while beyond them an outer band of trees moves your way (as the moon also goes with you) – so the quick trunks flee behind while the contrary trunks beyond keep pace to trap you at a standstill. However desperate you attempt to escape, all you can ever do is speed up this confusion and drive the counter-circling mazes faster.

I flagged. I gulped and gasped ratchets of breath painful as punches to the chest.

Both the near band of wheeling forest and the outer band counter-wheeling slowed down. When I stopped they stopped. I was a beaten man. They were trees in a land never used. Some memory of clocks ticked loud in my brain, I swung round – expecting to surprise my enemies as they closed in on me: the Master with his whip, felons slavering at the bloodhunt with murder on their tongues. Nothing. I saw nobody. Only the standing-still blackness of tree trunks and the pale grey and fragile pewter green of that sky-to-earth tapestry.

How difficult it all is to describe.

The frightful cackling laughter started again, after a gargle at the beginning. This time two voices laughed as rivals, their mimic mirth struck through me so that I felt cold, helpless to escape, helpless to decide which way to go or how to hide. I saw a pair of plump brown kingfishers glide down from a branch above me. They swooped toward a glint of metal on the ground ahead, dipping through matted growths. Vines with blunt hooks at their joints ripped my rags to remnants.

This glint was not metal. Let me say that I now believe metal is as alien to this land as beasts with hoofs. The glimmer came from a strip of still water. Perhaps the smell of this water was what the cow went on about back there at the dunes. I thanked heaven. A few minutes spent drinking here might save hours later. Thrusting my mouth in I sucked a bellyful. The taste, brackish and slimy, was delicious. I raised my wet face and the breeze blew cold all over my skin. Had this drink been fatal – the delay a minute of flight I could never have back? Fear got at me again. I was sweating and my knees trembled. I struggled up. I had to make good. I began to believe that, against all odds, escape was possible.

The black tree stumps ahead of me were not trees at all. Dumb with terror I swung round to bolt the other way. The black tree stumps behind me were not trees either, though they stood still as rooted things and old beyond the span of human generations. I had been trapped by weirds of a kind no book of travels ever described. Neither Sinbad nor Prester John came across such a breed as this. They had eyes and the eyes watched me from under shadowy brows, but they did not have proper faces or torsos; theirs were face-shaped clumps of feathers, and torsos of leaves. Nor were their arms ordinary arms, because the white bone appeared to grow outside the flesh. Where a man would have cock and balls some grew a thing like a melon. Where a man stands on legs they stood on a single prop. But though their heads kept as still as their sprouting bodies, the bird-eyes fixed on me moved when I moved, stopped when I stopped.

We were relics of ancient life suspended in the amber morning, for I include myself.

I heard cattle mooing, then a distant shout. And so, by the enquiring tension they centred on me, did they. One of them unfolded a second leg from the single stalk he stood on: he levelled a weapon at my belly, a blade made of bone by the look of it. He stepped toward me.

The menace of magic made the menace of British law and its bullies look bland by comparison. On my legs, arms and scalp the hair stood stiff in shock, I can tell you. My skin cringed. The creature holding his sharp bone stepped through the tapestry, treading where there was no floor, out of the vagueness, gliding into focus and showing himself for what he was. He had black skin, shiny on the shoulder but folded lateral across the chest as if tucked and sewn there. By the wrinkled belly I judged him quite old. Stringy arms were knotted up with veins. Between the toes of one foot he dragged a spear along the ground. With no warning, he stuck the blade in among his head feathers. Straight after that he flipped the spear up into his hand. He balanced it, a simple sharpened pole with no metal head, the tip steady, inches from my throat. In the other hand he held a flat wooden paddle with patterns cut into it. There was menace in this also. On the paddle lay divers items: a smooth white caterpillar appearing powdered with ashes, a tiny yellow plum, a leaf with three points, a pink mushroom and a root like a misshaped parsnip. I looked upon these articles, upon the paddle, the hand holding it out to me, and the wrist growing clumps of foliage.

I could see now that his entire body sprouted coverings, mostly clusters of feathers in a narrow continuous line beginning at the neck, branching in two to fringe both collarbones, looping down on either side to the elbow, back up to the armpit, looping again down to the knee and back up . . . until at the belly button the line around the left side met that from around the right. So these tufted feather lines drew the silhouette of a dwarf on the body of a man. You will forgive me mentioning his gender, I hope. I wish to speak as frank as possible at all times. His cock and balls hung unadorned amid dark hair. On this fellow's face and head were such masses of plumage that all I could distinguish of normal humankind were moustaches above a wide mouth and two piercing eyes fringed with fluttering pink down.

In the eyes, which I expected to express raw evil, I saw the most unlikely thing, a flicker of terror. Yes, and I could explain it: my blood-guilt must in some way be apparent. These were creatures sensitive enough to death to smell it on me already and to know me for a murderer.

Water dripped from my mouth. The manacle dangled against my leg, reaching the ankle. My freedom had lasted less than twelve hours.

Despite my father being determined that I would not be hag-ridden by superstition in the form of God or omens, I believed in one fixed rule: that action of any kind will be punished. I had escaped execution, so now it seemed I must die by poison. Let it be. Amen. Without hesitation I reached out and took the fruit. Bitterness dried my tongue. Pips stuck to the roof of my mouth. The creature made no sign of approval. I took the leaf and chewed that also, tough and stringy though it was. Numbness dulled all sensation around my teeth, which were never good. Still he held out that decorated paddle. Next I accepted the mushroom, which was now clearly a toadstool with gills the colour of cream, expecting this to be the quickest acting poison but surprised by the delicate smell it had to it and the lingering taste of pepper. The caterpillar I could not stomach. I told him I was refusing by shunning it with my hand . . . and then offered it to him, because the truth came in a flash that death by a spear through the neck must be more merciful than death by corruption of the vitals.

From all round the circle low cries were uttered, sounding like amazement.

The next of these strange beings to unfold a second leg also stepped forward, feathers and leaves set trembling, and took the caterpillar between finger and thumb with elegance enough for Lady Mary Montagu. He put it in his mouth and chewed. Odd, I noticed that the hairs on his legs and arms were bristling like mine and that every bare patch of skin was tight in gooseflesh.

From down at the beach came the whinny of a frightened horse, reaching us like a call to the heart, confirming what I was. One day and a night after I had committed murder, my conscience at last took control of my fear. The law was now justified in treating me as a convict. I could never again be innocent in my own eyes. My sufferings to that time had in all probability scarce begun. If you look at the idea of Hell, the truth of it is that no suffering can be enough once guilt is admitted. The guilty are hardened. Only the innocent feel true anguish. My murder made good the judgement passed upon me a year before.

Perplexed at what could be done, I did not move. No more did those feathered beings. My death would be too simple a way out for both of us. My death as a murderer did not balance Gabriel Dean's death as a bully. This was the ceremony of it.

They knew everything.

Wind rushed among trees, bending massive branches, tossing

a sea of leaves and causing a scurry among our feet. I had reached the hub of chaos.

The great sound made of a million tiny sounds was ruptured by words: Get at him! Do you see where the bastard went? By Jesus!

Sticks snapped, menacing snorts could be heard to the south of us, boots tramped not far off. The circle of feathered creatures remained still as God on their single props. So did I at the centre. I knew then that I was invisible. We listened while the chase approached in a rush and then passed away through dense scrub, returned, turned, split into a shout from in front and two shouts from behind. We heard the snorts again and shuddering breaths. So it was a horse that had got loose, after all! Something truly valuable. The whole while, the air ringing with interruptions, the remote ocean thudded. How familiar it sounded in a lost land – that unhurried heart of the world – the exact same sound as I remember from childhood.

Only when the marauders could be heard no more did we begin to move. I can not say whether the circle of figures around me took the first step or I myself. Whichever, we were soon stepping light. I have already described how the forest baffled me when I tried to run, a band of trees to either side moving back the opposite way and the far trees moving with me; just so, these weirds moved when I moved. After the first shock, I gave way to my fear. What use to pretend being brave? I made an offering of all pretence. I began to suspect that the fierce cold laughter high among the trees had in fact come from within, perhaps from the region of my navel. Also that the twin voices mocking me might be a single voice going one way while its echo travelled back the other, as the voice of a dragon is said to be two, both in the one throat.

Twigs crackled under my feet but not under theirs. Only the whip of a sapling bent aside now and again and springing upright marked the air with their passage. They stepped with bird feet, dipping their toes among hazards they were used to, dancing ahead on sprung thighs. Always they kept the circle complete and I began to find the going easier. Inside my head rang those alien words of English: Get at him bastard by Jesus.

I realized that what I had taken for murmurous foliage was the speech of these creatures. Talk flew among them, alighting on one and a moment later on another, till it took up a rhythm. The pulse of the sea drifted into their mouths and out again as chanting. We reached a ridge and began loping across more open ground through waist-high grass from which tiny birds dashed in a mad scatter of alarm.

I had arrived at a place where all my knowledge was useless. The joy, as I found myself filled with it, could not be described, the pepper taste still alive on my tongue.

Season upon season of smoke followed. Billows rose from that cup of land around the bay and drifted inland, carrying like incense. We wandered, seeing the smoke from afar as a mushroom on the horizon; or from the edge of the scarp smelling it mingled with seasalt on the wind; or as we returned stepping through patches of it caught among vines and star-flower bushes.

I had now lived with my spirit beings for long enough to be convinced they were men. From time to time they cleaned the feathers off their skin and shook out their long hair. Admitted, whenever they approached me they did so with ceremony, but as soon as they felt at a respectful distance they fell to chattering and bursts of laughter. Loneliness tortured me. I could not learn one single item of their language because they seldom said anything direct to me. I was beyond words.

Only on rare days did I see them dress so elaborate as they had at that first meeting, patterns of mud tufted with leaves and fluff disguising their real shape, though there was one time when they pranced around me on a grass slope, each man with a cross strapped to his back and held firm by a belt made of hair. The crosses were very tall things, spindly and wavering, and two or three times as tall as a man. Where could they have seen the crucifix? How did they know? Yet there they were, nodding crosses, painted with bands of colour and having bunches of leaves like a dead hand dangling from each arm and a third stuck up for a bush of hair at the top. These weird crosses swayed around me: something between a pilgrims' parade and the type of gangling sinister figure we used to see at Douglas fair when acrobats on stilts stalked in among the crowd. They kept it going until night seeped up out of the earth and swallowed the men entire while leaving their crosses to move this way and that, outlined against the sky. The moon did not come up at all that night. I expected the cold blade at any moment, I can tell you, a bone knife between my ribs.

At an early stage of our travels they took a dip in a pond and stood up all streaming. Their shoulders were glass and their wide wet smiles full of simple pleasure. Frogs croaked from the margin where I stood. But a terrible fuss broke out when I made moves to join them. Some shrieked, some covered their eyes, others messed up the water as they came churning out to cut me off. Little did they know how amiable I was. Not for the world would I trespass beyond the limits they set me. To my surprise, I realize now that I showed their taboos more respect than the taboos of my own folk. Such curious creatures we are, to be so fascinated by discovery, to have such a passion for things we can collect as items of strange behaviour. My protector – this is how I think of the guardian who first offered me poison – brought a wooden dish of the water for me to drink. A scarlet dragonfly darted in and hovered over its glinting rocking surface. For a moment I held back my thirst, waiting for the insect to dart away before I set my lips to the rim. By then a tremendous silence had fallen. The frogs themselves were struck dumb. The pool listened.

Even during that precious moment, which might be fatal for all I knew, I was aware of smelling smoke from distant fires like an omen. As well, I had to fight off memories of home and winter by the open hearth.

The light in here is very poor. I trust my writing is clear. I was always praised for my hand. I have to keep rubbing my fingers, so I shall wait until the morning grows warmer and the sun is really up. Then I shall write some more.

Now: let me explain about the journey I began to take. These Indians – and how queer the word sits with them – were on a quest, determined to keep moving but at the same time calm and refusing to hurry. The men and the women kept separate in two parties. I could hear this distinct, the low voices and the high, though I did not catch sight of either. In all my time among them only once did I see a woman – but more about that later. Most nights their songs and laughter reached out to me, punishing me further with desolation. Sometimes one or other would let out horrid screams, and each morning early they could be heard moaning in a choir with a sound like soft bagpipes. Often, in my circle, I came upon a mess of footprints pointing in all directions, also the remnants of two separate feasts. Each time overwhelmed by sorrow, the air around that place seeming more buoyant and touching me light as breath.

No matter how far we walked during those first months we could look back and see smoke clotting above the trees or smudged out along the far away sea.

So my spirit beings were human. That is the point. And while I decided not to intrude on their perfect chaos, routines already began to eat away at the grandeur of it. I even caught myself giving them a general name: Men. Well, the excuse was to hand, this was cleaner than clumsy dodges with roundabout words, which would lead to an even greater plague of English spreading in a world which English has no right to. Do you see what I mean? I hope I do not offend you with these ideas.

I began to see what order is. Order is a way of trapping anything wild, tricking us into the game of thinking we understand. When you come down to it, the need for order is the mark of a coward.

So each of my saviours was a man – and I prayed I would not be forcing them into a frame too rigid if I thought of them in secret as Men. It was Men who brought me food, food I ate with a will. Lengths of snake, roots and stalks, berries, bleeding hanks of meat in a crust of burnt fur. But not those pale fat naked caterpillars. They ate the caterpillars with gusto but never again offered me one. I came to the point of believing I might rather fancy trying the taste but I did not ask. First because I was too timid, then because I was afraid to risk the calm of my boredom. You see how quick our fears can be dulled?

The boredom loomed so great – and so much like a thing – I had to give it a name also. I called the boredom Hope. I had two words, then, and between them the span of daily life: Men and Hope.

Yet at first the days were never the same. We walked unknown ways, the water had a different taste each time we drank, we fed on such food as could be found, we slept amid undreamed dreams. The one thing that did not change was that if I made an independent move, even for a piss, the Men rose up around me in that silent circle to watch what I was doing. Each night we slept in a different spot except for the time when it rained eleven days and I was allotted a cave overlooking a river which flowed through a plain where herds of kangaroos flew toward the hills as the shadow of a swift dark single cloud.

This went on for weeks and months, through seasons of cold and seasons of heat.

Then one evening we heard a familiar rhythm, every eight steps we took: 'Boom.' Another eight steps through undergrowth: 'Boom.' The scent of the wide sea pricked my nostrils. As for the smoke, well perhaps a year had passed, so it was little more than a stale ghost of what it had been. Ah, with what longing and surprise I found myself back where I began. To be near the sea! The sea runs in my veins, of course. I feel as sad near the unseen sea as I feel near an unseen woman.

We came to the ridge and climbed it on the western slope. You must imagine that, without knowing, I had become a forest creature, faulty sight no longer a hindrance, having learned to feel the ground with my feet. I saw with forest eyes used to the gentle forest light. Indeed, I wondered whether my eyes might not have strengthened. Well, from the crest of the ridge the sight was blinding and so strange I could make no sense of it. Dazzled by all that brightness, I found myself looking down at an assault on the earth itself beyond anything I might have been ready for. The natural aspect of the place was wiped out. The soil gaped with lacerations. Alien to itself, the land lay wounded. From just below our vantage point a road, cutting between the dunes and the ramparts of forest, curved north as a giant scar. Dumps of stony rubble were heaped here and there to either side. Above the road stood tree stumps sawn short and charred, and whole ghost trees. Lopped branches and shattered logs sprawled at odd angles. Away to our left a few horses, penned by rough yards, browsed in the warmth, standing in various fixed attitudes, ignoring the two fellows in hats (this much I could make out) who plodded along the road. Down to the right and closer at hand some roofed dwellings were set square to the road, the grey sheets of roofing being bark or thin-cut shingles. They were lashed down with beams and rope. You may judge how this astonished me. The walls were slabs and in all probability thick enough to last out the century. Other roofs were visible through a patch of bush. From one of these a puff of smoke stood up. Breathing air fresh from the sea, I could not believe so much had changed in so little time. When last I set eyes on this place I was running through it, tripping and crawling, cursed by my own fear, expecting any minute to be caught again and dragged back to be chained to another murderous bully for the term of my sentence. Since then, that dense mat of undergrowth and close-set trees had gone. Wiped out. Raw earth lay open to the weather.

Please do not imagine I have forgotten what civilization is. I saw the road clearly as a road. The buildings as buildings. But I also saw, with the sight of Men, the horror of it, the plunder, the final emptiness. My protector looked around, long and searching, then turned to the others. But they could no more explain what they saw than he. I felt the puzzle as they did and even some of their fury as my own.

What is this for? My lips formed the question from the shock I saw in their eyes. Only later did I wonder at not feeling any longing whatever to go down and be part of the honest work of sawing timber, ploughing and sowing the fields.

Instead, the sheer scale of violence made the sight hard to grasp, so out in the open it was, and so ruthless. A glare of sunshine beat on the whole houses and the broken soil, exactly as rain must have slapped down on them a few weeks before.

It looked to me as if certain patches of the road might still be cut with troughs of mud.

So what was this for?

I answered myself as I might answer a child: to produce food. Although I had little doubt that the Master's sheep and cattle were somewhere nearby, it suddenly made no sense. As I saw it, he had taken a place, complete in itself, full of the food I had been living on, smashed it to fragments, then slaved at the work of carving out something in its stead, something different. But – how can I put it? – something no longer complete. His enterprise struck me as cross-grained if not downright contrary. Do you see what I mean? Does it puzzle you too?

As we stood looking, the sound of an axe came from nearby. Soon two axes were working. A ringing 'thwok' 'pok' told how big the tree was, just as the rhythm gave away that they were working at a single tree and not two.

The Men turned together to look to the south-east, agog at what confronted them down that way also. A spidery trestle stood out from the cliff – a landing-stage with a boat moored at the end, doubtless the pinnace because it had masts. Tucked inshore of the pier a kind of loose raft jostled slow and heavy in the shallows. This I recognized too. It was a jam of floating logs. Here the road ended.

I want you to come upon it all as we did.

Fraternity was nowhere to be seen. I thought of the deep water in the channel out there and the rigged ship I believed I saw underwater, standing intact with masts and spars, and I thought about us and what queer folk we are to be murdering and drowning for the sake of a quest after some paradise that can never be. A terrific conflict raged in my heart. I knew the risk, supposing somebody saw me there, but I was drawn to it. One day there would be a new town here.

Put it this way: I was living a life in which I did nothing for myself, indeed I was not allowed to do anything. If I had I would have offended them and their hospitality. Suppose I reached out to pick one of the berries you could eat: my guardians would call warnings, block my way, break it off for me, place it on the ground and smile when I took and ate. Though I longed to wash and to swim when we came to streams, they cried out in shock at the least hint that I might try. If we had to cross to the other side they made me lie on long poles, covered my face with a mask of reeds matted with mud, and carried me on their shoulders.

Of course I objected, but what good did it do me?

I contrived to parley by simple signals. We knew this between us. My right hand I used for subtle messages such as coaxing, a request for eatables, to signal pain or doubt. My left, with the manacle still hanging from the wrist, I kept for warding them off or for messages of power. In an emergency or when I felt helpless rage I got hold of the iron bar itself and shook it, the chain and empty ring clattering about on the end, and brandished it above my head. They also took my meaning when I turned a shoulder on them. Such were the rituals, and I only ever addressed my protector or, when he was absent, his deputy. In any case no one else in the circle had looked directly at me since I turned down the caterpillar and passed whatever test they had put me to. They kept their eyes cast and I obliged by gazing a bit to one side. Like being a king, such manners held my interest for months. I was engrossed in myself and my state. Let me say I had no interest in keeping count of how long elapsed since I escaped the Master because I never wished to leave the Men or go back to slavery. This way I soothed my guilt on account of Gabriel Dean, clear that I would never need to face a court of law.

And yet you may be sure the guilt gnawed at me. The torment of it, constant and dainty, did much to fill my life in the dumb solitude I was condemned to.

During our journey they pointed to every feature of the landscape as if I might recognize it. They behaved like family welcoming a cousin who has been many years away from home, reminding him of childhood games, making a tour of certain caves and standing rocks. They took me to admire particular trees with nothing remarkable about them, gnarled growths and even strange shadows on the soil. As I soon realized, they were never pleased when I showed the least surprise or wonderment. I was only able to gratify them by gazing long at what they showed me and seeming to recall it. How did I do this? Well, one gesture was to place my power hand across my mouth, the manacle banging against my chest. Then their occasional talk would quicken to a chant. I knew the exact game, I became an actor, I played the part of showing gratitude for treasures I had never thought to see again. Having lost so much during my life I could feign this easy enough.

You must forget that I was ever a plain felon assigned to a settler who might be called Atholl. I was the centre of the wandering circle. I was the one who had to be protected from being seen by women. You must imagine this: me as the shell of a dumb brute standing under the last of the uncut trees, agape at that loggers' road connecting jetty and farm.

The fellows in hats unhitched a couple of horses and swung up into the saddle. They came riding along the road.

At this, the Men exchanged wild looks. Leaves bunched on their wrists trembled.

What shall I say about the sound of horse hoofs coming near? They took me straight back to Kirk Braddon and the Douglas road, to my dear father and brother fastening capes around their shoulders, rustling through the kitchen and hurrying out into the night to meet the horsemen – whoever they were – then setting off on foot to a secret conference with others of their trade. Each time they met the horsemen they risked being caught. At very least they were likely to be away for a week, during which my mother would fret, strong though she was, and hide her tears. Horse hoofs on a soft road will always take me to the heart of my grief. Also to our morning vigil at the stone with the dragon carved into it. My mother had me believe the dragon would return in glory when the Sassenachs were driven from our sacred shores and their brand of Christianity with them. She held my father to blame because he took Hall with him at these dangerous times and because he was what she called a backslider in the faith, not giving himself to politics and rebellion, but only to adventures which she scorned for being mere scratches on the skin, as she put it. And there was some suggestion in her tone, when she read me Bible stories, of a commander teaching his scouts the enemy's language.

Close though the riders came I could not see either one clear enough to know him. They passed beneath us. Peculiar temptation: to shout Help! Or what if I dislodged a humble stone with my toe? Fear and longing raged through me. The ocean pounded in my breast, in my head, in my throat. This was exactly as I had felt when I slipped over the gunwale and knew my chance would not come again, that I must cut and run up the beach or be a slave for the term of my sentence. I was two persons, both cursed.

In my terror of being caught again I wondered if the Men might be planning to hand me over. If so, I could not raise a finger to defend myself because I was feebled by an unbearable ache to reclaim my right to belong in the hateful familiarity of meanings. No need to feign this.

Yet I was tugged in the other direction by pride in my new grandness. I, once terrified of being hurt by the manacle I wore, now struck terror into others by simply shaking it above my head. Was I to give this up for the sake of sentiment? The point is that neither the terrified person nor the grand person seemed to be me. I could no more accept myself as a convict than as a chief among Indians. Even the real murder seemed too tricky to grasp. I still found difficulty in believing that I had done this, that I had fully intended doing it, and that when successful I had felt proud and jubilant. Likewise, deep inside, I could not believe in the fetish thing I had become – despite the fact that I was quick to understand how to behave towards the Indians and despite the fact that day by day what took hold of me was a hallucination that this was indeed my natural birthright and that I really might be recollecting what was already fixed in my nature.

A separate matter was the fear of further punishment. I had been called a coward and I dare say there was some truth in it. Standing silent at the centre of the circle of invisible Men, I belonged among them. I repudiated those colonial fellows (what a great Biblical word 'repudiated' is). To cry help or dislodge a stone and attract attention could only bring the wrath of both parties upon me. If I did not die immediately by the spear I could look forward to being hung by the neck from the mast of the pinnace.

There is a flock of birds outside the wall. They are setting up such a hubbub they must see something I can not see. It is a grisly reminder . . . being shut away again. How do I help myself crying out and asking why you leave me locked in here? Well, I suppose you are giving me time to show you the whole truth.

That day the shifty sea trembled right out to a fixed horizon where the hot milky sky rested heavy on it. Two osprey shadows flickered across furrows and upturned tree roots. Nagged by anxiety, I worried about what would happen if the Men recognized where I had come from, with whom I really belonged. They might see in me the exact same thing I saw in those fellows on horseback down there!

When at last the truth hit me, it hit with full force: the Men had gone. Alone, I stood marooned between two lives.

I looked down along the new cut road at those approaching figures. I watched until they passed below me. Horses' rumps glossy and tails swishing in a remembered way, they rounded a bend among the treetops at my feet. Out of view, the beasts could be heard plodding on in the dust. They stopped. Why had they been reined in? I listened. Why? That moment the strangest sounds began: a wooden crate from another world being dragged across a warehouse floor, some huge disaster shrieking, the splintering crackle of glassy air splitting from sky to earth. A frantic wind puffed round me while the crown of leaves behind which I hid rushed away, breaking a passage as it went, followed by a colossal thud. Birds scattered from the felled tree, birds like those whose feathers I was given to stick in my hair, tiny blue fly-catching birds, pink-crested birds, even a hawk. The air was still full of the rhythm of the axes which had already stopped. Away from the shock a kangaroo fled, crashing past without a glance at me.

A curious pressure around my leg called to mind subtle memories. You must imagine it rising to my knee. And me, discovered there, understanding everything too late. I remembered: this was the clasp of a snake! Who had I become now? Never was escape more urgent.

What was that, then? demanded a voice below, while the kangaroo could be heard still breaking its way to safety.

I am expecting the savages, said the Master, we are ready. If that's you up there you can come for a dose of medicine, you heathens!

I heard hoofs among the stones and the two of them walked their mounts back till clear in sight and not more than a dozen yards from where I stood. The escaping beast still bounded away into the distance, heading up the slope as I had escaped an age ago – splintering thickets. The snake reached my thigh. There it hesitated. I saw the head waver as it investigated my manacled hand. I dared not look again. I dared not move. But I had glimpsed a twist of rose-red underbelly, glitters of sunlight on lustrous black scales, and pinpoint black eyes. A tongue flickered against my skin. I felt the snake's coils glide higher to use my power arm as a route for reaching my shoulder. The Master and his servant stared right at me. The snake's head examined my head. A comical thing came to mind, that snakes are famous as being near-sighted.

A shot, fired like a single clap, sounded ridiculous. There was no harm in such a puny thing. I stared at the Master and his levelled weapon, then at his companion. They stared straight back up at me. They were so close I could almost have spat at them and expected to find my mark.

Heathens! the Master sneered. And his trunk sat so firm he seemed part of the horse.

The other's hat nodded.

Only then did I realize an amazing fact. They were looking right at me but I was invisible to them. My snake rippled up over one ear. The rasping scales gave me the shivers. Into my hair the thing went tunnelling. The tail still reached down to my feet. A slender creature this was, filling me with nausea and pride.

If I am King of Men, I told my coward fears, then this soil is my soil. Toads and serpents belong here.

From down in the direction of the felled tree the long stroke of a saw began, rasp, pause, rasp. One of the horses stamped. Time enough elapsed for a war to be fought.

Or was I mistaken? Could the Master see me? Did he ignore me as not worth his anger? Did he think I was a decoy, to be left alone until I lured his true enemies within range of a bullet? Grief dug deep into my vitals. The pain grew unbearable. To be despised by him – an individual I thought less worthy than myself. I had to challenge him. Yes, this pride had hidden in my heart ready to betray me at the moment of my second escape. Was it possible to resist? Nature don't answer to reason. I was in the grip of forces beyond a person's control. Fate favoured me in my turn. My mouth opened and I shouted.

No shout came; only a gasp of something stale.

I swallowed to get my voice back, the voice which I had scarce used in all this time of being King. Why had I not at least sung songs to keep the faculty? Disuse robbed me of power. I tried again, but the snake came coiling round my brow.

I don't suppose we hit the swine, the Master grumbled.

The eggshell head (can you imagine the frail skull of a snake, so like a bird's skull?) swayed while checking my open mouth which, very slow, I began to shut.

Didn't catch any screams, did you? the Master laughed short and slapped his heels hard against the horse's flanks, moving off at a trot. A few extra words reached me garbled by the wind. The long saw continued rasping to an even stroke. A minute later the riders emerged again on the track above the floating logs. I could not tell which way they were now looking but they soon passed beyond the jetty and out of sight.

I was full of becoming invisible.

Rigid as a stick for fear of my dangerous snake, I made to turn gradual, seeking help. You may imagine how slow I turned and how hope leaped up in me when I found the circle there again, each man perched on one leg and the leaves tied at his wrists gently rustling. Their eyes would not meet mine. I came to the point. I could understand that I may as well give up hope of ever being helped. I was marooned in grandeur or in shame (it scarce mattered which), made untouchable by my struggle against fate.

Once you live by the rule of order you put yourself at risk if you are green. You can not win. The court proved this to me: I was transported for forgery to confirm the matter. My father denied there was any such thing as law or any such thing as smuggling. He treated his courtroom like a Punch and Judy show. My mother told me he scoffed at the judge and farted when the jury brought in their verdict. But I only remember the wooden way he stood up there to hear his sentence of death . . . plus the curse he put on them.

In my case the courtroom was to be just as strange to me but, without the good humour my father's courage allowed him, I wallowed around, adrift on a nightmare. Expelled in the dock, I had to face an old schemer dressed in silk and animal hair who never let me speak when I needed to. He kept cutting me off for breaking rules I did not understand. He had a mace carried around and set up in front of him and he talked in code. I had to crawl to him by calling him My Lord. As for the constables, the Oxford beadle and the clerks, they formed a ring around me. I was trapped. And I trapped myself because I did show them respect, my stammering a tonic to them. No doubt they enjoyed seeing me pale and scared. How easy it is to admit the truth to you! But at the time I had no idea a trial has its roots dug far down into the murk of our savage past. This time my mother could not be there. She knew nothing of what had happened to me. None of my kin were there, nobody from Kirk Braddon or even from Douglas, to watch the end of my bright hopes. I was just a cheeky boy, I suppose, jeered by the public with their Oxfordshire hee-haw.

So you are a skilled tradesman we hear? That is how the judge put the question. His voice went like honey. We do not question the quality of the work you were trying to sell! You assure us that this is a forgery and your own forgery. We shall not attempt any comment upon the art of printing in case we show our ignorance! His wit was greeted with general merriment. However, we are puzzled, he went on, as to why you have called nobody to give witness to your mastery of the craft or your good character, not even your father. We should hesitate to call you a bastard, he said. There was lots more laughter. Oh no? You don't say so? How very misfortunate – was it for smuggling we hanged him?

The country itself was hostile.

All my life on our little island I smelt heather without knowing it. The cry of seagulls and the sea's distant beat were in my blood, but how was I to know this until I no longer heard them? When at last the time came for me to tell such things the courtroom fell silent, even the scratching pens stopped while the clerks listened. I got going all right, so much so that I warmed up to the crimes of the Earl of Derby's family and the Scots before that, of Irish kings and the Danes in their longboats. I did tell them about the heather and lost cries on the wind too, but not about the dragon cut in stone. The name of the dragon was on my tongue but I held back. Nor did I say I had a brother named Hall, because if he was alive he would be certain to be hiding still.

We shall not deny you the music of seagulls, never let it be said, Judge Mitchell assured me from under his wig of a sheep, you shall feel most perfect at home in respect of gulls and squalor. I am sure His Grace, the Earl of Derby, will approve. You shall be held at Wapping until the first available hangman can carry out His Majesty's pleasure. Accept my regrets that I do not know of any heather at Wapping!

Where a grown man would have reacted with rage, I was still so much a boy that I just felt indignant instead. This was the first sentencing, before I appealed and they commuted it to transportation once they admitted my crime was only forgery and nothing worse.

You see how I wish you to know all there is to be known. My shame is the very last thing I ought to keep from you. I shall come to the tale of my appeal in good time, but let me confess here that even when they clamped me in irons aboard a transport bound for New South Wales I kept myself lofty. So pure and bold I felt.

As to the matter of the forgery, there was no dispute. I had planned it, set the text on the press, gauged the lead to a niceness, and paid due respect to the great man whose sign I copied – simpleton that I was and eager not to fall below his standard. I locked the type into the forme, ligatures snug and firm, painstaking in the matter of ink, worried lest it might not be as black and even as the real article. I started the coffin gliding to and fro. When there were enough copies to choose a clean sample of each sheet the practice runs were burnt. My crime called for skill – and love of English. You may guess that I felt confused on this score. Loyal as I was to my father.

My father spoke no word of English in my hearing ever. Manx was his language and he stood by his own folk. He was neither for the Goidelic people nor the Brythonic people: the fact that Irishmen and Scotsmen could make little sense of our tongue being proof enough. As for the English, how should poor father even know the law when he had no word of their rules in his head?

My mother it was who first taught us, Hall and me. She was quite another case, being fixed that an education meant the skill to make headway in life.

I should not want the lad's wife one day to accuse me of condemning her to the poverty I've had myself, she once said, so if he turns out to follow his father it will be because he chooses to and not from ignorance of any option.

As a girl she had been known to the Bishop of Sodor.

Your father may say as often as he likes, she told me, that we should call him the Bishop of Sudr-eyyars, but in my view that would be contrary. Sudr-eyyars is a name more proper to the dragon than either the Church in London or the Church in Dublin.

Being green (again) aboard ship brought more trouble. I had not imagined there would be allotments of power even among the condemned, privilege and rank. I was to learn that the rigid order of society is mirrored even more rigid in prison. The constable had his fellow bullies among the felons, like the judge had his fellow sneerer. Just as a nightwatchman ought to be cautious in case he offends against a bailiff's territory, so you can trace a ladder from such as myself on the lowest rung up to a murderer with the dignity of an Earl of Derby . . . only that the Earl has more anguish and more spilt blood to answer for than any petty copycat of the bottom deck.

I was green even on the quay at Sydney town in the bright drizzle of a new place, a stranger to the ropes. Again it was my downfall. When the gentleman arrived to look us over (does this call to your mind a particular scene?) I myself was insolent enough to look over the fellows I was mustered with. One commanding figure, a man moderate tall, of solid build but lean, still bore about his stance the independence the others had lost or had had whipped out of them. Simply to see him look the gentry over, quite the way they looked at us, gave me heart. So very green I was, I jostled among the ranks to a place at his side. Putting myself as low as possible on the ladder, do you see?

I would pay the price.

My sight again played me false. Once beside Gabriel Dean, having elbowed my way among lags showing no interest in the draft, this ideal rebel revealed his nature in disagreeable details: hard mouth, cruel eyes and a manner of flaunted coarseness.

Did he need some creature to cringe and adore him? Well, I was this creature. When those who were chosen to board the *Fraternity* were chained in pairs he offered his wrist alongside mine. We were joined together.

I'll keep the runt in order, he promised.

Saying this, he was speaking sidelong to the Master, as I have come to realize, marking the difference of their worlds by claiming a likeness between them. From that moment the Master would see how the matter stood among his felons: whom he must reckon with, and how vigorous a chief convict might act to force others of the serving order to obey.

I was nothing to Gabriel Dean. He didn't even need to look at me to tell why I was there. But once we were chained together his coolness showed as hate. I had served his purpose and he bristled at being yoked to me for three days. No sooner were we aboard *Fraternity* than he knocked me to the floor and, with one arm, hoisted me to my feet again. This was not for my benefit, I was nothing already, but for the others' – to show that there would be a vacant place beside him for the right candidate, for a lieutenant. Like his counterparts in society he had the vanity of cleanness and kept as free from filth as conditions allowed. But contagion is a thing unto itself and mysterious. No matter how the strong man twists or turns to avoid it, if it is in the air he breathes or in the water he drinks he is even more prone to contract an illness than a weak person – such is the divine law which levels everything – because he consumes more air, more water, more energy. Such contagion was already at work in Gabriel Dean. To tell the truth, he might have known this. He might have staked his claim when he did to get in first while still able to impress the rest of us, aware that he would recover quicker for not having to waste his strength coping with rivals.

At most an hour after we weighed anchor, the ship creaking into a steady swell, his bare arm against mine felt sticky with sweat. Having no time to lose, he smashed his chain in my face. He set me humiliating contests against him to prove that the effort of my whole body was not enough to match the arm I was locked to. He forced me to foolish gestures when he raised his hand and mine had to follow it. He refused me the simplest comfort of resting at ease by jerking so violent as to wrench my shoulder out of joint, not to mention more disgusting offences against my pride. This is enough.

By the second day, when the fever struck him severe, he was already warranted as our leader. I had served my turn. And yet there was a smallness in him so that he could not let up. I suppose he feared the fact that I knew for certain what state he was in, whereas the rest might only guess because being so few – just ten of us in steerage – we had room to spread out. This, added to the lack of any window, gave him the cover of poor light. He kept up minor torments, seeming satisfied as long as he made me gasp with pain. I dare say the thud of his blows impressed the others and confirmed the glimpse they had of my bleeding mouth when that hatch cover had been slid open for a voice to roar: Are you Frenchies or something, begging for a taste of the cat?

The third day he lay there, for the most part, inward with his illness, so absorbed by fever he took no interest in anything else, not in food, not even in tormenting me. A curious awe fell on the company. We began to hear the noises around us, not just the timbers under strain from the sea, but anxious animals in the hold bellowing and barking. The passing voice of a seaman, brisk about obeying orders, bare feet running across the deck above. Once a woman sang out, but we could suppose little from her tone except that she was displeased, though we held our breath to hear. Her accent declared her to be of the Master's company.

I thought about her. I tried to put a name to her but I could think of nothing new enough.

During this break I had leisure to take stock of what lay before me. Mischance had already marked me out for the butt of malice. Once free of our shackles, it would be anyone's guess how many lesser bullies might jostle me as an easy and proven victim.

Some I could fight, but most were like to find me as weak a prey as they wished. To think of it robbed me of manhood. I had a loser's heart. I slumped there. Meantime Gabriel, that fastidious ruffian, grew inward and slack. He snored while still awake.

An idea came to me.

Once the idea had come, many hours passed before I could take it in and hold it up to the light of reason. I felt knotted by doubts at what it would mean. You will laugh, but I even took into account that, as a man wronged, I had my pride and that acting on this idea would damage my good name. I have never been hasty. You may be surprised to learn this. But the habit of care had bred in me a custom of reckoning risks. In such matters I am used to being correct. With this in mind you may not now be surprised to hear that I valued my own notion of honour. My father had been a gallant man and an example. I asked: Did he die deceived in me? Were his affections so misplaced? He once said to me (though the poetry is lost in English): Being your mother's son will load you with enough to live up to for it to last a lifetime.

My mother, who made an enemy of Christianity, taught me the Psalms. We may not be church folk, as her saying went, but that need not mean we are Godless. That is how she was.

Are you ready to hear more about my crimes and not dismiss me as a rogue? What have I told you of my first offence, for which I was transported? You should not forget how hard I worked at it: I studied the document, set the type myself and checked each careful flaw to get it right, slaved over a tiny chip cut in an upper case H, the precise irregular lines, also that I went in person to the dealer in Oxford to sell it: my 'Commentary upon Twofold Victims of Fate in the Thebaid of Statius, from the Press of William Caxton, Anno 1491'.

The funny thing is that I still have little idea what the Thebaid of Statius is or what it might mean. It is just a name for a book. The original, nothing to do with Caxton, had been put into Irish from the Latin. This much I know. And I can recite the opening by heart, having tinkered with it for so long to get the print right. 'This tale of Thebes was written in AD 1487 at the House of Fineen, and in the same year died Ua Mael-Shechlain, to wit, Laighrech Ua Mael-Schechlain, son of John, son of Felim, son of Ferral Blind-eye Tiernan.' I was in love with the music of that. I used to chant it to myself as I trudged home on cold damp evenings. The commentary listed four items to be dealt with: twin heroes, the divine beauty of women, the death of a dragon, and a voyage to an unknown land. Each item had earlier echoes in Celtic beliefs.

Going back to the most ancient times before history there was a Goddess who took two bridegrooms each year – have you heard of her? – one for the winter and one for the summer. Each had the task of killing the husband who had lain with her for the six months before him. This idea could still be found, so the commentary said, under the skin of the Thebaid of Statius, enemies in pairs and friends in pairs. A warrior having a lion's mane, with a warrior whose bushy boar bristles rise like a horror of white-shrike wings when with wild angry terror he seizes his enemy. So in our Celtic tales the Goddess chose a bridegroom with a horse's mane for summer and a bridegroom with goat thighs for winter. The summer one twanged his bow to make warlike music. The winter one hooted through the cold dark of our secret self. Just as the Thebaid of Statius has women grey-eyed and distinguished like the Goddess, so our tale has a Goddess like a woman, crimson cheeked, crimson lipped, with fine calves, slender feet and rounded heels. In both there are fiendish mad monsters loosed on the land to devastate it – I wish I could remember the whole thing to tell you it word for word – monsters part serpent, part clawed beast, and journeys to strange lands.

Anno 1491, by the bye – did you notice? – the eve of Columbus's voyage to the unknown.

The commentary explained that the Christian imagination had refined those beasts of fable to achieve the glory of unicorns and other marvels, as listed in a forged letter from the supposed Prester John, beasts not content with being beasts but mixing the virtues of many kinds. A forged lion with parrot's feathers. Forged horses blessed with horns for use in battle. A magical bird of fire called Yllerion which made a habit of plunging into the sea where mortal birds, sucked down by the high wind of the plunge, drowned while Yllerion rose again like the Goddess, flaming up through the waves to fly into heaven. A pretty story. This Yllerion could swoop boldly on an armoured knight, catch him and carry him off into the clouds, complete with his horse, and eat him there.

So we fancy what we do not know. We dress what we desire in gorgeous hopes. And our ancient stories curl round on themselves to bite their own tails.

I was a simple boy and carried away. I did not miss the fact that this Thebaid of Statius, whatever it meant, was translated first into Irish and only then into English. For every reason I was determined to do a perfect job.

Can you want further proof?

I already knew about the Goddess of Kirk Braddon taking one husband at the feast of horse mating in spring and the other in autumn at the feast of goat mating. An old lady, a friend of the family who helped with our Melliah, many a time told tales of the kind, with the Goddess gorging the lust of each new husband while she got him ready to meet the death he was chosen for. (How he must have fought against fear of his coming death – and yet, would he not in truth be excited by the ritual also?) Storytelling is a great thing where I come from.

The Goddess still lived in the Isle of Man when Vikings began their raids. Each summer the longboats swept in. We needed leaders to beat them back. The stench of burning villages rose on the wind. Common folk were in fear of their lives. The time came when a horse king, who proved himself the hero of a summer campaign, stood tradition on its head. At his execution he fought back and the new winter king, in white goat skin, lay bleeding on the soil. You may know the story. The ritual had gone wrong. Christians were among us. So we became the nation we are. The past was dead. The Goddess lost her power. The age of kings began. There will be no end to wars until a second bridegroom brings back the peace.

My mother mourned the fact with the old lady. I suppose all this lay somewhere behind my choice of what to forge in the first place. However the rest of the island may think, we of Kirk Braddon were still the winter king's folk. I myself once heard his flute in the far distance on the night of a new moon. I heard it here too. Yes, seated at my table, blind and helpless in the dark.

By the way, I have opened the biscuit barrel. I do not mean to steal but I must live. I ought to record the strange crumbling of a biscuit in the mouth. I can think of nothing like it. Already this biscuit is itself a journey back to some strange place where I have been in dreams. I find myself hungry for the sharp taste of a beetle I know and the numbing juice of a green leaf.

Did I tell you about the forest and how, while I was escaping, I lay body to body with this warm unknown land, gazing up through the treetops at a shimmer of moon lace? Of course. And how freakish birds whistled and cackled?

Each day, escorted by the circle of guardians, I moved among charmed hills as I moved among my questions. And I saw with joy how disordered they were. Food was brought me without any need to lift a finger. Drink was brought. We left the place of the little water badgers with duck bills and webbed feet to set out for the place of winged squirrels. We found giant footprints where a two-legged creature had walked and left the ripped relics of a native dog to die from lion-sized bites. A passage through the forest of shaking treetops could be watched while the creature itself escaped being seen. Down through a gully he went, violent in his haste and invisible as wind, up and over a mountain.

If my names for these marvels do not convince you, this is not to say the marvels are not there – simply that English has nothing to know them by. I do the best I can because I want you to understand that there is something to be understood out there, something free of the law, free of any comforting faith in a God whose motives may be explained through our own, something that has become the map of my heart.

At last, I have dared confess! And don't you see? If once we gave things our own names we would have to begin destroying them.

Rain rained. Hail hailed. Frost froze the ground. Trees shed long rags of bark. Creeks ran and stopped running. Flowers opened to the moon. The sun grew hot again. Short nights bristled with mosquitoes. The earth baked hard. The water they brought me tasted of death. Still we walked and we slept in the open. Sometimes we paused on a mountain where the empire of leaves beneath us was all the same strange hue, not quite a green nor a brown nor a grey, but closer to green than anything else, leaves cloaking range upon range of foothills where hot air danced like a million daytime stars. At another stage we walked out from the forest shade to a grassy plain. Clay-yellow grass, silver at the tips, up to our chests and level with the horizon where tall mud spires stood, from which the Men dug termites for my dinner. Another time we reached the ocean, ginger on the sharp rocks among salt water pools, the damp air a blessing to my tormented skin. Feasting on lobster we heard the women, gathered just around the point out of sight, splash and shriek with happiness. Nothing was more foreign than this happiness, nothing was less English.

Once, we saw a ship under full sail standing away to sea. I could not make out if she might be the *Fraternity.* She headed south. My guardians watched her with dread. The great sky (and I believe you will accept that the sky here is wider and deeper than anywhere else in the world) showed us lessons in emptiness or shuddered with thunder or filled the mind with swiftly floating clouds. Skies drained white by heat. Skies glutted red with blood. Skies pink beyond the morning mists. Skies as a black field sprinkled with soft daisy stars.

A few times in our wanderings we came upon signs known to me but not to them. You may guess how threatened the Men felt when we discovered a shirt hung from a sapling. Imagine the witchcraft of a copper nail, or the imprint made by a cloven hoof! The knife we found became a sensation because I wanted it and was set on having it. I signified this by drumming my leg with the manacle to clear them from the spot and picking it up for myself. In the same way I put on the shirt to prove I could turn blue. They moved back a step. Perhaps they expected me to disappear altogether in the sky. The copper nail I lodged in my matted hair.

One more thing about coming upon that knife: the sight of it surprised me into feeling a surge of joy. Yet the important thing now was that I could not let the joy show. Joy was too human a thing. Impassive, I bent and took the knife with my power hand, then stabbed at my own leg to prove its point. They observed the trickling blood, also when it stopped and crusted over. Having nowhere else to carry the knife I jabbed it in through the fabric of my shirt and out again, hoping this crude loop would hold its weight.

The Men watched to see how I would use the knife and the nail. But I kept them to myself as too precious even for the ceremony of death when one of my guardians died. He had been stalking a kangaroo. We watched him glide in the squatting position with only the top of his head above the seed-level of the tall grass, when he vanished of a sudden. The quarry went about its quiet business. No spear whirred from the cover. No hunter went leaping to claim his kill. We found him twisted in a struggle against nothing, face etched with frightful pain, and an ant already at work on one open eye.

It fell to me to mark this serious day with my own ritual. And I did have the service by heart – or at least the right Psalms, as you have already been told. Strange that the first words of English I ever spoke in the presence of these people began with the text: I held my tongue and spake nothing; I kept silence, yes, even from good words; but it is pain and grief to me.

The sound of mumbo-jumbo, said out loud there in the wild, made me appreciate the dignity of it. Well, so much for the

Order for the Burial of the Dead. I did explain that I once printed it, I hope?

After speaking, I wondered what might happen if I produced the knife and cut a lock from the corpse's beard to see what they made of that, because I still knew nothing about them really. I thought thoughts of using a stone and hammering my nail into his skull. I thought of sacrificing my blue shirt to wrap him in. I did none of these things. God's words were enough, in the event. The circle moved on. Still at the centre and still untouchable, I was taken from that place as I had been taken from so many other places. But this time, once I was out of sight, people back there began wailing a chorus of long-drawn wails. One voice sounded like the dead man's own. I paused to listen, certain I recognized him. They let me stand.

Are you curious about how readily I threw in my lot with them? But did I, I wonder? Yes, because I felt so contented among them.

For their part: who was I to them? You see, in their way of looking me over and agreeing about me, there was what I can only call deep familiarity. This was a fact as tricky as quicksilver. At all times they behaved with perfect confidence that they knew who I was. Even when we came to have some sign language between us they did not ask me to explain my coming among them. You would think they had expected me, they were so little surprised or puzzled.

Can it be that these people have refined the notion of brotherhood among all mankind until they take no thought to defend themselves, nor even to display curiosity? What is society, at bottom? Must there be fences – some people inside and others outside? The closer a family grows, does this mean that anyone who is not kin will be all the more unwelcome and kept out? If so, how far may kin be said to stretch: to second cousins, to second cousins' spouses?

This sort of conundrum teased my brain while I walked in my cocoon of silence at the centre of that charmed circle, hearing nearby laughter and snatches of forbidden companionship. For my part, so little idea did I have of them that I still can not say if they even saw one another as individuals. Most duties they did as a group.

Yet if I ever tried to solve these issues by applying the question to myself I came up against the fact that I did not know my own answers. At the centre of our family were my parents – but could two people be a centre? My father had certainly been head of his household, but how often was he there? My mother, being born with a different surname, might have thought she belonged more to her father's family than ours, yet she was the anchor, the one we depended on. Were there two intersecting circles? Only two? In my father's line all the eldest sons took the Viking name Hall: so when had that circle intersected with the Celtic circle? And how about my Uncle Fox, mother's brother, also the jolly young woman he wed – didn't this confuse another circle with the two we already had? And so forth, until I reached a halt at the boundary of the entire island, the Irish Sea. This, surely, would stand as a limit to my belonging? But many a person went over to Glasgow to try his luck, or Liverpool, or Belfast, or even to France. So wasn't the sea itself enough, then, either?

Following this line led me to some pretty claims, until I recalled the Englishman who, unwilling to believe I had the skill to deceive him with my forgery, accused me of stealing the genuine article, a national treasure . . . which straight away branded me as a foreigner. I was too young then, though it is most likely less than two years ago, to dispute with him on that score. I had to accept exile to avert the worse disaster of being hung. So much for the brotherhood of man!

Then, if we grant the view that, as humans, we all belong within the one circle, how can a person ever be in exile? Add to this the extreme strange fact that when the British cast me out to the remotest strand on earth, the natives of this place – part man, part plant, part bird – recognized me, set their lives around me, and made room for the mystery of my being there in their routine day.

How did they feel kinship with me considering my clumsy ways, though? When we travelled they moved among the tangled plants without the least inconvenience, seeming to walk straight through a confusion of boughs and vines woven together as if on purpose to resist any attempt at pulling them apart. They paused, polite enough to check on my difficulties from time to time. I scrambled after them, forearms guarding my eyes, head down like a bull, cursing and panting, breaking a passage by violence and ill-judgement.

Yet, of course, they have their own circles.

I soon learned that the men and women travel and even camp separate. I longed to see how the children were reared and whether they took all men for their fathers and all women for their mothers. Having never fathered a child and being fearful that I never might, these were the times when I felt sorriest for myself.

I was still in my own childhood. All I ever learned of the deepest bonds I learned as a boy, as one who receives and has little power to give. Then here I found I had become the giver. Granted, they supplied my food, but I was not bound to accept it. Nor was I bound to do anything I did not choose to do, provided I remained within the circle.

There you have it. I hope you are not laughing at me. Like any other king the symbol of my absolute power was to be useless. They adored me in their way. The fact that we had no speech in common warranted my greatness, you see, and their need to serve me. If I had been able to make myself plain how could they fail to see me as a man like themselves. I was wholly alien: therefore, to the marrow, I belonged.

The Men kept me as their King.

I can not yet say how I should address you. My hand is trembling as I toy with Dear . . .

Do you remember how red my hair is? The beard I grow and

my chest hairs are the same bright colour. I have heard it said that hair is dead already, a dead part of the spirit being pushed out through our skin. My hairs were all I had to lose at one time, so I collected them. You will think this strange. Perhaps I do too. But it saved my life as you will see. Each hair that came away in my fingers, complete with a tiny bud of root, I rolled together with the others, using a little mud, to make thread. There was no plan in my mind when I began this work, but as the thread thickened to cord I thought it might one day be useful. I rolled it round my power wrist and tucked it under the lip of the manacle. Besides being safe there the cord served to dull the pain which never let me go. The new comfort shocked me because it proved that I had not let my spirit be broken. So I was not even wasting the body's failures.

The murder had been an earlier proof that my spirit would not be broken. The murder had given me back my courage and turned the beatings into a victory. Yes, to look back after so long, seeing myself dragged on deck while deckhands carried the body, seeing us both thrown down before the Master and reading disgust on his face, was also to see what the behaviour of the other lags meant. I did not notice at the time. But those chained felons, who crept two by two into a brilliant morning and turned their backs on the dazzling sea, watched. What they watched they watched with respect. They saw the carpenter come and kick that splendid body to clear enough room for his skill, then cleave the wrist at a blow. Fool that I was, I missed my chance; stunned with the guilt of the thing, I failed to see what the Master meant.

You owe me fifteen shillings for this man.

If he were squeamish, Mr Atholl would scarce choose New South Wales in the first place, nor would he be in possession of a large land grant from Lieutenant-Governor Snodgrass. No. And it was not only me he spoke to about the fifteen shillings, he had meant this for everybody. At last (and too late) the meaning became clear. It was a contract, wasn't it? He was saying, All of you are here as tools to be used while I carve out greatness for myself because beyond the vision nothing matters a damn – so whatever you cost you must pay back.

My fifteen shillings debt was to raise me to the leadership Gabriel Dean claimed when we set sail. That was a good man, the Master's words meant, so this must be a better: worth fifteen shillings extra.

The truth is that I need never have run away.

One day we followed a creek for hours, clambering up from boulder to boulder and reaching a high valley where the air was dim and green as lichen. Here we came to a forest of ferns so tall we walked under them among the bristling stems. The ground was covered by rocks spongey with moss. I wanted to rest and enjoy the song of one or two melodious birds in that quiet theatre but my guardians knew that we had not yet reached the place for sitting. Further we went, among darkening leaves, till we seemed to have pushed our way up among the tree tops, lost to any sense of direction. Then we broke through, clear of a sudden, right into the sky. The land opened below as a stupendous gorge. I felt my soul fly straight out of me and high above the forested hills so thick with the screech of a thousand cockatoos, launched into that valley of space.

Do you see it?

Such a place this is, with the sides of the gorge like long winding curtains of rock hung with ropes of white water here and there. The cascades seem to fall too slow and to defy nature, the far ones are heard like a long sigh in an organ pipe beyond a soft thunder of those nearby, while above everything countless leaves whisper supreme. You should bear in mind that I was living in the close and always changing places of a plant world. So now the vast and simple space with its vast and simple sky transported me into the life of pure light.

I know how an eagle feels.

My soul aloft, I could even render thanks to the dull past for growing thick upon me as feathers. I cried out. How shall I explain this for you? There is a word, but like a fool I can not be sure how to spell it! How embarrassing that my spelling should let me down when I most need to say what I mean. Exstacy (extasy?) was what lifted me up. But now I feel an idiot trying to call it to mind and set it down. What I discovered was that pain, even by itself, can be enough to carry the body in flight. Out over the killing emptiness I soared. Gliding on fear, the pure strength of invisibility holding me up. The wind my ally. Absolute confidence came to me. My guardians stood locked in their roots with the ground. I was alone. I welcomed the truth of it. Even as a child I was alone. Although Hall tried many times to break through, he could not. I suppose I hated the way he tolerated me. He was my hero all right and my friend, but he was already a man while I remained a boy. So of course he could not reach me.

Stooped over my printer's masterpiece, handling some precious vellum I had found in the stacks, inking the type for an even black and hearing the bed rumble on its sliding base, while beyond and above the workshop our town bell clanged twice across the square, cursing the lamplight I had to work by, eyes watering and wandering with strain, what else was I but alone?

What else am I, squinting as I write this, believing you are out there but not knowing?

At the gorge I could feel the actual world under my fingers and my own part in this world. I knew that a single doubt, a single lapse into worrying about some separate detail, would send me tumbling down to my death. Above, a true eagle watched as it went gliding, aloof but curious. Did I spoil his chaos? Was I a miracle in a world which could admit no miracles without losing its sense of being whole – or was I the invader who upsets an organized plan of food growth and food taking without understanding it?

The monotonous murmur of leaves and rushing water held me there.

Cliffs far down in the valley dropped into the green foam of more forest. Then I was dropping too. In an instant the world turned over. Yet I would not surrender, I would not put the name of cowardice to my cowardice.

Back among the guardians, I was leaning desperate against a bluff, fighting the vertigo which drew me to the brink. The odd thing was that even then I put it to myself that this was how I would one day come upon love.

Months later we reached the selfsame gorge from a different side and in winter. A still sea of mist lay in the vast space. Nothing moved. The slanting light of early morning showed the cliffs as a council of giants. This time I stepped to the very edge and dropped a stone, watching it hit the cliff once and bounce out into white emptiness, the tiny sound of impact as clear in the air as ringing glass. Silence rinsed my soul. Colossal breakers of mist rolled noiseless to collide with these shores.

Do you know what I promised? When I am ready, I promised, I shall step off into this and be part of the silence. I won't utter a murmur. I shall be gone.

As I write, a leaf has fallen on the page. It must have been caught in my hair. When I look close and bring it into focus, I see shape and I see colour: a curved dagger, and a riddle of green, green lying beneath a sheen of grey. If I break it open I expect I will find the blue of sky inside and the mottled brown of an eagle's feather. The scarlet stem, where it joins the leaf, branches into three – two outer edges as fine as scarlet thread, the main one a central vein. What does it feel like? Tough and velvety. What does it smell of? Ghosts. It fills me with longing. I have broken the leaf and hold it to my nose. I want to go back out there. The tang clears my head. What joy that I have found the means to sit and confess this to you.

I knew my guardians would see that I was planning one day to step off the edge. And yet I knew also that the silence included them. They watched as part of the silence. With their genius for such things they were also part of the emptiness. They could see my thoughts all right. They stood among the trees, each one carrying a bunch of leaves like this leaf, ready for the ceremony of rattling them when the need arose.

What can be said on the subject of the Master's wife? So we come to the brink indeed! Without ever seeing her eye to eye, I know what I need to know. And I knew from the day we embarked. She existed. She grew so strong that she left no room for anything else. More so when I escaped. The forest put me in mind of her. The mossy rocks. The gurgling creek. The bursting into light. The world silence. Flight. The eagle's eye. My mind was fixed on her. She haunted every moment. She had begun to be with me then, you see. Had begun to torture me. She kept off, yes, but that did not help. Her being remote was part of what made my heart leap. Wasn't I above clouds already, commander of space, able at a single shouted word to shatter that immense calm and bring the whole thing to centre upon me? So proud I was. So much a slave.

Do you agree that power, to be power, must be employed? This is why God, the image of power, ought not to be confused with Nature. God punishes and God rewards. Nature is neutral. I understand that the greater the power we have, the further removed we become from enjoying the use of it.

My guardians had power over the clan and I had power over them. Because I was so powerful I could do nothing. The mark of my power was to not even meet the people I ruled or know how things stood with them.

Let me put it to you that any man who is a slave to love can not tell whether, to other eyes, his loved one is handsome or plain. Nor can he tell this for himself until she shows him how he is to think of her. In the meanwhile he must wait.

What else can I say? This is what all my letter writing is meant to mean.

P.S. Note that my migration among Men has itself been a circle.

Not only did we come yet again to that part of the coast where I first waded ashore: during the final few days we made haste to get there. In all my time among Men they had shown few signs of haste before. I could see no reason for it now. The weather lowered and brooded but the food remained plentiful and the water good.

My mind, I suppose, was elsewhere in any case. Lately I had been puzzling over a new question: Why had my guardians never grown tired of me? Surely they will rebel soon, I thought, against being isolated by my isolation? Surely there are other things they would rather do? Surely they have had enough of this scabby foreigner and the servitude of feeding him? But if any such grumbling passed between them in secret they kept it among themselves. That got me going on the subject of good manners.

Can you see that this might be the highest human accomplishment, good manners? There is a lot to it, a lot more than sitting up straight and saying please.

Without letting any feelings show they fetched me my food, my water, watched over my nights and from time to time presented me with a black snake. The snake would be put on the ground and then they would watch with great interest to see which direction it took. They never caught the one which saved my life because none claimed me or tried using me as a tree.

A week passed after we left the grasslands before warm damp winds blew in on us as we entered the forest and fine rain fell, gusts of it being pushed in billows among the tall straight trunks and tasting of the sea.

I felt stronger than ever in my life. There was a toughness in me that I believe even Hall might envy. My skin, though a crust of sores and festering, no longer tormented me. Even my eyesight seemed a degree sharper. Maybe this was the freedom from close work; and close work had always fallen to my lot owing to my excellent vision at that range. Or maybe I simply no longer felt tense. By this stage I was without any fear of what was around me. Long since I had given up peering into the fuzzy tangle of the bush anxious because I could make out so little or be sure of distances.

I trusted the circle with my life.

We journeyed seaward, climbing small rises and strolling

down long saddles. The soft weather had a promise of summer. All this took me back to a memory of the life I led long ago on the Isle of Man: I was happy.

Then we came to a fence. Imagine it. The fence baffled me as if I had never seen one before. Most likely I cried out. The Men would certainly have no name for this thing so I gave it the name I had brought with me. Fence. But what would happen now that the world of dreams – where fences belonged – began to trespass on the existing world?

My subtle hand touched the hewn rail. This was the hand, you remember, able to signal dealing and falsehood. Like a blind man's fingers checking a forgotten face my hand checked the fence. The post was a crude job, squared with an adze. So it came about that the word adze required the object adze. My fingers said yes to the adze and yes to the fence. But not me. I felt a sudden flood of anger because our way was barred. Oh, we could easy climb over or duck between the rails, but what sort of answer was that?

I thought: I have given up everything to be as I am now – helpless. So by what right does anyone come along and tell me I should look after myself again? Or, to put it the other way about: by what right does the old taint that I am worthless come to shake my new composure in being supreme?

You yourself may judge me too, for all I know, and argue that I did little for myself. But this would mistake the appearance for the substance. I had been wholly alone during this time, perhaps amounting to two years, as I say. The point of my place among the Men was that although I gave signals upon which they might sometime act there was no give-and-take between us. What I did, they observed. What they did, I observed. That is how we were. (You can see that I would need to have been a fool not to note by this time how and where their supplies of edibles were sought.)

So I stood, confronted by the old lack. The fence brought the whole horror home again. The symbol of my power was nothing but a manacle which I prevented chafing the skin by stuffing my own lost hair under it. I must have looked no less nonplussed than the Men. The fence marked a boundary across changed land. Grass inside the fence, though it might look like grass outside, was not at all the same: that grass was Property, as this was Nature. Trees had been cleared from the paddock. And the soil, yielding a lusher crop, was being fertilized by cattle. The cattle eyed us over the fence, their great heads turning to follow each move we made.

Up to that point the Men were like adults while I was like a child. Now we were all children.

There were ten or eleven heifers. Behind me my guardians waited to be shown what this anger of mine meant and how one dealt with devils. When I was little I once asked Hall what he would do if he met our Kirk Braddon dragon in the flesh. He said he would ask it to light his pipe. The monsters, stock solid on four equal legs, faced our way. Who could miss in their glassy eyes suspicions as luminous as the dusky sky? Who could fail to be alarmed by such horns? We had come from a country of shy kangaroos fleeing with graceful bounds among other wild fleeing things. These were warlike animals quite capable of attacking without occasion.

Already the day passed and it was evening.

I stared at them as a person stares at death. I had become used to the free mix of wild species. Cattle were not part of that belonging, not even as food, being the Master's beasts. They could not mix with anything. Their portion was to continue eating the allotted grass and drinking at the allotted lagoon. Already their hoofs had pocked a deep trail down to the water, which I saw glimmering with sunset. The forest had been cut open for them. I recalled our arrival last year at a spot quite close to this: the Master and his servant on horseback, a sound of axes and crosscut saw, stripped logs floating beside the jetty. No doubt the logs were for sale, to be towed on a calm day to the nearest roadhead where hired bullock drays would cart them to a port from which they could be shipped to Sydney. In time there would be a bill of sale, a purse of coins. Such littleness, I thought. So much gone for so little return. The cutting of a forest I had once struggled through wounded me. My stomach dropped.

Thunder grumbled across the water, rolling in from the sea. Scuds of heavy cloud swept in. The cattle did not budge, but down at the lagoon two white horses looked up. By the tilt of their muzzles they were scenting the air. They began moving so graceful their hoofs scarce touched ground. Horses of mist. Ghost creatures from our fables. Hopes.

As the light began to die a slim figure emerged from the clump of bushes over to our left. Startled, she stopped. I could tell it was a girl, her supple movement and hesitating filled the emptiness inside me with joy. Not fifty yards off. She was caught facing us. In a manner of speaking she had fetched up against a sort of fence too – a fence no eye could see. She was one of the tribe, so already she expected what was to come.

Did the whir and whip of spears sound so entrancing to her? Her face still turned my way, her naked body pliant, she folded and fell.

The cattle, also intent on watching me, did not notice her fall.

Wild grief gripped my heart. I dared not run. But I had to know whether she breathed. Why should I care about my life if it cost her hers? Was I worth the two deaths the world had paid for me? I clamped a hand to my trembling mouth without even thinking it might mean something. Well, let the Men spear me too. Let them spear me in the back. I would never accept their offerings of food again. Either they could kill me quick or watch me waste away. Our chaste circle was broken by violence. Chain clucking, the iron bar thumped against my chest.

Until then I saw nothing strange. But that was when I realized something very strange had happened. An unearthly glow played about the heifers' heads, pale flickers, fitful prickles of white light dancing on the tips of their horns and wavering down the bone. When I say my hair stood on end, I believe it did. So some minutes passed before I knew that this was not the only reason why my head tingled. The light was on me too. I held still. I had seen St Elmo's fire only once before. But I had seen it and I knew what it was. I began shivering. For a moment more it darted around us, uncertain blue light, linking me with those dumb brutes, faltered and weakened. I felt it flare again as I turned to face the shadows (my guardians, my gaolers), to hold up my manacle and shake it at them, felt tiny thorns of light tremble on my hand while the metal came alive in my fingers.

There was no hurry now.

Under the gloom of baggy storm clouds, my sight further confused by a lens of tears, I strode through the grass to where the body lay. I fought to control my mad heart. I threw myself on my knees beside her and took her head in my hands – ordinary hands without meaning – a young man's hands – the hands of a lad who has known too little tenderness.

What I saw was that we were both young. She was a child from the women's camp, on the brink of being a woman herself. She might or might not have been beautiful, I don't know, but her youth was beautiful. Her slender arm, her smooth elbow, her cheek and long lashes. She lay on her side. My heart, so huge in me, filled my whole skin. The sight of her breast so tender and alive let loose a frenzy of grief. Both spears had found their mark: one pierced right through her neck, one dug deep in her belly. I sobbed dreadful convulsions. I had died and come back to find nothing changed. The old fears were waiting for me. I gave up with a howl of horror, such a long howl it left me fighting for breath. The voice blocked my throat. I struggled to draw the air I needed for life.

All this for this!

Alone, I was overwhelmed. Then came an answering scream. At first it seemed a thin sound, snaking up from the lagoon. The scream grew and swelled beyond human power. The shock of it cut like ice. I choked. I coughed out that solid plug of my own cry. I listened and listening gave me cold shudders. Returned to life, I squinted down that way, able to make out just enough. Pale forms plunged and bonded. The horses were mating. Spring had come.

At the time of my venture into the fine art of forgery I had been some years with a printer. We produced pamphlets, books bound in morocco, and everything between. I began by setting broadsheet ballads when I was fifteen, after four years an apprentice. Each broadsheet had a woodcut picture. As often as not I hawked the first batch in the streets of Douglas myself. They sold for a penny each. I was quite the young blade about town. But before long I was put on to more exact work.

My father thought the job a foible and not fit for a man to do. He said he expected I would grow out of it and take up something serious – perhaps in the line of his own work. My mother scolded him for a troublemaker. She encouraged me. As for Hall, my model in life, he brought us together by humouring our mother, following our father's trade, and singing the ballads I printed. His favourite would have you in stitches I am sure:

> Whack the folthe dah, dance to your partner
> Welt the flure yer trotters shake,
> Wasn't it the truth I told you,
> Lots of fun at Finnegan's wake.

That ballad, so filled with characters, was his favourite; not just for the tune, but because it sang the glory of getting drunk. In case you are wondering at his being christened Hall, his middle name was Henry, so both given names began with H. I thought this the grandest thing.

I was never drunk. Any time he led me on, Hall always kept a sharp eye on me. If I had had enough he invented some urgent call on our loyalty, a friend we must not let down, an appointment we must keep. I used to fret at this. I sulked a good deal, I dare say. I accused him of being selfish and maybe he was. But it is certain he loved me.

Your father is a man of trade, our mother said with a laugh and the wind dancing in among her hair, whereas you are a man of craft.

And what am I, then? cried Hall.

But she had no answer for him. Her eyes grew dark and her mouth helpless. Hall was her pet and she could not shame him.

I knew what was what, because she walked in her sleep. Into the room we shared, many's the night I saw her creep and stop in the sightless way of her ailment, facing his bed but not looking down at him. If you ask me she sensed him through her skin. Then she would turn and wander back to the dreams of her own bed. Our father knew too, proof being that he was often awake when she returned cold, because a quarter hour later their bedhead started banging up against the wall.

Then began the nights when she stood in her sleep knowing Hall wasn't there. Those same nights she would find her sheets cold too when she made it back to bed, and wake like that. I lay fired with jealousy, jealous that she loved him best and jealous of his freedom to go out with our father. Hall could now claim to be in trade himself. Sundays they brought home quail eggs and a purse of earnings.

Trade is about the size of it, Hall told her with his eyes merry.

He lapped up the excitement and couldn't wait to put her through the torment again. This is the life of the people anyhow: either they go along with the law or they damn it to hell.

Does he have the skill, she asked her husband, notwithstanding that he talks too much? But she knew the answer already and turned to me. So you're the last hope of commonsense I am left, she said, and if you must go to the foolishness of making a fortune make it of the skill you have.

Welt the flure your trotters shake, sang Hall, wasn't it the truth I told you, lots of fun at Finnegan's wake.

He and I went out to trap some rabbits. As we tramped through the crunching heather I told him about her, how she walked in her sleep; I told him she stopped by his bed and that was all. We walked. He could be quiet when the time called for it. He laid an arm across my shoulders to show he understood. Then we played at wrestling. Unless on his part it was not play but the serious matter of proving that my worries on his account were uncalled for. Not yielding an inch he could withstand whatever weight I threw against him.

Taking string for the neat little trick we had with loops, plus a sack for the catch and several sticks, we came to the dragon stone.

A fanciful notion, Hall replied, setting me straight when I began to speak in a low tone of respect, a fish's body, a tiger's feet, a bat's wings and a tongue of fire. He laughed, scornful. Meat for some hero to kill before supper, he said.

This was what sent me to the shelf of books in the workshop. I knew one flaky leather spine bore the title, *Heroes in History and Fable*. The first page told me that however important our history is to us our fairytales go deeper, that what we decide to do becomes history, but those actions going beyond choice fall into the pattern of the fables we are told. This book had a whole chapter from the Thebaid of Statius about two heroes, one called Tydeus, but the other name slips my memory. Then came the commentary, just four pages long. Such a very suitable length.

I took my mother's advice.

I had not expected Oxford to be a deceitful town.

I came on foot, avoiding Derbyshire, home of the deposed King of Man, through Solihull and Warwick, Stratford upon Avon and Edge Hill, entering the county from the north-west. My last stop before Oxford was Banbury Cross. I mention Banbury, although the cross itself had long since been destroyed, because there, sleeping under a hedge, I had a dream. The sound of harps called my attention to a courtyard in which two persons rode round and round on horseback. The horses cantered in contrary directions, a young woman making the inner circle and a man in rich robes making the outer circle. They kept the same pace. But as they went round, the bridegroom grew in power until I looked for somewhere to hide, fearful that I might be caught prying. His raised arm a triumphant gesture, he threw back his head till what I saw of it was a bearded mouth. The beard jutted black with threads of grey. I remember this because I remarked – in the dream – how the myopic person's dreams are free of myopia. I am sure you are familiar with that fault in a dream when you go absent for a moment to dream you are aware of dreaming. During this lapse the horses had veered on to the same track. The emergency gave me a jolt, especially when I saw them merge to a single horse, a single rider – the mother – into whose body the lordly man disappeared. She caught me watching. She tugged at her jingling reins, turned the stallion's head, and came at me.

I never had this dream before. And never since. So I can be sure it was once only. I woke into the night, scrambled out. By broad moonlight I stumbled down on to the road and set off right away for Oxford. I would not risk another hour in that ill-omened spot. Twenty-two miles or no, I believed in my heart that if I did not reach my goal before the next night I never would. Such are the foolish fancies of the young who set themselves goals. I am amazed to think that it could not be more than three years since this happened, since a time when I would swear that if I arrived at some signpost before a bird flew across my path I would have seven years of happiness. You know the kind of thing? Well, this time I swore that unless I made it to Oxford I would never grow up. My idea of growing up, I might add, was to be like Hall.

The fields were freshly turned, apple trees were in bloom, and all the way a cuckoo called to me, always too far away to be seen. The land lay full of promise. And I got there, though we are talking about that time of spring when the nights still fall early. By dusk I came in view of the spires. I took a room in a public house because next morning I must present myself spruce for business.

As I say, I had not expected Oxford to be a deceitful town. I mistook its charm. The inn was a coach stage and across the yard a smith sat early in the day shoeing a post-horse amid the hubbub of arrivals and departures. He hammered nails with deliberation. He chose not to notice me when I went over and stood near. Having wished him good morrow and taken my place among some children who watched, I offered a comment on the quality of the beast. Tis her ladyship's own, he growled. The hammer blows made a sharp unpleasing sound. Metal on metal. Up until then I had not known how hungry I was but now an aroma of fried gammon filled the whole yard. I must not be tempted; I had so little money. I took my precious folio, promised myself a royal feast when I returned, and set out along backstreets behind the colleges.

At one point I asked my way of a young scholar not more than a year older than myself, thinking he must surely treat me kindly if for no other reason than the fellowship of youth. I took the route he pointed out, only to learn that he misled me so that I had to retrace my steps. Back where I started, and quarter of an hour wasted, I realized my purse had been stolen. There were four pennies in it, enough for a full meal of the best cooking, enough for goodness knows what else. Yet I must not be put off. I had the future and my family to think of.

I found the shops of three respectable dealers. Which would I try? Courage failed me because I admitted ignorance: not knowing what to look out for. I wandered from one to another and back, peering at them from across the street, pausing to pat a cur, gazing at reflections in a tobacconist's window to tell what I could, hurrying away, returning, loitering and then rushing past. I had not yet learned that timidity is the most dangerous vice or that such simple dodges would be noticed. It is likely I would be there still, growing long in the beard with dithering, but that, as I passed one for the fifth time and read yet again the gold-embossed sign, the wine merchant next door struck a cask with his mallet – the tuneful sound very different from horse-shoeing – I saw the spicket knocked out, the cask being mounted on a counter just inside the door. He began to fill a jug with dark frothing wine. I don't know why but that decided me. I called myself to order and took a deep breath.

The dealer, when he stood up from his desk to greet me, showed himself to be a tall man of sixty years or more. The veins of his hand were dark and particular as the rivers on the maps hung behind his desk. The smell of this place put me at home in an instant: leather and paper and old size. When I brought out my Commentary upon the Thebaid of Statius he treated it with reverence.

May I hold it? he asked, letting his eyes pop up to meet mine for a second only, and wheezing with greed. Yes, yes, he muttered, very . . . so very . . . might I look at it by daylight? . . . too kind . . . Thomas, Thomas, come this instant and open the door for me . . . the light is better in the back lane, my dear sir, where ivy on the walls softens . . . you don't mind? . . . shall treat it with perfect care . . . in all my years this is exceptional . . . found where do you say? the Isle of Man? an untapped source . . . most exceptional . . . the back door Thomas, if you please, son . . . excuse me just a moment, I'll take my glass to look more close . . . need not insist on your coming with me . . . fetch a chair for the gentleman, Thomas . . . after you have opened the door . . . just one moment, sir.

This was the gist of it and the tone of his confidence. I have rehearsed the whole scene a thousand times since to convince myself how foolish I was not to see what he was at.

The dealer had scarce returned, bearing the vellum as if he had the Gospel there, written in Saint Mark's own hand, when Thomas set a bell dancing on its spring as he left us to our business. Already my heart was singing. But I was nervous in case I might not have the skill to strike a worthy bargain. What price would a professional man stick out for? You must see the problem yourself: how much was a unique handsel worth, a handsel printed by the father of printing, the master of us all?

You may not be aware, young man, that in the world of books one mystery outweighs all others, the dealer explained. We know it as the Old Hundredth . . . not the hymn, no . . . you might hear us say, the North Sea will go dry before we unearth the Old Hundredth . . . so-and-so will pay his debts when they find the Old Hundredth . . . this kind of jest. Let me explain. There are ninety-nine authentic publications from the Caxton press. One simply cannot conceive that the master would die content, in his seventieth year all said and done, without producing a hundredth. Even, perhaps, in his frail state not a full book . . . something brief and simple, but enough to bear his mark.

He bent his tall frame, stretched out his mapped hand, and pointed to the initials WC, a device I had laboured over.

The little bell danced again on its jingling spring. I did not look round. No doubt Thomas had returned. Of course I did not look round, my whole hopes were on my forgery. I willed my dealer to hurry up and name his price. He could have it cheap. He smiled.

There is no mistaking William Caxton's mark, he admitted, or this black-letter type . . . you don't find this in a modern printery. The qualmishness of his manner had gone, his hasty way of speaking gave way to a gentle summary. The only question left, he said, is how best to reward you for this priceless discovery . . . where was it found, do you say? in your family chest? . . . under the stairs? Remarkable!

A hand falling on my shoulder from behind made me jump. The constable flung his other arm around my throat and pinned me, sitting as I was, tight against him. His belt buckle cut into my ear. I cried out at the pain, comforted only that none of my kin could hear.

It amounted to this. A professor came to question me on my knowledge of the Manx language, which I was proud to prove I spoke. And then I was charged, as a foreigner in England, with theft of a national treasure.

Perhaps you do not need these things explained. Perhaps you know already or don't ever wish to know. Perhaps you can not be told but only made to feel. Whichever the case, you may think this letter comes from a disordered mind. So be it.

If I am putting the sublime and simple largeness of the whole at risk by focussing on yet more complications – supposing we mortals are capable of taking in the whole in the first place – you only need stand back a bit for these details to merge together, do you see?

So to the vexed matter of colonial prospects. The plan in many a good man's mind is to reach for great things, his vision being of broad pastures and himself raking in the plenty. He begins with a good run by ship from Portsmouth, landing sixty-nine days later at the Circular Wharf, enough pleasant company in the forward saloon to share his fantasy, with perhaps the surprise chance of the Governor's surgeon returning from furlough in Winchester on the same voyage and becoming so intimate as to promise he would press a friend's claim to a satisfactory offer of land. So we move along to the sighting of this land, a lovely cove, a cleft behind the dunes leading up to the belt of forest with the promise of natural grasslands beyond. Then the thrill of pacing the grant while deciding the spot for a house. The bush must be stripped and the timber sold in the next detail. But why go on? What is the point? You know this. And it can only be bitterness to me; denied even before I arrived. Let us not forget in what disgrace I came here and with what prospects of my own! But no, why should I flinch from listing the kitchen garden, the tomatoes and good potatoes? Even hardship and hazards may be welcomed, mayn't they – the torrential rain, the new road a frightful bog, all hands being called to drive a bullock team to the jetty with their freight of logs and then called to curb some skittish horses bolting for freedom (I see it all), the dray stuck on the slope and another squall sweeping in from the sea. Let us end the list with quiet satisfactions of an evening, lamps being lighted and a fire dancing in the hearth. What could be more vulgar? A novel, perhaps? Yes, a novel to be scanned but not read, or a sampler to be worked while the master of the house scratches his head over his ledger. An empire has been begun, leading in the end to visits from a bishop, a woolclip of three hundred bales and, crowning glory of all, a return trip home. Isn't that his style, to stride along a London street as a wealthy colonial?

Am I cruel enough?

When such sense has been made of the chaos here, success will give you leave to pity those who fail in their attempt upon the same goal.

But what happens if again we draw back from the detail and take more of the wild land into our view? A long stretch of coast? Are you with me? Your vision widens to reach a hamlet perched on the shore, an outpost of stone and shingles like any little English port (forgery), its church a smaller copy of the very church you were baptized in (forgery), the citizens on the street respectable in full skirts and frock coats (forgery). But spare a moment to see past the fashions, the fences and straight roads, to see marooned folk lost and longing for the comfort of their bosky county home and hedgerows and Sunday rambles, cursing the Indians who fail to live up to Man Friday's example. Is this order? Will it be seen as such by an order-loving Maker?

For the moment I leave these questions with you.

Draw farther back. More wild hinterland. A longer stretch of coast dotted with more hamlets. But what if you have to compass this whole sea? And the next too? What if you must take in China on your right and the Cape Colony on your left? Can it be said that the sense you make of such chaos is other than a way of avoiding the whole? Does it make any sense at all when the scale is so large? Do you achieve more than a small voice in the enormous dark, a voice pleading: Lord let me know mine end, and the number of my days?

Meanwhile, what of the chaos? Don't it go its sweet way as chaos still?

I ask such questions because – at the end of my wanders in the circle of tree Men and bird Men – I could make nothing of the fence. An old dream had turned solid around me to hold me in its spell. I would never wake up. But this fright was nothing beside my anguish when I did recognize the fence and I knew I was awake. It brought back the smell of prison, the smart of shame. I knew then that we had not seen the worst of it. The most heartless violence would follow if settlers such as the Master ever lost their fear of the place and its people: telling one another they had come to a primitive land possessed only by a childlike race and that such simpletons, furnished only with accidental food, could be saved and civilized, brought to God, and that it would be a mercy to rescue them from the doomed calm of their backward ways.

Then, as if to prove me a hypocrite, there lay the corpse of a girl, and myself broken with grief. To me she was innocent. But to her own people she was not. Right until that moment I could be proud of having fitted myself into their world.

That night I heard ceremonies and wondered if the dead girl had a family, or if all children were children of the clan. I listened, choked by guilt. But for me she would be alive still. Again I saw the sprightly way she had stepped from behind the rock, her sudden halt, her shock, how astonished she was.

But isn't the notion of an accident just another detail in the fraud of order? Given a state of chaos, can there be accidents? Wasn't it by accepting life as whole, as beyond progress, that the Men had no need to sit in judgement of her? Instantly they knew what must be done. I overheard no discussion. So great is their knowledge that a mere detail can not distract them. The fact was enough. Nor did they have room for the superstition that she might be an instrument of spirit forces, a sacrifice to the greater good. She stepped on to the scene as part of the scene and remained as much part of it with spears deep in her neck and her belly. I did not need to draw back from the moment to see this. I took the moment in my arms because the risk I ran was also part of the chaos and true to it. I cradled her head in my hands. Her black hair hung warm and silky between my fingers. Dust smudged her cheek. The last light of day sparkled in one eye.

So I saw the bird Yllerion. There in the eye of this unknown lass, a wing as sharp as a razor, the fiery point of a feather plunged into the sea. Ordinary birds swept around us, drawn to the fall by a high wind. Of course, according to the book from which I made my forgery, Yllerion will rise again. I know that.

If you are to understand how I came to commit murder I must face the pain of setting down the sick man's last try at humour. Can you picture us, the convicts, chained in pairs but otherwise slumped as we pleased under the fitful puddle of light given out by a swaying lantern. Gabriel Dean was by then so ill that each sally at my expense cost him half an hour recovering. But he had won his point: one sarcastic word from him and those other toadies obliged by sniggering.

This fellow here is called Suck-prick, or Shit-nose, he said, driving himself up on to the prop of an elbow to introduce me around, and collecting his energy in bursts.

Sniggers.

We shall leave Suck-prick for a better time; but why he is called Shit-nose is because his job will be to clean up my shit.

Laughter. Bones cracked in my shoulder as he forced my hand to where he sat and underneath his stinking pants.

Clean it all out, he growled hoarse. I'm a particular man.

Sniggers, also a single: Pieuw!

He sighed and let me go. You can eat it if you like, he offered.

That night I watched the lantern gutter – the oil had run dry. My misery stretched minutes out to hours. In these hours futile ideas churned in my brain. Then came a thought to stand like a bright presence among the dross. Everybody else slept. Soon the lamp would go out, its little tongue of flame dry and dying to a red ember. The wick smouldered. Meanwhile my tormentor rolled from side to side, slippery with sweat, strength drained from his boneless meat, the fever at its height. By morning, if he lived, he might be over the worst. And that was likely, his constitution being what it was. He would be ready to take up the new life awaiting us.

My idea stood so bright among the dross it bewitched me with its beauty: the only weapon I can use in my defence is myself.

I took scrupulous note of how he lay; also the exact position of his head. Each time he rocked or shifted I printed his new position in my memory. The hours crept on. Maybe they lasted half the night, I have no way of knowing. Then the tiny flame faltered, revived, flared up, and died to a glowing ember. The ember winked and went out. The dark in my skull burst as dazzling snowflakes. I listened for any footfall. The ship creaked a lullaby. Beasts shuffled sleepless below. I thought of Noah's wife and Noah, the sneaky way God played favourites to take the rest of mankind by surprise. I thought of home and the last war and Wellington's victory. I thought of the tale we were told of a French prisoner spitting in a British officer's face: I would be justified, the British officer said, if I put a musket ball through your head, but I shall not give myself the pleasure because I wish to show that I know better how to behave than you; I will add, however, that it is lucky you spat at me and not at one of my subordinates. Preachers went all round the Isle of Man repeating that. It may not be so lucky for those among you who reject Jesus Christ that you spit on me.

I raised myself to my knees. The silence itself seemed aware of my risky plan. I had to keep the manacled hand quite still on the floor, not to jerk his end of it.

Gabriel Dean's breath came shallow and fast.

Now, with the greatest care, I moved my locked arm, easing his as well, to give me room to twist round. I listened.

He did not respond. By the faint sucking sound I think he still rocked a little. I could smell his slather of sweat.

I believed. At that moment I believed in a forgiving God. The end of all flesh is come before me, He whispered, for the earth is filled with violence.

The weapon, as I say, was to be my body. I calculated its most effective weight to be at the solar plexus, which was also pliant. I did not throw myself upon him. Quite otherwise. From the kneeling position I leaned over, taking my weight on the free hand, intent on remembering the precise whereabout of his face, then lowered myself, very gentle, until I felt his nose touch me at the base of my chest. I shifted position an inch or two. Then pressed firmly down.

The turmoil of thoughts was gone: my mind empty and peaceful. His body thrashed in its coma. But his fever was my ally. We bucked together. Why had I not expected these horrifying jolts? From ignorance of what I was to do, you see. We pounded away with dull padded thumps. The other convicts woke: I could hear their unasked questions. The bucking grew more violent.

Please! I cried out in pain. Oh please, no!

They lay listening to us thudding on the planks. Dean's free arm flopped and beat at me. I gripped his head to hold it tight under me so that even when he lifted me by the power of his neck he could not free his nose and mouth. The pad I had made of my tunic held in place. I kept my midriff slack as I could. But the struggle went on too long. How could he live without air?

Help! I gasped with real desperation.

Certain that every one of them must now be awake, my hatred for them grew beyond any pain I might have felt at their betrayal. They knew I was being murdered. There were enough of them to save me. Yet not one uttered a word. The cowards lay, each man in an agony of waiting, until the difficulty was finished with.

But it did not finish. Spasms kept humping up against my flesh, eruptions and shudders. His body twisted, bridged. This bridging was the first sign of a stratagem. I was no longer suffocating an unconscious victim. If he got one breath of air he would get others. I knew I was failing. Even with his illness to help me I could not resist him. I saw flashes of red light in my head (that is what I remember now) while stabs of fire ran about my body, sharp in the blood, raking at the small of my back and my shoulders.

Help! I let out a yell of panic.

But the bridge had already collapsed. Gabriel Dean slumped under me and lolled as if his backbone were snapped. My tunic sopped up our sweat. I grew aware of myself, sprawled, one arm twisted against his at a painful angle, in agony from the iron bearing across my forearm.

Somebody let out a discreet play-actor's snore.

Fraternity creaked about her lazy business. Rat claws snickered across the deck to visit this possible meal then that. Could murder be smelt already? I slapped with my free hand to protect Gabriel Dean's handsome person from being gnawed at and began to free my shackled arm. I put my ear to his chest, surprised by the feel of springy hairs crackling against the side of my face. I could hear no heart beat. He lay dead, limp and invisible.

As I say – they let me cradle the girl's head in my hands and feel her warm hair among my fingers. Nobody speared me for it.

I had been asleep a long while when I woke to a disturbance, a steady spitting crackling noise. The world was still dark as the grave. Dazed, I wondered where I was, with a king's pennants flying in the wind, breaking to sparks and swirling past me down the hill. Points of fire winked across the night sky and left a cut of smoke in my nostrils. I sat up, fuddled and exhausted. From the ridge, back there where we had slept the previous night, little bobbing flames snaked in line. From the other direction, down by the bay, clusters of them gathered and crept across the sand dune. Beyond, wavering among forest trees to the north, yet more specks of fire arrived to converge with the others. Standing at my vantage point beside the fence I watched enthralled. I wished then for sharper vision because the prettiness of this scene was beyond fancying. The customary million insects trilled and chirruped. An owl screeched from a distance, the same owl had tracked us the whole way from the mountains, I was sure of his hollow ominous note. Otherwise all was hushed.

My protector and my guardians, whom I now swore to disown, were nowhere to be felt, not even at their established distance. By habit I was used to sensing their body heat, but now the air had gone cold. Just when I began to master the lack of being private, I was dropped into privacy deep as the ocean. This was not the aloneness of a Byzantine emperor, untouchable as the god he was supposed to be: I had been left where I lay, as a thing no longer any use.

By going to the murdered girl I broke the contract of my sanctuary, you see. During the many months of this sanctuary, layer after layer of aloneness peeling away, I had learned to live with what was left. Yet now, a total and naked solitary, I felt my lack of defences as a kind of security. I don't know how to put the point but, after the grief of holding that dead girl, I might have expected anything other than this.

Then excitement clawed at my whole being. A burden lifted from me, my spirit leapt with freedom. To accept was enough. Why should anything be thought about? I knew. And I knew the whole sensation of knowing as the blood pounded and set my head spinning. I soaked up the glory. There was a fresh warmth in the air, scented with woodsmoke and sea-drift.

The truth came on me, sudden as being taken up by an eagle: those flames flickering down there were justice for my wrongs.

Who is to call vengeance base? Or lust either? Do they not bring us to our most glorious flights? Clanspeople who had never seen me were settling my account. Yes, because I knew what that hollow held where they gathered. No sooner had I welcomed this than my excitement soured, the underbelly of revenge being guilt. This was proof that I had not yet acquitted myself of my crime against Gabriel Dean. Nor my passive crime against the girl. Not far under the guilt I discovered fury. Fury at the savage way I was punished for my original misdeed – that test to put my talent at full stretch – for attempting to defraud those who exploit us all the time and sit in tyranny over our island people. Fury against myself for speaking so feeble at my trial too. Many's the time on the voyage to Sydney I had practised the sort of eloquence I hoped to rise to, denying English law altogether, proud of being a prisoner of war, challenging the Earl of Derby to appear in the witness box and answer my charges, ending on a climax of damning the English for the mortal injustice of my father's execution.

If this was vengeance, then I lusted for it.

When I thought of my darling mother and her woe, my rage burned fiercely. I thought of Hall and his unknown fate, so gallant in following our father's profession. Hall, when refusing to let me take the same risks, unwitting that he thrust me into a more and more fixed determination to be our mother's hero, to outwit the enemy over there on their home soil through their vice of coveting things. To hell with it: how was I to know Caxton published ninety-nine volumes? I chose Caxton only because I had not heard of anyone else!

I was telling you, I think, that our house at Kirk Braddon stood half a mile in from the sea. Some similarity in situation here on this foreign soil damped the bright thought of flames. With no moon yet, the sea glimmered dully out there. Certain it is that I thought of home and the marauders of old burning down our monastery. Had I become a marauder myself?

Picture me: my scabby insect skin, stick limbs, and leaf veins down the inner side of thighs and forearms, rags of a faded blue shirt buttoned round my neck, the whole caked in a chrysalis of clay. I was what the Men wished me to become. I was, if it came to the point, what my persecutors also wished me to become, supposing they could ever conjure such a scarecrow.

The sheer number of flames appalled me. Whose hopes were burning?

Out to sea lowering clouds grumbled, the threatened rain held off as it did the evening before, when I had been touched by St Elmo. Meanwhile, over to my left a swift carpet of fire passed across the flat. The best I could make out otherwise was a chrysanthemum of glittering gold, which must surely be a bonfire or a whole building going up. Fine drifts of moisture being carried on the wind wafted down as a mockery.

I took my decision. Tying the knife to my waist with a shred of shirt sleeve, clutching the talisman of my manacle and stepping firm, I ducked through the fence where the cattle were kept and down a slope. No one emerged from the night to stop me. I could see quite well enough by the light from a screened moon. Reaching the lagoon, I came out from the fence and stepped on to the road.

You may not think stepping on a road could mean much. Well, nor did I. My feelings took me wholly by surprise. A long time had passed since I felt a road underfoot. It spoke to me by righting my stance. I had been out of touch. I had not even seen my own face since I grew beyond age. With no friend to help me escape, by mercy of a shot or a dagger in the back, I had become lost to myself. The chap I used to know was last seen shinning over the gunwale of a boat and wading thigh-deep at the edge of the ocean; the chap I used to know was a heart in a painful basket. Under the weight of that stormy night my relics walked, bones clicking into place as I passed along the road, on my way back to strike a blow, to win my brother's respect, to send a message home, to cry, Down with the King!

Several times I suspected that shadows were keeping pace with me on the far side of the fence, but could never be sure. Though I remembered some buildings from last time I was not prepared for the cluster I saw ahead, almost a village, where the livestock was already in full cry. Chickens raced, shrieking and night-blind, for their hutches. Two dogs jerked at chains, thrown into collision by the same frenzy, gashing one another as they bounced apart, to be tripped by their bonds and tumbled in the dirt as furry bundles.

Several gunshots went off: brisk and to the point.

A horse reared at the garden gate, striking the rail with a rapid thudding like the kettledrums people used to beat in the wake of the dead while winding along the streets of Douglas following an open coffin with someone inside. Again and again the horse reared up to pound the solid timber. Hundreds of wordless flares were carried dancing across the compound, eddying among the buildings. Unseen men shouted from inside and a scream flew loose above the shouts. I ran that way. And once

I ran I knew for certain that my guardians ran as shadows, keeping pace with me.

Bastards! I wailed at the same time as my heart sang to see a shed go up, flames catching the bark roof. The catastrophe came so quick there could be no stopping it. Glory! I whimpered when the roof curled in a single contraction and tore loose from the frame put there to clamp it down. A rampage of heat punched my body, knocking the breath out of me. Whose idea was this fire? And why? The Men could have no motive of their own: how had they been injured? Beyond this small parcel of land, our journeys through their country had never brought us to any other invasion by settlement. The only evidence of any stranger intruding on the dense disorder had been those few leavings we found, such as my knife. Not enough. No.

The truth was this, that while the Men knew no word of my language they must have known my thoughts. So, they had felt my fury and sensed my need. They had obeyed. I had given orders as sure as if I spoke them. Who knows whether rage shows in subtle colours on the skin to those with skill to see, as holiness glows about the heads of saints? They were innocent of blame. Thus I could point to no other culprit than my own anger. I was the one who willed this. In my divided and deceitful heart I demanded it, lusted for it.

The shed burned. The strong flames roared. The dogs fell silent in a heap.

Caught in the middle, where did I belong? I had long known I was like to be torn between great forces, but would not let such a thing happen. Until that moment I had kept myself from the real pain.

It does matter, after all, how we die. Between death and near-death I must put my proof to the test. Must I confess, then, that my enemies and I came of the same mould? Was my unjust sentence no more to be abhorred than an unjust acquittal? Was it all one, in the end, when face to face with this other thing, this pure chaos, this world free of categories, of individual choice or moral dispute? The joy I found in revenge, by the time it broke over me, was becoming a wave of shame. What had I led my guardians into? What fury of an eye for an eye might follow their victory? The redcoat garrison in Sydney hungers for just such an invitation to perfect their bloodthirsty skills.

A lick of flame shot up the side of the house itself while I watched. I do not know what noises I let out. By the time I came to myself I was gagging my mouth to stop a howl that seemed to have gone on longer than the lost air of my lungs. I crept near. A dark block of roof stood in silhouette against the steady glare from some fires behind. A house. The word stood up with the thing itself, its meaning solid as walls and as much at risk.

Do you see my dilemma now?

Shouting with joy at the Master's fall, I felt the ground shift under me. Was there ever a time in my childhood before I knew what a house was: the pitched roof, four walls, square windows, smoke which was supposed to spout from the chimney only?

I whooped encouragements. Yet I was like a ship whose hull sweeps on by its own thrust, well after the captain's command to heave-to is clear and the rudder has already been thrown hard over. Leaping out of the night, Men set torches to whatever would burn, raced away as far as the gully, and raced back up on the unseen side. Meanwhile this wonderful idea, this house, the uses of confining space and closing it in, whispered an irresistible call to my loyalty. The idea of a house was my inheritance which, however I might be convicted, could not be taken from me.

A rush of intense heat engulfed the timbers. The building fluttered feathers from between its rough cut slabs. Dazzling claws dug into the doorposts. I could admire how solid the frame was put up. Right across the roof the shingles were outlined with fluid gold. The making could never have been so beautiful as the destroying of it. The swarm of torches spilled like red mercury, forming a pool and then running out on a sudden, trickling too fast and unpredictable for a man to catch, a few beads broken loose joining together to dart out of an opening, only to circle as the land tilted, tricky, slippery. Voices chanted and flickered about me. A thousand black birds broke free and flew in all directions from the explosion of fire. The roof, bulging and wavering, shone like a live flank of scales; while from the end of the house a broad wing lifted, a wing large as a tree, lit along its edge by loss and ruin.

You will want to know if I saw any survivors after hearing those several shots.

Forgive me. The horror fresh in my head, I must put down my pen. Night is come. Darkness seeps in to swallow me. I shall answer you. I shall find the strength to answer tomorrow. For now I am lost and faint with confusion.

This morning I woke before dawn, thinking of what I wrote last night. How I came to shed tears I cannot now explain – unless because a burning house suggests the frailty of our strongholds. Was it grief for the Master and his hopes? Or for myself and mine?

A shaft of pink light has just fallen across the page. I am laughing because my nose almost touches it – such is the effort I must make to see what I am putting down. Impatient to have you read what I tell you, fear torments me in case my frankness offends. I begin to understand more about my untested needs.

I fret at having to suffer being shut away again and left here, this latest indignity, yet I shall never believe you are to blame. You could not be so cold. Meanwhile, I shall push on with the task. There is still much to be set down.

Let me take you back again to the fire. I mentioned several gunshots. Well, the house was already lost by then, I suppose. A door swung open and a figure stood there. Are we not used to seeing the past look out from a gilded frame, plump and self-satisfied, dressed in a Sunday waistcoat buttoned right to the top, beside a spouse in her Sunday bonnet? This, then, was the nightmare counterfeit of the same picture, the spouse being gone. It was, perhaps, the future which I saw in that gilded frame. And what a future, dazed by facing disaster, while tucking a flintlock under one armpit to tap more powder into the pan! As if shooting into the colossal night had not been futile enough, the fellow cocked his piece and made ready to fire again. The light being so hot and brilliant about him, surely he was too blinded to make out those shadowy forest spirits and their agile leaping? Yet he took aim and let fly. There was a wink of red fire. The sound of the shot could scarce be made out this time, such was the general din of popping and booming. Then, quite near me, one of the Men fell, even as he was running past. His fire stick rolled right to my feet. At close range I could now see that the stick itself did not burn: a thick bulb of resin sizzled like tar. The fumes threw me into a fit of coughing. I doubled up. I was still coughing and in a seizure when the next shot hissed past my head to rattle among shrubs at my back.

I hobbled away from the light of the torch, still in a hacking fit, to stumble among foreign shadows. I fell. I crawled.

Brilliant as sunrise the buildings burned. Winds whirlpooled from all directions, drawn towards the inferno.

Only at this desperate last minute did figures come dashing out. Impossible to tell how many, perhaps ten, perhaps more, racing clear of the collapsed roof. They dodged haphazard – and this was their downfall, because they collided with one another and fought. So it took a while for me to realize the spearings had begun. By that stage I knew myself for a traitor already and one who let this happen. You see, I did not come between them and their killers, although I believe my power was such that I might have stopped the butchery just by holding up my manacle, evidence of my disgrace.

What I want you to understand is that I did not notice the spears in time because my mind was absorbed by another task: to seek among those darting outlines for glimpse of a skirt. All my energy and powers were bent on the single moment when I would be most needed. I knew there was a woman around the place and I reserved my courage for her. The men did not matter. If they could not look after themselves, they must wait the worst. But I declined to watch her murdered the way the natives had already murdered a young woman of their own. I had no room for more than one pitiful memory of a pierced throat. And yet – and yet – the more I work here at this task and strive to explain myself to you, the more I suspect I am winning battles against my own truth. Each sentence I set down shuts me farther away behind a barricade of tidy excuses.

I confess I do not know why I did (or did not do) anything.

The best I can say is that I did not leap in among those frantic figures. I did not shake my manacle with terrible majesty. Nor waste an instant debating the case against myself. Nor indulge my grief or guilt. I watched. And took no part. I crouched. And saw pouncing forms, cowering forms. Torches snaked and fluttered among ruins, shedding sparks and puffs of smoke thick as clubs. The attackers sped from shadow to tactical shadow; they struck and struck.

The livestock panicked. I felt the delicate thrill underfoot as their bulky mass went pounding this way and that inside the fence. Voiceless and desperate they lumbered off – I heard them gasp and wheeze – only to come lunging back through the night a minute or two later, pumping at the terrible bellows of their despair. Huddled against the fence as I was, all I could see of them were fleeting glints of fire in their eyes or the glow picked on the point of a horn. All I could feel was that shudder of earth and the passing puff of damp breath. Meanwhile, high in the valley a vague cloud of sheep drifted across the hillside, compacted, broke apart and drifted again. The horse which screamed kept screaming.

Ash rushed up the funnel of flames, loosed from the bondage of weight. Months of labour, in the form of beams and rafters, swirled beyond reach. Space claimed them. They were gas, they were a spiral of light, they were the origin of a new star. While, answering that roar of loss, came the willynilly thunders from the storm just out to sea.

Still no shape of a woman ran clear, though by now it was already too late and the attackers cast away their torches, setting fire to crops.

From beyond the cup of firelight, when the noise began to

lessen, the funeral pounding of the ocean could be heard again along the beach. Waves could also be heard to joggle a barbarous instrument of timbers. Floating logs clocked and bumped in restless collision.

Tell me, are we in 1838 yet? I feel old enough. I am in my twenty-first year at any rate.

A tragedy sloughs off useless details and this includes time. The thing exists itself, with any rough corners knocked away and smoothed by handling. The frenzy is distilled as one clear simple scene, another clear simple scene, and another. Not that such scenes are tranquil even if we see them as still. They are charged with energy so pure it may inspire a man to heroic risks. I saw this and felt it. I saw a shadow wearing a hat, he stooped double to hurry out from the blazing barn, he was in the act of rolling something across the yard. He kicked at it. I wondered if this might be a large ball. Or a biscuit barrel, perhaps? Having sent it rolling and bouncing down the slope toward the house he stood up, a perfect target, and removed his hat to give a theatrical salute.

In the next scene the hat was tucked under one arm while spears flickered round him – some thonging the air, others stuck trembling in the ground – and an immense burst of light responded to his salute. The battleground was revealed: a few staggering defenders and an awed bunch of attackers, corpses at different stages of grasping the earth, chickens dashing zigzag from calamity to calamity.

When the blast of it hit me I heard my skull crack.

I picked myself up and all I could think was that I had lost my knife. I had to search for it on all fours. Why had I never used that knife? I condemned myself. If I had only thought of a use for it I might have staved off this conflict. Such was the childish way I thought. (Now, much later, I might defend myself by arguing that I could not be held responsible for what others did: neither the Master with his ambition nor the Men who wanted their land back.) After the explosion I shrank from new flashes of light, only to realize they were nothing more than the arriving storm.

So the settlement burned. The business of flames tackled this section then that. Once the living quarters were gutted a satisfactory start was made on the kitchen. Dark coils of shadow spent themselves. Is this what I wanted, I asked, a triumph of ruins? You already know about my habit of guilt. Well, the disaster was so tremendous and I wept so savage that I was brought to the point of groping for the blade. What else did I deserve but to fall on it? Wasn't I one of the Men, the very centre of their circle? Hadn't I let them use me as a mascot for their courage, proof that the invaders were not spirits after all? Didn't I, all unwitting, act as the medium for working magic? Such matters can never be known for certain, but what was sure was that my protector often went unarmed, yet I had made no attempt to go for him with my knife, and after all I am a man who knows how to plan a murder, even with an inadequate weapon.

I felt curiously like the eunuch in some pasha's palace, the harmless witness brushed aside by great events, known to the powerful on both sides but in each case let go as being of no account.

Ash and glowing debris sailed higher and higher. I crept through the fitful dark, the night itself seeming to flicker and fluctuate, hands groping as I went. The soil smelled good, already swarming as it was with alarmed beetles and centipedes. I jabbed my knee on a flint. The mingled violence of fires sounded more than ever like babbling voices, arguments and singing. I peered around but the place stood deserted. A lone chicken went belting across the yard and straight into the oven of a crumbling out-house. The fires crackled companionable together.

The Men were gone.

As a scene, this had the fancifulest beauty. Throat dry, I watched a family's hopes being eaten away by cankers of night, gobbled into that black mass bloating and swooping above the hail of ash. I do not believe I had given much thought to ideals for some time and the notion struck me as full of tricks: such a frail ideal as a new life or a new society will remain forever beyond reach. And the ideal of a farm carved in virgin territory is not far different from the ideal of justice in a court of law. Each one being suited to the fool who falls for it. I found my knife and kept hold of that. The knife would be enough salvation for me.

Excuse my clumsiness, but the blots are not entirely of my making. Your nibs are cheap things, a brand we would never use at the printery, not even for writing invoices.

Is this new one better?

I know where I left off: that dark wing as big as a tree and a roof being the dragon's wavy flank. Well, such dragons breathe pestilence too. Whatever burned with a foul reek burned amid the last sumptuous climax of fire. A gold pyramid sank and slumped and cataracted down as scattered jewels, while flurried plumes bunched and fluffed to soar away as whirling stars and popping blossoms of light, and the black wind scurried among stark statues of lightning – all suddenly netted in delicate silver ghostliness. Drifting every way at once, a glitter of air sealed the burnt-out posts and frames in glass. Falling falling falling. Timeless, unhurried, ever new, delicate among raging flames, falling from rolling upside-down hills, fragrant as the fresh sea: rain. Rain, bright with the prism of an insect wing, folded wavering vanes over the ravaged land. The parapets of bonfires burned more energetic. I witnessed the sky as a spinning muddle of lights that stung the eyeball and rested on the lashes with glints of chance green, chance violet, chance orange. Thunder wallowed around while the rain set in until the whoosh of the fire dulled. High along the ridge beyond the sheep paddock, one lick of flame poked right to the verge of the forest and then died.

While tying my knife into my rags again, the thought visited me that I had just watched weapons of war employed with the cunning of Napoleon – fire and water. The downpour moved inland in the wake of destruction, drenching a softer darkness where it fell, to reach right up among the wild hills.

Is the mastery of fire what makes us human? Is this the one thing denied the rest of the animal kingdom? I am reminded of the dragon, his swimmer's body, his walker's armaments, his flyer's swiftness, each one possible for other creatures. The mystery being his tongue of fire.

Yet, when you think of the individual human beast, who among us could manage fire without help? What a tyrannical master it would be! Just to keep the fire alight through all seasons, with never a day's holiday, never an hour, or it would be out and lost. Whole families must have dedicated themselves to a single fire. Whole tribes, as I see it, had to come together and stay together for that one thing only. They had to learn to manage fire. But where tribes in most countries settled to this task and nursed their gift in some sheltered spot known for safety, until they began building special shrines for it (you see how I work?), in this country Men dared a risk more skilful. Like jugglers they have found a way to keep it with them wherever they wander. The tribes of Britain or the Isle of Man settled down, having to be content with the same place every day for a thousand years, where these Indians are free to move and have always been free to move because they care nothing for any possession other than this one thing – they dedicate their lives to the miracle of carrying it with them, asleep in the sticks they rub together (I have seen it done), asleep in the dry foliage they pile up, asleep in their own breath, for all I know, with which they blow the smouldering leaves to life.

Think of the Library of Alexandria going up in smoke. What power did the printed word have then?

The blaze subsided. Oblivion rained on charred structures and on the earth. The occasional still-burning timber, eaten out by night worms, glared a moment and fell, kicking up a wreckage of sparks which were soon doused. The grey smudge across the landscape was as much steam, I suppose, as smoke.

My heart cried out. I stood up and rushed to see if there was anybody left to be helped. Lightning still strayed out along the horizon but it was not much use to me; in the main I saw by the sullen glow of the ruin itself. Groping across a slick of fresh mud, I peered into the victims' faces and felt for their hearts. Five dead. Six. All dead. I expected to recognize them. I plied my brains to match a nose or hairline with some memory, overwhelmed by my longing to be known – even by a corpse. If these were total strangers to me, so was I to them. Helpless. Frustration drove me on. I think I began shouting. All I asked was to rescue someone's name or voice, not even anything you could touch, from my days in Hell. Then I began doubting even such memories as I had. Soon the only ghost I could call up before my anger and put in the dock was Gabriel Dean. His face became every man's face. His voice, his smell, his sneer. I scrambled away. And tripped over another body. This one's hat, having fallen to one side of him, lay turned up to catch the rain. The light was so poor I had to put my face right close to his to see who it was.

The Master.

I felt no pity for him. My own needs were too demanding. Instead what hit me was gratitude. The enormity of this gratitude choked me and left me dumb. I laid my subtle hand, the doubter and compromiser, against his cheek. How could I thank him for being there, dead though he was, for reminding me who I had been? At last I knew what it was to give away the life of a god and be willing to embrace our shoddy human fate. Injustice too, yes, I embraced that as well. Yet I was not about to become victim of another ritual; if he was the first bridegroom, he could remain the only one. My voice did sound at last while more rain pelted down, whipping round me in gusts.

Why you? I croaked, as I remember.

The sound came guttural with lack of use. All around us, in the storm, the shell of his plan for the future glimmered. Beyond the shell, across blackened pastures, that miraculous cloud of sheep passed again, still clustering dispersing and regrouping.

Only then did a brief flare up of flame shine on the fallen man's open eye, bright as the back of a teaspoon, a watching eye, and I realized it was him growling: Bleeding traitor – I'll hang you for this!

I sprang back. He must have been in fearful pain, spears still stuck out of him. Yet he lunged at me. He grabbed my ankle, then my wrist. He held me.

I'll hang you, he whispered again as if the whole affair had already turned into a victory.

I wrenched myself free. But he caught the manacle and hitched the chain round his own wrist. Must I murder him as I murdered Gabriel Dean?

You heathen, his voice grew strong.

I knew him for certain. What was I to do? Was I to pull out one of the spears, though sick with death, and use it a second time? I could not rise to the deed again. I threw myself back. He hung on like a lunatic. I already understood what it was to be shackled to another man – and he did not. That was the difference. I drove my fist at his face. He astonished me by twisting aside and ripping my knife from the bindings I had made for it. My own knife. He stabbed at me, gashing my shoulder open, then slicing a flap of flesh under my good arm, then aiming for my head with a swing that lifted his trunk clear off the ground. Between each thrust I punched his face. I dragged him to one side as I threw myself back. We slithered in the mire with the terrible effort. I was sobbing. My knife was gone. He jerked at the manacle until the string made from my hair worked loose and flopped about, growing longer as we fought. Those lost hairs had been the only measure of my time among Men. Years of hair. My ritual observance was to keep what could not be had again. My sufferings were coming loose and being thrown away. Such loss could never be replaced. While I wasted a moment trying to stuff the long end back, the blade snicked my thigh. The Master grunted. The hair string, itself bonded with clay, fell apart and more slipped out. I could not stop it. Again the Master raised his trunk, dragging at me so that I strained to bear the weight of him. I tumbled back into the slime and rolled down the slope. My bones knew what my exhaustion had no mind for catching up with: I was free.

So thin had I become that once the hair packing was gone the manacle slipped off my wrist.

My bones propped me on my feet and set me staggering away along the road. There my mind caught up. I knew the truth. My mind took over and directed my drunken totterings as if now the bones had grown soft. I drove myself. I had to get away. I would survive in the wild. He could not follow. So I turned my back to the fire and made what haste I could. Stopping on the road only once to catch my breath I wavered there. At that moment a figure loomed out of the night to come right upon me, flapping queerly, heading in the opposite direction. I dodged aside. My ankles gave and I collapsed. I picked myself up and faced death. But the figure had gone. Slipping and grovelling, I made my escape. The storm crashed over me. Repeated stands of lightning now lit the country as a sequence of pictures. Sea thundered along the sand. My blood pulsed with its own thunder. I did not look back. The last of my blue rags having been ripped off me with the knife, my sores stinging like hornets, I fled up along the boundary of the paddock to where fence timbers hung smashed from the posts. A piece of splintered rail pierced my foot.

The cattle were out.

I reached the spot at which earlier that evening – a century earlier – I had wept for a young girl and believed no worse horror possible. I did not stay. I pressed on, gasping for strength to reach the trees where I last saw my guardians stand still as sticks and calm . . . though I knew that on the ground beside each man lay a spear, held between two toes, ready to be flipped up into the hand.

I detest what I have become. You bring out the worst in me. Day after day I labour to recover the truth. I was all right before – I could abide my faults. But now I come to the point of seeing myself as a dupe and an idiot.

Why should I not be loyal to my parents and my homeland? Then again, supposing all trade is trickery in some degree (which I swear it is), why am I suddenly worse than another and fit for the hangman? Ought I to be afraid of saying I hate your England simply because I suppose you are English?

Well, I do not care to have sympathy on those terms. As for the wrong I am thought to have done respectable persons, let me say that the most respectable have been brutal enough to me – from the lackeys of Derby to the mealy-mouth gentry of the courtroom. If I am to offer you anything, let me offer myself whole, heady with anger and despising those who persecute me.

As to my reason for writing at all, this must be clear by now. You are my hope. I think of you the entire time. I wait for you. I listen for you. I ask: Have you no heart? I curse you and then my eyes fill with tears and I turn the curses against myself. I think of the future (of you on horseback, for some reason, at full canter, and I fear for your life). I think of the past (of you seated in lamplight staring at the hearth, startled by some presentiment and yet basking in comfort, unable to shake off the pleasures of ambition).

Then I think of you today, living in hunger and fear, and I say again: Come to me.

Let me show you my notion of perfect order. There it is, a tiny island. By kneeling on the English shore and reaching out you could take this island, cup it in your hand and lift it, dripping, from the sea. It is the world seen through a lens, details sharper than life, with a single specimen of each thing needed by a world: one good harbour, one mountain, one ring of standing stones, one earth fort from prehistoric times, one castle, one dragon.

To the north of the mountain lies a fertile plain, to its west a clean-swept stony ridge, to the east a wet vale where herds graze. To the south of the mountain lies a pocket of tropical palm trees planted by one of the Goddess's doomed bridegrooms who still carried her palm frond and her blackthorn in his hand and who stuck them in the ground together on his way to death in luxury.

The island stone is old, the river is old, the story of courage is old as the river. There has been time for everything. Order rules. Fields are ploughed in furrows straight as combs. Orchards are planted in rows. 1 2 3 4 5 6 has been called mathematics and carried right through to a zero for ten and two zeros for a hundred. Musicians take the trouble to tune their instruments. Nothing gets wasted in this little world. Even the sheep's back is clipped for wool. Not only are there laws but agreed ways of breaking laws. Legal ways of smuggling. And, among those who smuggle in a manner considered rude and blameworthy, there is humour. You see how perfect it is and how complete?

I am peering through my lens. I see miniature folk who build stone houses with slate floors and slate roofs. They live in families. They know nothing of the loneliness of chaos. Look close. Although you have had to reach your hand as far as it will go to take hold of this island, every leaf and whisker is perfect. So soon the gorse dries out on the hills. Today is the day of the Melliah because a corn crop has been harvested from all but the last corner of the last field. And now the job will be finished. People laugh while they work with sickles. The farmer already sets up a keg of ale. Young wives arrive and lay their infants down to sleep on shawls spread in the shade of a hedge. The heat is getting up. If you put your ear close you can hear this heat as bee wings humming. The older ladies make tea at a trestle table and pour buttermilk into cups for the children, who gallop through stubble and call for the feast to begin. The prettiest miss has the honour of reaping the final swath and she does it at a blow. Men mop their heads. They unbutton their waistcoats. Women loosen bodices and throw down tools. They gather at the table to be thanked by the farmer, who looks like my mother's old man and speaks directly to God to thank Him too. But look closer – even while he thanks his friends a lass comes running from the farmhouse, don't she? One clog slips off and her ankle turns in the ditch. She reaches for his shoulder. She hangs her weight on his shoulder. At first he can not make sense of what her gasps are saying. He calls his married daughter from where she drinks ale, also his grandson of thirteen years busy celebrating the glory of a man's work. This farmer excuses himself from the Melliah but begs his neighbours to do justice to the spread. How clear we see the three of them, figures so tiny they could stand together on a nail's head. They enter the farmhouse, where all is quiet as Sunday: rugs spread on the floor, a fire banked up with turf, kettle singing from the slowrie, a fly measuring the quietness wall to wall, whips hung on pegs and boots hung on pegs, hats belonging to the working folk hung round the kitchen wall. In the quiet they share the news, the woman having only one question she needs to hear answered (just as the island has one mountain). Was young Hall arrested with him? she asks.

Are you there? Do you still hold the island in your hand, this model of order and the benefit of law? Evening stands around the house clear and fresh. Herring fishing ends for the season with the herrings salted down. Rooks caw and flap among elm trees at the edge of town. We see inside the Doolish Courthouse. A half-wheel section at the top of each window being propped open on a brass catch to let out the hot pleasure of spectators. Now the sun sets. Flames are brought for the candles while the High Bailiff announces a verdict. The spectators dare not breathe lest it be known what evil lurks in their hearts which they might not wish to let show. But one voice does speak out. My father, from the dock, replies in his quiet and casual way: Narra noain dhyt!

Do you hear that as you read my words? Do you know the grief we know? Does life mean what you thought?

Out into the night we take those words my father spoke, down along a shadowed lamplit lane beside the court house and into the black tomorrow: Your fate come on you!

On the Governor in Government House too, my mother adds, also a curse on the Atholls and the Stanleys of Derby.

You hold in your hand the harvest of order. If there is any pain in your knees from kneeling on the rocky coast of Britain, please feel free to set the island back among its waves, you need not bother with it any more, you may leave it to the mercy of contending enemies.

My brother escaped to sing 'Finnegan's Wake' another day. But we never saw my father again.

I knew nothing of letting go. I was too young to imagine anything beyond the dead littleness of life: my routine as an apprentice, the craft I set out to learn, even my mother's promise that I would be a poet one day, considering my gift with words. Neat and tidy and all of a piece. How could I be expected to imagine what I found here: an endless land with a maze of jungle ridges fanning in every bewildered direction as various and grim as a choppy sea, where each landmark is set among a thousand thousands like it, or the inland plains under vast skies parading clouds that can be seen raining a hundred miles away, a continent of yellow-grey grass littered with pebbles which, seen closer, are bigger than barrels, bigger than carts, bigger than houses, until when you come right up to them they are too big and round to climb, but a dozen men may sit in their shade all day, gazing out at a galaxy of those other boulders you will never visit. All this was indeed a strange world. Back home I thought it a long way to walk the half mile downhill to Douglas and the half mile uphill for tea.

Printery – Established 1619. That was the sign outside our shop. I don't believe the machines had changed either. You could never call the island rich. Yet the printery produced work second to none, as we told our customers. Thinking back, I begin to wonder whether a deeper promise already called me. Don't you see? Is there ever such an odd thing as chance? When I set up my forgery was I answering the promise though I had no idea I was hearing it? Was ignorance the one quality required by fate – the mere thought of my mother's grief would have bled me of courage – ignorance, and talent too perhaps? Talent because this is what led me to the wilderness. I was so steady that I was the only one let supervise himself. Every fact fits, right through to my chancing upon boxes of old blocks and packets of vellum in our storeroom. I was in full flight and headed for my downfall, my capture, my hurt . . . and my escape. The fact that I had courage put the issue beyond doubt and forced me to my destiny. The best laugh is that if I had been wild like Hall – neglecting to study, breaking my contract, worrying our mother out of her life – I might be there still to comfort her.

One skill I shall need to learn all over again, and you shall teach me, is to laugh. I do remember laughing and laughing a lot. More of this later. There are yet more confessions if I am to be honest with you.

We must go back to the fire.

Scrambling up the hill away from the smoulder and ruin, I knew I had been corrupted, the turmoil in my heart nothing more than mawky. Glimpsing the house as an idea I had had as a child took me back to childhood. I wept for my father. We were never to sing, for him, that he had a sort of tipplin' way, with the love of liquor he was born; and to help him on with the work each day, he'd a drop of the craythur ev'ry morn.

> Whack the folthe dah, dance to your partner
> Welt the flure yer trotters shake,
> Wasn't it the truth I told you,
> Lots of fun at Finnegan's wake.

I was not such a fool as to return to the fire and risk being caught, but I was curious to know if anyone survived and what they would do next; like being a child who learns by watching adults. Would they take the pinnace and chance the current, or would they wait for *Fraternity* to show up from wherever she had been, bringing whatever she was expected to bring? Did the Master survive and would he lie mending while he ordered the fence fixed, a palisade built and a new house begun? I hung around at the edge of the forest. I listened out for the signal of hammers and saws. I wanted to hear them.

What I did hear, one night, was a man crashing among the vines and bracken. I sprang up from where I lay. I crouched in the dark to listen until listening hurt. This was no kangaroo nor any native Indian. Dead boughs split and snapped under his boots, green sprigs thwacked at his clothes. He came right upon me, snuffling, letting out desperate grunts. He passed so close I could have tripped him. On he blustered. Keep going that way, I thought, and you will soon come up against a clump of trees grown so close together you will try in vain to force your way among them, tough stunted tress with papery bark flaking off them. He crashed ahead. He called out each time he stumbled but I could not pick any word I knew. Not one. I, who had been so vain because my mother boasted of my way with words! Well, those trees stopped him all right. I waited to hear what he would do next. I thought about my weakness and the cant of it. Was I still green? A million trilling insects left off their chorus too. We listened together. All quiet. He must have fallen. He must be crumpled there, beaten by the jungle, staying put until daylight. Exactly as I once did.

You will say I was mad to tarry, that no matter how swift I moved in the morning I must face the danger of being caught. True. But when dawn came I had not yet finished turning my thoughts to the dark. In the glimmer of morning the bush woke without charm. The overcast sky faded from the colour of soot to the colour of ash. I squatted in very much the place where I broke and slept that first night of my escape, hemmed in by dense tangles of dead and sprouting plants which, to my eye, matted like a tapestry without form, blocking the whole world, hanging from the sky right to the ground underfoot, so deep as to have no depth, so close as to be never reached. In effect a screen. Even though I made no move I knew I could walk into it when I chose and find the screen renewed yet still complete. This one skill I had learned – I could gain ground through that maze with scarce a rustle to give me away.

There was no mistake, the small furry animals sat tight and put off their usual business: an intruder lay there, less than fifty yards on.

Birds began their tit for tat while the light grew strong. The ocean still made itself heard, methodical and sullen along the beach. I stared near-sighted at where I knew he would be, alert for the first suspicion of movement.

So, I thought, I shall not escape, after all!

Looking back on it, I see that a deep need held me prisoner. Freedom is not the greatest force. The call came; more urgent than escaping into my chaos. Did I know what this was? Perhaps I did. Then again perhaps not. Yet I found the courage to face it, to put salvation behind me. Once my mind began slithering down the slope I gave myself to the thrill of letting go. Could that sleeping man be the Master, half-dead with wounds? Or was he an escaped convict like me? Of all questions the most curious was this: Would the fellow wake to find himself in a circle of Men?

I looked for them. I applied to my ears for what they might tell me. The air, full of chirrups and scuttlings, was void of human sounds – only that expectant stillness of an alien body just come to its senses, before it begins to stampede about, hunting for a path where paths have never been.

Not yet too late, I could still creep clear and make my escape along the ridge to the open forest. Instead, I plucked a couple of berries from a shrub, bit them open, dug out the pips as I had been shown, and ate the fruit.

He stands without warning. Though I have waited I am not ready. He is closer than I thought. My scalp freezes. I am spellbound. When he turns to look he will catch me. However still I stand I will never again have the skill of Men to be invisible. He has his back to me. He wears a thick shirt and breeches. The Master. Yes, he has the Master's build and rubs the back of his head with one hand. Surely this is what the Master used to do? The other arm hangs limp at his side. There is a message in the set of those shoulders which I can not quite read.

Still having time to duck down, to worm my way along a gully I know and give him the slip, I do nothing. The spell has its claws in me, because how could the Master be on his feet again and why come crashing through the wilds at night? He does not appear to carry a gun. But if he is looking for someone it must be me – or else why don't he call out? And why else stand so still? He is still as a hunter. This shocks me to my senses. Inch by inch I back away.

Leaves betray me with their whispering shadows.

He turns. He sees me. We are face to face. I squint to be sure of him. The sinister pull of the world of Easter and fairgrounds, of ventriloquists and devils on stilts, drains my heart to emptiness. He holds up his arm to arrest my escape: an arm without a hand.

Do you understand that even then it was not too late, because I knew that place and its secrets? How could I be stopped but by a bullet? I knew now what held me so enthralled. This was a dead man.

I waited for him to wade my way among tangled vines. And he did. He thrust himself mindless into the thicket and broke a passage through. Step by step I got him in better focus, that handsome fellow. With his cruel arrogance he had entered his own chaos and been lost. He peered out from under a jumble of hair, eyes anxious and glad. He uttered cries in a language I no longer knew, supposing I ever had known it. Yet the Master's curse, the previous evening, was not lost on me.

He reached with his good arm to grab me by the throat. You will hardly believe this, but I let him do so, being helpless with astonishment and in a sweat of terror. Then instead he took hold of my shoulder, his fingers still thick with strength. He pulled me to him until my face was close to his and stared at me, absorbed, taking in each feature.

He is remembering, I told myself, our three whole days together. He remembers his arm against mine when they clapped the manacle on us, the bashings, my humiliation, the effort as he jerked me to my feet for more punishment, my nose running, my secret tears. He remembers his fever and the onset of weakness. He remembers forcing my hand under him to clear away his filth. He is looking back to seek some clue which he ought not to have missed at the time, some giveaway sign that this cully was capable of rebellion. He remembers my dead weight smothering him. He may even have hovered in spirit above the deck to witness his hand chopped off.

Then I saw that he recognized nothing. I made to loosen his grip. As I lifted my arm he shielded his face.

This was not a dead man driven by unforgotten angers, knowing he once suffocated under my loathsome body. This was not a ghost hungry for vengeance. This was a man heavy with blood and solid in the early light, crushing the plants as he trod them down. He clung to me and cringed. Until that instant I do not believe I had reached the true bottom of anger since, as a boy, I had to stifle my helpless rage against a judge passing sentence on my father.

I had seen Gabriel Dean dead, and now I saw him alive. His legs were functioning, his eyes saw, his mouth opened and shut. If I punched his face a bruise would begin to gather. How this could be was beyond me, but without doubt Gabriel Dean did stand there, all the more certain alive because so changed. I had thought my adventure unique; I never expected to find that during the same period even stranger things might have happened to him. His cringe sent bitterness thrilling through me. Was I to be stripped of all I believed? Was I to be left with nothing of the past though I had paid my life to renounce that world of order? Might I not be spared the bully as a bully? Beauty as beauty?

One thing I did know: you can not be a leader and live in chaos as well. I struck his arm from my shoulder.

Keep off, I barked.

Cackles of mocking laughter came from the tree above us; it was those birds with their uncanny call, egging each other on as they do. He lunged at me with a cry that might be mistaken for misery, but I threw him back. My flesh shuddered at the touch of the unknown. He stood arrested, mouth sagged open. Wrist stump hidden behind his back, as though that might be to blame for my ill will, he made pleading gestures.

When I turned to go, Gabriel Dean followed. If I paused he paused. When I went on again he kept me at a fixed distance. He became a clumsy replica of me; and I could guess how my guardians must have despised my own early efforts. The faster I walked, though too proud to hurry, the more he crashed in my tracks, gasping and desperate but without complaint.

In this way I brought him to a pool. Water lay still and dark under the trees while at the far side reflecting bright clouds. I bent down to drink. I showed him how. But he propped. This he would not copy. He stood back from the bank, eyes fixed, wonderment around his mouth widening across his cheeks.

He took my leadership away from me.

I looked where he was looking: mirrored clouds slid over the glossy water to vanish in a net of shade, glittering for moments like golden thorns. Drips fell from my chin to shiver the surface where swift circles opened, rings of dark ribbons and bright ribbons – gone – again the same repeated swiftness – while out at the brink even the glowing silent clouds were touched by a gentle waver. Bewitched, Gabriel could not hear me. He could not be persuaded he ought to drink. Even though I grew furious at his stupidity and so far overcame my fear that I tried forcing him to obey me. Feeling tall, I thought of throwing him in. I tried. But, to my shame, was unable to shift him. He did not argue, he just resisted. And had lost none of his strength. His body took root like a tree.

You could smell more rain in the air, yet it did not fall. I was hungry, which was bearable; and peevish, which was not. I felt ashamed of my petty feelings. Chaos is too large and simple to leave room for such childishness. The clouds billowed solid and grew dark as they slid across the pool. Yet still I could not persuade him to follow me away from the dangers of the coast and into the forest, where we would not be caught. I admitted that I wished to leave him and be free, that I had not asked for his company, that I knew he was dead, that I shivered when he took hold of me. All this being true, my course lay clear. What was to stop me going alone?

Evening drew in. I left him happy with a lens of cloud cities and cloud mountains gliding across it. I left him.

For years now (this being the length of time I put on my freedom) I had gone where my guardians went and eaten the food they brought. Isolated as a king, I had done nothing for myself but wait and watch. Now I put this knowledge to good use, picking my own fruit and digging for roots. I profited by that copper nail, which I found still tucked in my tangled hair, when poking grubs out of the tree bark where they burrow, those fat pale caterpillars. I ate them raw. A nasty thought stopped my blood and interrupted my eating: I had only dreamed I suffocated Gabriel – dreamed it while awake – much as my mother walked about her business when asleep. Perhaps the problem ran in our family. Whatever had happened that night aboard *Fraternity*, the man's mind had gone before his body could call it back. But did I know this? Could I be sure? I ought to go back and see. So I went, flitting among trees and under vines, noiseless as my teachers who had worshipped me.

Gabriel Dean was a burden. I wanted nothing more to do with him. Nevertheless, I took a few juicy morsels . . . and thus I set about throwing away my freedom, that total freedom of mine, that joy which I can find no word for. I was going to let him rob me of me. But why? Why should he not look after himself?

He had not stirred, of course. A dusky purple cloud slanted across the pool. At first nothing I could do would win his attention. Not until a glittering sheet of darkness folded over the surface did Gabriel take the food. As soon as there were no clouds left to watch he was pleased to have me back. Drinking, he made a thin greedy sound, quite a feminine sound, which he kept up from time to time between gulps. He took his food: the root, the pink mushroom, the tiny yellow plum, the leaf, and the grub. He refused nothing.

Since I was anxious not to be stuck at the pool all the next day too, I set off straight away. Up the ridge I strode, satisfied by hearing him follow. Then the awful truth of this staggered me: satisfied! Just so. And wasn't I already on the lookout for landmarks known to me, picking my way through the bush as if following a path? What next? Chaos with a path through it is no longer chaos. In the end any such path must lead me back, whether I wanted this or no, to the ruined farm . . . to a fence, to a window with bars.

Gabriel stopped. He shook his shaggy head. And spewed the food I gave him.

By the time we lay down to sleep I had only one thought left in my head: escape! I believe you will understand. I believe you will see that I had to save my life. Yet I lay, still awake, divided and uncertain.

At dawn, red clouds filled the sky above the trees. They sailed in from the sea, a dumb procession puffed up with dignity. Gabriel remained on his back, eyes as wide as they would go and a beetle drinking at a tear stain. No sooner did I decide he was dead than he moved. He lifted the arm without a hand and placed it across his chest. He did not turn to look at me even though I brought some berries. When I put food in his mouth he chewed. But he wasn't going to miss a single cloud. I asked how he felt this morning. He stared past me. I saw them there in his eyes – plump pink cushions in miniature, clouds to suit an island so tiny you could take it in your hand.

As for his hand, the lost one, it filled me with fear – being more there than the one he still had. I reminded myself that quite ordinary folk may have a hand missing. There was the mill worker who lived near the old Douglas crossroads and lost his in a crusher. There was the doorman at the court house even, whose one hand qualified him for work. Each of those missing hands meant a simple loss to the shrivelled arm inside a sleeve tucked in a coat pocket. Gabriel Dean's lost hand had become a mighty thing, the lone survivor of a lost body, a perfect cruel hand still full of the grace gone from the rest of him.

The distance boomed with muffled drums. I experienced an overpowering desire to smother him again. This time I would really put an end to the creature. I felt so strong. But first I must place my ear on his chest to hear his heart, to be sure he wasn't a ghost, because trying to murder a ghost might lead to problems. I looked up and saw what he was seeing: scuds of cloud with edges bright as knives. Again it was the silence of their passage that gave these giants such strange power.

I did not dare touch him. My needs went begging. To hell with the idiot, let him rot.

But I could not help myself. Something in my childhood made me stay and look after him. I hated him all the more. He would not get up. How was I to bring water to him here at the edge of the forest? The question fretted me as I set out, busy gathering more food for two. You see how quick I took to my new spunkless servitude? But no – there were strong arguments against delicacy.

Would I leave him or look after him? I could not decide. Even when I returned to place his share beside him as an offering. I set off again.

I was alert for signs of Men and often stopped to peer among the trees expecting to find my guardians in a circle around me. Or expecting they might switch their loyalty to the cloud-struck Gabriel. And that afternoon I did come upon some half buried embers of a fire. Still warm. The watchers were near, I could feel through my skin that they watched. But, all eyes though I was, I caught no glimpse of anybody.

Another thing: I found myself constantly pausing to check on the sky. These pauses grew longer. I saw fascinating banks of cloud drift and collide. The mere air grew in my mind to fill me with a drama of merging vapours. Next thing I had hurried back to Gabriel, master of clouds, to warn him that these pretty games of his were about to rain on us and the rain would be a downpour. Of course I was hoping he had got up and gone, died or become lost. Yet my heart jumped with relief when I saw him there still.

I bent over him – this man who once insulted and oppressed me, this victim of my murder – careful not to get in the way of his sky. Were the true clouds happening in there: being born in his imagination and thrown up as giant shadows on a distant wall? Might he, in other words, be commanding this rain? Afraid to interrupt, I placed more food in reach and stood back to watch what he did next.

The downpour, when it began, made him blink. Was he a conjuror? Did it rain harder the harder he thought of it? A monotonous patter settled among the leaves. He blinked and stared and thought. Rain came teeming down. His clothes were soaked. Trickles of water ran under him where he lay. This time I did not lose patience. He was not clever enough to realize that if he made the rain too dense the sky would go a general grey, sink to the level of treetops and blot out his clouds. Finish. He turned aside from it and crammed some food in his mouth. So he had known all along: he had known I came and what I brought. I smiled. We were friends, then.

We slushed off on our journey together to the grasslands. I now saw that I intended to make a full circuit of the territory known to Men. This was my ambition. Gabriel would be shown what I had been shown. The gifts given me would be offered to him. I helped clear his way, pointed out pitfalls, chose the least tiring alternatives in that trackless country. And once, when we overheard people talk and laugh in the distance, I hastened towards them, never suspecting this might be dangerous, eager to show them that I was not a freak, that here was a fellow of my kind. How weak! I would present them with a friend who had proved himself the better man though I defeated him; who, now he had returned from the dead, must be kept alive.

But the talk and laughter fled at our approach. No silent Men, part-tree part-bird, stood and watched or flipped spears off the ground with their toes. No one threatened us or tried to influence the way we took.

Gabriel spewed again.

You must understand me, I was not unselfish. I taught him to sip rain from tiny runnels coursing down the tree trunks. I began taking pride in my care of him, in my skill at finding food – the food he still could not digest – in my skill at choosing our direction deep through that confusion.

Three cloud-rich days passed. On the fourth, the sky filled up with white tops too massive to move. They bellied and sagged, billowing and building gianter than anything on earth, until Gabriel grew exhausted with the effort and fell into an uneasy doze. As soon as he slept his white tops collapsed, mountains broke apart and dragged away, leaving pink scars from horizon to horizon of the evening. Before sunrise he began on filling the morning with fog. When he cleared it, he must have been remembering a sandy beach because the blue sky was all ribbed and scalloped. As before, his duties lasted the whole day and he only got up at twilight, when there was nothing left to do. We walked under a moon with a halo, myself as guide and him still in the musing way of an artist who looks back on his inspirations. By the sixth day I found I had been leading us, aided by the call of soft constant thunder, towards a waterfall. We had come to a place I never saw before. The creek rushed solid down to a midway basin and then spilled over to plunge into a pool hollowed from rock. Fern trees grouped round this deep clear pool. Flowers grew from cracks in the cliff.

Naked I slid down the rim into the cold water. While my body sang at the delicious knowledge of what it was to swim I wept again for lost memories. I stayed near the edge, splashing, dipping my head for the amazement of water washing among my hairs, the freedom of feeling it lay them flat.

Gabriel looked hard at me when I crawled out. He was seeing me as he had not seen me yet. Did he recognize me without my disguise of filth? Then perhaps I should be ready for him to rise up and take revenge for his lost hand and lost mind. This made me nervous. I invited him to drink, squatting to show him how. He watched. But stayed where he was, propping himself on his one whole arm as he sat shedding sleep.

I knew I would accept my fate.

You see how far I had come since kicking the officers who dragged me from the courtroom at Oxford? I was not going to run away. Indeed I went towards him, my wet feet slapping on stone. So I found my courage at last – but only with the aid of poor sight, as the affair turned out, because once close enough I could see that it was not me he stared at. He stared past me to where the churning water smoothed to its edge as a clear surface holding the empty sky. That mirror was what he watched. The blank of his slow face opened out to terror. There was no sign of a cloud. The blue showed bluer the more I looked into it. Deep air stood steady. Gabriel refused to drink cloudless water.

My arms and legs gleamed. What did I have to be ashamed of? How else ought I to be? Wasn't it the wonderful comedy of the world that human beings are made of skin and hair, knuckles and nails?

Just as once he had been at my mercy thanks to the power of a fever, now, thanks to the power of the clouds in his brain, he was at my mercy again. If I led him on into the land of food which he could not stomach, offering him water he could not accept, I would kill him surely. He had no manacle to brandish, no power to make me do his will. How could I bring myself to murder him twice? What say we retraced our pitiful progress, turning our backs on this journey through the whole country of Men as I knew it – even supposing Gabriel consented to travel while the sun was up – I would still need to support him for at least two days before reaching the coast. Once there, I faced the risk of being captured, the Master surviving in some corner of his burnt anger, his agents returning by ship in time to charge me with the disaster.

Such ideas presented a set of pictures on stained glass. Myself depicted as a lesson for others.

The fact was that only Gabriel could save me from being a leader. The plan to return would fail if he dug his heels in and refused to follow. This was my chief hope when I set out without a word to him, my clean feet stepping delicate among roots and rotting mulch. I would test him. He was to be given a chance of redeeming my guilt by saving the man who had murdered him.

These are the things I need you to know.

I am just looking back over the last page and hoping I do not alarm you with my ideas.

Let me try to put your mind at ease. Through all my misadventures what troubles me most is that my folk have no idea what has happened to me. You may guess how a mother would feel. The blame must fall on the stubborn secrecy of my resolve to live up to my responsibilities. You see, I set and printed the Commentary upon the Thebaid of Statius entire in my own time at night and then signed it with the great man's mark. I could not confess to my mother or even to Hall what I had done. Anyway, I suppose it struck me as more of a prank than a crime. I felt damn clever too.

Did something warn me my skill might be out of hand and putting me beyond my depth? Not until I turned my back to the island. Fool youth though I was, my teeth did chatter when I set foot on the packet for Liverpool. So how can I say I was innocent or expect you to believe me? Yet I do.

You may guess how proud our family was. Me, for a start, taking on the work of an English master to baffle a university dealer, hoping to return home with money for my mother now that my father's smuggling had brought him to the Earl of Derby's gallows. Madness. But I was full of vim and my childhood had been carefree. When anybody asked my name as I walked across country to Oxford I told them John (which it is not). When I was sitting in fatal comfort, hearing that little bell behind my back jiggle on its spring, the dealer looked past me to see who entered his shop and asked my name.

John Stanley, I replied pert.

The composer of *Oroonoko*, I presume? he kept up the joke in a kindish manner. Oh yes, he was kind.

How should I have heard of any John Stanley except the first Earl of Derby, who took the title King of Man? Or any such thing as *Oroonoko*? Or any such person as Mrs Aphra Behn? Only when the Reverend Davies came aboard our transport at the Cape of Good Hope did I learn about Mrs Aphra Behn.

Throughout the trial they referred to me as the Supposed John Stanley. No torture would have wrung from me my father's name or mention of my village. Indeed I lied, I told them that although I came from the Isle of Man I was said to have been Irish, an orphan born at Drogheda on the Boyne.

Even the Pope expressed satisfaction, the judge remarked, at the defeat of your people by William of Orange – what do you think of that, ay? But I suppose every kind of lesson is lost on you. Well this one won't be, let me assure the citizens of Oxford. We shall not be indifferent to the theft of any part of our national heritage. And Ireland being as much under English law as the Isle of Man, the citizens of Drogheda are bound and protected by the law to the same degree as these good people here.

So the joke was that I needed to prove my forgery was a forgery and not a theft. No one believed me. They mocked me for my presumption. I was even stood up in front of the court to answer the charge of throwing doubt on Caxton's fitness to produce one hundred editions. And now there was no point in calling attention to the concealed initials FJ, because why FJ if my initials were, as I told the court, JS? Yet anything was worth a try.

Well, said I, my mother christened me Felim John Stanley, so I've been told.

The best they could make of it was that this did amount to an answer of sorts; whereas there seemed no immediate answer to why old Caxton, whose mark was already so prominent as to risk seeming too forward, should slip in a secret FJ signature. I saved my neck by winning an appeal – this meant paying the only shilling I had as a bribe to be allowed to show my trade at a proper printery. And what a sharp place it was, with a score of the most modern presses.

I gave them proof that I was a forger and not a thief of treasures. My reward was to be sent in fetters to New South Wales.

I shall make you smile when I confess that there was a moment when the trial became so interesting that I began to enjoy myself! An expert was called in to give evidence on the latest craft of copying documents or works of art. He told us that in France is a camera obscura with this difference from ours – it can fix the picture inside by engraving a square plate of silver. Nor is this witchcraft. Even in England they have tried it already and made it work. He was a most honest kind of expert. He told us that with spectacle lenses such automatic engraving will soon make portraits and landscapes. I can't fancy how. But he said so. Imagine! Nature engraving herself!

I realize I ought to have called out: What will become of the law against forgery then? I ought to have said it. But I was too busy learning.

I once had the chance to look through some spectacles at the fair. I never saw anything more beautiful. Every tree had a hundred twigs. Birds could be seen flying high in the sky. A clown on stilts was pulling a face. They brought things so close that I could read the word FAIR right across the common.

At any rate, forgers are friends of the original. Why? Because the forgery is only worthwhile when the original is one of a kind. So a forger brings an artist respect. And yet judges do not have artists led away in chains.

Speaking of chains, I noticed on the manacle a locksmith's mark stamped into the iron: FJ. As if it had been made for me, forged for me, you might say. Even my imagination was given no room by fate.

As for guilt – and I must be frank about feeling guilt – I

suffered horrors because that shilling had been borrowed, also a further elevenpence, from my brother's box of papers. I had not asked him; and now I might never be able to explain or pay him back. He will think badly of me. This reminds me of something worse, speaking of the box. Not only did I take his money but I also stole a look into his soul by reading a letter from some woman. Heart of my life, she wrote, and all mine, even your lovely goat legs, when shall we make the eight-shanked beast again? You are less my friend, she wrote, than the friend you keep hidden.

It astonished me how she knew about this hairiness. I guessed the friend he kept hidden might be myself. I could never ask him, that's obvious, but I still carry her words as a talisman. At work next morning I told the whole workshop that my brother would as soon make the eight-shanked beast as be seen in any church. I hadn't meant to let it out. But I did not expect what happened. I was caught by the ear and thrown into the street to enjoy some rain for half an hour. That should cool your blood, said the journeyman who bolted the door, and when I let you back you can keep your hands busy with cleaning the racks (these were racks where we stored the fonts) instead of taking your Saturday afternoon off.

She must have been an educated woman, that friend of Hall's, writing like she did in such a clear hand, though she was a hopeless speller.

I am sorry I took the cash. But I do not regret sticking my nose in his affairs. What else are older brothers for? And this woman's secret words are the only love letter I ever had the chance to look at. You see my plan? I sit here day in day out to work at the task of teaching myself to talk again. Soon I shall be ready for facing you in person, for the joy of hearing your voice and asking you to believe my answers to your questions. I tremble with excitement to think how great an idiot I shall seem. I imagine the things I shall find myself saying to you. Such things!

Gabriel, having excellent sight no doubt, could see what I could not. Yet all he did was watch clouds. And what use was that? For the most part he stumbled behind me, weak from hunger and thirst, shaking his head at the tidbits I found for him but alert if we came upon fragments of laughter still haunting the air, or the smell of roasted meat (probably the Master's beef!), as on the day we reached the coast again. I shrank smaller while he grew cheerful. He knew he was on the way home. Also he still knew what laughter meant when he heard it. I reckon that a person is never lost for good if he remembers laughter.

The moon set not long after the sun that night. Clouds stood up over a far-off sea as flat and still as glass from where we were. Gabriel gazed at the sight for an age. And when he threw himself down beside me on the tussocks I noticed the glass edge of his eyes. I wished he would eat but he would not. Neither of us slept, he in his grateful swoon, I weltering in fear at having risked my life to come back so near the Master's fences.

I pause here for a marvel: a void. I am at the brink of a chasm, pen in hand, because who knows what you think of this? Will I fly or fall? The only certain fact is that you are still reading. You might be bored, angry, disgusted . . .

At least, do you agree that it is best to face a crisis with laughter, leaping around as the mourners at Finnegan's wake leapt, welting the floor and drunk like the dead man himself would have been for sure. Well, you will excuse me the liquor I made free with this afternoon. As it happens I am not a man with a sort of tipplin' way. But what choice do I have? The writing comes slow in any case – with me sitting here and nothing else to do.

So, to press ahead. By dawn the chances of being killed seemed to outweigh any hope that I might deliver Gabriel to safety and get clear again. Either the Master's shot would get me, or a native club. Yet not only did I still lead the way towards this fatality with a sort of pride at doing my duty but with a light-body feeling like expecting a birthday. Mad though this was for sure, it seemed to be catching. Gabriel's face broke with lopsided happiness while he watched me swilled clean and cavorting. I dug more caterpillars for him and picked more berries. He did not seem to mind that he brought them up as soon as he swallowed them. I looked on the bright side: this was all I could offer and at least he agreed to accept it. What's more, he drank again from the pool filled with clouds. If you ask me, his instinct told him he was well on the way home to bondage. No wonder he felt glad!

For a moment I suspected his happy mood had the same cause as my madness. Duty. Maybe he saw visions of the selfsame person, down there among charred rafters, aiming the same carbine. But the idea was fanciful. As a man in the full power of my intelligence, surviving adventures enough to kill many another, I put it behind me. We went forward.

Right there, in the middle of a place never tamed or tampered with, what should we come upon but a dead cow. The carcase had been butchered and singed, the hind quarters part buried in a trench of warm coals, perhaps still waiting to be dug up and eaten. The flesh was torn away from shoulders and flanks so the skeleton showed through and shreds of blackened hide dangled thick with ants. The cow's stricken face was turned up towards us, so you might think she still had life in her and she required an explanation of the horror – her horns alert, mouth open and the tongue gone. The head was propped, as I then saw, by the shafts of some broken spears stuck in her neck.

A new era began.

Who was I to care? I pranced ahead in the grip of this ridiculous mood. You would have called me a child rather than a man of twenty or twenty-one (I cannot be sure which).

It occurs to me now that Gabriel's satisfaction might have been solely on my account, because at last he had me at the mercy of his will. So confident was he by this time that he stopped to gnaw the carcase, mad with gratitude, ravenous for half-cooked flesh of a taste he knew. As for me, I could never stomach such food again. I confess this to you so you will be ready for how strange I have become: a meal of moths is more to my liking.

Down through the clump of close-grown trees we wended, me slipping nimble among them, Gabriel crashing along, and into that tangle of undergrowth where I had found him, to the foreshore of flowered shrubs, to the embankment above the Master's logging camp, and to the Master's road.

The pinnace had gone.

This was as far as I would risk taking my charge. From here on Gabriel must make his own way. Hadn't I put myself in danger enough? (The proof is the four walls shutting me in now as I write.) I remember a cold shock of commonsense. What sort of rash fool presents himself a second time to be shot? Or to be chained, for that matter, or whipped as a deserter?

I had delivered him. He knew where he was. I wished him goodbye, patted his shoulder and turned inland again. But Gabriel caught that patting hand. He was already in the act of stepping down the embankment so I found myself wrenched and dragged, staggering on to the road. The animal in a trap knows everything in a flash. Fear of the trap is in our blood, known by the deepest instinct. I fought to shake him off. I lashed out at him, I twisted and cursed, I kicked and used my elbows. Most of these blows hit their mark. Still he would not let go. By now he had hold of my arm. I could not break his grip. The nerves were dead in him, most likely, because nothing hurt. He made no attempt to kick me as I kicked him. He did not even try forcing my arm the wrong way. He held tight and plodded ahead, fixed upon reaching the farm ruins.

While anxious to make as little noise as possible, I struggled like a wild thing. Once I tripped him and brought us both down among loose sharp stones. But he held me firm, lumbering to his feet with no resentment and taking up his task. If he had only conquered the fever and found strength sufficient as this aboard *Fraternity,* he would have thrown me off easy and seen me hung. Waving that handless arm, although nobody appeared, he bundled me along.

All my energy left me.

The picture I must show you is of a clothed man bringing in a naked savage. This is a picture which we know from as far into childhood as we can recall, is it not? A British picture.

The beautiful chaos back there called. Birds with no name called. Scents never before smelt called. Greens not green and browns not brown, leaves hanging vertical from their twigs to cast no shade. The looseness of the place lodged in me as an ache. And where was my circle? I believed my guardians had seen enough by now to come and rescue me. I saw nobody. What use was their knowledge of eternity if they did not foresee this? I had proved my power to them. Who could take away from me those minutes when the snake peered in at my cry of fear in time to stop it coming? Who could deny that St Elmo's fire played about my head or that the lightning did not strike?

I knew then what I feared – not the Master and his carbine, nor being manacled to Gabriel's one complete arm – I feared being seen naked by a lady! Isn't that enough to make you sick laughing?

I offer it to you as the real test of whether a man is civilized.

Night again here in my confinement, with just enough of a fading dusk left to jot down another thought for you. This afternoon I wrote about the clothed man bringing home his captive and about my worry lest I was caught naked. I should make clear that the people I have been living among wear no clothes. Even their feathers and bunches of leaves are not placed to cover nakedness, being mainly decorations on the head, arms, chest and thighs. Also I must report that after only a few days, to my surprise, I no longer noticed this.

I was brought up a modest boy. Therefore I believe others would find the same thing and soon get used to it. I put it to you that when we give up the habit of clothes, you will scarce notice – provided the weather stays warm.

Mind you, if it became general, this would end the comedy of fashion. A terrible pity too. There is nothing at heart funny about the body, which is either beautiful or tragic, whereas clothes are always good for a laugh. Frilly bits and fur lining, the responsibility of matching one pink with another and risking eternal damnation if the length of a hem is not right. True, without clothes, people's lives must lack passion and scandal. Not to mention a severe shortage of jealousy and snobbery.

Yes, I take it back. Who cares if nakedness would soon pass unnoticed among them? Let them have their foibles. Let bottoms be all the more padded and waists pinched. I am starved of laughter. We cannot have too much laughter.

But for you and for me – good night.

Morning.

Lord, let me know mine end, and the number of my days: that I may be certified how long I have to live.

Isn't this the prayer everyone prays? Such folly – to hope that if once we were prepared, being allotted a fixed span, we would live more contented and die without anguish! The fellow who wrote the Psalms knew how to get under your skin.

As to Gabriel and me, wasn't it true that for both of us our return might well number our days and no mistake? Bearing in mind the lessons of religion, no doubt my own end ought to be sweetened by the satisfaction of bringing a runaway back to the fold. Wasn't it worth losing my freedom to take his away for ever?

Instead, my capricious heart, my despot, felt sad. Seeing the wreckage of the place did this to me.

So the Master dreamed about Virginia, did he: rich plantations, a neat church, labourers singing in the fields? In his dream I suppose he saw himself looking up along this wild coast to where an orderly town might be built, where ships might tie up to a stone quay and dandies doff their hats to ladies. Or perhaps he dreamed of Jamaica: black slaves flocking down a hillside of tobacco fields, the women's laughter on a fruity breeze, tools being stacked in the barn where hogsheads would be broached and the slaves allowed their songs and dances under supervision, just a few heads needing to be clubbed before the procession could set out from the church to the waterfront, a statue of Christ with actual hair, a general looming of hysteria, candles in branched candlesticks guttering and smoking inside little glass chimneys, and a fantastic voice from the crowd singing lewd wild things from a fog of incense, but fear of the lash holding them, at last, in check and the day passing off with no more than a couple of deaths, the crop safe picked. Or did he dream the town as a planned place right where his gutted house is now, with civic offices each side of a clock tower, taverns on corners and a chapel behind? Well, what he achieved was one erect wall in which a single pane of glass held good, the charcoal shell of half a dozen outbuildings and kitchens, two standing sheds, one with the roof half gone, the other intact, a stockyard where a dead white horse lay as close to the water trough as it could stretch, and an empty paddock closed in by a broken fence.

I do not mock him. My own dreams are too breakable.

While I pause a moment I hear, down at the cove, that loose raft of logs clocking as the tide comes in. There. And again.

Yet I have not finished telling you about my return to the farm and Gabriel bringing me. Once I had stopped struggling he let me go. So simple. He was not bringing me against my will. He wanted me to be glad. I suppose he wanted a friend. So tight had his grip been all this while that I still felt fingers around my arm – as if he held me now with his missing hand. The place was deserted. Even the bodies among the ruined buildings were gone. Someone survived to bury them. I walked wary. Then a teasing thought came to my head. What if Gabriel had been neither lost when I found him in the bush nor wasting time hunting me but had offered himself as bait, certain of my being out there and certain that when I heard his blunderings I would be too curious to pass up the temptation of seeing who it was?

Do you notice that, released and given this further chance,

still I did not learn, still I did not seize my freedom and clear out?

All I could think was that the farm and sawmill being abandoned provided proof that he had not run away. He had been left. Why this filled me with such fury at the time is hard to say. My life was always rich in lessons, yet it struck me as brutal that whoever took the pinnace did not take him along too, this broken soul, dumb with surviving the deep fears his body must remember from being murdered.

Gabriel himself knew enough to spend some minutes scanning the sea, seeming to expect their return. I was ashamed at suspecting him of treachery. He needed me. So great is his heart, I said, that he can find it in him to love any person who fills the void, no matter how base. He showed me (me, first among enemies) a nest in the part-standing hut, his dirty heap of rags. Then he guided me to the shed, the sole structure left untouched by fire, waiting in attendance while I unbolted the door.

I peered into a darkness smelling of sheep oil and stale smoke. By the stripes of daylight slashing across the room from gaps between the planks I soon came to see what was there: twenty pair of folded blankets – a hundred pair maybe – suits of clothes, boxes full of gift knives for natives, scores of tomahawks stacked on a shelf among looking-glasses for native ladies and a heap of scissors. On the floor stood the station flour stock in sacks besides casks of grog, biscuits and salt beef. I could also see that the place was built of the stoutest timbers to foil theft and withstand attack.

My amazement that the Indians did not plunder this store gave place to respect: they had not wished to steal, despite a good portion of their land being stolen, they just wanted back what had been theirs before. The gift trinkets were doomed to remain covered with dust. Or was it more like a question of ignorance, the Indians failing to imagine what all this stood for, flour being foreign, corn being foreign, even the idea of things stored in one place foreign, and bribery being foreign too.

On a small table I found account books. Also a tray of paper, several jars of ink, some nibs and a pen (the very pen I am now using).

Gabriel stood back while I poked around. We had all the time in the world. And yet I scarce lost a minute before giving in to the old corruption. Torn between longing to set a mark on paper – a single letter of our alphabet would do – and the need to cover my nakedness, I took a shirt from the pile. I slipped my head in its noose, arms stuck up in the air. During those few seconds when I was blind and helpless he ducked out. The door swung to. The bolt shot home. So much for Gabriel being simple! This was my punishment for treating him like a child. Fury softened to fear. Trapped: I had put myself right back where I started in Oxford. Just as the dealer tricked me into the wasted time of being polite, so Gabriel Dean did the same. Our manners are a weapon against us.

There was no use banging on the door. I stood still to think. Hollow.

A haunting odour mingled with the sheep oil and smoke, some delicate thing of suggestions. It took me back to memories of our linen drawer on the landing in the Kirk Braddon cottage on the Isle of Man. Could there be a bag of dried herbs here among the blankets? Yet no sooner had I named the memory as herbs among linen than my nose lost it. The faintest trace, like an echo, seemed to linger on, a mere suggestion in my wishful thinking.

Nothing could be done until the gaoler came back with food. I felt sure he would come back because, if he was deft enough to throw a bolt, he could be nowhere near as helpless as I had thought. And he must want me alive, or why use so much cunning to entice me back, why not kill me out there where my remains would never be found?

You will know me well enough by now to see how typical it was that I took refuge in sorting through the choices offered. One was a plan to trick him by showing myself as his creature, being dressed in clothes and having a weapon already hidden among them. Another was to use a tomahawk and begin hacking away a section of wall. No, I must think of something quieter, something giving Gabriel less time to be ready to murder me the instant I showed my head. The best way out, I decided, was through the door. Meanwhile, I had to keep him calm by doing nothing. There was no hurry. It would be too much bad luck for the pinnace to arrive back right then. In any case, the sensible idea was to break out after dark. While puzzling over these plans I occupied myself by getting dressed. How strange it felt. The stuff touched me where I was tender. I tried sitting on the stool and remembered this too. What a great satisfaction it was to rest my elbows on the table and find it just the convenient height. I fitted a nib to the pen, dipped it in the inkwell and made a mark on a sheet of paper: I.

The thing looked graceful, a tiny vein traced down the middle where the nib spread at the top of the stroke. My eyes swam with longing. I think I was never so homesick as at that moment.

I heard Gabriel come stumbling around. I called to him with more pleading in my voice than I wanted him to hear. He did not answer.

I can tell you the exact moment when I knew you were there. Of course I can.

I confess it took me a long time to solve the mystery of that trace of fragrance which came and went several times. Once it happened when a bird sang, once when a shadow passed, interrupting my slit of light. But you must excuse me – how could I guess there might be a lady out there still in that wasted havoc? I failed to read the signs.

The day after I broached the grog and biscuits I heard a voice. Quite a long way off. At first I took it for an effect of the sea. You must have noticed hearing a lonely cry when at sea, or the chatter of crowds, only to find no one there. Then I knew, from the matter-of-fact tone. This voice was a voice.

To go by the rules the Master laid down before we set sail from Circular Wharf, any woman joining our enterprise must do so within the strict rules of decency – as a wife wedded by

Christian wedding to the man she came with. Only one such woman sailed aboard *Fraternity.*

So I knew.

The fact is that I could not discover any surprise at you being here. Once I realized this I knew I was expecting you. This expectation had tugged at me in secret to draw me back under false colours as Gabriel Dean's guide and protector. He had been more in my power than he knew. So! What do you make of that?

The door closed. The bolt shot home. I was captured again. But this time I was not your husband's prisoner. That fragrance kept me from despair. Again and again. Until my being shut away began to take on new meaning. My mind filled with other plans and guesses, nothing to do with escape.

No sooner did I pick up the pen than I felt joy go wild in me. I had been given a purpose. Selecting a clean sheet of paper, I commenced with a sentence I mulled over for hours to get right. I must face the fact that you will have forgotten who I am. And look how many pages I have filled since then in order to put the full stop which I now make on this one.

Heart of my life. If only I can think clear I shall know what to say. I am breaking rules. These letters do not attempt to put our lives in order. They are part of the muddle. And part of the muddle of all letters this moment crossing paths in that terrible scramble forever going on throughout the globe. They are meant to throw you into utter confusion.

I have set down my faults and my claims as true as I am able. How delicious the hope that you will find in my confusion a new country to claim as your own and possess.

Will you forgive me my goat legs, my scaly hands, my beard grown thick, and my childish dumps? I promise to be happy.

My dearest,

One favour I beg: do not be too proud. My pain brings me some slight pleasure. But pride, in you, can only bring you loneliness and power.

We cry out when hurt. This is natural. Forgive me, then. Even heroes whose deeds set them far above us must be the same as other men: they must suffer or we would not recognize them as heroes. This is my excuse. You nor I can afford to seem polite. Only a barbarian dies smiling.

There, you see how I have conned my book of *Heroes in History and Fable*!

The one fact I can not escape is that you never come. This cold tap fills my veins. The terrible harmless cold goes pumping through my whole map of loneliness.

How disgusting that I go on living. Why won't I die? All I have, cooped up in silence in this mockery of gaol, is my own stench. Was it for this that I stepped over the gunwale of the boat, let myself be lifted on a wave of courage, and kept going up the sand, though I knew any escape into so strange a place would be an act of treachery?

Under my belly, while I strove to keep it soft enough for my crime to succeed, I felt Gabriel Dean's nose press against me, his brow, his chin. His mouth was moving.

You can not imagine the anguish you put me through. Nor how I fear that you may not be trying to hurt me, that you may be doing it because you feel nothing at all.

Our Lord, so the Psalm tells us, shall go up on high and He shall take captivity captive. I know how this feels. My present captivity has no power to confine me. Here in this dark store, among the paltry sort of gifts we offer in return for the luxury of being destroyers, I have reached the freedom to say what is in my heart.

In the courthouse at Douglas I sat on a wooden bench. My fingers played with a fold in my mother's skirt. Up there in front stood a man with shoulders bundled into a jacket too small for him. The suit was made of some rough woollen stuff. His hair had been wetted and brushed to one side above a face which was a clumsy wooden copy of my father's face. When asked to speak, the marvellous wooden mouth opened and there was even a ventriloquist voice that came out parroting my father. I looked round for him so we could smile together and I could let him know I thought this pretend person looked idiotic.

Speakers droned on. Much later the ushers brought light for the candles. The man in the woollen suit was led away. My heart stopped in a grip of ice when on a sudden he came to life and in my father's strong clear voice called out: Narra noain dhyt! and that toy face broke into my father's wonderful fierce smile.

My mother, who had been soft and absentminded, not too interested in what was being said, jumped up. Tremendous tall and proud she was as she marched me out through the crowd without a word about why they stared at us. Only when we reached the lane with its dingy lamps sputtering did she start sobbing sobs that stood my hair up under my cap.

*

Let me tell you I was surprised when I set eyes on Sydney. We were brought in right alongside the wharf. There was none of that clambering down rope ladders to board a lighter, an awkward matter after being shut away in the dark. They marched us along a plank in comfort. You will scarce believe I felt like singing.

So this was New South Wales, the exile we feared.

Across the harbour lay a peaceful ridge where a couple of windmills turned slow, also a church and a scatter of houses, each house with its own field. I could not make out more detail than this, but it all appeared pretty well established to me. Light grey drizzle gave the place a dismal aspect. The water was heavy as lead. Our side of the harbour being built as a stone quay, on which we stood, a fully paved roadway led up to the town. I had expected a tropical stone quarry where chained skeletons swung sledgehammers – anything but hansom cabs lined up outside solid buildings, gentlemen on horseback, ladies with umbrellas, and sailors unloading crates of cargo. At one doorway stood a queue of respectable people getting wet. A dog curled for shelter under a barrow. Merchants wore top hats, if you please, and frock coats. The port presented a forest of masts and spars asway on the tide while rigging slapped and hulls nudged the timbers with much bumping and squealing. The whole place was alive and going somewhere. Even the horses trotted with purpose.

Curious, though, the buildings already needing repair. You could not miss noticing. And we are uneasy with the decay of the new. The whole port – not yet fifty years old – had a worn-out look. That is how I saw it. But it smelled good. It smelled of horse dung and chandlery. Not like Douglas or Portsmouth (where we sailed from), which smelled of dead fish.

How does my sketch strike your memory?

Voices were shouting, such voices I had never heard – men become bulls. This was my first taste of what the next week in barracks confirmed. A fellow here may be respectable without hiding the beast in him. Or a woman too, for that matter. Everyone had someone to bellow at, warlike bellows, most of them, bullying and cheerful. Even the redcoats had showed up different the moment they stepped ashore. There was no mercy to be expected of them, as we knew already, but here they had no need to bother hiding it behind a mask.

So this country, I said to the next man, is a place to be reckoned with?

He spat in my face.

It was one of those fresh damp mornings. The drizzle had just stopped and some young ladies were braving the puddles to come and look us over and murmur sentiments of a Christian kind, nothing of the warrior or the beast to be seen in such modest girls. One of them took up my case and rounded on the fellow, telling him he deserved no better than a harsh task. Being spat upon, as I could have told her, was the least of it. He did not seem to hear. We just stood there, chained hand, foot and neck. She was a most uncommon young person. You could see she would soon make up her mind to something. She glanced about like a nervous hen, pretty as you like, then darted forward. Her eyes were fixed not on mine but somewhere in the region of my shirt button as she reached out with her handkerchief and poked at the mess on my face. It must have been torture for her, she went so red. She wiped it off and flung the handkerchief away. I watched the white thing flutter down into the harbour and settle on the water where a bitten apple core bobbed beside a drowned cat among curds of scum. Next thing she burst into tears and buried her face in her sleeve for lack of a second handkerchief. I never saw so tender a nape. I decided she was eighteen – like me – but I dare say she was less. How hot my face was. She hastened off with an older lady in a bonnet, leaving her handkerchief afloat on some bright little ripples slapping against the quay. When they marched us away I thought of my wet feet squelching on the exact same stones where her dry ones had trod.

By God's mercy the fellow who spat was drafted to a different gang or she would have had me murdered for her tenderness.

For as long as you keep away you can not complain if her voice is the voice I hear as yours, your hand the hand I feel wiping my cheek, your eyes the eyes I see cast down so modest. Does this make you fierce?

My love,

Love is what I hope to learn from you. Isn't it true that your body, like mine, rebels against being lonely? To have left you here alone, your husband must be dead or insensible. I mean insensible to your rebellion too. Dare I say so? My sufferings are enough to justify me.

This stuffy hole is dark with the beat of my heart and the thudding sea. Wherever you hide, out there among the ruins, your heart keeps time with mine. Feel it now. You can not escape me. If I am a prisoner, so are you. And I thank heaven for my new imprisonment anyway. Do we not all wish to return to our past for the chance to live it again with the wisdom of later experience; even to suffer the most painful bondage and find it blessed?

I think about your body and the mystery of it.

If you ask me my intentions, I intend having no limits.

My brother is a good man (if he has stayed the way he was) and I hope to prove as good. But I must confess to you that the act of love is the thing, and it is one thing I don't know that I know the first thing about.

My body is still a stranger to me. I knew my body when I was a boy but not any longer. Its shape and length of bone, hanks of hair and ugly health are none of them the way I thought manhood would come to me. Only my smell is homely. We do what we can to be as we wish, but Nature goes its own way. Did you lose the girl you were? We must talk. As for me, I had a fine idea of just what I wanted. Foolish hopes. The mischance is that we grow to hate the half-and-half mongrel so many of us find we become . . . all the more when we notice ghost reminders of our grandparents too.

Forgive my goatishness before you come to look at me. If you will, then I shall forgive your beauty.

What next?

I am caught. I must confess my needs. To declare myself. I come to those lovely simple names we have for making love and for the tools of it. Each like the blemished note of a bell. Such a coward I am, I dare not write them for fear they might ring too cold and vigorous. Shall we be free to say them when we are together?

If I make myself a fool here it is from respect for you. Those solid simple words must wait until we are face to face. All I shall promise is the violence of my body, which makes me gentle. I believe I might explode at your first touch. So you see how little of you I need use up! One touch. Only promise me we shall make the eight-shanked beast: and you shall find I can please you. The flesh, being fixed in its designs, sets the mind free to be tender. Please have no fear that I would hurt you. I beg you to judge my passion by my courtesy.

Dare I call you my love yet again?

You are still reading.

If I understand the poets, perfect love is an island. But not like the islands we know when we are children, each with its safe sea around it. Each with its sad coop of freaks whose babies are doomed to repeat the same freakiness. On this island we have come to, how else should the lions be but feathered red and green like parrots? The horses here damn well ought to grow horns and fight in battle like the men on their backs. In this place there might as well be all tongues spoken or none. Dwarfs and giants will of course be met with and sacrifices fed, as they are in fairytales. The place is open to those clean dangers gone from our modern world since pleasures began to be made in factories. What else should forty-two kings do but bow down to the one who loves?

We need never again be alone, you and I, from the moment when you call upon me.

You might not guess from these careful words but I am become lunatic. Shut away in here I speak filthy things. I sing for you. I lie on the floor, too weak to stand. I am driven to get up and to scrawl yet another pitiful secret letter. I pardon myself by saying that the longer you put up with me the better my opinion of myself and the fuller the opportunity I am giving you to prove your greatness of heart.

Take me. I do not question the world's judgement that I am least and ugliest among men, a forger and a convict. This, I put to you, is the very reason you should accept me.

Can you imagine how caring the forger must be, how exact with his craft, how much in love with what he does? First he must grasp what he is to achieve and then keep this general understanding in mind while he goes over the parts in finest detail. He must look into each detail to see details within a detail. He has to love the whole piece in the very act of loving these details within details, otherwise he will never make a forger. And where he finds a fault in the original he has to feel joy; and the same joy at making the same fault. The artist may be dissatisfied and unsure. The forger is his opposite. The forger knows just what to do and has perfect confidence in the work the artist does. The forger is a happy man. He is generous and easy pleased. He is not jealous of the original, he loves the original. He is not profane against God, because he does not presume to put forward rival creations. Last, he is a stickler: if his labour is to pass for the real thing he can not leave off halfway, as the artist might; he can not allow himself to falter.

This is the kind of man who writes to you, using words to take captivity captive.

As to my eyesight, you may know that the sufferer of my complaint has compensations, his near sight being exceeding sharp. By nature he can see such fine points as others may detect only with a magnifying glass. His hearing is acuter, his sense of smell more delicate. Agreed, the universe beyond reach of his hand loses its detail and fine lines: yet he recognizes a garden as a garden, a church as a church and a mountain a mountain. A tree may be a block of foliage and never a thousand leaves, but it is still a tree. The near-sighted person moves in a bubble of complications through his simplified world, more aware of being private than others and less brash in what he claims to know. Before he leaps he does his best to look. You may think him a sorry creature, yet he knows himself. This he does know. This is within his range of clearness. Dear love, believe me.

I have returned from peering out through the crack. I heard a flock of birds fly away chattering, headed for the forest. The thought of it makes me anxious. I want my own freedom, please. The land calls. But I shall not expect you to feel the land as I feel it. There is plenty of time. And I am used to being questioned. You may ask what you like.

If you are hoping for a slave, let me say that I have served my apprenticeship. If a master, I have studied with qualified tyrants. Allow me to go further. Suppose you want both: a slave one moment and a master the next; then who better for your purpose than a forger?

Can I believe what my heart tells me, that you watched your husband die? Was this because you wished him to die? Was his death not enough to touch your pity? Was it your plan to have the native Indians swarm down with flaming torches and leave his dream gutted because he dared make a dream beyond the dream of keeping you? Did your blood rejoice when you heard the spears hiss, when you saw him lured out from cover to kick a powder keg in among the cinders as his desperate bid to frighten them off before they finished him? Did you feel the first spear dig into him? Was it joy you felt? I can understand it. Another. Another. Had you known you were trapped in the prison of his needs? Had you confined yourself to narrow hopes so the soul might survive by scarce breathing, by drifting with the tide, by not even wasting the energy needed to call for help? I understand.

At first when I knew it was you I saw rush along the road

from the jetty I thought you were sleepwalking. But I once knew a sleepwalker and how she walked. She never hurried, that one, nor did her breath come so fast. You may not have guessed I was there when you passed me in the dark. Well, I am used to the night. I am used to its faintest noises. The flapping of a skirt astounded me. Meanwhile, your husband lay clutching the knife he got off me. I would not put it past him to notice if it had once been his own and might have been filched. Was he base enough for this? Was he dying? Were you flying there to help? You know best. I only ask because I want to understand. And I believe you will agree that love admits no moral; just a body which takes – and gives nothing in return.

You can not shock me. My love will swallow all. As yours will too if it is to be love. I welcome whatever horrors I must suffer for your sake. If you agree to accept my beaten face and my back, raw wrist, the hump of hate in me and the jealousy. I would have them doubled to test your taste for me. I would have my sores break out again and suppurate, I would crawl in fear and commit the basest acts of cowardice just for the joy of entertaining you with nonsense.

Say nothing but vile things. Beauty added to your beauty would pile too much grief on me, making me falter under such happiness enough to remember who I am.

I shall prove I know you better than you believe I can. There is a precious secret between us which at all costs I swear to keep from the world. A few steps closer to the blaze, staring at what the flames themselves were showing you, I reckon you stopped. Is this right? I stopped also, in terror that you had seen me. I did not look round, let me be honest, but I heard the harsh sound of your lungs and heard it falter. At that same instant I heard something else too: the tumbler clicked against the sear when you cocked your pistol. You let out a hiss of air, closer to fury than to fear. I heard powder being tapped into a pan, no mistake about it. None. And then the stuff of your skirt slapping against your legs as you hurried on, with all in readiness.

Was your bullet to set him free, or to set you free? I ask it of my heart as a conundrum with back-ways of delicious doubt.

How did you know to take a weapon with you if you had left your husband's bed before the attack began? On the other hand, if the attack had begun, how strange that you left at all. And stranger still that you did not rouse him with warnings.

This is my treasure.

I have confessed to you how I murdered Gabriel Dean, how I found him alive again and fell victim to his trap or to his need (it scarce matters which), never doubting myself. Why? Because the body willed it. I was drawn by the magnet of your nearness.

So now, when I declare myself your lover, do you begin to realize what I mean? As I write, the truth comes in a flash: you – the only white woman for a hundred miles – killed your husband for my sake.

Dearest. I am thinking I should rip the whole thing up. Tell me I have not lost you. What I wrote about your husband was because he did not deserve you. Also because the spark of fire I saw passing me in the night could have been his fire in the mirror of your eye.

You are passing me still, forever passing. And taller than I thought. You were outside my wall an hour ago. Your perfume haunts the place. Someone else came after you and tried the bolt. How many people are out there? So easy it is for fancies to become fears.

But should you have taken my part? I was honour bound, as the second bridegroom, to do the deed myself.

Again and again I tried to see your face. You were on the wharf at Sydney and you turned away, as a flurry of that amber dress, settling yourself in a landau while I caught only a whiff of your light. Once aboard ship, when sailing out through the Heads and the hatch was not yet closed, I glimpsed you gazing astern at the wake. Thinking of England, I suppose. Or grieving for some lost lover? You had a flower in your hand. Do you remember? These are fragments I treasure. Also your fantastical moans through the swaying pitching nights and that same voice, one day, speaking sharp to a sailor. Then came my last glimpse, when you were ill and being helped down the rope ladder. That is when you gave me a gift! You filled the Master's arms. He had to give you his complete concentration while keeping his balance. The boat rocked and yet he did deliver you safe to bondage. You gave me the gift of those minutes I needed in which to claim my freedom.

You see how much we have between us? This is my hoard of treasures. And of course there was the outline of your back, seen against the fire: yes, the truth is that I did look, once I had begun running again. I glanced over my shoulder and saw your back bent over, engrossed, while lightning flashed around you. Were you unscrewing the cap and shaking out more silver powder? What did you think about? The task of priming that pistol? Or the prospect of what you had to do? So it is your back, above all, which I remember.

I am in a rage at knowing this. As I bring the scene to life again I want to shock you into turning round and seeing me.

He did not love you. He did not. I will never believe he did. So – have you made love to yourself? Or will it be the first time when you come to me? I wish I could be forty, with the gift of experience to give you as well as the gift of my youth.

My angel of the sharp tongue,

I dare say you will be curious to hear what I did out there during that tribal journey, having so much time on my hands. The answer is nothing. Well, I believe I was born with a gift for indolence, thanks to which I could go blank enough to be open to knowledge. The knack was admitting that there can be no such thing as the discovery of a land. Does this surprise you? Granted, we hear tales pitched at having us think there is nothing in the world so interesting, from big discoveries by Marco Polo and James Cook and company, down to little places called Somebody's Folly. But what do discoverers do? They put names to landmarks unknown to them and not named by anybody they ever heard of. But do we imagine the Cape of Good Hope came into being just to be called that name? We might as well talk about the discoverers of ignorance.

All that happens is that words and numbers are written down. The chart is a big blank except for a squiggle of coast here and a river mouth there: a scatter of names on a clean expanse of ignorance.

You will object that Botany Bay, for example, was discovered by Cook because no other Englishman landed there before him in time to call it Dog Inlet. True enough. But what did he do when he chose the name? The place knew nothing of Botany Bay. He put a dabbler's limitation on it; and admitted he had such a poor huddle of categories in his mind that this was the best he could do for the infinite strange place he chanced upon. Bay, cove, inlet, sound, gulf, kyle, harbour – what else is there? This little list will do. You see my point.

So while the place crowded his senses with a thousand impressions, a riot of bird song and busy animals, wind among forests of chance leaves (let alone the massed ghosts of the dead and the unborn crowding upon his spirit), he ties it to the noble ideal of greed. How can this place be used? It is a bay. He does not hesitate. He invents what he sees. Nothing was here before he came. He knows this because the chart is blank. He takes an accurate bearing and writes numbers among the words. He takes up his pen (as I also hold mine) and prints BOTANY BAY – so many degrees so many minutes south, by so many degrees so many minutes east – where before this there was only untouched ignorance.

For my part, I hope to show you something less simple about the country we are in, something outside the categories you know. The day will come when we shall have space to discuss this. My wedding gift to you will be to open your eyes to the beauty of things without meaning or use.

When it comes to the issue of two worlds I can not sit by. I must take part on the savage side of the question.

As for James Cook being rowed ashore by sailors with hats

and striped vests. You can see them in your mind's eye with their trews rolled up. Their bare feet splash in the shallows while those still aboard are shipping oars. You can look out at them from the shore and watch them reflected in the broad mirror of wet sand when a wave pulls back. The ship is at anchor in a deep channel. You can watch the great man leap out – success makes him young and springy – wading ashore to print the sand with the first boot mark ever made here. Well, aren't a hundred other eyes also watching? Don't the ocean wash away the imprint?

Nevertheless the first boot, being the first boot, you argue, must have been important.

Did it not take aeons for this place to be created, I reply, is it not old as the stars? So, what about a boot mark in the sand now?

We shall have wonderful arguments.

Let me give away all my secrets! I plan to stand by and wait until this land, which is so near you and so unseen, enters your heart too. I shall be there to whisper then that it needs no names. Your husband has had you in bondage to his cause of creating a counterfeit England by cutting down strange trees and digging out plants with no name. He has had you in bondage to the comfort of being able to call this thing a cabbage, this thing a peapod; of fencing animals you can call a cow, a horse, and keeping them fenced in case they recognize freedom with less trouble than civilized man.

This I can offer you.

I have already lived a life of knowing about marked limits and being kept in or kept out – of family and foreigner, owner and thief, tax agent and smuggler, artist and forger. But answer one question: Who makes the rule that certain things may be copied and certain things may not?

Each moment of life out there inland of that ridge is new. On my journey, gathering time, this was what I came to know. You can predict nothing. So much happens that your body tingles. The newness invades you, not just by the nine openings but by hundreds of nerves, thousands of hairs and pores. The person who is determined not to limit the risk is set free by risk. The body is part of the risk. So I can say that in my life up there I discovered nothing. And, at the promise of setting you free too, my heart sings. This will be my gift.

I wait for you.

Some days I have stopped writing because I could not go on without a drink. All I had was grog. And, my darling one, I have sworn to woo you sober. Being thirsty for so long and grown giddy from lack of water, I have promised to believe in God now the rain is beginning again, and for the moment I do believe. Sticking a knife through the roof, I have made a nice little trickle here and I am using a hat for a basin.

The light is awful poor. I work with my nose on the page.

You do not come.

I think of that sunk barque and those who might have gone down with her.

You must have noticed that I whittled a slot in the west wall, the wall without shelving. I can see out. I see, for a start, the dead horse still there.

I want to be seen myself. I want to be known. I want to feel what it is to offer my body. I want your cool fingers to touch my arm. The memory of that young woman's handkerchief on my face sends fires racing through me. So I know what I am talking about.

If only Gabriel would pass by, I might make him understand how to undo the bolt. Or at least he could deliver these letters.

And with them my love.

Heart of my heart,

I heard you at the door last night! I blessed myself for not giving up. I might have broken free on any day, armed as I am with more weapons than a man can carry.

In matters of love I admit I am an apprentice. But so was I an apprentice forger – and I foiled the experts. What a laugh. And

I am happy now. You did not stay. But you came. You listened and then crept away on tiptoe. I called. You ran. You know this is the truth. The thing is that, when you ran, you ran with my message in your ears. You had to carry it with you. You could not escape without it. It must have filled your head, so big it was. I have nothing to add. That was my whole message: I love you.

My plan is to stay awake all night, waiting until you come again.

My dear one,

There is no use lying or pretending. My visitor was not any other person but you. I know the smell of your clothes and the rustle of them. Also your exact light footstep in the gravel. You came. Did you want to make sure I am still alive? You did not speak. Does this mean there is somebody else out there, somebody I can not hear who watches you?

Can it be that Gabriel thinks he should be the second bridegroom and not me? How long has he been given to press his claim? Why did I not make some record of the days? Have I been here a week? On a sudden I need to know. But this is madness, he has nothing in his head but clouds. Forget my foolish worries.

I heard your clothes brush against the wall. The aching in this body of mine, this stranger, kept me awake. An agony of hardness shivered through me. I trembled so much with unspoken thunder I had to cling to the lamp hook by both hands. To be outspoken, convulsions shook me. The cordial shot right across the room, on and on, so that had I been as calm as now I must have feared some damage to my health. It left me feeble.

Do you wonder if I dare not think about your lips. I am in alarm at the power you have over me. There is so much to learn – and I dare be open with you – such adventure. I shake when I think about that tender hidden passage into the life you are keeping secret for me.

I heard your clothes brush the wall and I cried out to you. Yet

I was glad you did not come back. How could I have cleaned myself? When we are lovers we will not be shut away or seek shelter. Let us wander the hills and be free of shame. I plan to take you to a pool where we may bathe together. We shall eat oysters and periwinkles. On our journey inland I can find you parrot eggs.

Let my voice work in your mind. Do you hear it repeat and repeat: I love you? By a mercy there was no time for adding anything. This was all you had of me. Your brain can not repeat it more times than I cry it now in here.

Your ever loving lover.

Dearest of all. I find feverous relief in writing another letter. Here is a tale from a book I read. A young man travelling by foot in ancient times met a ghost woman. Of course she was lovely and she welcomed him. She took him to her house, where the chairs were plated with gold. He was a quiet fellow not given to pursuing his lusts, therefore he had made himself helpless against love. He stayed a day or two, a week or two, and at last he married her. Among the friends at the wedding was one with skill to see her for what she was and to see that her golden chairs were no more solid than reflections in water. When the friend spoke to her of this she ranted and stormed, she commanded him to hold his tongue. But he would not. He spoke out until all her gold, her house and she herself vanished as vapour. Thousands of people were witness to the fact of it.

But the book gave no answer to the question I wanted put: Was the young man cured of love or did this leave him worse afflicted than before?

Such love is more terrible than anything. I look at where I am. I count folded blankets. I toy with knives. I stack my written papers ready. I can not bear to think of all the truth I have put in them, or of you opening me as a book. Even the midday light is too dim today and my eyes too full and sore to read.

Where is the justice? You despise me without knowing me,

without hearing what I have to say. As dogged as justice, as prejudiced as the law, you cast me in exile here. So long I have been waiting in this coop, patient because I know you are out there. Am I wrong to have taken your watching for interest? Are you more coward than curious?

Gabriel heard me this morning. He did not run away. He tried to work out the bolt. And at last I lost hope. I told him how to do it. Good soul he did his best. He panted at the task an hour at least before he gave up and prowled around the place. He came back again and again to the puzzle. So someone else locked me in.

I have left myself trapped by my own evil, afire with shame. Does this please your cruelty? Well, let me also confess that even when I am heaping the vilest curses on you my desire is kindled.

The rain begins again. The sea beats up. Think of me and my freedom when you come to look at the splintered roof. This is the best way out, the walls are too thick. I am claiming my freedom and you are to be thanked for it. Whether you wished to tame my spirit or betray me to the courts I do not need to know. The treachery would be the same. You see I have regained the full power of speech.

Your silence itself has become a routine: that is what gives you away.

Suppose I am wrong . . . then you need only set foot in the wild. The tremendous shock of it will widen like ripples on a pool to be felt for miles around and I shall easy find you. All you must do is hazard starvation or hazard chancing upon some sight not meant for females.

My last folly being sentiment, I still hope.

My dear despair,

Remember this: I am a convicted forger proud of my forgery.

Ought I to sign myself your slave? I would be short-sighted indeed! I begin to suspect you have little sense of humour.

The point is that the forger dedicates his skill to worthless labour. Does this mean that you forgive me because, in the end, my crime was against myself? Meanwhile, I have this to be proud of – that I did not fall into the evil habit of niceness.

To hell with the Psalmist praying: Lord, let me know mine end.

Life will not be trapped in boxes. These letters themselves, after all, my dear, might be forgeries! The end will always come as a surprise.

The rain has stopped. I think of all the clouds swarming into Gabriel's emptiness. What if he sees more beauty in the sky than you do? Unbearable thought.

Mrs Atholl,

I am in terror that you are dead. Gabriel is back. He heard my axe. Read everything. I shall escape as soon as he is out of the way. Read it all.

P.S. My last hope is that you have wished to drive me away to freedom.

To Mrs Atholl.

Madam,

I have done as instructed. I have read these papers from beginning to end, and a disagreeable task it has been. I shall not set out to enumerate the contents, enough to acknowledge that you were right to suspect this of being a confession. It is indeed. You may recall, Madam, there was a fellow escaped the day we first landed here. At that time your late husband – God rest him – said we were better off to let him go and be rid of a man who would not stop at murder, because anyhow he was sure to die in such wild country. Well, the author of these papers is the self same person but, I fear, still at large. His confessions being so perfectly brazen and circumstantial, I believe this whole affair is become a matter for the authorities.

There is, I would suggest, if I may be permitted, little need for you to bother yourself with the actual papers, all the more so as they are filled with viciousness and indecencies from which I consider it my duty to protect a lady. I must confess that there are also threats made here against your person, which I am convinced you would find distasteful. However, I am firmly of the opinion that the new Governor, Sir George Gipps, must be indebted to you if you was to dispatch the letters direct to him with a request for action. He is doubtless in need of information on the behaviour of such villains, the more so if there be any truth in the rumours I heard in Sydney that he is determined upon being soft with the convicts; also for the assurance that he will find courageous settlers like yourself in the colony whom he may consult and upon whom he can rely as the backbone of society.

Accordingly, Mrs Atholl, I have packed all the papers and sealed them with wax ready to be sent to Sydney. For the rest, Madam, I venture to suggest that an accompanying letter from yourself ought to secure the matter; in this case I do not doubt that you shall see redcoats arrive here to make an arrest as soon as they can be sent. Indeed, why should His Excellency not consider establishing a small garrison in the district for the protection of British rights, exactly as I have heard you say you wish to see it?

Your obedient and obliged servant,

Wm Earnshaw

From Mrs Edwin Atholl,
'Yandilli',
New South Wales.

March 12, 1838.

Your Excellency,

I take the liberty of sending you the inclosed papers to confirm the report sent by my late husband in July of the year before last, concerning the escape of a convict assigned our service. I write also to intreat you to occasion a patrol being despatched down this way to effect the capture of this criminal, who remains still at large, beyond doubt being succoured by savages.

Should you consent to deal summarily with them, which is the savages, I doubt not but they'ld yield him up. Thereby your action would serve the double purposes of bringing a miscreant to justice and punishing his protectors for murdering my husband (also eleven of our assigned workingmen, two pigs, half a dozen sheep, a heffer and an *excellent* blood-horse), also the distruction of our fences and our farmhouse, also the kitchen and outbuildings which were burnt in the fire – not to mention the spearing of a paid servant and the unknown fate of two others.

I dare persist that I still hope to see the object of my desires fullfilled as my farm flourishes, to produce grain and timber for the betterment of our colony. To this end, I beg you, make haste with re-inforcements for the assigned workmen who are due to arrive here shortly. The truth is that I mistrust the suitability of convicts to be given arms, in consideration of their past crimes. I await your speedy decision.

Meanwhile, kindly permit me to explain about these accompanying papers and how I came by them.

To go back to our catastrophy – well after the fire the quarter-master and our few remaining men sailed our brig, the *Fraternity,* to report the tradgedy and the savage character of the blacks in this district. Then he was to fetch help and a fresh assignment of labour to replace those killed.

When the 'Fraternity' sailed I watched her out of sight. I shall not attempt to speak of the fears in my breast, nor the *resolution.* I could not face the journey, as I suffer 'mal de mer' to an appalling degree. Three servants remained with me, also a harm-less creature, Gabriel Dean, a convict who is maimed and has lost his wits, but fond of me and *devoted* to my service. We five were to make a start on the task of rescuing what could be rescued and setting in order those articles left to me – which by great good fortune encluded our store room filled with pro-visions and tools. However, the very next evening when the poor half-witted creature went missing, two of the servants set out to look for him. They did not return. I went out myself, armed with my husband's best piece. When I returned, with my skirt covered in burrs and my face scratched, I found the third servant dead of a wound to the neck.

To be brief, day after day I called to the missing souls. I risked lighting a fire in the hope that my smoke might guide them back to me; but naturally this put me in fear for my life on the mischance of the blacks being far more likelier to see it instead. I took to concealing myself in a cave which I knew of, down near the jetty a half mile from the house.

Your Excellency, you may imagine how *flabberghasted* I was when, four days later, on the Tuesday, Gabriel Dean imerged from the woods beyond the sawpit, dragging a naked creature by the arm!

I observed their actions from my hiding place. To be frank, I was in terror of being seen, as you may imagine, yet taking care to check that my powder was dry and my weapons stood ready. I should explain that I have salvaged several guns and a pistol.

There was still no sign of the two servants who had been sent in search of him – and indeed they have never been seen since.

The convict dragged his captive along the road towards the farm ruin, a creature fighting and struggling the intire way. So soon as they were lost to view round the bend, I creept down and followed, but only so far as I need go to obtain sight of the place. This fellow, Dean, did not let go until they reached the store room, which as I have said miraculously survived the fire, and there the loyal soul and I locked him in.

I still could not be sure of Dean's intentions so I thought it prudant to retreat to my hiding place. There began my vigil. My first fear was that the good Dean would turn on me too. In this I did him a grave misjudgement. My next fear was that the creature, having plenty of tomahawks in there, would chop his way out and then come after me. Such is the life of a lady in the colonies! I am blessed, I am happy to say, with a strong constitution – my one weakness being, as I have explained, that I fall seasick the moment I set foot in a boat. Even so, I felt under some considerable threat.

The dilema was that I could see he was a white man! Naturally I debated the justice of keeping him inprisoned, also the legal point, lest he might be merely a survivor from some legitimate enterprize, a wrecked ship maybe, perhaps even being a gentleman driven to wildness.

Strange things have been known in this colony, as you will discover when you have been here longer.

Some days elapsed, I must say, before I decided to take my life in my hands and go down to question Gabriel Dean as to whether or not the prisoner still lived and where my servants might be. I should point out, Your Excellency, that this Dean neither can speak nor clearly be said to understand. Communication with him is difficult. The fact is, however, that he greeted me with touching pleasure and led me to the store, where he slapped the bolt with his hand (he only has one), giving me to understand that his answer regarding the prisoner was positive.

I returned to the store hut several times during the next week.

But I dared not let the prisoner out. I feared him dead almost as much as I feared him alive.

Still no relief had arrived, there was not a sign of any sail, and neither of my helpers returned. I began to grow desparate with the worry and responsibility, at a time when I already felt that, in justice, my burden was heavy enough and the task confronting me arduous almost beyond hope of success.

Once when I listened at the wall of the store a voice within uttered an awful cry. It was the roar of a wild beast shouting amorous words which I'ld blush to record.

Who may not imagine the *confusion* of my predicament, the terror, the relief that I did not have the fellow's life on my conscience – or the outrage and the *nausea* at his sentiment? One issue at least had been answered: this was no gentleman. I decided my most prudant course was to take vittals and water again to my hiding place, keep myself armed against mischance or siege, and wait out the perilous days until the servants returned or the quartermaster brought the *Fraternity* home.

The prudance of this plan being confirmed by an onset of drenching rain, I began the last stage of my vigil.

One farther difficulty which I beg to lay before Your Excellency was the necessity of keeping Gabriel Dean ignorant of where I hid, for evidant reasons of decency. I prayed that he might at least take shelter from the rain, also that he had learned to cup his hand to drink from. Convict though he was, and wretched in the extreme, it *wrung my heart* to watch him down there wandering back and forth, desparate for some person to have the charity to take care of his simple needs. My worst fear was that he would find the means to open the bolt in order to have the naked fellow for company.

Strange as it may seem – and perhaps unaccountable viewed from the comfort of a Sydney parlour – when the ship returned I *missed seeing it*, so sunken was I in misery. The pinnace had already put out and nearly reached the jetty before I heard voices hailing me across the water.

I gave thanks to GOD ALMIGHTY for my delivrance.

Now, if I may be permitted the liberty, Sir George, I ought to warn you against a *perilous* tendancy in our colony to indulge the convicts. My late husband, I regret to admit, was guilty of this, although a good man in other respects. You are new to New South Wales and I am convinced you will not take amiss the concern of your conscientious free settlers that you should be made aware of the true issues.

I resolved to establish a new order of strictness now that the task of working the property had fallen to me. In this I am given *great* strength by precious memories of meeting Mrs John Macarthur, whose fame will doubtless be known to you, as it is in *Westminster.* Mrs Macarthur successfully conducted business at Camden during her worthy husband's several *long* absences to further their case in the old country, and I trust she is still hale and healthy.

It affords me satisfaction to be able to report that, carrying a musket, I found strength to go down to meet the pinnace and insist upon the quartermaster's arresting the next man to show any such *disorderliness* as to feel free to shout for me! I felt it only fair to be clear that they were under a new regimen. Also I took the precaution of giving orders that the newly assigned convicts were to remain in chains for the time being, until duties could be allotted them, also that the lash should be employed against the least disobedience. This done, we went very quietly in company to inspect the condition of my prisoner – I having apprized the quartermaster (William Earnshaw, by name) of the crisis.

To put it shortly, Your Excellency, it is my duty to report that we came upon the convict Dean laid out dead among his blankets. We could find no sign of struggle. It appears that he crawled on to his rude bedding, which he had piled in one corner of a half-demolished shed, being apparently in some extremity, and died there.

As for the prisoner in the store, the long and the short of it is that he was gone without trace. He is still at large.

You will be wanting to hear about our stores, which we had

been so grateful to find saved from the fire. I confess to having been somewhat amazed when we looked into the hut. We found no damage, apart from a panel of the roof partly smashed, a barrel of biscuits broken open, and a hogshead of grog with the spicket knocked out. The several blankets evidantly removed for use were folded neatly enough and returned where they belonged. The place stank of the fellow's bodily necessities, yet he had done what he could to conceal this inconvenience. A suit of brown holland clothing, soiled, was placed on a stool beside the table, while upon the table itself we found a sheaf of papers.

I could not bring myself to *touch* anything so insanitary. The place reaked like a sewer. At the thought of his labouring over these papers and fingering them ... not to put it too indelicately ... I declined to have the least truck with such filthy stuff. However, I did glance at the top sheet, enough to be surprized by the fair hand it was writ in. For the rest I desired Mr Earnshaw to look them through.

Having apprized himself of what they contained, he reports that they amount to a full confession by the escaped convict, who did indeed survive among the savages and by their help. As it seems, on Mr Earnshaw's insistence, to be a matter of some consequence to your administration during these troubled times, I venture to pass this packet on for your perusal.

My one hope is that such vicious confessions might stir the spirits of those among your staff reputedly under suspicion of showing indulgance towards proven offenders.

Lastly, Sir, to do justice to my own danger, I should point out that the savages in these parts must already be armed with modern weapons. Allthough my late husband was speared three times during the attack, spear wounds did not account for his death. He died of a bullet in the head. I saw the injury for myself. I was not able to write officially of this before dispatching our ship for re-inforcements, owing to the emergency and the *extremity* of my need, not to mention how beside myself I was with *grief*. But I confirmed this highly disturbing development when, with the servants, I buried him.

May I, in closing, Sir George, reassure you that I give no weight whatsoever to rumours that you yourself incline to softness, either towards the savages or the convicts, nor that you would be party to the iniquitous suggestion of imposing land taxes on the very pioneers who are risking their lives to open the country to a great future.

I should like to extend you my warmest congratulations upon your appointment as Governor of New South Wales and trust that you will take *expeditious* action in the matter of establishing the Rule of Law to prevent and discourage mutiny in new districts such as ours.

Ever very truly yours,

Mrs Edwin Atholl

P.S. A firm stand in the matter of keeping felons in control becomes especially urgent here, as I hear that a convicted person, having a ticket-of-leave, has arrived to take up the neighbouring property, an Irishman with the confidance to call his selection 'Paradise', if you please!

The Grisly Wife

Queer thing – but yes – we do mourn for the England we lost – maybe because the darkness of the tragedy awaiting us in New South Wales has left the memories of our youth bathed by contrast in clear simple light – and after so many years of exile one's gentler adventures tend to rise to the surface more and more appealingly –

But the day we set sail from Bristol I doubt if a tear was shed for home – England being so given to licence in those days and ourselves so out of step – I believe I speak for everyone including the prophet – this was to be our adventure in self-sacrifice and despite the fact that we were never exactly missionaries in the usual sense we did speak of this place as a mission right from the beginning – just as we accepted that we were the Chosen Few –

Being the Chosen Few meant we had a great deal more to look forward to than we had to look back on! – but *you* will never understand – no one born over here can have the least notion how desperate people were to escape the smut and futility of England then –

The whole enterprise depended on the prophet – the idea of the mission – the inspiration – the firm sense of being in contact with the Almighty – without the prophet's powerful personality the tragedy would never have been possible – oh let people say what they like about him being something of a weaselish specimen (I've heard it myself) and admittedly he does have a small face but a face simply filled with features – big ears big eyes high cheekbones thick brows – not to mention the perpetually big amazement of an individual determined to escape something in his past – something conceivably stupid – though once you startle him out of himself his eyes come so alive they astonish you and he can smile a whole gallery of teeth and show himself in a trice so handsome it hurts your heart to see his black hair gleam without a trace of grey –

As for his not being masterful – didn't he sweep us off our feet? didn't he gather us together as disciples? didn't he unite us as a family of women? – though he could neither read nor write didn't he succeed in firing us with his vision? wasn't the passage out merely part of his purpose? weren't we ready to faint when we first walked into that great draughty room at Bristol docks only to take comfort from the way he barked at the porters? –

I remember a salt wind blowing in from the open sea – mixed with a down-to-earth hemp smell – the blend intoxicatingly new to me – like the whiff of a fabled creature I had heard of but never encountered –

A clutter of heels knocked hesitantly on the flagstones while we presented our papers to company officials and fussed over the necessities of labelling baggage – echoes echoing in the heart – only to watch our pathetic few possessions trundled away on barrows through an archway where we glimpsed the ship's dark sea-stained timbers – with two sailors at a section of rail scouring the brass to sluice off an accumulation of rime –

The prophet did not flinch – even at the sight of that dismal tub and the way she diminished our future – and I trailed after him – though the odd fact is that we had no sooner climbed the gangplank than I was possessed by fierce regrets that the ship was not smaller and not more squalid!

Excuse me a moment – this country is too infernally *hot* for a person to draw breath!

The source of his power was a gift from God – an amazing talent – a secret – and I knew what this gift was – I had sworn never to tell – he bruised my arm when he made me swear so that's how important the secret was – until such time as he would need to come out into the open and use it to confirm a miracle –

How thrilling the future sounded then –

Still a girl and very giddy I used to whisper what I knew – always in the dark and always only to him – when I needed the comfort of reminding him how strictly I was keeping the news from everyone else – or if I needed to feel we shared something in our lives – he being my husband you see –

No sooner had we possessed ourselves of a berth each and gathered again on deck than Beatrice took issue with the prophet over his use of the word 'ocean' and treated us to a disquisition on oceans in various biblical contexts 'For the entire *three* hundred years from 1611 to 1866 – ' she pursued her theory through several translations of the Scriptures and enlarged on it with such impressive confidence that her cavils and polite contradictions once again drove him out of all patience – though she apologized as usual before proving him wrong –

And she did pay her own way it has to be said –

We guessed what was coming next because we knew her well though she had probably been with us less than a month at that time – and sure enough she proceeded to cite the true meanings of biblical symbolism (water as the symbol for people – day the symbol for a year or a thousand years – beasts for kingdoms – fear for love – and whatnot) – she was so positively fired with her own rightness she fell foul of Ann Whittaker too – you surely remember grumpy Ann who was such a saint underneath? –

Well there we were on board a ship and not one of us had even so much as glimpsed the open sea before –

It rocked about in a most sickening manner from the moment we cast off – sailors swarmed up the rigging to take their posts aloft like large dismal birds waiting for the tug to finish drawing us out into the channel where we were told we would catch a fine breeze – a fine breeze! – this violent wind slammed into us whistling among complicated ropes as the sails roared open and snapped tight –

The vessel thundered –

All passengers were ordered inside out of the way – so much for leaning on the rail at leisure to watch the Somerset coast dwindle while we fostered expected regrets concerning our recklessness! –

the weather closed in almost as dark as night – 'Night' Beatrice persisted breathlessly and coughing 'steals on the house like' she coughed some more 'like a murderer' – Ann sniffed – frantic sails began slatting – the mate who had welcomed us suavely at the companionway such a short time before now let loose halloos in a wolf's voice – the elements sent a violent thrill through the boards – 'All snug!' a sailor bellowed back right in my ear – the ship already sheered along a swell though we had not yet reached the Atlantic – the tall clumsy apparatus tilting dangerously – an unbelievable volume of water gushed past driving regular crests to slap its hull hard and send spray whipping at our backs as we retreated to the saloon door – we plunged in among scores of frightened gentlefolk stopping their mouths with handkerchiefs while a few experienced colonials strutted from table to table offering words of comfort (such as 'This is nothing to what you may expect!') and sipping punch –

Out there wild whistles shrilled from every direction as men galloped along the deck thudding past on bare feet –

I felt an urge to be in the open to face the danger so I elbowed my way back to an exit where the prophet and two stewards tried to restrain me – struggling with the brassbound door I slipped out despite a fierce funnel of wind – the hail of icy spray instantly shocked all breath from my body – I clutched at a deckchair rack to save being flung overboard –

Already drenched and thrown off balance and with drops of water dangling from my eyelashes I watched gangs of men rush helterskelter to humour the gale –

The masts had become useless tons of timber pitching about for no better purpose than to throw off any clinging sailors left up there fighting with canvas thick as wet carpet – this is what I saw before my mantle collar flipped up and blinded me forcing me to turn aside for the wind itself to free my face whilst I lurched back to safety – even then I only just managed to grasp the handle in time to avoid falling and rolling under the rail where the next wave would surely sweep me away –

The men who had stood peering out through salt-spattered

glass assisted me in over the step meanwhile loudly condemning my folly – I dare say I looked a sight trembling and staggering about with hair plastered flat – then because the whole company mutely accused me of irresponsibility I cried aloud 'I've never felt more alive!' – a fat lot of good that did me.

Well thanks to a courageous crew we hung on as far as Madeira where the ship put in to port until the weather cleared – which it eventually did –

But even with bright sunshine and a stiff breeze the trials of patience were not over – this particular wind being in a contrary quarter we began the maddening process of tacking about in an attempt to cheat it at a rate of one mile's headway for each three or four travelled – the whole contraption hopelessly inadequate –

Though soon even this was to seem purposeful compared with the calm that enveloped us – glassy water barely heaving – we lost headway till our gentle purling grew so quiet we might have been drifting backwards for all anyone could tell! – each day stretched longer than the last – the memory played tricks – the sea a mirage – within a week we forgot the dangers so recently survived and began to suffer that special boredom unique to travellers – the shipboard world being very small and amusements few – particularly for a closed household set apart from the rest by piousness –

Actually I have to admit to being visited by a wicked idea at this time which perhaps had some bearing on what happened – are you ready for ideas?

Far off course – out in that transparent universe – floating on the wide Atlantic above sunken mountains and valleys of sea monsters – with nothing the captain could do to turn the bow even a fraction of a degree – abandoned by the last gasp of breath and left helpless for eternity in a bubble of space – afloat on a soundless mirror where not a puff of air could reach us to nudge the sails –

In this era of steam you young people forget how difficult the old ways were with all the bother involved in mazes of rigging – and I suppose you've never thought of the sails themselves being especially heavy have you? well until I travelled neither had I –

Day after stifling day we drifted about in the tropics – our food stock dwindling – the fresh meat being finished we were down to dining on what a steward announced as 'Salt junk with pickles if you please!' – we passed our time lounging in the shade of canvas awnings and only made shift to fan ourselves mechanically – the liveliest thing was a doleful periodic ringing of the bell which was occasionally done by a vastly handsome youth with wild fair hair – while Ann Whittaker complained that we should never have left Madeira –

Several others discussed in undertones the curiosity that among the four Gospel writers neither Mark nor John makes mention of the virgin birth – and I had my wicked thought (much as I later wished I could take it back!) – what proof was there – I thought – that the virgin birth happened at all since God had never shown the world another in more recent times (which He could easily do) to have it verified scientifically?

At this moment the void around us was invaded by a faint noise of galloping horses – the entire ship's company strained to hear – passengers peered in every direction for some explanation of this impossible thing – horses – far out across the Atlantic Ocean! – indistinct as they were at first they soon grew definite – there could be no mistaking what we heard – yet the ship floated steady – web of ropes silent – spars dark against a brilliant sky – hatches open as if the vessel itself gasped for air while at all points of the compass the horizon presented a ruled line as flat as that – distant bugles sounded *tara-tara* and the thunder of hooves began to spread wider the nearer it came – we looked around in mystification – we looked up among the steeples of taut ropes – out between curtains of slack sails – astern among capstans and tackle – forward to where the bowsprit barely wavered – well! for a full twenty minutes those horses bore down on us from nowhere and went galloping nowhere until the din of their approach loomed tremendous and you could hear hundreds of individual animals gasping – riders shouted military oaths above a warm sea sluggish enough for glue – there were witnesses because this was heard by everyone gathered on the deck just as the baking of bread could be smelt wafting out from the galley –

'Well I never!' said Ann crossly –

Big guns began to boom and invisible confusion took over with cavalry charging from opposite sides to swarm around us and converge above our heads – struggling and milling in every direction while we lolled on comfortable chairs and stared in amazement at the fascinating emptiness of a diamond hot sky where muskets apparently popped and soldiers apparently shouted like beasts only to be cut short by unbelievable blasts of nearby artillery – being answered with far-off grumbles from an enemy battery – and then in a lull came weird screams like the whistles of the Great Western Railway except that these came much faster and more terrifying as they whizzed past causing frenzy up there and stirring renewed outbursts of shouting and fresh bouts of musket fire –

You could say it was a kind of music – the way it came and went in rhythms broken by brief silences or swelled toward climaxes of confusion with sobbing choruses accompanied by whoops and snicks of bullets until finally the whole battle as a complicated symphony drifted away (making a good deal more sense than some of the pieces I heard at the Melbourne Philharmonic Society a few years back by the bye) – then the sun suddenly set and we sank trembling against the headrests of our deckchairs with no one daring to utter a word while the lurid and bloody splendour spread around us – we were filled with lingering horror of a sort hard to explain unless by recalling the single voice clearly heard to cry out 'Keep going men – keep going whatever! – O God!' while the tumult drifted further away toward the distant band of sea which had already turned mauve where the rising night stood as high in the sky as the water was deep in that deepest ocean on earth – till the last horse snorted and the last spur jingled and the last glimmer of dusk faded – the Bengal lights were lighted while still we sat as if we ourselves were prehistoric sea monsters caught in a basket being pulled up by a net of cords –

Strange – beyond question stranger than the rickshaw boy we saw later in Durban with buffalo horns growing from his head or even the pagan woman who let herself be burned alive on her husband's funeral pyre beside a canal while the crowd of other ladies under umbrellas pleaded with her not to weaken – and the meaning of this battle in the air was plain to all but the most obstinate –

There was a lesson in it – Beatrice told us 'Our hopes are destined to be marooned somewhere remote – untouched by the world's turmoil – somewhere deprived – ' and she tottered away to her cabin –

With little else to think about during the aftermath I entertained another of my wicked thoughts 'What if – ' I whispered to the prophet who having stood rigid beside me through the whole drama now bent down and let a damp lock of hair brush my cheek 'what if *you* were to blame for this?' – he looked at me with such intense interest I ached to make the point stick 'So now I dare say you will calm a storm if we run into one?'

I do hope in the next world to be spared meeting anyone the least like myself as I was in those days – but to be honest I can't believe I knew I was putting temptation his way – and despite his divine secret I didn't in the least believe he *was* to blame – yet shortly afterwards I had to live with my conscience because he was destined to face a most appalling storm at sea when maybe he thought he could control it and couldn't – then again in the matter of our awful tragedy perhaps he –

As for the rest – well the rest was little more than routine except that the delay meant we were running short of supplies as I say and had to put in at the nearest port – much to the relief of Beatrice Offley who felt dreadfully ill – even though she did find enough energy to dispute the idea that the invisible battle had been a sign heralding the Last Judgement – 'With my training in the physical sciences' she said 'I believe it was more likely an acoustical freak and a lingering remnant of the American War drifting in a lost pocket of air – they *were* American voices after all – '

The prophet didn't bother to hide how furious he was with her –

I believe she would have been glad that he so far forgave her secular opinion as to make no mention of this error of hers when giving her a decent burial at Ascension Island where we docked to refill our depleted water casks – yes she died poor thing – can you see us gathered round her grave while the captain read the service and my husband preached a sermon beginning 'The House of the Dead is the place of birth'?

The mere thought of such a text makes me shudder now – with all I know –

The desolation of that island could hardly be imagined though the inhabitants began by welcoming us with wild demonstrations of jubilation and curiosity because they had not expected us to anchor any more than we ourselves expected it – but they shunned us when news got out of a death on board and a death which might be contagious.

The prophet called us his Household of Hidden Stars – being a secret order – the other eight members (surely I do not need to introduce myself into the picture?) – well you should place them in your mind on that stark and sweltering little island which is really no more than the one tropical mountain crag sticking up out of the Atlantic Ocean and adorned with big spiky plants – an island with a single harbour where miserable huts have been built of loose stone against a background blasted by the sun and grim enough to hope that neighbouring St Helena was as uncomfortable for the ogre Napoleon when he lodged there –

Imagine fifteen or twenty huts on a stony slope all but lost in a swirling cloud of seabirds so numerous you could not conceive how such thousands came to assemble at the one place or how they fed themselves or even found sufficient foot room to settle – the flurry of wings set the ribbons aflutter on Lady Edwina's bonnet as she stepped forward to drop a flower in –

The first of our burials and I wish with all my heart it had been the last!

Charlotte Smith was the dainty one who always put me in mind of celandines in mossy dells – the daughter of a mayor it was rumoured that she had shamed her father by an endearing native clumsiness – unlike clever Elizabeth Eyre who was her constant companion and took her hand at this crude graveside – indeed Elizabeth was forever taking Charlotte's hand and holding it too long – but I wouldn't have you think Charlotte was uncomplicated indeed she could be a conniver – and as a coward expert at having herself included at the centre of every plot – the necessary confidante to every meanness – we cannot all be perfect –

Now let's think who was standing next to them – Martha I believe – well Martha Sparrow used to puzzle me because she nourished some sadness which no amount of coaxing would induce her to confess not even to Hester Partington (if one credits Hester's word) who was perhaps the only truly wicked member of the sisterhood and therefore a person in front of whom things could be let slip with less than usual risk to the soul –

Flora Gilchrist stood to their right I recall – as ever habitually setting herself a little apart – she had been seven years old before she began to talk and the consequence throughout the rest of her life was an awkward disinclination to make friends – her father was quite a famous botanist I believe and so was her grandfather – indeed the grandfather had been the scientist who proved that forest trees attract rain (well I agree one would not think so right here and now with our drought!) but there must have been something in it because the government actually passed a law – don't ask me when – long before my day – to grow forests in Tobago for the sake of improving the climate – last century sometime – and she repeatedly boasted about one of her father's students who brought in the law to protect birds in Tasmania – a lovely idea – oh about thirty years ago – so much for Flora –

The fidgeting person was Lavinia Dudgeon – marvellous that a doctor at the asylum where she had been confined recognized her for a saint and not a lunatic at all –

Lastly my special friend Ann – dear tenderhearted Ann – almost a mother to me – author of the needlework you see on the wall here – no not that sampler this big piece which in case you are wondering is a chart of the more gruesome prophecies in Daniel and Revelation as they have come to pass in modern times with a great space left at the head of the design for the Advent.

What's that you say? Yes you are quite right you would remember another Elizabeth – Elizabeth Canning – she joined us in Melbourne as the daughter of an Australian merchant who lacked the refinement to know what to do with his money – especially since she had the lower half of her body missing altogether so she could not be expected to need a dowry – yes Elizabeth Canning became a favourite with us all.

The wind on that beastly island! and the birds! birds whirled and hurtled among us as if we were caught in a storm of big tropical flowers while we filled the grave with clattering stones and set up a cross – *Beatrice Ellen Offley* burnt into the wood – *R.I.P. In the bosom of the Lord* – then the prophet turned away and led us down the hill again –

Not till we reached the wharf did he declare his belief that Beatrice died in misery because she doubted we had been granted a premonition of the Last Judgement out there at sea – he confessed to taking the guilt of it upon himself for failing to bring her back to the faith in her last hours so he swore from that moment to bury the name he had been christened with – bury it as we buried her – 'For a penance' he vowed 'I shall become a new person so from now on you must call me Muley Moloch after the infamous Irish apostate and I shall bear the sins of the real Muley Moloch until I raise him from ignorance wherever he might be and save his soul despite himself – in return for the loss of Beatrice' –

So our prophet became Muley Moloch – we were astounded as you may imagine and I had a wicked revulsion against becoming Mrs Moloch but I dared not interrupt him while he was inspired – he promised that the electric lamps illuminating

Buckingham Palace for the marriage of the Prince of Wales would one day be seen throughout London and would light the streets of every city on earth even in the colonies – that a misguided American lady would soon pretend to offer a key to the Scriptures all her own – that there would shortly be a showdown between Germany and France (which did break out as we know) also that Germany would win (which Germany did) – oh and he prophesied other things I have forgotten – no doubt they came to pass –

For a whole day after the burial a guilty constraint fell on us while we remained at Ascension Island – we ought not to abandon Beatrice – I was nagged by a suspicion that she expected us to live there for the remainder of our lives but as Flora Gilchrist said 'The deed is done' – they ferried us out to the ship – we clambered aboard as it weighed anchor – almost immediately a brisk wind set the timbers creaking and squealing and rumbling and altogether sounding like a factory afloat while waves flew past dancing in sunlight –

All Beatrice's possessions and clothes were bundled up and cast into the sea –

I might say the captain made no end of fuss about changing our names on his manifest – arguing that it conduced to illegalities – but relented in the end and when we landed at Melbourne we stepped ashore as Mr and Mrs Muley Moloch and party.

How did I come to meet a prophet in the first instance? well to answer that one must delve right back into history to the way I was before we met – a capricious girl of fourteen – I still think of her as my true self – at that time I had a friend (actually this was a cousin whom I did not come to know earlier because her family was poorer than ours and lived eight miles away) – this friend came to stay and slept in my room and then I was allowed to visit her house for a week and sleep in her room which was above the farmhouse kitchen so that each morning we woke to a sound of clanged pans and water tinkling in the yard and the air full of bacon frying while we turned on our narrow beds to look at each other across the room – we fell in love you might say in the innocent way of young girls so we could not bear being parted – even when we got up we would stand side by side with our arms on the same window ledge peering down across a wall at the muddy drive and the duckpond beyond to guess what the weather would be like for us – we confessed our separate plans of marrying remarkable men –

We saw ourselves – poor hopeless copy-cats that we were – as brides completely bound by our husbands' fortunes just as we would be liberated by their talents and money because they were always to be respectably ambitious – my cousin's name was Dora –

Her father called her Theodora and I might describe him as a man who resented how niggardly God's gifts had been in the matter of good looks while (as he complained) over-endowing him with intelligence of course and then failing to put suitable opportunities his way – Uncle Herbert his name was – an unwilling farmer just as his beasts were unwilling beasts and his crops unwilling crops – he was even an unwilling uncle to me – but this made no dint in the fact that I adored his damp farmhouse and cold stone kitchen and adored his meek silly wife and wished she could be my own mother and envied him his chickens which I walked among while throwing grain for them though I danced on the spot in terror of being pecked – the excitement of finding warm eggs buried in the straw nests was something I shall never forget – any more than wandering through barley with the tassels of it brushing my legs or Dora and me making ourselves sick eating elderberries – where was I?

Unwilling – yes.

My father would squeeze up his face while he commented that needless to say the farm was not Herbert's own and that Herbert merely rented it from a family called the Honeywoods – so the more I grew to love Dora the more I became aware of how shameful it was that her father had let his family down by owning no property because my father (even though a clergyman and everybody knew how poorly clergymen were paid for

God's work) had amassed quite a comfortable little fortune through thrift and a good head for figures.

Judge Honeywood lived in the mansion called the Hall – Dora's farm was attached to the Hall – as indeed was the whole village of Cold Dean which it seems the judge took tremendous pride in (despite a rumour that the Coney family wanted to murder him) because all the villagers said he kept the closest eye on their affairs even to the thrill of privately dishing out alms to people in need and the thrill of privately punishing those who deserved punishment – he insisted on being godfather to every male child born there – and insisted his daughter should entertain the cottagers' children once a year at a Christmas party – what's more this party was not held in the servants' quarters (perish the thought of such missed opportunities for showing them their place) he would order the great front doors flung open so they could be led in through his hall among all its treasures to take high tea in his dining-room properly waited upon by his footmen in livery and received by his daughter precisely as if they were duchesses and ambassadors –

I'm telling you this because I once went with Dora and was fool enough to feel proud when an old footman with two silver pots leaned over me to ask 'India or China madam?' and I promptly said 'China' because he didn't know that China was my favourite country or that marriage to a missionary was among the adventures I entertained while lying in bed with a square of moonlight falling on my face as I gazed at the ceiling confessing to Dora my plans for my husband to convert the heathen if he were handsome enough – or that I had already begun collecting Chinese things such as the tiny silk painting of a coolie given me by another uncle and a packet of paper seeds which would open out to flowers if placed in a bowl of water – I never did place them in water because then I could never have them back as seeds though I was perfectly content with my faith that they *would* open if I chose to put them to the test –

All my life I have been an adept where faith is concerned –

The footman smiling gravely poured me this pale yellow tea from the full pot and then went on down the table asking 'India or China sir? India or China madam? India or China sir?' and without waiting for answers poured them all tea from the other pot so I felt important until I tasted the vile stuff and knew I was honour-bound to drink it –

This was what privilege amounted to.

How did we get involved in such an old story? oh yes because of what happened later when my father cut all contact with Uncle Herbert and refused me permission to see Dora even to the point of repacking a little birthday present she had sent me and posting it back despite my howls of rage and grief or perhaps *because of* my howls of rage and grief but he never did explain and the only way I ever saw Dora from then on was through Judge Honeywood's daughter –

How to do justice to Miss Honeywood? – well she had spent the best years of her life perfecting the bright manner of someone who would never marry – she was dedicated to being a good sport and a cheerful breeze around her father's house in which there was nothing that was not precious and very little that was not fragile – she was the one you always saw (indeed at that stage I had never even had a glimpse of the old man) she made the cottagers' children feel – as she put it – *at home* and organized party games in the ballroom where she told everybody who had shoes to take them off – and she was the one to care for their spiritual wellbeing throughout the rest of the year by presiding over a private Sunday school class every second Sunday in the small drawing-room –

Dora and I were her helpers being of gentle birth and she treated us as little nieces to be bossed about in a way she never bossed the others – besides keeping us back for a quiet chat over a piece of cake when they trooped home to the market square with their catechism still to learn – I loved the cosiness of this time spent sipping Indian tea and shaking our heads over the vulgarity of the uneducated while waiting for my father's curate to call as he now did to preserve me from having to stay at the farm – the point being that despite Uncle Herbert my father valued his contact with the Honeywoods through me because they were people with such lovely manners as well as being rich – well on one occasion Miss Honeywood suggested we carry our refreshments into the garden and when she returned indoors to call somebody to find her shady bonnet (leaving us alone) Dora became suddenly agitated to my astonishment and struggled with what appeared to be an attack of dumbness – remaining dumb for the several precious minutes we had together which was not like Dora – nor was it like Dora to blush and twist her fingers in a knot –

She never got to the point –

So the months passed and we tried to remain as close as ever but something had come between us and I believed it to be my father's insult to her father so I told her I was all burning up with hatred for that man (my father) which was a daring thing in those days and almost as terrible as blaspheming against God – yet even this fell short of the desired effect and we never recaptured our closeness until one Sunday she met me as we walked in the side door of the Hall ushering the freshly scrubbed children before us and took my hand on impulse carrying it up to her lips – '*Now* you will see!' she whispered – you may imagine how I trembled with excitement – well what I was to see was nothing more exotic than a preacher brought in by Miss Honeywood to inspire the village urchins with an enthusiasm for God's work and I was only struck by the queer fact that he spoke to the children in their own rough language which he had mastered perfectly – and that his eyes were such a deep violet as to be almost black –

The very next fortnight Miss Honeywood greeted me with a shake of her perfect head and murmured 'The less said about poor Theodora the better perhaps because after all no one can pretend it was altogether her fault' – I was agog! – so after suffering the adoration of those little ogres with their grimy fingernails and after swallowing the lumps of cake I was privileged to share with Miss Honeywood I clanged my cup in its frail precious saucer – I invented a few excuses and rushed out – across the road I ran hoping to reach the farmhouse before our curate came bowling down the lane in the ancient brougham he used on his rounds of the parish –

I hurried in through the little old stone gateposts and down the drive to the farm not caring a fig about my new button shoes nor my bonnet being tugged by the wind and pushed back off my head to dangle behind me where it flopped about – until I caught sight of the low stone house jolting there before my blurry eyes and I stopped to get some breath back because the scene was just the same as ever –

Yet it wasn't the same – the dogs had gone and the ducks and chickens too – a couple of thrushes trilled in the deathly silence and then the single bell of a distant church began donging and the hollowness measured an immense silence to call up the saddest feelings which seemed to stretch back to a time before I had any memories at all –

I pictured myself hammering at the door and calling out or weeping and rushing round the back and I pictured myself throwing gravel up against the pane of 'our' bedroom window or pushing open the iron gate and taking myself off to mope beside the duckpond or kick my heels in the kitchen garden or run through the fields beyond but I did none of this because I knew nobody was home – I knew it by the coldness on my skin – also that nothing could be done –

Once you start submitting to fate there's no end to it – I truly believe this was when my stoicism began – a stoicism that led to a life of humiliations – what I did was to set my bonnet straight and turn away with a vow to put all the happiness of that place behind me while I concentrated on walking like a young lady and concocting a good excuse for my emergence from the wrong gate – together with an excuse for the agitation which must show when I came to climb into the brougham and confront the curate's inquisitorial gaze.

Curates are without doubt the most hateful species in creation – but why on earth am I telling you this old stuff? excuse me –

Coughing.

What were you asking? ah yes of course I promised to get to the question of noises in the night didn't I? though you may rest assured on the issue of occasional screams at any time during the past thirty years that this may be simply part of our religious practice –

My father used to be very much attached to such comforts of his vocation as afternoon teas – with endless opportunities for airing the right opinions and harvesting agreeable little tiffs and even more agreeable little reconciliations to be concluded with a homily in support of his acknowledged superiority in matters of the conscience – do you think they ever grew tired of his overbearing attentiveness? not a bit of it! they pressed him to come back as soon as possible – so his life passed in a turmoil of arbitrations before it was time for port after supper –

However where I was concerned – and this goes for my mother and my sister as well – the truth was that my timid sentimental father became a tyrant at the least upset to his routine so when I was fifteen and taken by Miss Honeywood to hear her visiting preacher deliver a sermon at the chapel in town (how was she to know about my father's lifelong abhorrence of chapel?) I was more excited by the combined thrill of doing wrong and maybe finding out what Dora meant when she had whispered '*Now* you will see!' than by the visiting celebrity's brash manner –

Not until I was in there and trapped in a pew by a wave of shyness did the full force of my disobedience come home to me – together with the profound disappointment of no one handsome having sat beside us and nothing scandalous having so far happened –

The chapel was startlingly different from our lovely dim old church – instead of carved stone and worn paving this stark room had plain whitewashed walls and a crude silver cross on a table which had been spread with a cloth too small and the wrong shape for it – even the faces of the congregation appeared scrubbed clean of expression – they stood up sat down knelt down and stood again like a regiment that knows its drill – they sang their hymns in sober voices and seemed not at all to mind the predictable harmonies – such a contrast to the unearthly boy sopranos in the church choir – the service itself was as dressed-down and doggedly plain as the congregation – so Miss Honeywood with her embroidered bodice and her shrill confident inaccurate singing became so very noticeable I had to repress my pride in her – and I must say she behaved most handsomely during the sermon letting out appreciative Ahs and surprised Ohs when he said things like 'Your souls are diseased – or rather dead – dead in sin – so now I am calling on you to wake up – be born again – arise from the dead for Christ to give you light' – that sort of thing – I know it so well –

In the end this sermon in fact made a notable impression on us all though at first my mind was repeatedly elsewhere –

I could not have been less interested in the preacher – his ears stuck out and his neck was not firm enough to fill the collar he wore so I entirely missed the text on which he based what he had to say – missed the part when no doubt he laid in the first broad strokes of his accusations against our sloth and corruption – but as he got wound up he broke through my indifference so that I grew to relish my strangeness in that place – I enjoyed feeling superior to the young organist who sat at his keyboard gazing raptly at the cluster of ridiculous pipes painted pale blue with the most laughable gilt rims and fipples (a hopeless player I might add as well as a hopelessly insignificant male with his spindly fingers) – the preacher said 'No free society ever existed without free women' which arrested my attention – and I was further alerted by hearing a curious reedy richness enter his voice as he went on 'Because morals are the work of women!' I looked up to find him gazing at me – I was doubly astonished – 'Women are always the first to heed the word of the Lord – so you ladies are our strength and I want you to know we need you in this place – we weak men – you have already seized the privilege of freedom and the humble evidence is that you were able to decide to come to this service today –

a freedom to be treasured because in other parts of the world you would be prevented – in Catholic countries young women are less mistresses of their actions than in England – even during these wicked times!'

That naked room took on a new character because now I saw details which were to remain in mind as pegs on which I could secure the sentiments I most wished to remember – at the same time I suddenly found myself annoyed by all the coughing and shuffling going on around me –

A shaft of light fell aslant a wall where I studied the text painted above the vestry door – *He that hath ears to hear let him hear* – while I grappled with the strangeness of the idea that it might have read 'She that hath ears' and 'Let her hear' – the preacher went on 'The virtue of women secures order throughout our whole nation' – I stared at a brass candelabrum hanging by a chain far thicker than necessary – his argument branched out in a new direction 'As there was a beginning so there will be an end – because the very idea of Being depends upon an end to it – without an end there is no proof of a beginning and therefore to deny the end is to deny the beginning and to blaspheme against God's word in the Book of Genesis!' – stared at the hymn numbers displayed like Egyptian designs in their little bracket as his voice rang out even more compellingly 'By no means does the end destroy the value of life – what is precious is only precious because it can be lost – and *will* be lost! Friends – the end will soon be among you and for this you should give thanks to the Almighty – it is not because death will bring an end to my tribulations that I give thanks but because death will bring my joys to an end – my faith to an end – my riches my happiness to an end – this – this is why we must avoid sin – because the end of sin can only give meaning to sin and you need to strain every sinew of the soul in denying sin the least hold on your life – therefore keep alert!' – by now all shuffling had ceased – the congregation listened with an unaffected piety – 'Sin will creep in by whatever means the Devil can find' he continued 'even food may become evil if we are tempted to find it tasty –

lots of sneaking tricks – and those sins we have not avoided we shall need to root out in a hurry before the end is upon us' (a lady cried aloud for mercy) 'before Jesus walks the earth once more – because you may be sure He will come as simple and pure as a flame' (she cried out again) 'He wishes to find us burning with faith and eager for the moment when everything and everyone we hold dear is struck away and destroyed!' these words flashed like lightning in the hush – he seemed about to add more but thought the better of it –

I noticed he looked drunk when he left the platform uncertain of where to place his feet – eyes huge and shining – then a chapel elder twice his age bowed before addressing him in a croak as 'Our blessed Father in Israel' –

Afterwards we took refreshments in the vestry and the preacher continued to fascinate me though he appeared much smaller than in the pulpit – back to the way he had been at the Hall – all the more disturbing then that people were now calling him a prophet – Sister Briscoe took his arm 'The Lord visited us indeed' she murmured –

I was flattered when he remembered me and took a few moments to ask after my health before coming out with something commonplace and neutral 'The times call for uncommon deeds!' as he turned to devote himself wholly to Miss Honeywood's complaint against Jesus' preference for Charity over Faith and Hope – 'Um – Um – ' he contributed while vigorously nodding though Miss Honeywood scarcely noticed because she never expected anything other than acquiescence – an amazing tingle fluttered in my throat – I was alert with astonishment – my instincts told me it was for *me* that he kept her there – for me that he proceeded to consult her not only on such topics as peacock butterflies but oddities like the correct number of waistcoat buttons gentlemen leave unfastened when seated as distinct from when they stand –

By this time everyone else had given away vying for the least particle of his interest and of course they themselves were aware of the honour of having the great lady come all the way to town to join them at chapel – especially as she had previously been known to favour the highest church practices –

Even then I wanted to laugh at those primpers rinsing their nonconformist cups and dusting crumbs from the table – my sense of fun had not yet been put to the torture – I wanted to laugh at the ushers straightening chairs and beginning to bolt the doors so even the judge's daughter shot a look at the blessed clock and said 'Is *that* the time!' as she smoothed her gloves to a satisfaction over each elegant finger and then in an abstracted mood stretched out the whole arrangement palms up – then backs up – 'Now come along Catherine' she bullied me affectionately 'say thank you for the inspiring sermon and lead the way' – however we had scarcely passed under the iron arch of the outside gate than the preacher appeared at the door calling 'Oh I say Miss Byrne excuse me' so I glanced up and caught his ecstatic expression and left my protector – drifted back again among those flurries of dust perpetually patrolling the footpaths of Stroud –

In a trance I climbed the stone steps – delayed briefly when my skirt caught on a rosebush and I stopped to free myself – accidentally pricking my finger and tugging the glove off to protect it from being stained with a blood spot –

I recollect to this very day hesitating on the threshold to lick my finger (too innocent for understanding omens) while he invited me in with the explanation that he had a text for me and that Miss Honeywood had left her hymnal behind too.

Do you know Gloucestershire? well someday you will I am sure – beautiful Gloucestershire.

He was standing in the dim room between the lectern and a table covered with a thick cloth (I can still see a fringe of little pom-poms) – and then right there in front of me he began to rise up – glossy pumps lifting clean off the carpet until I could have passed my hand under them while he gazed down at me from a brilliant face full of features!

Thirty-two years ago – and all this while his miracle has been kept a secret between us! – but of course I may be wasting it on you – you may think flying nothing so very special.

When it comes to the point I suppose *I* didn't know what to make of it so I just went along with things as usual and expected that even this would end in disappointment.

You will call me hopeless of course there is no getting away from that but I was haunted by what I had witnessed –

It was odd enough to be sure (I beg your pardon? no matter) because not only were the visiting preacher's shoes rising off the carpet but he – and he had struck me as stern during his harangue in chapel – he came alive with laughter 'Hope!' he cried in an adolescent voice despite his twenty-eight years 'Hope is the greatest of the three!' rustling towards me inside his hot suit like a bird –

I dared not meet his challenge or watch his floating feet so I stared to one side at a framed etching of a lamb hung up by a belt around its middle – well that was the moment when I knew this business of flying was not quite decent and would need to be kept secret from the world –

My whole story is a catalogue of secrets if you like –

One thing led to another and the young preacher was invited back to the Hall but that week the Sunday School had to be cancelled owing to Miss Honeywood's headache – you may imagine my discomfort with a whole hour to kill – until the obliging fellow volunteered to walk me in the garden where he soon confessed that he hoped to live a private life of secrets too huge for telling – I was captivated – we strolled – engrossed in profitable conversation – I had never felt such happiness – we listened to bees hum around the dusty perfume of lavender bushes – he boasted modestly about his father having died Warden of the Worshipful Company of Cordwainers which is to say bootmakers – I couldn't think of a boast about mine – meanwhile his father had passed on the whole art – mine had passed on nothing but rules for table manners – his father had taught him everything from how to soak tannin out of oak bark to how to stitch flat seams around a welt – I was speechless and all the more speechless when the preacher dropped to his knees – surprise upon surprise he grasped my foot which he placed in his lap to show his skill at fitting customers by the feel of their toes through the uppers (this was when he discovered I had a toe missing) while advising them on the superiority of local Stroud products over the finest imported leathers from Cordova – carried away by enthusiasm he promised to show me his realm in all its manifold prospects – beginning with a tannery – an offer which struck me dumb –

Naturally my moment of silence was interpreted – there have been many such moments for which I have had to pay during the rest of my life.

Funny you should ask because in fact he did suggest a visit to the abattoirs as well if I wished to appreciate the true provenance of shoes – such shoes as I had worn until then all unwittingly – what a prospect! – I recall fumbling for the handkerchief in my sleeve and pressing it against my nose while the garden brightened and the perfumed skies went to my head –

I declined –

But I never could resist the thrill of adventure for long and I suppose I fully intended to visit this new world of the tannery plus any number of abattoirs as well for that matter even though he warned me they were beyond doubt 'grisly' – if only I could concoct a clever enough stratagem to keep my father from knowing – yet the lure of the thing lay in the power it gave me to let loose a tornado of parental fury if I chose – just think of the crimes I was accumulating – an interview with a chapel man including a private conversation in Judge Honeywood's small drawing-room and a walk around the garden during which I had let him kneel to take my foot in his lap while he corrupted my virgin fancy with horrifying visions of flayed carcases and of skins being salted while the meat was lugged away for carving into the separate categories of delicacy and offal.

Can't you just picture my father making ready to kill me? –

his neck swelling purple inside a tight collar and his bald head starting with perspiration (dear Reverend Byrne!) he was so very English –

Come to think of it everything we suffer as colonialists in Australia might be because we are from England and this land doesn't like the smell of us – do you feel it? – but no – how would you?

Back home people carry off their hypocrisy with unbeatable grace – which I regret to say you local types have never mastered – and the secret of this grace is an Englishman's tact – by the bye allow me to warn you against confusing hypocrisy with tact – what could be more different than a person who pretends to be what he isn't and a person who knows when and how to respond out of consideration for others?

Come to think of it maybe the reason I could never please my father was because I had no tact – I could never tell when or how to respond –

Yet England used to be a happy place for a growing child and I feel sorry for anybody without the sort of recollections I have – scuffing through drifts of fallen beech leaves in autumn to churn them up and kick yellow cascades in the air – lying down among them if it wasn't raining – gazing at the sky through new bare branches –

Glorious!

As a child I was a wild thing who had been trapped and apparently tamed – a child not often praised and then generally when I stayed out of the way or when I showed a talent for obedience or when I kept my pinafore clean while playing out of doors or when I did well at elocution or practising scales but never for my lively mind or my pluck – I decided I liked everything about my new friend the preacher except the warts on his hand which could be felt pressing on my fingers as he first took me into the dark by which I mean not only the dark of superstitions but his actual world –

He had no idea his darkness was dark at all so he offered it to me quite as a favour and explained that in the interests of the maturity which would be required of me by his imminent fame I ought not to pass up the opportunity of watching him at his humble craft (you see how little his insight helped him foretell his own future?) – and a pair of shoes he had promised to make for Judge Honeywood would provide the means because they were to be of the finest box calf so he would have to attend to every detail beginning with the choice of leather –

Meanwhile events moved faster than I knew – at least between him and the Honeywoods –

I suppose what gave Miss Honeywood such a nose for matrimony was not being married herself – and for a similar reason I found myself in some sense ashamed of the preacher's peculiar powers now I suspected I would marry him –

The first I knew of a change was the frightful scene between my father and the curate who was supposed to have monitored what I did when I went to the Hall – though the poor horrid creature had nothing but guesswork to go on and was left with very little option in the matter really since his duties were simply to set me down and then pick me up eighty minutes later – culminating in the fellow's dismissal and our immediate departure dressed in our very smartest clothes bound for the Hall which we had never before visited as a family –

You must picture us arriving and being intimidated by Miss Honeywood's cordiality as she conducted us across the hall to the large drawing-room – a splendid blue and white affair with huge chandeliers and floor-to-ceiling windows from which velvet curtains were drawn aside to open upon a view of the garden – while gilded chairs kept sentry duty either side of the doorways in a manner forbidding to anyone tempted to sit on them – I remember some delicate tables placed under the mirrors too – yes yes and a pale blue carpet lying like an immaculate patch of sky separating us from a double door at the far end of the chamber – you would never find anything to equal it in the colonies – the carpet was of such soft luxurious stuff that everywhere you trod your footprints remained clearly marked –

For once I had the advantage of my father – being a familiar in the house and the one whom the footman smiled at –

While we assembled there suitably diminished by the setting I found myself fascinated by that chaos of ghostly shoe-prints trampling round in a bewildered patch – then the two halves of the door swung open to reveal an astonishing little man wearing a powdered Captain Cook wig as became gentlemen of the old school – he had knee-breeches with buckle shoes and was already shuffling towards us on bandy legs.

God must be like this – limping across the sky – twisted by age and frail from his burden of sifting the world's dross for each rare grain of truth –

I had never before seen such an ancient specimen – he wore lace at his cuffs and collar with the air of someone hastily dressed – but there could be no doubting who he was though it suddenly struck me as funny that he should be spoken of in hushed tones and sent messages of gratitude – even by his own daughter –

His lean face folded in on itself to shape a permanent smile which surely must have mystified the criminals he despatched to the mercies of Bridewell (such a name for a prison!) – my blood stopped at the sight – he stepped out of the last century with that peculiar grandeur which seems to our modern taste next door to obsequious – watching us shrink as he dragged one foot and primly placed the other like a marionette –

He babbled greetings – toothless gums slapping together wetly – as he waved an arm behind him to beckon somebody forward – then who should I see letting the weighty drapes of the portière swish closed as he emerged from the private chamber – draining me of blood while at the same time pumping my heart with cold air and then hot air – who but my very own preacher? –

The palpitations grew worse until the room became a bellows – by turns pressing me down and puffing me up –

Judge Honeywood proceeded to behave for all the world like somebody ordinary – introducing the preacher to my horrified father my mother my sister and to his other guests that day – a neighbour called Major McDonald and the solicitor Weedham's widow who later gave it as her opinion that one knew enough about the poor fanatical young man's family just by their ugly name –

Do you wonder if it makes me shiver to think back on this and face the fact that it was not a scene in something tastefully hilarious by Arthur Sullivan? – well I stood like an idiot and gaped – I who was supposed to be so famous at showing nothing and keeping secrets!

The judge piped up and promised us a 'special treat' as he put it while his little white eyebrows wiggled independently 'this being a remarkable fellow and a remarkable occasion all things considered' – or something of the kind – then to my amazement actually took my father by the sleeve bringing him face to face with the preacher – as close as this – and pronounced the engagement 'a remarkable match' brightly offering us all glasses of hock – including me.

The Honeywoods were one of three wealthy families in the district – squires on a grand scale and notable throughout the county – as well as owners of the best living for a parson –

'Yourself being a man of the cloth and all that' the judge continued with his voice sugared by the wine – all the while tweaking my father's sleeve 'you will not thank me if I offer you moral advice I dare say and I'm sorry for it with all my heart as I am sorry you will not need reminding that if there is one thing more delightful than memories of having raised a fine girl tis I am sure the gratification of passing her future into the care of another' – but if he noticed Miss Honeywood wince he did not hesitate –

Habitually quickwitted thanks to his suspicious nature my father soon saw what matters were afoot without his knowledge (without my own either I might add!) – but I'm sure he never guessed that my mind filled with a single thought which was not 'Am I really to marry?' but 'Shall I really escape?' – and although I felt a tremor of happiness please do not imagine I had planned to marry anybody yet – let alone a common bootmaker –

'Nowadays soft kid is as rare as salvation!' the judge prattled on –

My father prepared to explode – not least because his suspicions must have tweaked him now we could see that both cobbler and patron suffered the selfsame limp which gave them an appearance of conspirators in some mockery of the Creator's work – but people who prepare to explode seldom do do they? –

The judge invited us to cast a more exact eye over the cut of the shoes while his voice trembled as he explained 'So you see why I am all the more to be thanked for agreeing to let the fellow go' – go *where*? I wanted to shriek because this was all too appalling and too great a relief – then I remembered having confessed my Chinese ambition to Miss Honeywood! – but how could I deny that mad fancy at this stage – good heavens I had only chosen China as my favourite because the very word filled me full of fear – like the word 'missionary'!

I suppose I expected somebody to comment on my betrothal if that's what it was or at least say Oh my goodness gracious what a *wild* girl (which might have given me an excuse to slip out of the arrangement) but instead they looked at me as though I was doing something I had always done and would never grow out of –

My father was on the brink of bursting with rage at any minute but in the event he showed none of the courage he threw around so recklessly when the butt of his anger was only my mother or me and took the easy way out – I dare say he lives with the disappointment of having missed his opportunity –

And any anticipated disgrace to our name must surely have paled beside the reality of me managing my skirts up on the roof here a couple of months ago with nails clenched between my lips and hammer in hand pounding away in an effort to repair a leaky slab of bark before the oncoming storm – can you imagine!

I was sure to have made a mess of things even if I had been wooed by a regular dullard in the expected manner – so I probably did the best thing given the circumstances – and then

Judge Honeywood led us outdoors to present us with a wedding gift – the very latest foible – a lawn-mowing machine of the kind tried out by the Queen herself.

My full name is Catherine Jane – née Byrne – I was born on the tenth of March 1850 at five-and-twenty to two in the morning at home in Stroud so you may deduce my present age for yourself now there is apparently no such nicety as concealment left me at forty-eight – and I wish I could be sure that I am a good person – but what I can say is that I am a person who has quite given up the vanity of expecting to get away with anything –

That may be to do with being a Byrne – because when I think of my family I cannot believe in myself – Byrne is supposed to be a Catholic name and yet we never had the least taint so far as I ever heard – even Catherine creates doubts because one has to deny being Katherine with 'K' or Catharine with 'ar' or whatnot –

I think I ought have been christened Alice and that our family ought to have been Middletons – I am convinced that Alice Middleton could nowise have become engaged to anyone so hastily – the shock hit me twenty-four hours later – I knew I had to escape him or that together we had to escape respectable society –

This idea continued to seethe in my head when I plunged into working with him on his ministry – finding I could be useful because I knew so many of the county identities besides knowing (from my father's table conversation) their chief frailties –

A week later Flora Gilchrist chanced along –

Flora had the advantage of being grown up and able to do anything she wished – maybe she could persuade him to marry her instead? – but no – only later did I realize she was to be the first of many trials I must undergo for the sake of keeping my faith – and oh how I envied her because she knew how to flatter him and improve his arrangements without treading on Miss Honeywood's corns as his patroness and yet be safe from his advances – I envied her also because she proved she could speak his language when she said 'Life is an unexplored country the wonder and beauty of which calls to me every hour of every day.'

This was at a time when I had to face the embarrassment of his visits for dinner – my family staring in complacent disbelief while he toyed with cutlery he had never been taught to hold correctly – he chewed with his mouth open and every so often ducked his head down to the plate – not to mention his habit of licking his knife and fork clean when he had finished or replacing them on the cloth exactly as he had found them before he began to eat – or gulping Mother's pudding or guzzling Father's port – until the household buzzed with a general air of justice being seen to be done –

I made a virtue of not showing how ill I felt – the same when he perched on the sofa and picked at his fingernails or primly set his hat on his exasperating head while indoors and still with the ordeal before him of having to kiss my mother's hand – besides the outburst of titters he provoked by calling her 'Mum' –

We had to endure the whole catalogue of niceties each time he was invited and although I gave him hints as to what was wrong he refused to listen – indeed the more discreet the hints the more they galled him – and yet – and yet he did offer me freedom and his unconventional ideas did open whole worlds of bold new vistas –

Is it any wonder if I looked to the colonies as the best solution once we were married? –

Curiously enough he was the one to give me my chance of breaking our engagement 'You can take yourself off home to the parsonage' he growled one afternoon 'because I cannot carry you on my conscience' – 'I shall not do any such thing!' I retorted and this checked him – 'There's no comfort in my life' he explained quietly – 'Nor in mine' I replied – 'Do you understand?' he shouted – and I shouted back 'No I do not!'

Then I added in a more ladylike manner 'If I go home to my father it will be because I have decided to go' – 'There's nothing more to say' he said and yet that night I wept into my pillow and in an agony of mind silently vowed not just to abandon him but to abandon religion – I would leave him to Flora! – I went on raging like a mad creature and only brought myself to reason by crawling out in the cold to kneel on the floor until I nodded off halfway through my prayers –

It brings me up short to think of my casual tone when eventually I came out with the suggestion that we escape to the colonies and how serene I was in my ignorance of the size and violence of the oceans one had to cross – but do we learn? can even risking our lives teach us? –

It's the trivial things that catch us on the hop.

'Our mission' Flora agreed when my idea was put by our leader as his own 'will be purely and simply perfecting ourselves.'

I've told you about the voyage – us becalmed and burying Beatrice Offley – well there were storms too and days of misery belowdecks – so you may imagine what we thought when we docked in Port Melbourne and drove to the town after months of travel – supposedly at the ends of the earth – only to find people exactly like the people we had left behind at home! hundreds of comically respectable idiots strolling around sunny streets in frock coats and crinolines wishing each other 'Good morning' under the huge blank sky! –

I could have killed them!

That very year Melbourne was declared a city – proud of its Botanical Garden and on the eve of greatness with gold about to be discovered – indeed as we drove along wide streets one might imagine we were in a real capital – all very dignified – provided one could ignore frequent glimpses of the huddle of tin buildings tacked on behind the columns and porticos – Mr Moloch appeared enormously relieved but from my viewpoint it would not do – nor would people plainly given to wild notions of respectability as their right! –

Apparently I was fated to have no peace of mind in Australia either unless we got away from the city's false façades and the horrors lurking there (Melbourne being a town where no sooner does a good clever man arrive than he finds himself caught up in a public-house brawl and has his skull cracked open by a pack of brutes) –

So soon as tickets could be arranged we took berths on a small coastal packet and headed north seeking somewhere innocently primitive – the prophet blowing the clarion and rallying his Household of Hidden Stars – we sang 'Onward Christian Soldiers' as we trooped aboard eager to do battle on Christ's behalf –

Meanwhile at close quarters I had discovered that our ladies were not so perfectly good as they had seemed in England – I grant you their spite was a refined class of spite and their coarseness seldom physical (being mainly coarseness of sympathies) but spiteful and coarse they were – and there's nothing like a voyage to bring things to a head –

The little ship proved much less comfortable than the big one thanks to the shock running through its whole frame every time a paddle vane struck the water – thanks to the soot forever raining on deck too – and thanks to the cramped quarters – not to mention an added worry that in place of an interminable ocean we were now presented with interminable unbroken woodlands stretching the full length of the coastline – the Australian wilderness – with not a solitary sign of civilization for days on end until we reached the whale butchery at Eden –

With the stench of Eden behind us we arrived in Yandilli at last.

You may think Yandilli all right but let me tell you the port looked ridiculously rudimentary to us – indeed until we rounded the point we might never have guessed it was here at all – so when the packet tied up to a rickety pier very few other passengers got off with us (I am talking about a time before the days of the Illawarra and South Coast Shipping Company) and they soon disappeared along the shady lower level of a two tiered structure – we took deep breaths of wild air and waited to watch the boat depart without us – our last link with England

– its paddles beginning to slap the water again – the deck visibly shuddering – tall funnel puffing black smoke – booms swinging over as the ugly little sails tugged taut – then I remember my husband suddenly becoming furtive and herding us along the wharf like the secret society we were – we left our baggage in a pile – trunks and suitcases stacked round the crate containing the lawn mower – because there was not a single porter in sight – only a couple of bystanders who lingered to look us over in so frank a manner as to risk actual rudeness – fragments of the picture remain painfully clear in my head – they stared at everything from our hemline to our bonnets while we climbed some damp steps to the upper level where an open-mouthed child watched us emerge into the light and clung to a man who crossed himself –

We were among Catholics!

Very moving it was – no I don't mean to sound sarcastic! – we were isolated by our faith in a place so bare that our message had never before seemed more beautiful or more fragile –

At one stage the district had been a single property but folk soon told us there was a curse on it thanks to that lady who murdered her husband – Governor Gipps had to send troops in – what was she called? – she ended up becoming the first gentlewoman hanged in New South Wales which provoked Mr Moloch to joke that he hoped in his case there would be safety in numbers! – setting Flora Gilchrist and the entire mission laughing at my expense –

This was the fifth of March 1868 – and the horror had taken a step closer – so had Louisa –

There's no doubt I found the jibe quietly upsetting but I would also have to say that to some extent I tend to feel more satisfied when I am quietly upset than at most other times –

Poor things – those people who built 'Yandilli' – both of them – especially because many wives might contemplate murder without necessarily knowing how or even having any real intention of putting it to the test though I do not mean to implicate *myself* nevertheless I would suggest that murder may not seem so very out of the way if once we have the privilege of looking into the souls of quite ordinary folk –

By the bye I hope you do not mind our cats – actually they are Louisa's now – I've lost count.

Not a happy history – well I heard that the local community sighed with relief when all but the logging camp at the south end of 'Yandilli' property came to be pegged out by a surveyor – it was sold to us at auction just in time for some harebrain to discover gold in the creek – so we had to face the fact that within a week a thousand diggers might descend on us.

Was that your father who found the gold? I believe it was! but in the event there was not enough of it to stir any real interest –

The point is that when we compare truth with lies each item of the truth looks sadly simple beside the variety of lies one could possibly tell instead – comparing one's actual life and one's hopes for one's life is a little bit like that too.

What's that you say? how did we manage?

It was difficult because the prophet recruited gentlewomen with ever more obvious disabilities – a missing ear a missing breast a missing nose – until in Melbourne he converted Elizabeth Canning who was on crutches – bravest of the brave Elizabeth put a strain on the rest of us not to help her or keep fussing around her when she seesawed along till eventually we procured the only wheelchair in the district (you probably remember how you used to jump when you heard it rumble across the floorboards?) – don't ask what Louisa is missing –

Once we settled at the mission we found ourselves spending more and more hours of each day being brought face to face with the most horrible realities and laying bare our tender hearts in order to clear out every taint – well – wickedness and vanities – often enough I sit here with my eyes closed against the day blazing out there while I marvel at what we survived – such scrutiny and punishments – not to mention monstrous expectations –

All people live in fear of the afterlife no matter how great their faith and this applies especially to those of us who study the Scriptures and understand what a riddle the whole caboodle is – so no wonder we do our utmost to recognize signposts in this life to prepare us for the next – and why shouldn't there be equivalents for everything in Heaven just as humble habits reveal profound truths? –

So the voyage which began as a grand adventure ended in stagnation? – then this had to be faced up to – simple –

The idea of a *continuing* journey took hold though we had no idea how long a journey it might be nor how many wrong turnings we might take before tragedy caught up with us to bring us to our senses – as Christian says in *The Pilgrim's Progress* 'things pleasant and dreadful go hand in hand' – which they did –

It has to be admitted that we were mainly happy in those days – singing to the sublime swish of brooms and clash of buckets because we knew we had been accepted as God's elect thanks to Mr Moloch who preached that 'Woman is to redeem Man by becoming his second bride which is to say his second Eve' – a text quite explicit concerning his choice of spinsters as disciples – besides being another riddle – for a while our days were filled with hard work and merriment but soon the suspicions began seeping back and once again we had to be vigilant about our thoughts because otherwise things went wrong – a back-door key mislaid – hens failing to produce eggs – the prophet himself suffering a bout of flatulence – such problems multiplied and had to be investigated –

Investigations became the centre of our routine –

There came a time when I was made to lie on the floor in the shape of a cross for seven hours so that our mare would not die of the foal she was struggling to produce – then poor Lavinia who always had to hunt down whatever word she needed bustled in all of a bother and announced 'Kick – um – desperate – quick – no – the heartbeat – what do you say? – thorn – thirst – it's born – '

For the rest – well – after breakfast we laboured in the field as the Bible exhorts us to do (or else in the house like Dorcas if the weather was wild) each duty a joy so that every small pain helped fortify us against the great void – my main challenge was to keep up to the mark and not fail to be worthy of the example set by the others because one thing for sure is that Flora Gilchrist and Ann and Martha and the rest (except Hester Partington) proved themselves better souls by far than I and I envied them the ease of their goodness while my goodness had to be squeezed out of me if I was to produce any at all.

What's that you say?

On the contrary I do not recall a single instance when Mr Moloch laid a finger on anybody either as punishment or encouragement because he kept a very proper distance and even during the fiercest beatings he was scrupulous about leaving it to us and never taking part other than to clarify the nature of our faults for others to judge and act upon –

True – while I lived from day to day it seemed a hard life with not enough joy for a fair share but now I look back on it I can see straight away that it was probably a good life – even though the punishments started very early in the piece – perhaps the best kind of life imaginable –

Our very first disciple – Flora Gilchrist – who had been a leading Stroud Methodist made it her special role to take up the least thing my new husband let fall and magnify it into a doctrine which she then policed with the utmost rigour –

Throughout our early years together she performed this duty – the moment any problem of faith arose Flora set to work on it like a crosscut saw working a deep cut when she applied her principles to it this way then cutting deeper by dragging the same deadly edge of righteousness the other way – again remorselessly and again – she had absolutely no sense of humour – so you may imagine there was never much love lost between her and Lady Edwina Wyntoun – the one who brought us enough money just in time to fulfill our plan of sailing for Australia – but who was not accustomed to being ordered about – especially when it came to the proprieties –

Before she fell ill Flora had been quite pretty in her own way and proud of her golden curls – whereas Edwina who could never have been called pretty made a point of her fine discrimination – I believe they both thought me a ninny and I was one of the few subjects on which they could reach agreement in a perfectly amiable way –

Naturally I could not boast of the power I had over the prophet although every decision he took began with a suggestion from me – just tuck that away for future reference (though you should remember that this influence was utterly without effect when it came to drawing him close or to satisfying my needs or even to luring him to take my hand for no other reason than to show me he knew there was panic knocking at my heart) – I had the unfair privilege of pretending to appear quite helpless and of laughing off any hint he let slip in private by saying You will make me split my sides with your suspicions my dear I do declare I could never dream of any such *thing* –

You see what we were like?

I have already confessed whose idea it was to flee England together and set sail for the colonies – I dare say I deserve no sympathy if I complain that I spent a good deal of the voyage as my husband's secretary taking dictation while he was inspired to compose a book of rules for thwarting Baal and thirty-eight prohibitions necessary for reforming chapel worship – all the while the important thing was that I should protect him from guessing I was less ashamed of his illiteracy than his lack of manners.

As for the question of appearances – it is no use looking for evil in obvious places – Flora helped by criticizing my handwriting.

Yes for several years Yandilli did seem secluded and primitive enough – but then our privacy began to be blighted by nosey parkers and we became victims of gossip – with neighbours discussing Mr Moloch and myself (as husband and wife) speculating on when they might expect the first sign of fruit from our supposed labours – and taking it in bad part that we presented them with nothing –

I dare say even the sisterhood began to blame me for my apparent barrenness – and quite suddenly I found myself overwhelmed by a new desperation to hide somewhere even more remote – matters came to a head one morning when I went to the Yandilli shop to buy some haricot beans and sell some spinach – interrupting Mrs McNeil who had just said the whole world wondered at such a weedy chap being able to keep up with the many demands made on him! – of course this was unbearable especially as I was still untouched myself –

I pretended to have forgotten my list – as ladies we were condemned by our genteel upbringing and I dare say in my shoes the others would have blushed as painfully as I did – and I *did* despite being the only one of our Household with the least claim to know what carnal knowledge is –

I am glad to be making progress against the horrible habit we are taught of cushioning the truth for the sake of saving face –

I was so desperate to get away that the minute we heard of a suitably barbarous place being up for sale I nagged Mr Moloch to set off after the owner who had gone to the goldfields – 'Very well' he said quietly 'I intend following your advice but this will be a new beginning for us all and from now on you must no longer share my bed' he silenced my protests with a raised hand 'it is God's will that you sleep alone – don't ask me to explain' –

He gave no reason and brooked no opposition – I leave you to imagine what state such sheer unfairness threw me in though I excused him by privately blaming my cough which must have been keeping him awake at night – and thus matters between us remained at sixes and sevens while my illness worsened until I was too disastrously weak to care anymore and collapsed on my lonely couch with a sigh of relief.

I am doing my best to explain the circumstances of the whole story as fast as I can – trying not to get it back to front –

I was so ill – the Lord's hand lay heavily upon me – He cut off every comfort at a blow – He smote me with a fever and a consumption and a guilty conscience – all but carrying me off – night after night I read about myself in the Book of Job 'Terrors are turned upon me' you know the passage? 'they pursue my soul as the wind – and my welfare passeth away as a cloud – and now my soul is poured out upon me – the days of my affliction have taken hold upon me – my bones are pierced – and so forth and so on – ' I read it over and over 'by the great force of my disease is my garment changed – it bindeth me about as the collar of my coat – '

If you ask me I caught the disease kissing Beatrice Offley to console her on her deathbed when no one else would touch her – I remember she whispered as we made ready to lower her into the pinnace for rowing ashore 'There's nothing of me left to save' – then when I had comforted her she added 'I have been hollowed out' she coughed 'All that's left of me is my skin' and later as the oars fell to with a rhythm and we drew near the quay she added 'Completely filled with foul disease' –

Odd that when my own crisis came I found I could face hidden truths about myself as if I had become a separate person appointed to the task of judging me – for example being able to hear my father's accent in my own voice – and (when the evil Hester held a mirror for me) seeing a person with my grandmother's nose which I would never believe I inherited as well as Uncle Herbert's ineffectually villainous contraction of the eyebrows – all of which explained why I was left to suffer alone in my silent bed apart from fleeting visits by only the kindest and the cruellest of the Stars even though I lay on the verge of death –

In this condition I sought the Lord but He gave no answer – He afflicted me with helplessness – He scared and terrified me with dreams and brought down the night upon me at noon covering me with shame until I cried out 'I am vile – I am afraid – help me!' only to have Hester's puffy lips smile into my face and open to ask 'What did you say dear?' –

I no longer thought myself a whole person – just a thing which must breathe by fighting for each breath with skill and courage – the skill of securing enough air to survive until the next heartbeat but not so much as to provoke fits of coughing – the courage to try for another –

Incidentally people who regard coughing as a mild inconvenience do not know what they are talking about – some coughs shake your soul into bleeding fragments –

I punished myself with complete surrender to the illness until it struck me blind and dumb and I remained insensible for days with my eyelids so tightly closed they might have grown together and my mouth sealed on my tongue – so far was I deceived that I mistook this flowering of my illness and the severity of its climax for something wonderful happening to me –

A great white hidden tree-root nearby broke the ground to hump like a naked back then opened out to stand up as the risen God (Oh you may be sure He won't arrive in a chariot of fire swooping down among massed crowds of gaping vulgarians!) – this white tree-root remains a disconnected fragment among the memories left over from my coma –

I also remember the vast sky beginning to rock and scatter chaotic light to invade the hearts of the most doubting and shine on their faces dissolving the shadows till the air around us shimmered with flocks of angels' wings while Mr Moloch praised the ancient tree for its fertility and two horses outside the window also broke into light and bats rose as a white glitter of squeaks – leading the prophet to explain sound itself as no more than slow light – oh how the pulsing wings fluttered around and how radiantly the shadows trembled with bass notes and how the whole sky breathed a colossal harmony of C major too massive to be heard! –

Immediately the tree-root and the dazzling harmony of light became part of the soul's holy fervour and I felt myself 'an Israelite indeed' and linked my convalescent dreams to my conviction that the Second Coming would happen in the quietest wildest least touched place and He would arrive among us almost unnoticed except for a soft breaking of soil and a sigh of moist mosses – and the more often I dreamed about it the more I found I was the one to say yes that we were ready for the Messiah – so He came to step forward for us to clothe him in a clean embroidered shirt while Mr Moloch bowed down to the ground in that fawning way of his and took His feet fitting them one at a time with handmade shoes of the finest kid –

The strange part is that in my weakness I dreamed I recoiled a little as if we could smell something faintly evil in the Messiah's paleness – there was a certain hesitancy about His smile of a man wondering whether or not we would forgive *Him* and this seemed curious – there was even an air of evil about the sinuous way He moved – so I suppose I ought to have been warned! –

Neither the leaves in wind nor the ocean away down there nor our creek rushing through the gully when the rains have passed could overwhelm the harmony of light and the tree-root at its centre – nor could those wild parrots swarming among the trees interrupt it – nor the harsh cackle of laughing jackasses – and this was when I understood what my husband meant by Earth storing its light as music – yes he often said Earth stored its light as music – do you like that? –

Mr Moloch – though packed and ready to depart for Melbourne – hung round anxiously and even came to preach at my bedside – he took as his text 'Thy light shall rise in obscurity' Isaiah fifty-eight 'and thy darkness shall be as the noonday' – I suddenly felt desperate to penetrate what this meant.

Do you know what a consumptive suffers? well the first symptom is a cough – and of course your friends have it too – all at different stages – so everybody is coughing and wherever you go these little coughs and big coughs may be heard – at the dinner table or across the garden or in the dormitory – apologetic but irrepressible coughs – while word flies round that evil thoughts are in the air until this lady or that finds hers taking a turn for the worse.

Well one's chest knots tight in a spasm resisting some enemy pressing a gentle hand there perfectly on the beat – the hand releases you a little when you breathe out only to press more firmly at the next breath – and firmer still at the one after – until it pins you down and you struggle to get out from underneath and fight against suffocation –

Horrible pains fling you about till you are too weak to fight anymore –

Later you bring up ghastly quantities of phlegm (excuse my mentioning this) and you measure the disease as a load which bears ever more heavily on your spirit till you are not fit for work and you disrupt the midnight confessional with uncontrolled coughing so that you suffer the disgrace of your failing twice over – especially because surely a *man* would not be ill with so disgusting an over-abundance of illness –

Then one morning you wake in a drenching sweat – you have shrunk to the size of a stone – helpless against the desperate seizures of coughing – the hand which had remained pressing on your chest for months is now thrust down your throat – stuck – until in a paroxysm you finally retch it up and discover blood on your handkerchief –

It is difficult not to give way to feeling depressed – so very few sufferers do manage to come through and they seem to be those who catch it young –

Although the entire household has noticed you losing weight does a single person venture on the truth to point this out? their manners are too refined if you please! they feel they are left with little they can do but pray – how fervently a sufferer herself prays also in the panic and the secrecy of thoughts too lethal to be put into words –

Without a government medical officer in the area – this was well before Dr von Lossberg's time – what kind of help could be called post haste from Bunda or anywhere inside a hundred miles of Bunda? with the port at Cuttajo not yet built and all the services you take for granted including the telegraph still to come? – it is true that Martha Sparrow had been a nurse and midwife but how could she help when it came to treating scarred lungs and chronic inflammation?

So there you are in bed being watched over by poor Lavinia – a perpetual fleck of dribble at the corner of her mouth which she wipes away when she thinks to – using one fastidious finger –

And there you remain too lethargic to rouse yourself though somebody keeps coming in to insist that you are needed outside to help dig a well because the work is so slow and that your selfishness will be punished – while day drifts into night and you perspire more than ever until by morning you have to strip off your damp sheets for washing and hang them out to dry or there will be the humiliation of being made to confess your problem plus the anguish of watching one or another of your friends singled out and punished for causing your misfortune – because as I have said already if something goes wrong somebody must have made it go wrong – there always has to be an inner cause for every outward manifestation – or what would be the point of our faith? –

At last voices begin to talk behind your back saying you look as light as a skeleton – you long to contradict them and explain the truth that you feel heavy beyond human endurance but this would be too provoking even if it were physically possible – and in any case you are falling into such a feverish doze you cease to register the difference between night and day while fearful headaches clamp your head and blood thunders and lightnings flash along your nerves and a wind blows through your bones although you doze by chance for a few minutes during which Tuesday merges into Thursday week –

This is what I underwent with the consumption and I am sure it was the same for others – I have heard it said that illness makes a person interesting – though I cannot imagine how! –

Not until Mr Moloch finally decided I would survive and so he could decently leave on his trip to Melbourne did the hateful thing which had invaded my body and threatened my soul for months gradually begin to withdraw – worried faces broke into tired smiles around me as he wished me goodbye and assured me he would return soon from the Ballarat with a title deed to our new mission property in his hand –

I felt giddy and ached in every bone –

Then he was gone and I could smell a disgusting staleness on my skin – I wondered if he had smelt it too as he bent to kiss my brow – oh I wanted him back so I could present myself sweet with soap – but I heard the outer door bang and his footsteps crunching away down the rough road while in the distance a bell was being rung on deck to announce the imminent departure of the packet – and I slumped back on my pillows with the gruesome conviction that I would die after all –

What sprang to mind was a vivid memory of the first time I walked out with him in Stroud – taken aback by his sudden familiarity now we were betrothed – not to mention a manner so assured as to be almost tyrannical – we made our way at his direction – to the tannery –

My poor nose! a nauseous stench poisoned the air for a distance and the closer we approached the more ghastly – so intense it squeezed the stomach – but what troubled me more was a little matter I could never have mentioned in those polite days – one's mouth fills with saliva even while the living flesh shudders at contact with the ultimate enemy – the charnel house – I was fainting with nausea and leant so heavily on the preacher's arm (whom anyone from our circle would have immediately mistaken as my seducer) that he had to carry me under the grim brick arch and in among stained walls – you know the kind of place? – verdigrised taps dripping – pools of brown blood swimming with bristles – and strange gobbets of viscous membranes touched with a blue sheen and showing veins –

I held my skirts as clear as seemliness would allow but imagine my ankles turning on the cobbles! and the risk of falling!

The workmen knew my companion and acknowledged him for the most part sullenly while they stared at me and made no attempt to spare my modesty or restrain their amazement that I was intruding on their world –

The stench of what they did made me gasp and gag – delving

into the pit of my lungs to press against my entrails and butt up against my heart – I felt invaded – my flesh being soured and polluted – blood contaminated – the stench stuck to my hair and plugged my pores leaving the skin sticky and tear ducts gummed up – my stomach turned and bile rose tainted – though all this was nothing compared to the shame of seeing the preacher mortified by my weakness –

Looking back our tannery visit seems like a trial being survived by somebody else –

The arrangement of the yard was rather in the fashion of a cloister with thick wooden pillars supporting an upper storey – the ground floor where the men worked under shelter at sloping tables remained open – so all round us were labourers bending and straining at their violent task as they scoured cow skins to scrub away a curd of raw fat and blood – drudging with their sleeves rolled above the elbow to show arms roped with horrible veins and while some looked up at me tipping back their cloth caps to show leering faces flushed an ugly dark red others mutely bent again to work with renewed violence –

Have you ever suffered the sort of period of repeated nightmares when even during the daylight hours you can't contemplate bed without cringeing from the terrors almost certainly awaiting you and yet you feel drawn to sleep by desperate overtiredness? – this was how the tannery affected me as if I knew it already and had already found myself unable to escape the shackles of sleep that held me prisoner there – I could have left him and run away home to safety yet I did not –

As it was we walked in through a second archway with me stumbling on the step because I was so frightened by the gloom – missing my balance and going down on one knee while I clutched at the damp wall – well no amount of surreptitious wiping could rid my glove of the contamination of that contact – but already worse and more urgent horrors confronted us with the shapes of whole flattened-out beasts being plunged in a pit full of bubbling liquid where they puffed up to wallow and loom among others being hoisted out (the skins doubly heavy for the fact that they streamed with putrefaction) to be slapped on cobbles and shown as the scraggy remains they were and then dragged away in a welter of nauseous steamy smells to the scourers we had just left –

Seeing how feeble I was my escort hurried me off into a gas chamber where the workmen who looked after this stage of the process were concealed by hanging sheepskins so only their boots could be seen moving along the rows – 'Hung out to rot until the wool loosens and falls away' he explained – and added 'valuable wool' giving me an odd look as I recall (perhaps the reason for this was that he could only see my eyes since I muffled the rest of my face in a handkerchief) – even so he saw enough to realize my retching had been brought to a crisis 'Not in here!' he whispered furiously and dragged me to a little lane connecting the factory's inner and outer buildings just in time to be ahead of the next spasm – the irresistible spasm – during which he looked the other way.

No – my impression was that he felt impatient to get on with the business though he did have the grace to offer me his arm as we climbed a flight of wooden stairs to reach the heart of the operation and stepped right among the most clotted billows of the stink which so sickened the surrounding districts –

The entrails of those dead domesticated servile and mostly female beasts – their spongy glands and heaving lungs – had been boiled into gas until the residue of it smeared every surface of this male world – every greasy wall and step – every lump of machinery slicked with viscous fattiness thudding away with a sweating secretive intestinal heat – the gas like a collective spirit of the slaughtered slicked every surface – a corruption and at the same time a clinging skin –

Fellows in long aprons dipped poles into a line of vats hauling out slimy hides naked of fur and slithering with greenish creamy ripples that seemed supple enough to be another form of life altogether and – watching the men lean back on their heels their faces puffed with concentration – I was once again struck by the ugliness of male strength – their eyes showed raw pink around cold blue pupils and drops of sweat hung from moustaches – their stubbly chins were tucked against shiny creased necks while the pungency of what they created welled beyond description – one of the ogres leaned on his pole to call mockingly 'Tell us is there any hope for us in Heaven John?' – another grinned at me around his broken teeth and uttered the word 'oak' nodding at the vat –

'Boiled oak for tanning' the preacher translated –

'Dog' the ogre pointed helpfully across to the other vat where some dwarfs were adding ingredients and then standing to watch a moment with glazed eyes – trails of sweat trickling from their hair to run down across their bulging foreheads –

'For softening the finest leathers' the preacher explained 'a warm mixture' then hastily led the way down some stairs flush to the far wall and stepped into a room on the next level where he headed straight for a fat old man pulling chamois skins from a giant drum set on its side and being mechanically turned by a system of chains on cogs – he flapped each skin before consigning it to a stack –

Liquid dripped on his boots but I dared not speculate what this liquid might be while watching him extract a desirable item to drape over a sill and then wipe his hands on buttery flanks by way of preparation for leading us past presses where hundreds of skins were being squeezed under heavy blocks and out along a gallery with daylight streaming among racks of spreadeagled animal shapes – every one as flat as paper –

Our conference was to be held here and I gasped the open air with relief – legs shaking and head pulsing – so rather than offer myself for introduction I hung back to stare at those flat outlines larger than life with their crucified limbs – while buyer and seller passed samples from one to another for assessing between finger and thumb – and for reassessing until the choicest skin at last was found to be fine enough for Judge Honeywood's new shoes –

Only then did the truth hit me (a truth I suppose I have

always been too mortified to confess to anybody) that this might be the price my suitor had agreed to pay for me!

I shut my eyes to save seeing actual money change hands though I knew quite well that the money was only part of the curdling in my heart which I believed (wrongly) would never go away – well because there was no answer to why a miracle-worker could not have worked the further miracle of obtaining family consent without a bribe of shoes for the rich man who was to appoint my father to a comfortable living – the whole squalid transaction suddenly clear – I believed absolutely in my preacher's gift of levitation and I believed absolutely that he could perform whatever other marvel might suit him – so there must be something I did not understand –

The tannery was worse than the worst ordeal I could have imagined – and I still had to survive the journey out again to the street –

Feeling giddy I leaned against some shelves scarcely bothering to check how filthy they might be – I felt soiled beyond rescue – breathing the slippery stench with its iridescent sheen – the novelty was that my suitor sounded gay and tender when he came to warn me we must return the way we came – I felt his hand on my waist for the first time – though I was afraid of him I knew then that he was to be mine –

'You brought a real little lady there' the dealer remarked to give us the satisfaction of hearing lascivious envy in his voice –

Away we went among muggy fumes down rows of split sheepskins and flattened-wide lizards dangling by a wire through their eye-sockets while behind us the fat man slammed his iron drum shut with a terrific clangour by way of comment (so I thought) and set the shaft turning – steam hissing round his feet – until the whole contraption rumbled and chugged – from the opposite direction a wheelbarrow came bowling towards us pushed by a pale boy of no more than ten – I wondered what had become of Lord Shaftesbury's new law but dared not open my mouth –

I noticed the barrow full of dung –

'From dogs' my friend confirmed with a pleasant nod as he raised the rolled hide he had purchased and sniffed it exactly the way he had put his nose to the inner side of my wrist at our last meeting – then became brisk and faced me about for the ordeal of wending our way again through that maze of horrors 'The vanity of the flesh' he explained while supporting my elbow with an insistent hand 'is skin deep – thus I have shown you the skin and all that its beauty amounts to – so now I shall lead you through life – out into fresh air – which is as much as to say that the Lord has chosen me to set your spirit free.'

Day after day in my convalescent bed at Yandilli I dreamed the same odious memory until at last I slept without dreaming and woke to a cavernous appetite –

I am told the colour had swept back into my cheeks and that day by day I could be seen to gain strength – the worst was behind me and Mr Moloch would be gone for at least another month – birds sang! ladies chattered and coughed quietly! my nightmare of errors evaporated in the sunny air – I came to my senses blissfully afloat in clear morning light while the discarded darkness sank down like an insect's horny casing folded away –

I had returned to life exhausted and I knew that – though I would survive my illness – something far more deeply troubling was afoot – was in fact happening in my body – something growing assertive as the consumption weakened –

Signs were soon manifest –

Unmistakably I was expecting a child – I knew nothing about it! I was terrified disgusted guilty baffled and disbelieving! what's more I would soon find myself faced with an impossible task – how could such news be broken to my husband on his return (no matter how passionately I might declare my innocence) without branding me a wanton?

No one can despise my cowardice more than I –

Let me assure you it is still mortifying to look back on after all these years – especially considering the way I taunted myself to the point of contemplating a fatal accident (my own) only to be discovered dozing with a smile on my face – and woken out of a dream in which Mr Moloch was the one who met with the fatal accident – on his sea voyage home from the goldfields –

Remember Beatrice Offley's interpretations? – a day was indeed a thousand years – and if fear is not necessarily love – beyond question love can be fear!

The saintly Lavinia kept bursting into my room like a lunatic – by turns interrogating me about my lapses of faith 'Why are you swallowing your pill – the space you leave – what is that dratted word – trumpets – swallowing your medicine – I mean – surrendering – yes!' only to collapse on her knees to sob on my breast – where she would be found by Hester (the evil Hester) arriving in from doing the garden to offer me solicitude and to provide herself with another opportunity for eyeing me closely –

I had to keep my secret from everyone – not even Ann could be told something so unnatural – anyhow it might prove to be hysteria – maybe the radiance I felt would simply go away – and I prayed that it might.

Can you imagine what it is like to be a lady dreaming of having a stronger body than a man? this was how powerfully the tide of recovery flowed through me – so that I fell to wondering about the others and whether they also entertained shameful fantasies while serving tea and primly dabbing their lips with table napkins –

We were all from good families – you see – and this would have made us oddities in Melbourne let alone Yandilli where our library was enough to arouse deep suspicion not to mention the grand pianoforte – talk about oddities! – nothing like us had been seen before in this raw heat of a forgotten little port on the east coast of Nowhere –

I was soon out and about and able to participate in the gentler pursuits – my easel set up among the rest and my paintbrush jiggling in the water jar while I frowned at an inadequate sketch of *Platycircus elegans* the matchless rosella (it is so important to give everything its proper name don't you agree?) and this was fun enough for a while – pleasant despite Ann's habit of spilling her jar and despite our nagging worries concerning Flora – Flora had come down with my disease but seemed to be enjoying no such revival – while we painted the crimson plumage of that shot bird propped up before us (shot by my husband as a parting gift) our thoughts wandered back to a shallow grave in the stones of Ascension Island – the screams of a million angry seabirds wheeling about us like a cyclone –

With our poor pinch of skill we struggled hopelessly with landscapes copied from Constable – just as we laboured in Schubert's wake at the pianoforte – and don't mention our attempts at emulating the divine Jane with embryonic novels set among our memories of Stroud! though I suppose the harmless twinge of failure is what one means by 'having a jolly time' –

The jolly time was darkened by taking turns to sit at Flora's bedside – and by several others beginning to cough seriously – then came a period of weeks when we were confined indoors during bad weather with the coughs becoming more strident – we sewed and cooked while accepting that the gales would delay Mr Moloch for at least another week – furious squalls sent low clouds trailing torn edges among the bent trees – rain lashed the mission completely flattening our garden and yet (such paradoxical creatures women are) we felt ridiculously lighthearted at being left a little longer to our own devices –

Tenderness grew among us – beginning perhaps with caring for Flora – whatever the cause we softened and talked among ourselves about other things than salvation and duty until we reached the stage where all but me took to embracing (I dared not in my secret condition) and the sharp words of our vocabulary fell out of use –

Even making allowances for my unique problem I realize I did behave rather more pettishly than necessary and set myself rather too publicly apart – making it hard for them to forgive me later – the idea did not once enter my head that we might someday learn from this month of tenderness or look back on our period without a man at the mission for hints as to the way life might change permanently for the better.

I sat apart while the other ladies showed off their education – embroidering slaves and factory children – tuning our pianoforte because the instrument was in great demand not only for hymn singing but when they treated the wallabies to some Haydn trios or Edwina and Hester scared the rosellas off our crops with Chabrier's transcription of the 'Eroica' – they sang Thomas Weelkes madrigals with the bass line picked out on a cello and the tenor sung by Elizabeth Eyre who could manage anything down to E – then Elizabeth was joined by Charlotte declaiming bits of Shakespeare's histories at Flora's bedside – and the sick Flora herself with her feeble voice pluckily dismissed Zeno's paradox of Achilles and the tortoise – mainly she said from moral repugnance on behalf of that bewildered reptile fleeing ahead of the beastly Achilles for interminable ages by ever diminishing degrees –

It all comes back to me now – the sheer miracle of not having to cut short these dizzy pleasures in routine self-surrender at confessionals which had been known to last well into the night – peeling away the layers under Mr Moloch's leadership – excuse this cough – each laying bare some crime of petty shortcomings – excuse me – exposing a flayed soul as pathetic as our bruised ugly bodies – before we could settle down together round the kitchen table for a nice hot cup of chocolate and a chat about tomorrow's tasks in the vegetable garden – well it would be soon enough to resume confessionals when the prophet returned –

A letter arrived to say he would be on his way directly and giving a date but that very day Flora complained of frightful pains in her marrow – the horror of her crisis was what broke me from keeping aloof and finally drove me off my convalescent couch – unable to lie helplessly in hearing of her gasps because no medicines were any help at this stage and nothing but death would staunch her flow of murmurings – I had to be up so I could creep away into my own peace –

I took to waiting in the front room – standing at the window gazing out to sea (with the pretence of watching for the flag to be hoisted at the jetty to announce the packet's arrival) because for me the sea represented freedom – in wild weather or fine – and to be honest it also represented home – contact with sweet moments of the life I led as a girl in a Gloucestershire town watching the maid scatter damp tea leaves on our floor and then sweep up the dust in little balls –

Nothing can be done for consumption except rest and Flora did rest – but I was growing too robust to quell my agitation – part of it being the strength given me by that inexplicable pregnancy and the baby just big enough to be felt with my cold hands – I stood at the window and willed my husband not to come home – never to come home.

*

Don't you remember the shipwreck? don't you remember the cyclone and those frightful gales when roofs blew off? then you must have been down with chickenpox or something of the kind – you never saw such a drama once the packet went missing and everybody guessed she must be in trouble –

My perverse heart went out to Mr Moloch – seasick as he must be – who had gone away on his errand purely to satisfy my demand –

I felt most terribly powerful and at the same time most terribly ashamed to think that on my say-so he would probably also imagine he could calm the storm – and with more days of suffering ahead if the captain decided to stand offshore until the weather improved –

Some other ladies came in to join me at the window until it quite fogged up with our breath –

We muffled ourselves in outdoor clothes though this was still early morning and the new wild day had not long drifted ashore as an eerie mist – light positively billowed in to push away the dark and blind the town with luminous whiteness – broken by glimpses now and again of foam thick with flotsam being dashed to fragments surging among the jagged rocks –

Even though I had felt more lonely with my husband by my side than with him away I said to myself – disgustedly at that time – 'You are infested with love!'

Imagine our shock when some person banged on the back door – who ever came near us? – we were considered out of bounds – he shouted his news that the packet had missed the mouth of the bay altogether! – while I stood paralysed I felt Earth turn because my husband was the only person alive who could question the legitimacy of the child I apparently had to have –

I pulled myself together – though still terribly weak – ordered horses harnessed in the sulkies for collecting whatever farm machinery Mr Moloch might bring home – two completely unknown boys helped us – and within minutes we were driving along to Yandilli wharf – close though it was – the boys riding on our tailboards – long before we'd found places for our horses at the hitching rail we were drenched –

Ghosts of the future were already with me – strapping a gag over my mouth and nose – already sticking pins into my palms and already squeezing my heart –

The crowd of jostlers knew the worst of course – some going off to saddle their horses and others begging rides in carts – while hampered by clumsy rain capes we struggled back into our own sulkies and drove to the crossroads – by this time I had forgotten we didn't belong – being among so many worried folk – and you would never have thought more than a dozen families lived in the district! – all as swaddled up in their outer garments as we were in our guilts – nothing showing but tense white faces with pinched mouths – eyes wide enough to see right in from helplessness to helplessness –

The pandemonium itself was sufficient to put a person in a panic – boots thudding and wheels squealing – not to mention some child letting out hair-raising howls against the gale – when it came to the point just the wind alone could deafen you like a higher pitch of silence – yet in the middle of all this I found a moment for telling myself 'I am an unhappy person' – miserable little drab – as if I mattered! – while horses panted and iron-bound wheels grated on and on among popping stones along a road recently cut through some scrub – trees swirled for all the world like desperate things trying to ward off the sky – and loosed dozens of mad black hunchbacked cockatoos to sweep across our path letting out witches' shrieks –

Cuttajo cliffs are as sombre and uncouth a place as mortal might ever wish to find – we waited there among neighbours we had never said much more to than a hasty 'Good morning' – your own folk among them I have no doubt – O'Donovans and McNeils – as well as those Earnshaw men looking more handsome than expected – talking to a fellow whose name I never knew though I would recognize his face anywhere because his casual conversation struck me at the time as a very great kindness – also the giant son of the Irish convict next door – oh and who else?

Poor exclusive outcasts that we were – we savoured this tragic hour of shivering among familiar strangers as the rain pelted down – catching sight of Mr Moloch's ship in time to watch her sink behind breakers with only her bare masts in view – shreds of canvas flapping from the yards – she canted into the mist as she rose through a dump of surf – a black wet sidelong senseless shape just beyond the reef – looming like an object from my troubled fancy and quite the sort of unsavable something I lived with all the time – and came on just as if the rocks were no more than another ridge of the swell – we saw her bow tip in the air – foam massed and cascaded across the deck to sweep over a cluster of humans swarming down the hull into madly bucking boats – boats being lifted level with the rail and then a moment later sucked down lower than the reef where the ship's keel lodged – then up they'd swoop again – oars at odd angles and tillers useless – more bodies dropped into them – though most hesitated a fatal moment and fell floundering into the surf of breakers instead –

The retribution which hung over me was moving closer and I knew –

You cannot imagine what horrible jubilation took hold of me despite myself and my upbringing in the church –

I strove to ward off the blame but more and more I began to believe I had been dreaming this disaster for days – and having dreamed it I must have brought it about – beyond question I had wanted to prevent Mr Moloch coming home – so great was the pressure of this guilt that I confided in Ann (though I made no mention of my baby) – whispering into her dripping ear there and then on the cliffs – while whips of escaped hair cut at our faces – only to be scolded for my sin of pride –

Among all the ladies at the mission Ann was probably alone in having no axe to grind – she said the whole catastrophe was too big to be my fault –

We shrieked till our voices grew ragged – calling in vain 'Mr

Moloch Mr Moloch!' – before following Charlotte Smith's lead (more about dear Lotte the conniver later) singing 'Eternal Father strong to save' – we sang it out – 'O hear us when we cry to Thee For those in peril on the sea' – and lo and behold against all probability this worked – because minutes after the last lifeboat went down to be lost the tide rolled a man's body on to the beach – just one poor puny indestructible man – we watched him stagger to his feet in the shallows – and all my old helplessness recognized in him what I did not choose to recognize – that far from wanting to be free of him I wanted him to be exclusively mine as I was his – and drew me instantly into his orbit –

Can you picture me in my green dress with purple satin panels and pagoda sleeves which I had foolishly worn with a view to enchanting Mr Moloch afresh in the event of the Almighty's failure to strike him dead? when instead of a husband I was confronted by this miserable creature who came hobbling through ankle-deep water only to be buffeted by the next wave swarming up to his waist and then just as violently swarming back down to drag a mat of sliding shingles from underfoot – yet it *was* my husband who had survived despite my wickedness you see! leaving me engulfed under tides of hopelessness – then a second sodden object rolled in on its tummy and rolled on its back and rolled on its tummy and finally in despair was let flop to one side – but the power that sucked all strength from me suddenly pumped me full of double energy when the first survivor began wading to the rescue – he blocked the body to stop it sliding out again – well I dared not think why – so I acted instead – despite my delicate condition – and promptly led the way slithering down through wattles and spiny grass though I felt that knives were gashing me with every breath I took – oh yes if I ever hoped I had not given in to love I knew better at that moment – but by the time I reached him – the seething tide flooding into my shoes – some Earnshaw men were already respectfully keeping their distance while Mr Moloch in his waterlogged suit warded them off from a drowned woman – insisting she was his and his alone to drag ashore.

*

During my years with the Household of Hidden Stars many's the time I swore to run away and never come back but sure as eggs the moment I took the decision things changed – I would see a brighter side and feel surrounded by affection – besides the faith we had in common – so I would stay – I stayed because I believed in Mr Moloch's special powers too – also thanks to the simple fact that he was a man – if you see what I mean – and the fascination of this – a strange creature with rituals of shaving and fixing his collar stud and a prickly temper – not to mention his vanity in needing to be right especially when he knew he was wrong and especially needing to prove his strength when a task was plainly beyond him – a typical man I think we could say –

As for the vicious things (there were vicious things) I tended to accept them as somehow – well – comfortable because these were only household cruelties – you don't so much mind your arm being pinched or your hair pulled or having to endure cutting remarks when you are trapped together by a country so alien it reeks of fertility and suffocating age – apart from which Ann was always available to cut things down to size with some such comments as 'Won't it be more serious if we have a heat-wave too?' or 'Tell me about it when you've fallen into a ravine and can't climb out!' – then if any of us continued to make a fuss she'd point out that we would have been worse off drowned – or frozen to death – or stuck in a cannibal's stew pot!

Indeed yes some people *were* eaten I have no doubt just as others drowned – we heard tell of a sunken ship just off the reef at Yandilli where the lads used to go diving to prove what men they were and risked their lives to bring back a porcelain dish or two for trophies or a few scraps of lead ballast worth a shilling at most – and you yourself among them at one stage – next thing these same lads went to prove how good they were in the ranges from which if the wind blew from the right quarter we used to hear remote songs of lost souls flying above the high gullies – though what those expeditions were to prove I'm sure I don't know because you young hopefuls had little to show for your pluck apart from plenty of lacerations – unless we count one breathless boy stumbling in through this gate here to tell us he'd found blood spots on a flat rock somewhere up the mountain! I remember every detail you see! and I believe what I was told –

I must pull myself together.

You are surprised by my memory? well we shall see what you think when you hear the things I have been keeping secret in this head of mine – how we faced the tragedy and how eventually we learned to laugh again – there's nothing new about tragedy and anger ending in laughter – even our present arrangement of living in separate houses has its interesting side – do you think I don't know what I am talking about? or that I can hear the clink of crockery from over there without feeling a savage pain in my heart and a longing to set out on some long journey – to stand under a beech tree while a thrush bursts into song overhead – to be free? – because all my life I have wanted happiness – and yet really I am such a perfect colonial I shall never go home –

If you think this is not what you came to hear you shall soon discover how wrong you are –

Let me take you back to the shipwreck and the exhausted Mr Moloch buzzing like a hornet while we crowded round him 'Keep away! get out!' he shouted at me and then looked up to address the air above us (like this) because now he had an argument with God 'All right all right!' which was when I knelt to check the woman's heart and breathing and found none of either so she was dead as a stone – and this I would swear in a court of law –

When I told him she was dead he accused me of desiring it – which came like a slap in the face because I was his wife – and not until much later did I come to see that I *did* desire it and my intuition had told me the truth about her – so this may give you some idea how well he understood me – also how he understood that I was swooning under the pain of watching him stoop over her and watching his breath of life being breathed into her –

because I at last knew what it would look like to have it breathed into me instead –

I do not believe he ever came to suspect me of calling up the storm itself –

You know yourself how treacherous the coast is here even in fine weather – with sharp rocks under a glittering mirror of reflections – well that was me and the fury in my loving heart too – let alone when surges come fuming inshore and night breaks your sleep with muffled thunder – don't ask more –

So having slithered on seaweed dollops stinking of iodine (without a murmur of complaint even though I could scarcely stand at that stage so oppressed was I by the weight of the sky I had to hold up) I came to look upon this interesting young woman and saw a mere lump of flesh bandaged in tight fashions all sopping wet – deliciously caught and knotted – you must imagine colourless lips and blue storm smudges and closed eyes and a nose pinched white at the nostrils – imagine hair fairer than wheat but darkened by deep water and strapped round her chin as if while strangling her someone had also bound it under her jaw and then up over her head to keep her from calling for help – she looked perhaps twenty – a year or two older than I – her solid neck jutted at one end of her dress while at the other a marbled ankle appearing every bit as obscene stuck into its boot from which laces snaked with the receding current while a few flags of seaweed hooked on a bodice button snaked the same way – she made a dramatic impression – you might say she had such training in striking poses that even when dead and without her guidance her body struck this last pose for itself – I was a child being bullied by each new surprise to ask what was expected of me by the older people among whom I had to make my place –

I mention her training because she turned out to be an opera singer – as you shall hear –

Ann arrived muttering against any interference in others' troubles and sniffed at the sight of our prophet crouching down again to place his swarthy cheek on that dead Jezebel's pallid one –

I have already described how Mr Moloch's big mouth big nose and big dark eyes could suddenly come to life with astonishing effect – well there below the cliffs he grew brilliant in just this way and if anybody in creation could raise the dead it was him with his big ear listening to her transparent ear which looked as though she was showing it by the light of day for the first time in her life – his black eyelashes brushed her eyelids –

Do you want to know more?

He was an elusive character and you had to catch him at the right angle to see what he was like at all – if you know what I mean – rather like a Daguerreotype plate on which the image is sometimes vividly clear but then – at the slightest trembling of the hand it may become a mere ghost of itself or be lost altogether –

I should explain that in his darkness he was a child of sunlight – this was the mystery of it – while in her pallor she looked to be a netherworld creature only ever seen by the glow of footlights – and I might add I did not need shouting at – already weighed down with the despair of how she brought out more beauty in him than I ever had except for a private occasion in a vestry which seemed too long lost to matter anymore – but the point was we were not alone this time – so once again he shamed me in public with his violent lack of discretion – and I became too much caught up in my own miseries to realize that no one but Ann was watching us – the rest were frantic figures in oilskins clambering along a groin of rocks toward large broken boxes which only minutes earlier had been a ship – and then the Earnshaws found time to step aside a moment to offer us a blanket for covering the dead which Mr Moloch accepted out of a misunderstanding because he spread it flat and lay down on it himself before wrapping the both of them together – him and the woman –

I was totally disgraced –

All I could think to do was look away toward remote shouts

reaching us from the rocks where the rescue party of fellows pressed ahead laden under coils of rope and grappling hooks – silhouettes against a blast of white spray with their balanced arms outstretched while spindrift sank from the sky or great feathered sea shapes clutched at them – and the rearing sea beyond heaved up another cavernous broken box with two masts still stuck out of it –

Her world of the theatre was taking over ours –

The next roller flung down a fresh burden and with it the first lifeboat – a nimble sleek upside-down thing – horrifying because it skimmed like a porpoise until the shore party rushed among churning waters in the shallows to secure it and turn it over and display its emptiness while further in the foam several heads still bobbed and were buried under a suffocating thunder of foam –

Birds were blown by the wind with crooked wings and bony pink feet clenched on nothing and beaks gaping while they screeched at us because (poor feeble sinners that we were) we had been no help to anybody and then they were whisked away among the souls of the dead as I've mentioned – up over the forest like heathen creatures calling to Baal who was as big as a whole mountain and blinked his million eyes among the leaves – can you imagine? – the Earth shook each time the ocean was flung against it so we could feel a living anger underfoot while the tempest howled and hurled down torrents of rain to block out all vestige of the hills of 'Paradise.'

Excuse me.

Yes for all I know there were screams last Monday and for all I know they were mine but this would not have been the first time – and if you still do not understand you should accept that you know little about the true faith in Jesus Christ.

One has to seek perfection from oneself – you are my witness that I am not at all a colourful person though we live in colourful times – the fact is that things go wrong and when things go wrong somebody must be to blame – the worst punishment let me say is to be given hours of silence and yet one never hears complaints in the district about silence –

Where was I up to? – I mustn't lose the thread – yes the mournful cry of gulls blowing about and the wind tangling our hair as we strained to see if anybody else might be rescued from the disaster – 'O Christ whose voice the waters heard and hushed their raging at a word' we sang while figures fit for dreams of happiness teetered further and further away out along that jagged finger of land – 'who walkest on the foaming deep and calm amid the storm didst sleep' – to where masts tilted uselessly and frantic little canvas hands flapped from the yards –

Our shrill voices sang 'O hear us when we cry to Thee For those in peril on the sea' as we glimpsed other rags in the pounding waves being churned under – jumbled about brutally with limbs and trunks still in them or dead arms flung up or hands lacking bodies – I felt how pathetic we were and how daft a creature God had bred in us – do you see our waterlogged bonnets with the quilling spoiled? bodies clutched by cold dresses? well this was what we were reduced to while we apologized for upsetting Mr Moloch and backed away murmuring self-effacements which could not possibly have aggravated even the most sensitive of bullies while he cupped that stranger's head in his hands and a cry broke from him to coil away like the crack of a whip –

Then I'm telling you we saw her body flip over of its own accord convulsing free of his grasp – kicking off his blanket – and heaving while her smooth statue's face flushed dark as a plum to vomit a bucket of clear stuff for each spasm that doubled her up –

Womenfolk from Yandilli township and from 'Paradise' came sloshing and flummoxing our way (I cannot put it better than that and you will know what I mean with your mother one among them) gathering their skirts and managing baskets of food for nothing better than rescuing Muley Moloch's opera singer who might have been his paramour too for all we knew – small wonder I felt ashamed of my husband's ignorance concerning the decorum expected of a churchman – yes she was a common opera singer –

Martha handed him a flask of brandy – Hester offered to take the drowned female's arm and help her up – Charlotte of course offered the same service on the other side – I accused him bitterly saying 'All the time you were away I had you and only you on my mind' (yet I dared not admit my guilty reason) –

In that uncivilized place my aloneness was brought home to me by his cold stare and tightening mouth – I knew I must face ostracism – even among those close enough to me not to feel outright horror at the sight of my pregnancy –

Yet I was not inclined to submit without a fight – I neither liked the bond between him and this new individual nor felt called upon to disguise my dislike – I threw it at him that I would be grateful to move away from the port into obscurity – pointing inland as I did so – and then I looked up in that direction to emphasize my anger – only to see a strange figure perched on the cliff – head like a little black tent supported by three flimsy stick legs and two sturdy human legs –

A single round expressionless eye observed us –

I said to myself 'This is the end of the world we know – nothing can be private ever again!' and I recall thinking 'Yet there will be no more lies because every fact can be proved from now on' – no more crime – out loud I said 'Let's for goodness' sake hurry!' – hearing Hester ask was the thousand-year kingdom to be entirely photographed? while she and Charlotte laboured under the weight of assisting that huge pale Goth of his – 'May I introduce' he remembered his manners ridiculously 'Miss Louisa Theuerkauf?' –

I had already turned my back – it was no concern of mine that she looked half dead and not fit to travel for a long time – I could find no room for mercy – we had planned on going straight into the hills to claim our new property so that is what we would do – promptly next morning – I told myself I did not care if the journey killed her.

*

What a wind! what clouds! anyone would think the sky is flapping away to China it's in such a hurry.

Yes there are simple answers to your questions because every question does have a simple – but this won't help you understand what you are asking – not a bit – I cannot possibly give you answers just like that until I have taken you right back to the beginning so you'll at least have some idea what they mean –

As for religion *this* is my religion – these shacks and hovels that hold the relics of our hopes – bless you – certainly I shall show you around in a few minutes although you'll remember the mission I dare say –

Not much changes apart from bits falling off and roofs leaking – yes that building was the prayer hall when you were here and except for the couple of pews we chopped up for firewood during the recent floods it remains pretty much the same –

The worst things I suffer are in my mind – much worse than the shortage of breath – chronic though that is – left over from the white plague –

Those were the stables down there though all except one of the horses died of melancholy – but you know enough about our stables – doesn't it make you hoot to think how cluttered we are with things decaying before they even have time to get old? (including me!) well we are a puzzle to ourselves for sure and in my opinion this is thanks to the fact that the moment people think of something sensible they do the opposite! what else!

Proof? what more proof do you need than *us* trailing out here although we had been settled comfortably in our cottages at Yandilli? – maybe we need never have moved – because the point is that when I went slithering down that muddy slope to the beach – acutely aware that nobody knew how petrified I was of jolting the baby in my womb – I vowed to put all our plans at risk – though I didn't care if the journey inland killed Louisa Theuerkauf I cared that my baby might be born in guilt if his secret remained a secret – so clearly I should take the punishment on myself and tackle the problem straight away –

For a while I weakened – something had happened to me beyond my control that disgraced me and soiled me (despite the fact that it also filled my blood with fire) – maybe the true alternative was not a confession but an earnest prayer for the Almighty to strike us all dead in His vengeance! –

Yet when I lost my balance momentarily my whole life sprang alert with the need to protect the baby – wasn't the baby's safety the very reason I had been more shocked by seeing my husband stand in the foam than by seeing him washed around like a corpse? – I returned to the nausea of my decision to let the truth out so it could never be taken back – to be free of it – so as I say I was rushing over the brittle shells towards my husband and heedless of his own extremity I opened my mouth to cry out 'I am with child!' –

He cut me short before I could utter a sound – he looked up from the drowned creature at his feet and shouted right in my face 'Keep away! get out!'

Imagine a string of five vehicles – four sulkies and a spring cart – ready to set off from Yandilli to carry us inland to this place which we had purchased with Edwina's money but which none of us had seen – our guide being the young Irish giant from next door who drove the leading vehicle in which Flora's mattress had been put and Flora lifted up to lie on it – then Mr Moloch helped his invalid opera singer on to the step and climbed in beside her – leaving me to manage as best I may –

The owner clipped the tailboard in place with the special care of a man made proud by his brand-new equipment and then stepped up with us and took the reins –

My husband sat defiantly while the meaning of that defiance pierced me to the heart – and I took my place facing them – determined never to take my eyes off them – to save my dignity and because of the contempt I felt for them – determined not to let my suffering show –

Flora gave out a few murmurs and when neither of the others appeared interested in listening I leaned down (still watching them) to ask what she wanted – 'Did Beatrice die' she pleaded in gasps 'because she argued with the prophet?' – it frightened me – yet I knew without meeting her eyes that she meant my husband to answer –

'Flora asks' I shot her words at him with so much venom I astonished myself 'did Beatrice die because she defied you?' and the sulky jolted into motion while the driver's back listened to us – we went bumping down over a gutter and swung up along the smooth road – the Goth wobbled imperturbably – Mr Moloch's silence concentrated in his eyes as an exceptional power while he stared me down with that brilliant dark look of his – to Flora he said nothing – even when she put out a feeble hand and held on to his shoe –

All along the high street folk watched us pass – you could hear how glad they were to see us go by the greetings they called to Mr Jack Earnshaw who drove the second sulky (the other one with passengers – Ann Lavinia Charlotte and the two Elizabeths) – the three buggies loaded with our furniture and tools were in the hands of Hester and Martha and Lady Edwina –

The rude priest who used to be at Yandilli in those days stood at the door of his iron church and drew the only words we heard from our driver 'Morning Father' the giant called and then mumblingly reproved us for our lack of respect 'Father O'Shaughnessy don't you know?' – young Billy McNeil was struggling with the blinds to help open up his parents' butchery – and I fancy we may even have seen you holding your mother's hand because we certainly saw her – she crossed herself – her superstition made me want to stop the pony and leap out and shake her! – in that same moment my mind filled with mutiny at the likelihood that Beatrice had died thanks to the resentment I felt whenever she put my husband in his place as a man who could neither read nor write –

Then we were out in the country and quite suddenly overhung by trees from which trailing vines brushed our shoulders and twigs snagged our woollen jackets – the road shrank to a track jostling us roughly and the sound of hooves was muffled by soft evil silt while our wheels lurched against roots and skidded into potholes – I felt awfully queasy and headachy – the air filled with such huge shadows we ducked and shielded our heads against them – all except the opera singer who had made a remarkable recovery overnight –

Louisa Theuerkauf was firmly determined I should feel her resentment at my watching her – which meant she must have recognized my *right* even in the absence of anyone pointing me out or explaining my special status as the wife – though indeed she worked herself round to half face my husband so he could not help seeing how she registered neither surprise nor apprehension at finding herself driven into a wilderness (a reminder that she had been to her death in order to follow him so what else was there to fear?) but she also faced him so he could not help watching her cut me out from the silent communications they shared under cover of indifference nor fail to catch the quirky tilt of her chin when some thought came into her head which she intended imparting by telepathy – not to mention what meaning there might have been in that intense possessive questioning frigid look of hers –

We trundled out of the tunnel of leaves into sparser bush with splashes of sunshine on the ground – an eerie sense of expectation filled the air – and I realized that if once you were to be lured into leaving the track you would never find it again – all the trunks being identical and identically spaced – no horizon visible or anything beyond the trees themselves – you would be lost in five minutes –

Never was there any place so shapeless or nameless or bewilderingly closed against being understood – even the birds swooped around in silence – 'Mr Moloch has said' Flora hissed at me from the floor as several bumps threw her about among shafts of pain 'we must beware the Devil and all his works!' even her weak voice sounded too loud in this brooding place –

I hoped our land at the mission would be different –

The prophet neglected Flora perhaps because he felt helpless to cure her – I don't know – however at last the Goth condescended to stare down at her coldly – showing about as much tact as a mincing machine – meanwhile they both continued to ignore me and left it to me to console the poor creature besides looking after my own fragile health –

By contrast Mr Moloch frequently enquired about the Goth's comfort and her restored strength or such trivialities as her satisfactory placement in regard to the wind if you please! the amazing thing was that her vulgar coquettishness appeared to escape him even while she made use of sunlight and shadow much as if they were stage lighting which she turned to such marvellous effect that her unmoving face appeared animated by constant variety so flickers of brilliance darted in the corner of a still eye and her large simple cheek was endlessly remoulded by the changeable glow and veiling –

The previous day's storm having dispersed left the air entirely cleansed so as to seem too neutral to sustain life – broken grass lay combed out along the verges – our guide drove undaunted along a track never better than greasy and sometimes completely under puddles – the pony appeared in positively carnival mood skittishly kicking up its heels and flattening its ears –

Voices carried from the other sulkies – little clusters of conversation budding on the passing air and briefly flowering – but in ours any such effort withered under the tensions created by our driver's disapproval (eloquently expressed by the most massive back I had ever seen) and the angers passing mutely from one side of the sulky to the other – not to mention Flora between – letting out desperate groans which she had abandoned all attempt to suppress –

By lunchtime we reached the tall trees and I decided maybe we *were* lost – the track becoming drier and stonier the wheels rhythmically jounced us about with such relentless violence I longed to cry out 'For goodness' sake stop right here and let us at least get down and walk!' but shame kept me from complaining and I could not tell whether the others (who were not in my condition) might have been enjoying it – meanwhile the lofty gloom struck me as not just hostile but hostile in a queerly challenging way – so untouched by civilization and having a certain grandeur of senselessness (yet if you had told me I might someday surrender to it like one intoxicated I would have laughed in your face) – leafage loosened during the storm pattered around us and settled as a cushion to muffle the dainty hooves padding along –

In the sheer wildness of that era we must have been an astonishing advent – our procession of bonnets and fluttering mantles – our fragments of laughter –

Although we felt a great deal of apprehension about the future we also felt relief at leaving Yandilli brooding on its past of scorched walls and ruined outbuildings – besides I need hardly tell *you* that two years in a tiny seaside village in New South Wales is quite enough to addle the brain and altogether squash the gaiety from one's animal spirits – you have been here a whole lifetime after all –

So we were escaping – yes – but at the same time we knew this put us beyond reach of help – including the doctor's help (though I dared not commiserate with Flora on such a matter because I dared not explain myself) – we had trotted far out of sight of the last pasture and up among boulders – joggling and shuddering over ruts to wend our way through a forest rising on all sides and cloaking the ranges like the gigantic rustling waves of an unbroken sea –

Down into a gully we swayed with overtaxed springs thumping against the frame and into a stream – watching the following carts crawl and slew as they set my friends rocking and holding on – also hearing Jack Earnshaw sing out to us that this was called Burnt Bridge Creek – well we could have done with a bridge because we stuck halfway across! – our driver cooed at the pony and clicked his tongue to encourage it and murmured endearments which came strangely from so taciturn a specimen while the poor beast heaved and trembled without success – eventually the fellow jumped down to put his own shoulder to the wheel – give him his due – immediately we lurched out of the hole we were in and bounced up the slope with him striding beside – boots spouting water and trousers sopping – he only jumped back on when we reached the crest –

In this country sons are always taller than their fathers – but I might say he was providentially ugly –

On the hill climb to the summit I wondered about that burnt bridge and when it might have been burnt – surely precious few civilized folk had settled this district before us? the question let a draught into my soul –

We trundled along the top making better progress despite many diagonal gutters across the track which caused us such discomfort I believe Flora several times lost her senses –

Louisa merely adjusted the set of her head to present her brow for the green shade to accentuate her majestic mound of hair which she wore swept up in the secular style – the changes deepened her eyes –

Please do not think I intend sounding spiteful – nor that I am taking a belated opportunity to pitch into her – I simply have to tell what I remember as I remember it – everything matters –

When we came upon a solitary hut in a clearing I feared it might be our new home but as we drew closer we could read a sign over the door *The Brian Boru Inn* – the publican came out to salute our guide – evidently expecting anyone who passed that way to stop – however Mr Moloch insisted we keep moving and refused to sanction even five minutes' rest for the ponies at so sinful a place (this was before the establishment moved to the new village of Cuttajo) – so we pressed on – hearing Jack Earnshaw's voice call a greeting and the publican's answer like a lonely echo – up the winding stony track in a gulch with a perilous drop inches from our wheel – we were heading north now and when the trees thinned we were surprised to find we could still catch glimpses of the sea –

Nobody can tell what will lead to what – you may trace any catastrophe back to issues of dwindling importance until you reach some miserable bubbling spring so feeble you could plug it by sticking your hand in – and the same with each tributary of the river – well here is an issue of little importance to start from -

As soon as our leader agreed to a break the ponies gathered to wheeze together with the sulkies standing at odd angles – Martha drove up in the last one complaining that her vehicle had no springs while ours was new – and read aloud the freshly painted lettering on our tailboard 'Paradise' – 'Oh Mr Moloch' she tittered 'you are there already!' –

I have no reason to suppose she was commenting on the fact that my husband sat beside Louisa Theuerkauf – nor that Martha intended any unkind comment on my being obliged to face them and watch them sway together (despite the good springs) shaken by the same jolts – but if somebody had told me then that Louisa and I would one day live together and that she would lead me to freedom – well! –

'Look!' called Ann from the next sulky 'is that a grave?' and she pointed among the moss-grown tree trunks – unmistakably there was a mound of newly heaped soil and leaves –

'Grave?' Flora croaked in alarm from where she lay too weak even to prop herself up on one elbow 'Why would anyone be buried out here?' and added 'unless they were murdered?' –

The prophet stared dumbly at the mound but Farmer Earnshaw smiled and explained that it was the nest made by a forest bird – a kind of turkey – and that the mound of mulch was for keeping the eggs warm – Muley Moloch decided against a sermon on that occasion so he sat down abruptly and ordered the Irishman to drive on.

In the mid-afternoon we arrived – or at least we came to a gate where we stopped – I believe we all felt a little like trespassers even though we knew the Barnetts had already moved out –

But not Louisa –

Stillness watched us – stillness listened to us – and Stroud seemed far enough away for Miss Honeywood to have been no more than a witch in a fairy tale – yet at that instant I was overpowered by nostalgia for the lawn at the Hall where I used to sit among daisies on the clipped grass – nothing seemed more unlikely than that we ourselves might have just such a lawn here one day –

Of course our new mowing machine was in among the luggage but Mr Moloch felt so tremendously proud of it he had not been able to bring himself to soil it with work in two years – maybe because his ideal lawn had to be somewhere permanent – as a promise of gentility –

We gazed around us at the outlandish wilderness which was to be home – our silent driver though familiar with the place did not open his mouth to explain a thing – when Lady Edwina dismissed his surliness on the grounds that he was a known Papist Ann Whittaker retorted that he might have been as horrified by finding himself in so remote a spot with us as we were at finding ourselves with him – yet I believe it was more a question of his belonging and our foreignness – because after all hadn't the Anglican Earnshaws married into the Roman Barnetts? – Oliver Barnett and Jack Earnshaw being cousins? –

Does it not strike you as strange that English people are so seldom touched by experience? that whatever happens we remain unchanged? and for all our tenacity in the colonies we have acquired no more in the past hundred years than possession of air and water? – certainly on the afternoon in question I felt it was only because we had lost everything and gained nothing that we were doomed in all honour to stick it out –

We haven't *learnt* much collectively (have we?) which we could not have learned at home – apart from the sentimental value of lost origins –

I squeezed Flora's hand when she took hold of mine because I guessed she dreaded dying in such a barren waste – but now I look back on it I wonder if she foresaw what was to come for the rest of us – the poor thing wept openly when everyone crowded round to lift her out and settle her in a patch of sunshine –

This much I do admit that though I love to chew over a good

memory I never had any talent at guessing the future – hence my perpetual New Year resolution to be obedient –

I looked over my shoulder in time to glimpse our guides shaking their shaggy heads while they unpacked the heavy bags – carrying the last items past Louisa who sat gazing ahead at a huddle of little rooftops half-buried in shrubbery and showing no sign of alarm maybe because she needed to concentrate her energies on recovering – or maybe simply because she was a stodgy German potato as Ann used to say –

The Irishman offered Louisa his arm so he wasn't wholly dead to chivalry while my husband took the other side and they led her away to the gate – meanwhile perhaps because the load had been lifted the ponies began bucking at phantoms – the shafts clashing together – but we could not quite make out whether anything else might be the matter until one pony's hoof caught another on the side of the nose with a terrific smack – the Irishman's sulky jerked back and slammed into a tree where it fetched up askew while the frightened animal shook her head and bared her teeth – well this wasn't very important except that when the fellow ambled across to calm the poor thing and lead her away from the others we could see one axle had been damaged – 'He might fix it for the time being but it's his father's' Jack Earnshaw explained.

The wheel wobbled.

Mr Moloch watched without interest but you mustn't forget that being a prophet his attention was generally on matters beyond the immediate present – unless the grimness settling in his face was an effect of those nagging aches which went with his touch of lameness – in the meantime madam had shown herself as the type who has never been taught to climb into a brougham let alone how to step down gracefully yet she looked very imposing standing still –

Plainly our drivers regarded Mr Moloch as a charlatan and were displeased when he waved them off without the least gesture of hospitality while to us he said as reassuringly as he could 'I believe we shall find the house complete with furniture left by the Barnetts' – oh yes those Barnetts got out with nothing more than the clothes they wore and the hopes they had of Digby Barnett returning from the Victorian goldfields a rich man – as well he might because God moves in strange and contrary ways – none stranger than to think that even when we first discussed moving inland He must have known Louisa's opera company was already propping up its pictures of disaster and hanging a canvas tempest for a backcloth at the Melbourne Theatre Royal while singers gathered to do battle with the inadequacies of a colonial orchestra and what this would lead to –

All the colonies went mad over gold in those days – though it seemed to slip through people's fingers – the cities spent it on celebrations and entertainments and the diggers spent it on grog –

We watched our guides set out for home and then pause far off along the track to rein in their ponies while that nice Earnshaw man waved us a final goodbye – the Irish giant kept the rock of indifference turned against us – probably still sunk in worry over his wobbling wheel –

Being so impatient to inspect the house we did not immediately unharness the ponies though several ladies remarked on how nervous they seemed –

I walked apart for a minute or two just to try confronting the enormity and sameness of the bush – saying to myself 'We have arrived' but the idea of this as arrival made little sense in such a limbo – the laugh I suddenly let out died on my lips – another of my thoughts had come to me – that the usual picture of Hell is of familiar sins and almost domestic sufferings (fire and pitchforks – bleedings and beatings – very much our own penances on a larger scale) whereas it now seemed more likely that an effective Hell would be to suffer in complete meaninglessness for absolutely no understandable reason – can you imagine? –

I developed this – wasn't it arguable that even the old idea of a Hell constructed from experience might work more painfully in meaningless surroundings? – wouldn't this throw the sinner back among her sins – to live in a world of memories? – and we already knew about that – the anguish –

Lost in thought I suppose I did not bother to listen to the voices behind me or try putting meaning to what they said – syllables completely adrift – weird as utterances from another world (which is what they were) surviving in this trap of repeated shapes and monotonous colour – I believe I wept –

Ponies whinnied – one voice at length broke through to me calling 'Look sharp!' – I dashed some blinding tears away to find myself confronted by a horde of demons prancing out from among the trees – a squad of them sidling this way and that and beginning to wail tunelessly – ferocious horrors with arms hung down to their knees – things stuck into them and other things stuck out –

Mr Moloch thundered at us to avert our eyes while he dealt with the menace alone – goaded to a fury he was – having so recently performed the greatest of miracles I suppose he was full as a drum with pride and in common with most men felt an urge to strut – fortunately the demons were not to know what I knew – that under his breath he cursed himself for not carrying a loaded gun – curses being a sure sign of fear – and he rushed up to me at a limp –

Will I ever be free of this problem with –

My breath?

I stood petrified where I was – glancing back only once to where Flora lay helpless in the gateway to see Hester (give her credit) hurry that way in case Flora needed somebody to ward them off but no one knew I myself needed special protection for the sake of my unborn child – more perhaps than a dying woman –

So along came these ugly demons in all sizes from huge to tremendous confronted by puny little Mr Moloch making good his humiliation at not being able to drive a cart by rolling up his shirtsleeves bunching his fists and dancing about as he had been taught in the slums while Lady Edwina called 'Come come!' from where she yanked at the snaffle of her frightened pony which had not yet been tethered and was crabbing with its buggy into a ditch but nobody took the least notice of her –

I was amazed to see – behind vicious masks watching the prophet skip unevenly this way and that – eyes full of good humour and eyes full of fear – while it was my husband who gave a desperate shout like the sort of noise you'd expect only a dog to make –

As for the fact that he did begin to carry a gun after suffering this fright – well we were to find out the consequences of *that* later on!

Intense light and shadow swirled round us as gusts of wind crowded among the trees and dashed against my skirts and sent massive chunks of sky flying at my head while I caught at my husband's sleeve to restrain him – he wrenched it free and flung a few words at me so that I stood dazed and bewildered trying to grasp the meaning of what he said – 'The grisly wife as always!' –

Was this me? Was I in the way? –

I knew by the stab in my heart at his familiar word 'grisly' – he and his opera singer had coined this name together – no use excusing his crudity on the grounds that those closest to Jesus were fishermen and carpenters – not to mention a wild man in the person of John the Baptist – I believe I felt a surge of hope when the demons responded by aiming spears at him – might they achieve what the shipwreck had not? –

They jabbered and waggled their snouts and bared sharp teeth and shuffled webbed wings – not at all the type of congregation Mr Moloch was used to at the Methodist meeting houses in Cleeve Cloud or Chipping Sodbury – 'What do you mean – the *grisly wife*?' I shrieked – anger lifting me beyond fear – like a hero – 'In the Lord's name' he roared as he marched right up to them 'get thee behind me!' and actually laughed (which sent shivers through me) sounding like some demented being very much bigger than Muley Moloch –

So this was to be the future! this was to be our home which we would make decent enough for the Visitor – the returning

Christ – oh yes that was the idea and nothing less – to make ourselves worthy as hosts for the Second Coming in this appalling hole with the peaks of rude shingle rooftops already announcing what squalor we should expect – not to mention the scatter of battered cans and smashed bottles littering the place and scraps of paper blown in under the bushes or the torn shreds of coloured cotton snagged in the branches or the lingering stench of unsanitary living – I drifted into a chasm of self-pity –

I did not care whether I lived or died so I turned my back on the danger and there before me I observed a huddle of women in neat dark clothes – some with cashmere mantles others with pinched waists and lace revers – their bonnets cupping faces wide with horror and eyes so shocked God knows what they thought they were witnessing – whether insects as big as horses or birds with teeth or giant eels coiling through the treetops – and over by the gate where Hester crouched I saw Flora's head on the mattress wag from side to side as they whispered together –

'Come to me Charlotte' Elizabeth Eyre called and took her hand –

What about my baby – I wanted to demand – but all I could manage was to shout after Mr Moloch 'If they bite your face off you will be no further use to the Almighty or to me either!' and then my heart emptied of blood at a piercing note which was not a scream but had the pitch of a scream and lodged in the ear as vibrant and pinching as a clever kind of torture and saw Louisa Theuerkauf having shaken off her exhaustion assembling her vast bulk to march forward – impassive like the ivory statue she had seemed to be when washed up dead by the ocean – she took one mechanical step at a time carrying her bosom prominently and her manly shoulders squared and her face nothing more than a frame for the cavity of a gaping mouth – her fair hair ballooning round the whole arrangement while with head well back she uttered this superhuman (what did I decide it was?) top D or top E flat –

Well the demons might have encountered the like of the prophet but they reckoned without Louisa – their hair stood on end between the clumps of feathers and bloody bird-gizzards they decorated it with and they scattered – all but one – tails and appendages flapping and the animal pelts slipping crooked across their shoulders they scuttered and dodged away among the forest trees with weapons rattling –

You should bear in mind that it was I who first introduced the idea that wherever our mission might be we must make it a decent enough place for the Lord – my husband and I had been walking back along a Gloucestershire lane with hawthorn bushes at either side and enjoying the buoyancy of his latest successful sermon – he had taken up a stick from the grassy bank and broken it to a convenient length – so he began to invent our future beginning with a group of select disciples to follow the true path – perhaps in secret – 'However' I said 'my dear man' relishing my role as an adult 'the Visitor will need to recognize how decent it is' – which led to the question of location because how would *our* decent place be found in England for example when England despite its corruption was still so full of the wrong decent places? –

So to the mission in the hills –

This then was to become the decent place – here among jungle demons – the very improbability would offer our best guarantee of being found by the Messiah – this rustic slum with its first candidate martyr already laid out at the gate to gasp in extremity while her forehead was bathed by the most evil of women dipping handkerchiefs in water – and I (as author of the journey) discovered I had already become the victim of a private jibe enjoyed by my husband and the opera singer who might very well disqualify us from our purpose by making a mockery of decency –

The only person I could bear to speak to was Flora because Flora would soon be dead –

She was all smiles as she whispered that she had not once coughed since we unloaded her – I felt terrible and I believe I did have a premonition then of some dire tragedy awaiting the rest of us – perhaps aided by Hester – Hester who stood back a little and stared down at me as she asked whether I felt perfectly well and only released me from her enquiry when Martha turned to us to report that the demons had entirely disappeared and to hope very loudly that there were solid locks on all the doors –

Mr Moloch strode back taking longer steps than were natural because plainly he expected credit for the rout – and it must be admitted that Lady Edwina was our sole casualty – her pony had forced the four-wheeler right into a ditch pulling her so violently down the bank she lost her grip on the bridle and being chiefly angry with herself did not stint in her outburst against Louisa 'That was a damned fool thing to do!' – she was raging I can tell you from the ignominy of her muddy hole – though true to character she immediately recovered her spirits and called up 'But effective!' –

If only to prick Mr Moloch's complacency I too complimented the opera person 'How nice that your talent survived after all you have been through' I said but she wasn't to be provoked into listening to any wife (grisly or otherwise) because the world was going to consist of no one else but herself and the prophet who was all for explaining the demons' defeat along the lines of an answer he had from God but the satisfaction gathering and spreading around Louisa to poison the very air we breathed made plain that she knew otherwise –

And soon enough she was to find her speaking voice too because we overheard her cajoling him saying '*Herr Doktor Moloch Muley mein liebschen* such a saint is born in a thousand years exactly only once!' –

We knew enough German because we sang lieder –

Actually when it comes to the point Louisa was quite a famous opera singer though still very young and discovered by Richard Wagner (he is a modern composer so you will probably not have heard of him) a controversial individual who took her up and she sang in his opera though I have no other authority than herself – she toured to Melbourne and the goldfields to sing the same part and this could be checked because Mr Moloch showed us the Ballarat programme adorned with a Romantic etching of cliffs where storm clouds shot zigzag lightning at a ship carrying the lone figure of its captain wrestling with the wheel –

He confessed he had attended her performance as a celebration after registering our title to the land – which I suppose means little more than that he was starved of entertainment despite having more than enough women waiting at home to dance attendance on him – and yet how had he dared? – he must have felt a fearful dread in his soul knowing he trod forbidden ground – especially as he later recounted the story of two people who had been trampled to death when crowding up the very corridor he himself had used only minutes earlier –

Apparently Mr Moloch waylaid her at the stage door and made her feel so important she determined this was the way things were going to remain (wife or no wife – mission or no mission – wilderness or no wilderness) so please don't imagine I am failing to face the truth just because I can talk cheerfully and because I have only two eyes like anybody else –

This is not to gainsay his claim that he *is* the prophet or to deny his gift and I might have done far worse in life even without taking the adventure into account – the point is that years would pass before the truth dawned on me – those demons were sent when we needed them – and Louisa likewise –

Our whole life being such an adventure seldom anything lasted long enough to be dull – even the sturdiest trees had their tops constantly raked by the speed of earth turning on its axis to tip out a rainbow of parrot wings and cast down a puzzle of sunshine on hillsides simply alive with lizards – even on the way in through the gate wild orchids drooped to touch one's head with stale fleshy petals and in the garden shadows leapt around brandishing clubs – all sorts of surprises –

We decided to embrace the fact of those filthy huts when we saw them despite having paid good shekels – the more primitive the better we said bravely – cant I'm afraid – pure cant! –

*

I could not understand my husband and when I went to him he defeated me with a new considerateness which betrayed the fact that he did not love me – and whereas I had once been at fault for just about everything which went wrong including the weather he soon began sharing the blame among the others (I felt increasingly baffled that he had ever married me in such haste) so as usual I was caught standing still while the world rushed by! do you see where this is leading?

May I freshen your cup?

Yes well I suppose you find it inconceivable that such a trivial thing as an oblique and unfinished remark overheard in a grocer's shop might goad me to insist on quitting the coast at such risk – but this is precisely the nature of respectability because naturally one would rather die than look foolish –

As I have said – if I am to answer your questions I need to go right back to the beginning and tell you everything – which I am willing to do – so long as I can get the picture clear –

Our first experience of the huts was unforgettable banging open doors and recoiling from the filth of stale rags and putrefying kitchen waste – I swore to remember each painful detail beginning with Louisa taking it upon herself to decree 'The kitchen shall be kept clean here for I am angry against dirt!' (though I simply cannot begin to describe what we were to think later when we saw the way she washed herself!) another thing – yes she turned her attention to the two dwelling huts and selected the larger – herding us in – 'That is the place for everybodies' she decided as she turned about and marched back to stand in the doorway blocking out the day – she challenged us with her pale eyes of a brine-pickled herring which neither blinked nor flinched –

Would you believe that I still did not take her meaning until we returned to the smaller hut – the original house – boasting curtains at the window with a border of handworked lace – she declared '*Ja!*' like an explorer who comes through a desert to the shores of an inland sea 'this will be for Herr Moloch to sleep' she measured the inner of the two rooms with arms spread wide while we tried peering past her 'here his bed is' she blocked it in with a chopping motion of the hands 'here he himself washes' she blocked that in 'here he writes and here on the floor he prays' she then swung round to address the outer room where we were gathered 'here' she announced with finality 'he sits for his pleases' she blocked in another oblong article 'here the couch is where I sleep' and she concluded such arrangements satisfactorily by bringing her big sticky hands together like a gun shot –

Lady Edwina's opinion was that we should find her a suitable butcher and marry her off without delay –

For my part I can tell you I was going to murder Louisa – I was going to strangle her fat neck or poke her eyes out or pour arsenic down her throat or push her into the fire or drown her in mud or tie her to a stake for ants to eat the flesh off her bones or at very least offer her as a sacrifice to the demons to keep them occupied with good works – I was ready to forsake the chosen few and join the damned – my pregnancy gave me the courage and I thought I had strength for anything –

But I was not strong enough for what I encountered that very first evening as the sun was going down –

I had been assigned the kitchen to clean and I had broken another cup of Edwina's precious tea set – I went outside to collect my wits – well Mr Moloch having raked together some scattered leaves and twigs had set them alight – the ladies sweeping and scrubbing our quarters emerged now and again to feed the fire with bits of rubbish – I myself would soon contribute my share – the little kitchen building I might say stood separate from the rest for safety's sake because sparks from the tin chimney tended to shower the shingle roof so Digby Barnett had left a clear area of packed earth between – this was where the fire was –

The point is that I hid my crime of the broken cup – so you see how vulnerable I suddenly felt in my own home – and I was looking for a means of disposing of it – I leaned on the door frame beside a bucket of mouldy scraps and crumpled boxes for consigning to the flames when an unpleasant and familiar odour distracted me from my plans – how can I explain? – I want you to smell what I smelt – I want you to see what I saw there – out in the yard the fire burned energetically with a heap of dry branches crackling in the flames and a column of smoke with a fancy head to it blossoming in among the tall straight trees –

We were making progress –

Ann Whittaker could be heard from across the way softly singing a hymn while she sat at the table working with the sewing machine which I heard start and stop and start and stop – otherwise the place seemed suddenly deserted (I later learned that most of the Stars had gone off scouting for wood) though a couple could be seen drawing water down near a vegetable patch the Barnetts had once dug but then with their characteristic sloth let run wild – they drew small pails from the stream for emptying into a bigger container – Hester Partington and Lavinia Dudgeon – Lavinia had once been in an asylum you know – then they stooped together to lift the large pail using a pole thrust through its handle – they approached in a wobbling awkward way and even at a distance I saw the sides of the pail sheeted in slops as bright as glass – Hester with her missing nose –

Let me get my breath a moment.

This old trouble!

The obnoxious odour turned out to be common enough – the tart stench of burning cotton – cotton which Louisa Theuerkauf poked into the flames while presenting a view of her mannish back with the straps of a borrowed apron cut tightly across it –

She had a way of being busy without moving much –

You could almost imagine the whole fire spouted from her stick as she stirred a smoking mess of something white and black-edged which flopped about and practically put the show out altogether like the turning wing of a dead white eagle – she prodded it and lifted it to let a draught revive the flames – this absorption was unlike her usual composure – I found myself tantalized until I hit on the appropriate word – she was *enjoying* herself –

The scorched rumplings of stuff caught and a renewed gout of evil smoke thickened till I thought I would be sick on the spot but what was there to complain against? and nohow could I demand she stop what she was doing without speaking to her! so I made a great matter of fetching a tablecloth I had rinsed and I hung it out letting the fabric slap damp and cool against my cheek –

The water-carriers drew near – the wicked Hester calling cheerfully 'Pooh pooh pooh!' as they crossed towards me and staggered up the steps to my clean kitchen – while I took root by the clothesline with the crinkled cloth faintly steaming like an animal skin and refusing to hang square – 'The floor's not dry!' I warned as they put their pail down on the top step and propped their pole against the doorpost – leaving a flat bright world of light to tilt and rock on the water's surface they set off to tackle another chore –

'Buck up Louisa!' Hester honked over her shoulder –

I knew I was screwing up courage to face what was happening and yet I had to be prompted by hearing my husband's boots on the verandah of the private quarters (this house we are in right now) and seeing him emerge carrying a bundle of cotton clothes tucked under his arm as if he hoped he would not be recognized – when at last Louisa herself looked up she reached out to take the bundle and straightway flung it on the fire –

They stood side by side to watch it burn while the flames wilted under the extra burden and she coaxed them back with her stick –

So far they had not noticed me but now I did not care if they did and I rushed over to the dormitory to burst in on Ann who was serenely singing above the whir of the sewing machine '– for virgin souls laid up on high And ready keep her lamp at night To hail the Bridegroom drawing nigh And surely Thou at last didst come To end the sorrows of Thy bride And bear her to Thy peaceful home With Thee forever to abide' – the sewing machine was said to have cost Lady Edwina ten pounds – Ann was feeding a seam through while the needle stabbed and stabbed it at a terrible rate – she glanced up ready to scold me but then half rose with concern at what she saw – I am sure she had no intention of letting me see the full length of the new garment but on recovering her wits she gathered it swiftly and whisked the hem up off the floor –

This garment was a man's nightshirt and she reached out to take me by the hand as one might offer to protect a small child (the poor poppet) from unnecessary fears 'He needs a fresh one' she explained 'now the others are to be burnt' –

You see how good I am? you see how I can look the fact in the face? how I can tell you about even the awful things? – how the nightshirts he had worn in bed with me were treated as contaminated?

I did not show myself at dinner – nor did I move from the dormitory so that by evening when the others came in to prepare for bed I was already there – with no mind to deliver my full feelings as to the treatment I was suffering – the door was shut and padlocked on the outside by our jailer – we had to cope packed into that squalid little shanty with scant room to move among so many bodies jostling in a rustle of crinolines and yet instead of moaning against our discomfort the rest tattled and made the most of it by commenting on that woman and her surviving voice – 'The most absolute dragon!' Lady Edwina said to help me out of my difficulty – besides gossiping about all manner of interests from news of modern scientific opinion that a person might die and yet leave some isolated part of them still palpitating (such as a live heart in a dead body or a live hand by itself) to niceties of description concerning a drowned person's jellied eyes and seaweed lips or to marvels such as feet being so saturated they squidged a trail of colourless blood or to persons giving off the whiff of a bedraggled turkey in consequence of not washing –

Meanwhile hairbrushes whacked at loosened tresses and teeth glimmered and stays whipped and pretty noses grew sinister so

I was released from my knots to loll about and dream how I would one day show myself for the brilliant person I kept hidden – then I well remember Whatsaname (this wretched absentmindedness of mine! there are times when I don't know how I shall remember to take the next breath!) well anyway it doesn't matter.

Flora began coughing – did I say? –

In England and on the voyage out I had been protected from overhearing their spite because I was the butt of it but now they included me so at last I belonged.

I felt I might burst if I did not let out the secret filling me with terror and unthinkable power – well you must bear in mind what a torment it was to my conscience and my decency because I felt all the more violated for being so totally innocent and so totally helpless –

The sheer mortification.

Mr Moloch's mission was exclusively for the female sex with himself the only male on the place – so it was small wonder we had stared at those fleeing demons and especially the one hesitating long enough for me to see he was a callow ogre with a boy's mouth and sinews trembling under polished skin – wings of woody growths flapped on his back when he also fled away and I held him captured in my mind – absolutely complete – his wonderment and his runner's body –

Poor Mr Moloch never looked like that though I am sure none of us would have dared think of him in those days as poor anything –

How life changes other people and yet leaves oneself untouched (are we never prepared?) – leaves one lumbered with the useless baggage of security property etiquette etcetera – leaves one lumbered with memories – in this case with the sight of ladies bustling about though their bodices were unfastened and myself for the first time placing my boots on the rack among theirs while we agreed in concert to condemn that Jezebel who had lived the sinful life of the stage –

Beyond question we believed in Mr Moloch and his inspiration when it came to explaining the nature of the Holy Ghost yet we doubted he understood the first thing about Louisa Theuerkauf and let me tell you it hit me like a thunderclap that therefore he might understand nothing whatsoever about us either – this hurt because the plain truth was that we followed him like martyrs so even if he had wanted somebody *killed* I suppose we would have dispatched the deed without a second thought and simply to reassure him –

So I came to belong among the Hidden Stars in a dormitory smelling of undergarments when a voice shrieked 'Listen!' and we froze but Flora Gilchrist's laboured breathing drowned out anything else that might have been heard – we simply exchanged glances by the fitful lamplight –

You could picture us as fragments of Mr Moloch's single creation crowding the tiny dormitory so that the room became nothing but a box crammed with parts such as one lady's dimpled elbow joined to another lady's rounded shoulder and hands of several sizes making nearby gestures while others fluttered in the distance to touch locks of red hair or brown where someone's malicious sneer was returned and someone else's fawning eye faltered with alarm – you should imagine us sharing all eighteen legs and ten torsos and you should imagine us sprouting old creaky flaps of skin among young breasts – imagine a nest of restless passions and a rack of used air – because we were the one beast Jealousy with a bristly mole on a jaw otherwise hidden from view and two knobs of a spine where someone bent to unlace her boot unaware that her straight leg might show swollen veins behind the knee or that the person she half-obscured might be polishing a set of claws or that twin heart-hairlines side by side might suggest duplicity or the hollow at the base of a throat might echo an empty mouth above it from which sobs would soon escape –

The thrill of a bullet could hardly have been more rivetting than that sudden rigid silence revealing us as degraded by an appetite we never confessed to (so that any quality or quirk which might have saved us by recovering the identity of Lavinia or Elizabeth Eyre or Elizabeth Canning had been lost) but I believe we gloried in this bestiality because if we could not be avenged on Mr Moloch we would be avenged on ourselves -

Now will anyone kindly tell me what other choice was offered us – being only human? – and whether in my place they could have told a single soul about their agony or about the even stranger satisfaction soothing me like a caress and making my skin tingle? –

Eventually the silence in the dormitory broke into titters and a flurry of petticoats – such simpletons we were that I believe most of us assumed our laughter did less harm to Louisa and Mr Moloch than to ourselves – though there was little call to indulge in merriment apart from wounding them by forcing them to hear how cheerfully we had settled in.

I would rather you did not sit with your back to the window because I cannot see your face now the daylight is so dazzling out there.

The point being that Ann Whittaker stared and stared at me as I stood revealed in my camisole so I saw (by the way her eyes darted from side to side to check if anybody else noticed what she had noticed) that she knew my secret – the bond between us became in that instant a tremendous conspiracy and I immediately sat down – piling a loose garment on my lap –

Would I be able to speak to her of my fears and my bafflement? could she perhaps help prove I was mistaken – that the sparking flashes in my blood might be no more than symptoms of hysteria and probably a belated consequence of my recovery from the consumption? – when I imagined how peremptorily my parents (in her position) would judge and disown me I felt so grateful to Ann I lost my voice and could offer her no more than a pleading look –

Excuse me a moment.

Come to think of it one might say that our unseemly laughter had been let loose by the corrupting air of this colony where nothing matters yet if Mr Moloch had presented himself in the doorway at that moment we were so well-bred we would have affected ignorance of the least scandal despite the fact that he was shutting the woman away with him – almost certainly we would have asked whether he was comfortable in there while declaring ourselves content with the quarters we had been allotted – if necessary we would have invented pretty lies to account for our boisterousness –

He did present himself too – that was a frightful shock – him in a fury scrabbling at the padlock and then thumping the door so hard he made the wall shudder –

We kept him waiting because our cheeks were still flushed with echoes – meanwhile elbows dimpled again and white arms plunged into dry sleeves to box the starched folds out of them as we made ourselves decent – we also had to face the possibility that we were mistaken in our faith because despite his miracles Mr Moloch showed signs of being only human – perhaps he may not know what he was talking about after all – he certainly risked making a fool of himself hammering for us to invite him into our hut –

You should picture our heads butting out from neck-holes like nothing so much as plain caterpillars who have left it too late to take wing on the butterfly colours they lust for (oh I belonged among the rest already I tell you) with the dim lantern light sputtering because we had used up all the available air in our gladness that I had fallen from my high place –

How odd – I was about to be confronted by my husband as nobody with more right to courteous treatment than a washerwoman – which accounts for the ladies' gruesome interest when they caught my eye – not even my friend Lady Edwina knew the right thing to say to the terrible question of his mute presence in the door frame – when I spoke up –

What's that?

I am told I had gone pale as death and I can recall wanting the earth to swallow me but my voice came colder than Edwina's even at its coldest – just as my words were words one might have taught a foreigner rather than my own 'Kindly spare me a minute in private Mr Moloch!' –

Ann collapsed against the cupboard.

*

I wonder would I have found the courage to confess even then had not my husband led the way back to his room and ushered me in without a word? probably not – but as it was – there in the light of my own lamp which I had chosen for my personal pleasure – Louisa Theuerkauf stood up to face the intrusion so I found myself caught between the two of them and in an eruption of rash anger launched my attack 'I think you should know I am with child!' and held my breath at the enormity of what must follow though I did not dare look Mr Moloch in the face 'I have been with child for four months!' –

The lamp burned – flame steady – and my pink shade cast such gentle light I admired it as if I had never seen the thing before while Louisa simply cocked her large head to squint the more shrewdly at me and then cocked it the other way to gauge my husband's reaction – just from this I sensed that they had been in each other's arms – oh yes I knew – as certainly as if I had come upon them by surprise and seen for myself – I knew – meanwhile insects screamed into the night –

The dormitory next door stood hushed –

I had indulged my madness and I tried to read Mr Moloch's reaction in the mirror of Louisa's next move but I could make no sense of it because she came up to touch me for the very first time – a most unexpected thing – 'The child lies quiet' she reported with her possessive hand flat on my tummy 'like an old man already' – by her stiff manner of speaking I guessed her latest twist of cruelty – now she was hatching a scheme to rob me of my son at the moment of birth – to bring him up as her own because she was not content with having robbed me of my husband –

I pulled away – covered my face with my hands – poor mite with the spirit so easily knocked out of me and no premonition that one day it would be left to Louisa to restore my sense of humour my right to be angry –

I was in the grip of the unknown so no wonder I fell to my knees quite incapable of further speech while all my rehearsed explanations crowded at once into my throat and choked me so what else should I expect but that he would cast me out and disown my unnatural baby? –

Mr Moloch said 'Is this the sign we have been waiting for?' and asked it in the tenderest manner imaginable – you may guess my amazement – and he knelt beside me as he added 'the greatest miracle of all?' – he smiled his gallery of teeth –

Had I won him back at the very moment I thought I must lose him forever? and had the Devil prodded me to speak for no other reason? and did the Devil or something of the same ilk guide Louisa in her turn –

There was a moment during which her stolid face underwent the changes of a developing idea – so that at first I expected her to scream at me – next I expected her to scream at him – then she mustered her professional training as she met my defiant gaze – there was only a hint of haste – only the very slightest edge of hardness to her tone to show how she managed it as she said 'Our divine child!' – yet she knew she had betrayed herself.

I could not leave well alone!

What did I do but tempt fate by pestering my husband to continually assure me that his mind was quite at ease about the baby? I forced him to listen again and again to my fierce dogged insistence that I did not know what had happened to me –

To give him credit he became so very handsome during these harangues that I almost always broke down and begged him to tell me what it meant – or to condemn me – yet I knew when I encountered no resistance that perhaps I just wanted to have him to myself and possess him and swallow him whole – crude manners and all – don't worry about his stuck-out ears because even at our wedding he had been the radiant one while I remained confused and conceited and suffered two pimples on my chin besides a soggy nose – well at sixteen years I was nowhere near ready to address the question of whether light bounces back off objects rather than spearing through a shell of appearances to be lodged within or whether that rock at the mouth of Christ's tomb might have been blasted away by light rather than manually and clumsily rolled aside – but this is to tempt us into a discussion of theology –

Meanwhile the life of the mission took on an ecstatic turn with every routine a celebration of the coming child – we began shortly after dawn each morning sweeping and scouring the huts and tucking our bedclothes tight as boards over the mattresses – every stick of furniture had to be waxed till it squeaked and the walls whitewashed – we starched our blouses and dressed our hair while listening to extracts from the Holy Scriptures – then filled with joy we hastened into the yard for hymns before breakfast – our breath steaming in cold weather – this outdoor singing lifted us free from all the shackles of uncertainty –

Those years in England when we had not been living in the spirit came to seem more like a previous life than an earlier period of this one (which incidentally helped us have compassion for our parents' faults and let go many foolish attachments once thought to be friendships) though Lavinia who feared her family particularly welcomed the chance to hold them in disdain and forgive them with the highest motives –

We threw our energy into civilizing tasks – we were translated as Shakespeare would say – no longer the same people – we taught the prophet to read and write –

As for Mr Moloch his civilizing task was to mark out a lawn and begin pitting himself against a tangle of waist-high weeds – you know I could never bring myself to call him 'Moloch' though in moments of tenderness I have many times called him 'John' which was his given name –

I might say he'd always had a poor opinion of families – and resented mine – the one thing he dreaded most was that we might walk out so he liked to be certain we had nowhere to go – which also explains why he discouraged us from reminiscing about our childhood – and why he put a ban on letters home and confiscated any that came in –

Occasionally I found him chuckling over those letters because he could have quite a sense of humour provided you tickled the right spot and once in a while he would look up at me and pass me a page with portions snipped out – jagged scissor cuts chopping short a dozen lines here and half a dozen there – from time to time I would accept one such broken-backed object to spread it on the table recognizing the hand and seeing my own name with the end snipped off and I'd stare at a frightful hole in which calamities might have been reported (or love confessed – who knows?) while he got up from his chair scrumpling the censored bits into a ball and kneeling down to burn them in the grate – on other mail days he might burn the entire bundle –

But who is to say he was wrong or that we were in a position to judge for ourselves? in those days before Louisa made her mark we were grateful for what we received – we accepted that an offending passage may simply have seemed to us like town gossip when in fact insidious ideas were slipping past our guard disguised as comic doings of a distant cousin – or whoever – it is certainly not true that my husband did such things in secret –

We had already made our commitment to Jesus and once the baby arrived we knew this would cost us a great many more contacts – so having previously given our families into his hands we began to be relieved – if you like – that he found them guilty enough to hack their messages up and that he refused to allow us to send them our news –

For the same reason Christmas was forbidden at the mission – our once-a-year greetings had to be sent at Easter instead – this we did seated together around the big kitchen table each holding in mind a different face – and I confess we were torn – many a secret tear being mopped or dashed aside – which is odd when you consider that we had all been desperately unhappy back there – I suppose it was our perversity – rebelling against the idea that the main function of these Easter greetings anyway was to prevent some nosey relative posting us as missing persons and setting the British authorities on to our leader –

I did once receive a whole letter with absolutely nothing cut out of it – the chill of apprehension! – though curiously it was a letter full of rejoicing at Father's elevation to dean and of course I too felt gratified for him (as well as grateful to the censor) because of all things I believed being dean might bring my parents some contentment at last – and some proof that I had not permanently blighted Father's reputation.

The months and weeks ticked by in precious minutes – we were all so breathless with waiting that we never let the waiting alone – meanwhile my baby became quieter and quieter until he lay still in the womb whether because of the anxiety around me or not I can't say – imagine my terrors! – yet he was not dead because he grew steadily larger and weighed me down at a time when already I had the gravest difficulty managing my own weight – the mirror confronted me with the frail fleeting papery mask of a stranger disturbingly like I used to be and yet even more disturbingly unlike I used to be –

So – not only did Louisa claim to be the latest of Christ's converts to be raised from the dead but claimed a place in my most personal affairs by referring to the baby as '*our* divine child' – in addition to which she immediately set about removing Mr Moloch out of his room and advised him to make a bed of hay so he could sleep with the animals in the barn while she remained faithfully where she was on her selfsame couch with new duties – from then on I had the extra burden of her watchfulness –

My husband took his expulsion remarkably tamely because after all he was (and still is) a devout man well versed in the Gospels –

But none of this endeared her to me or lessened my hatred for her pallid skin and fluffed-up hair and her large gestures – nothing to lessen my hatred for her froggy fingers with suckers or her huge feet and solid ankles or the effort she made to control her cold assessing stare and private little smiles or her manner of superior simplicity which one could easily call the vast spaciousness of the woman's ignorance – whereas Muley Moloch welcomed his discomfort which seemed to rouse his spirits until he positively revelled in humiliation and waxed so gloriously eloquent that I never entertained the least suspicion of his sincerity in caring for me and the child.

I was installed in comfort and the worst guilts were behind me – like those frightful weeks which had culminated in the shipwreck – I was one of the rare ones to recover from the consumption – indeed the only one among those who caught it at our mission – Dr von Lossberg tells me this was because I had the luck to have contracted it when I was young – but my husband has lately begun citing my recovery as another of his quiet miracles – I don't know – and whatever anyone says now I had mixed feelings then – suffering the sharpest anxiety that my pregnancy could still be used against me and that my good fortune could end in punishment – suffering the insidious fears of an invaded body anonymously possessed – who had done this? who? who? – suffering because I did not know and because I had no idea where to look for the answer – being left with nothing but a constant smothered scream of disgust – the wreckage of my trust – a frantic fruitless effort to grasp at thin air – although well on my way to recovery from the illness and lying in state in the most private of sanctuaries gazing up at the moon as I had once gazed so long ago when Dora lay likewise awake on the next bed I was the prisoner of self-interrogation – in a ferment of perpetual wariness about the least noise – the place was full of practised eavesdroppers who might be able to read thoughts by now –

This was my condition when the Voice spoke to me!

I should explain that I am forever stopping in the middle of doing something to listen inwardly because I feel an essential word about to come – but this was different –

Don't ask what the Voice sounded like because although it has since visited me many times this is a question I cannot answer to my own satisfaction except to say that it speaks without actual words (I have to find words for it afterwards) – as to the tone of what I hear it is a kind of warmth – certainly less than the communications Mr Moloch used to have when he told us God came to him as a well-set-up man with the finest manners imaginable and friendly gestures –

My Voice gave no messages suggesting those might be the last days of Earth nor calls to bind Satan – it just reassured me with feeling 'You may depend upon it that the Lord is coming!' while moonlight around my pillow broke into the most beautiful scene of a hundred fluttering angels' wings – the softest caress of something joyful –

Next morning Louisa came and sat on my mattress to confide in me – she *had* entertained the ambition of a spiritual marriage with my husband believing he gave her good warrant – but now she repented because during the night she had been shown how wicked this was in the event of my carrying the miraculous infant and so forth –

Instead of slapping her face soundly I admit I softened as an exhausted child aching to be cradled in somebody's arms – at least to discover what that would be like –

Louisa talked until she brought herself to confess that she first came to dedicate her life because she had never been able to contemplate allowing any man the least liberty – then her quest began for a Husband of the Soul who would be no more to her carnally speaking than a being from another world if such a thing might be imagined –

It would appear that the Almighty intended preserving her purity for my service and support –

But this was not what dazzled me with amazement –

What dazzled me and confused me was how painlessly the crisis resolved itself – how readily my dear husband had heard me without once doubting my word though the matter of it was strange indeed – I arose feeling wonderfully refreshed and determined upon universal forgiveness when I glimpsed a fleeting dark body emerge from our larder to vanish in the jungle – I nearly cried out but caught myself in time to realize that because of what the Voice told me I must take special care of the local demons who were neither more nor less than lost souls – God delights in forgiveness –

I dreamed that I myself might run away! – though naturally I told no one – not even my dearest Ann who behaved like a cross but loving mother to me –

'Scholars are writing how Saint Joseph made eighty when Jesus was born' Louisa reminded me – also that Joseph is not mentioned as being present for the actual delivery of the Christ child in either Gospel dealing with the virgin birth 'however' she added significantly 'Mary was not lonely by herself already – no – because she had with her a lady – yes – a lady she called her cousin' –

Louisa was so filled with jubilation she grew inexhaustible – she would declare God's glory among the heathen she would reproach and scorn whosoever deserved to be scorned she would rejoice as a bride rejoiceth over a bridegroom and set up the tabernacle of Moloch – the tabernacle of witness in the wilderness as required in the Acts of the Apostles – with her own hands she must erect the chapel immediately which she would consecrate to our coming child –

No one knew how to plan a building but Elizabeth Eyre was willing to try (I might say she drew so beautifully her uncle had once sent her drawings for publication to a firm in the Haymarket) and produced a sketch for Gordon Pringle to check – the elder Gordon Pringle of Cuttajo who had already approached Mr Moloch to ask whether we allowed new people to join the mission or attend our services – because accepting neighbourly advice on the matter of the chapel was one way of rebuffing the man without offence – allowing him to have some part in putting up the building he was to be excluded from and at the same time securing help at less than the ten shillings a day being asked by workmen.

Oh you may laugh young Arrell but isn't this exactly the kind of thing going on all around us now with talk of Federation – insisting on boundaries?

The chapel was built and the prophet named it the Ladies' Chapel because he had told us we must keep the real dedication secret in case some Herod might have the boy murdered (some Sir Hercules Robinson or who you will – though come to think of it Sir Hercules was not yet in power was he?) –

The hardest thing over the years would be to keep the secret from the boy himself to give him a chance of growing without vanity and being open to learning his father's trade while living the same simple life Jesus had lived – but more of this in due course –

Despite Ann's forebodings we borrowed some convicts for the job of stripping bark slabs from the trees – each sheet had to be soaked and flattened ready for nailing to the frame – you seldom see a job done that way these days – the same for the roof except that we also had to make a grid of lashed poles for laying on top to save it being blown off –

The convict builders protested against the lack of a window

on the grounds of civilized precedent but Mr Pringle said not a word – he knew our services were private now – so the chapel was completed and once the door closed we were left with only a frail net of light glancing in through the cracks and joins above and around us which allowed us each to make out other praying silhouettes –

That was the coldest place in winter –

You may imagine us in our simple clothes – having long since given up fine fabrics – emerging from the dormitory in pairs to walk across the yard holding our breath as if about to plunge into cold water – our fingers made soft and insensitive by gloves clutched tiny Bibles with bone covers and brass hasps – as we filed in to establish our solitude among others in solitude while the door swung to behind us and Muley Moloch's shape trod to the front where he began preaching one of those fierce inspired sermons beginning with 'Except ye see signs and wonders ye will not believe' or with 'Ye shall be witness unto me even unto the uttermost part of the earth and so forth' with the words flashing like drawn swords to cleave us asunder – after which we would hasten to the table for our morsel of bread and our sip of wine – kneeling while the prophet performed the ceremony – then returning to our pews with glad hearts knowing that once outside we would burst into song with 'What if death my sleep invade Shall I be of death afraid? Whilst encircled by Thine arm Death may strike but cannot harm!'

I see your point but when I say we knelt in seclusion this was a seclusion made possible by knowing we knelt *together* because surely society is necessary to seclusion if the seclusion is to be neither desolate nor threatening? and since many of us were at one stage or another of the illness we were grateful to conceal the difficulty we had breathing – not to mention the chance of concealing our sunken looks –

Although we sang hymns all day we never sang in chapel – the special appeal of chapel was the silence enveloping us once the prophet had spoken – the healing tranquillity of a sanctuary from punishments – which lasted well after Mr Moloch walked back to the door and out – leaving us with the purity of being women among women.

How can I hope to explain what this meant?

You are a man so perhaps you are not aware of the world being jealously possessed by men or that regardless of how indulgent a man may be he won't let go once he has some little bit of it in his fist and feels he has the right to mock or revile anything not yet in his control.

I mentioned a slim demon flitting away from our pantry and I ought to have added that such raids became common – during our first few months here we often saw these lost souls clustered at the verge of the clearing to mock and laugh us to scorn while we directed the borrowed convict labourers to beat back the forest and dig a new vegetable garden (it was considered especially humorous for one of the ladies to give an order to a man and for him to obey) but eventually the audience shrank and took to shuffling on the spot and retreated under giant ferns – which we accepted as a sign of growing respect until Lady Edwina slapped her thigh and declared that they were able to smell the sickness raging among us –

When coughing spread until virtually the whole mission began to weaken the demons stayed away altogether 'They've a nose for death' Edwina confirmed 'and it terrifies the poor lost creatures' – tragedies kept happening which were not my doing at all because I was never inclined towards vengefulness and was as much left gasping at the shock as anybody –

Once we finished the chapel the next big job was to dig a freshwater well but by then the first of the convicts had fallen ill too and their owners took them back for fear they might all be lost if they remained – and in any case we had embraced the opportunity to do labouring work during the day which was a strange liberty – then we sat round in the evening discussing my pregnancy which some of our maiden ladies found fascinatingly distasteful – being ignorant of whether matters were progressing satisfactorily (you may include me also) – indeed had it not been for Martha Sparrow with her experience I believe these discussions would have driven me to a constant panic.

The first sign of life in the womb is a flutter so gentle you think perhaps you might have a touch of wind but then in a flash of awe you recognize the spark of creation and come to hear each little tremor as a word spoken in the blood – Saint John one one – In the beginning was the Word and so forth –

You cannot imagine how far skin will stretch nor how huge a baby feels when you are carrying it around inside – just to lie on one's back becomes desperately uncomfortable in the late stages and throughout the night one is driven to shift from the right to the left side – using both hands clasped around this other life to support it – and by then the flutter has developed to a tyranny of activity so that sleep is impossible while the unseen baby kicks you and sends lightning bolts along your nerves – nausea sets in with the horror of outrage that you are host to a parasite with a will of its own who drains you of strength till you are tortured by cramps and your back aches – not to mention waterbrash rising like acid in your throat each time the heartburn takes your breath away until you begin twisting and turning to escape the inescapable – just to draw breath – just for an instant to throw off the suffocator's pillow – that's the truth –

The pregnant woman also squirms and turns in her heart to find some way of staying as she was but she is bound to be changed because at the deepest level of mystery the new life has already made a monster of her pride (oh yes) – you've no idea – and even the fear you experience can become a weapon for making your husband feel ever more hopelessly excluded from the female power over life –

Meanwhile you suffer humiliating appetites – you have a craving to eat earth and no matter how guiltily you go about digging with your bare hands numb and tingling somebody is sure to catch you at it –

Even so in my case I flourished because I am an optimist and because the more often I am cast down the more surely I raise myself up again –

So my baby growing huge and alien in the womb was a source of power as well as the cause of acute anxiety even while he hooked his little feet round my ribs to give me terrible twinges and I watched one after another of our ladies register creeps at placing her palm there to feel how wilful he was and how independent of me long before he was actually born – not to mention the nauseous business of breasts weeping or the many times I needed to rinse my garments to save others the embarrassment of knowing about my bodily changes –

Where could I turn for advice? –

Regardless of what anyone says pregnancy is tedious and exhausting – only lightened by occasional bursts of inner radiance (but maybe this was because mine was a special child so for others you ought perhaps to discount the radiance) and he *was* a special child –

Louisa managed the whole affair – from caring for my comfort to telling the prophet how he ought to adjust his daily routines and prepare for the role soon to be entrusted to him – he never opposed her which made me suspicious because I knew how hotheaded he could be especially when touched on the raw by any suggestion that lack of education left him less fit to decide what was proper or where wisdom lay – but how about me? – was I supposed to forget the nightshirts she had burnt because they had been contaminated by contact with me?

You see how involved things were and why I grew so very angry?

Meanwhile more ladies fell ill and I was kept from seeing them because the child had to be protected – so for a month I saw only Louisa and Mr Moloch (not even Ann was allowed near though she seemed mercifully immune to consumption) – during this time Elizabeth Eyre who could sing a tenor line down to E and was commonly supposed to have been born without a womb died unexpectedly and then they told me that dear Flora was finally in extremity –

There is no doubt Flora had been a trial to me from the outset when she became the first disciple and right till the end refused to give up her function of converting Mr Moloch's passing remarks into articles of dogma –

What made the news of Flora and Elizabeth worse was a conversation I overheard through my open window.

Lack of breath again.

The other Elizabeth – Elizabeth Canning – and Charlotte were telling Hester Partington how the prophet had explained that it is the animal within us which gets out of control and how Flora had responded by whispering 'We want nothing – from anyone' – when Hester cut them short by snuffling that the old system should be brought back because someone must be to *blame* for spreading the illness which could not be passed off simply as contagious – it must be faced for what it was and the guilty person punished – even if that guilty person was in a delicate condition! –

Who else could she have meant?

I knew exactly what the punishments would be – picturing myself being once more thrown to the floor for my hair to be pulled – the fear I felt taught me how much I loved my baby because this was a new fear drenching me in coldness and quite unlike the routine trembling I knew from previously falling short of God's standard – the difference was that it roused ferocity in me now – such that I knew I would not be hit without hitting back in defence of my little one – she had made a grave mistake – she was not dealing with the same Catherine Byrne she had so summarily dealt with in times gone by – and yet the fear still gnawed away at me – my first defence must be to defy the confessional itself –

What a tremendous thing! – leading even to the notion of renouncing rules altogether –

Hester went on to confirm that my child must indeed be a divine child – that is to say 'wholly mysterious' – but she questioned whether due weight had been given to Satan's powers or Satan's habit of modelling his wickedness on God's finest flights –

When my friend Lotte interrupted to whisper that they might be overheard and cause distress I wished I had not so often been sarcastic to her – nevertheless Hester knew what she was about and kept them where they were until she had delivered her poison to the last drop – wishing she could be quite *quite* sure the baby was the promised Immanuel and not a changeling who would bring ruin upon the world and confusion among the faithful –

I heaved myself up in bed and although I could not catch them at it I did see into the hut across the yard – a curtain billowed from the open window to bloom with light – such a pregnant fullness and yet so elegant – I was fascinated by that curtain as a beautiful chance event until the instant when it curled slanted and slipped to one side before puffing out again – an instant long enough for my eye to photograph two figures embracing – but not long enough to see who they were –

In a flash the truth inspired me to whisper out loud 'So we are in Purgatory!' with Good clearly on one hand and Evil on the other – with the possibility of ascending directly to Heaven a mere step away from plunging into the bottomless abyss –

The next morning as soon as Louisa had told me they planned to bury Elizabeth Eyre just up there – you see the clearing on that hillside? – a tremendous hubbub broke out in the forest and even the prison of my comfortable little room resounded to the multitude of bellbirds and the screech of crickets –

I was forbidden to attend – what did this mean? –

The din lasted until they had carried the body to the chosen site and planted another pepperina tree to absorb the germs so that the chipping of pickaxes could scarcely be heard from here – nor the scrape of shovels – then mounting above this storm of little sounds came a remote pure voice rising from syllable to syllable holding the vowels until sometimes they rang out and at other times sank before gathering strength again or sinking yet further from a mere expression of human grief to an impersonal lament for the fleeting joys of this world fading to a resignation so profound I wept despite the cruelty swelling my heart because having feared Elizabeth Erye's unnatural interest in me I rejoiced at being rid of her – and now this melody pierced my heart with knowledge that in death souls may be united –

So music brought me to face my guilt after all and might have tortured my conscience had not Louisa's elegy been echoed by a soft humming chant from among the trees where I saw (and you may be sure I *did* reach the window this time despite my lumpish condition) a dozen demons in full animal splendour of feathers and tall pointed hats made of sticks –

They were briefly there and soon gone but it was evident to me that they knew more about us than we had ever believed possible –

I remained leaning on the rough sill right there – like this – staring out among the tree trunks when a whole tribe of women appeared before me encouraging me with smiles and open hands in no way like demons' hands and there was little doubt they called to me personally because the rest of the Hidden Stars were busy burying the dead – soft gentle female shapes partly naked and partly dressed in left-off oddments they had had from the townsfolk I suppose – how could I be angry at their shamelessness especially as I marvelled (when they walked into a fresh clearing of sunlight) at how the glory of the Lord shone round about them – and saw by their eyes that they were afraid –

Yet the boldest of these females persisted – even coming right up to the wall – and she reached for my fingers on the sill – 'If only you knew how terrified I am' I thought 'of Hester!' warm soft fingers touched mine 'how terrified I am of carrying Satan's changeling instead of God's child!' the creature's gesture was so tentative I knew the Lord God could mean no harm to her or her tribe so I said 'I bring you tidings of great joy which shall be to all people' – because these were not demons – they deserved as much pity as ourselves – and when they called me to the door to stroke my arms and lead me away from that place of misery – out where there were no paths nor any sign which the memory might catch hold of as a guide for finding one's way back – I thought I might go –

Though I hesitated – yes hesitated in the doorway – while staring beyond them seeing again that vivid scene of Louisa tending a fire in the yard – of my husband looking on and seeming not to notice the foul smouldering smoke waft round him – of her lifting a shrivelled black skin of a thing from the flames and holding it on the end of her stick while she let out the only laugh we heard from her that month – and a pail full of water as treacherous as mercury left standing on the kitchen verandah for the dazzling blob of light reflected from its surface to waver in the lens of tears at the corner of my eye –

I scarcely knew which way to turn –

Anguished memories flooded my mind with a chaotic jumble of wounding little occasions – I felt as if shattered glass crunched in my hips so although I had wanted to take my boots off and throw them away because Mr Moloch made them for me I could not face the pain of bending down to undo the laces – I wanted him there to see me scratch my cheeks where his kisses were stored – I would willingly have washed my fingers in acid because they knew the feel of him and poked out my eyes for the way they had looked at him just as I would have welcomed devils gnawing my belly until there was nothing left but a hollow of torn meat and would have wanted my skin stripped off with a surgeon's care to be scoured by a man with a steel comb in his hairy hand and immersed next in warm infusions of dog droppings to violate every pore then primed in an oil barrel before being hauled out for stretching drying and buffing so a perfect stranger's finger and thumb might acknowledge that I had my price at least as an article of commerce –

The thin skin of a sentimentalist –

The mourners on the hill surrounded Hester who was doubled up and seemed utterly broken – I know I generally describe her as quite awful really yet sometimes she could be nice and this moment I ought to have been able to feel sympathy but I could not while my own troubles outweighed even death – so I stared at those bonnets and clustered backs gathered around Elizabeth Eyre's grave – until my staring caused Lavinia (I can see her with her hair flatly braided and coiled behind) to turn and look down my way – meeting my eagle eye – but I was too angry to offer any other gesture before I joined the visitors and set out across the yard unable to feel the ground beneath my feet so perhaps I had learnt Mr Moloch's gift of flight with the slanted morning lifting me along –

There had been no need to come to a decision because I recognized those few seconds as though I knew them already but I didn't give a hoot about poor Flora (the only person apart from Ann never to join in punishing me) who I had been told was in extremity and who had not gone to the burying but lay looking out through the dormitory door watching me accept the firm dark hands of my guides –

I remember a flicker of dappled leaf shade across my shoulders – and as I look back on her now Flora's mouth is twisted with anguish –

I heard Lavinia wail from up at the gravesite and by her tone I knew she was letting go and that when she collected herself sufficiently to blubber a garbled alarm (the dear soft creature) such as 'Getting wild – gate – singing – no – free away – ' Mr Moloch would bit by bit assemble it correctly as a warning that I was gone – meanwhile I had precious minutes to make my escape – I was out of the clearing and still walking – past the garden then across the footbridge and up the ridge beyond the creek –

We reached a place deep in the forest where little crimson birds darted through the gloom among fern-trees – and furry animals took refuge in the high branches of the upper tier despite the reptiles there – how can I describe the effect? – this was – this was a place of fungus and juicy undergrowth where sap burgeoned amazing crowns of heart-shaped leaves and fan-shaped leaves – whip leaves and spade leaves – as well as an uncanny creeper with masses of tangled stems and tendrils but no leaves at all –

Here the women stopped to touch me and marvel at my skin and admire my growing child and trace the smooth shape of my fingernails – all of which they checked in the profoundest silence – meeting each other's eyes but never mine – then they harvested berries for me which I dared not taste for fear of poison especially on the baby's behalf – whispers agitated the forest and there came a sudden scurrying of small animals running away from us in every direction – whether the women at that point understood something I did not or whether they simply despaired of pleasing me I cannot say – but all at once they cried out a single word and ran through the undergrowth – I watched their dark shoulders bobbing and the pale soles of their feet –

They absolutely vanished –

I was alone in a place I had not seen before – I never felt so far from the gardens of the Hall or Miss Honeywood's voice cooing at her peacocks or the smell of new leather harnesses in the judge's stables – I began coughing but managed to keep it smothered – helped by the curiously sweet water I scooped from a basin in the rocks – several drips pattered back setting rings fleeing across the still surface – it was then that I heard an approaching wind among treetops and birds chancing a few calls while I imagined the soil being packed in around Elizabeth Eyre's corpse and heaped on top of her – I thought the air smelt of my own approaching death even though I felt full of vigour – perhaps because such peace would be exactly the peace one ought to embrace ready for the final surrender –

I had no fear of it – I only marvelled at the puzzle of how my baby was to survive – as the Chosen of God *must* survive – supposing it was not a changeling –

The forest had never been so shot through with enormous beams of light nor had the trees ever been so like iron or the sense of strangeness so strange surrounding my death which would be very unlike the maelstrom of icy water from which Mr

Moloch saved Louisa Theuerkauf when she appeared as unimportant as a torn rag thrown against the rocks in a daydream –

People used to say that to decide to die – and to make it happen simply by deciding – was the only thing beyond the power of the mind but I refused to believe this because I had discovered the frightful truth that what I felt for Muley Moloch was as near to love as anything I knew and that there was no other reason why I found myself driven to trail after those native women or let them abandon me.

Let me explain a different person inside me.

I was always puzzled that I so seldom wanted what other people wanted – not interested in money or possessions or marriage (to be frank) or even happiness – I was like a creature of some rare species without any likelihood of meeting my soul's companion – which was why I felt so shaken when I read Mr Howitt's account of his search for poor Burke and Wills when lost beyond Mount Hopeless he came upon the hoof marks of a horse! did you ever read his story? and then he saw the horse straying across that biblical wilderness – a lone beast appearing as fabulous there as a unicorn in your garden and the truly amazing fact was that this horse had not survived from Mr Burke's expedition after all because it turned out to have belonged to Charles Sturt sixteen years before! just to think of it makes my face seize up as hard as a mask even now – this lonely creature watching flocks of birds go by when the frost came to the desert and watching them flee back when the summer returned again and again the passage of so many birds while the lost horse wandered over a desert of Australian stones never setting eyes on another of its own kind –

I dared to consider myself a freak of sorts – so I had less difficulty believing I carried God's child than most women would have faced – for the same reason I cannot say I felt any overwhelming pride – just fear because such intimacy involved me too closely with the source of power – and worse fear if it was not God's –

I know I am always taken for the one with no special skills

who will fit in with what is needed – whether as a third player to read through Haydn's London trios or to roll out the pastry while others spice the rabbits and quarter them for baking *en croute* you know or to hold strips of padding straight while the experts begin tacking a length of quilting – or even such humble and essential jobs as checking that the outdoor oven never drops below baking heat –

And yet perhaps I do have special skills which are of a kind beyond the simple uses of housekeeping or the democratic arts – I feel a certain thrusting in me – some unnamed talent ready to rise from the dark and claim recognition – so there is another Catherine Byrne by no means content to remain mute or unnamed.

You remember I told you about Judge Honeywood and what happened as soon as he announced my engagement? well when I left the Hall with my parents we were accompanied down the lane by Major McDonald which put a constraint on us so by the time we squeezed out the courtesy of wishing that empty old soldier goodbye and took our separate way my father was ready to explode with fury 'A common bootmaker's wife! is this what you are to be Miss? and how did that stuffed dummy – in his silly wig? – be damned to him! – how did he dare – senile as he is?' –

My poor mother offered moderate explanations but he rounded on her 'There is no question Mrs Byrne! none! so kindly do not raise your eyes at me!' his face went mauve and bloodless which I associated with frightful things because once before when this happened he had slapped my face so hard I thought my jaw was broken – the point being that despite his show of agitations and convulsions while he stamped along the lane between hedgerows I still managed to amaze us all by speaking up 'If Judge Honeywood wishes to test your loyalty because he wants to be sure of getting the best man for the living at Saint Philip's – four hundred pounds a year Uncle Herbert says – then I do not think the price too high' –

To this very adult speech I added something much more in character and not at all sarcastic 'Why should I value myself so greatly?' –

My father boggled at being accused of selling me for the lovely old church with its square tower and melodious bells – but it was unreasonable to expect him to understand that I perfectly accepted his right – nor could he possibly know how determined I was that neither he nor anyone else would prevent me marrying a suitor who could fly –

Why did I begin on this old story?

The point is that I was out in the forest where the native women who had been leading me ran away in fright.

Once I begin to live it all again I can recollect every detail – my desperate state of not knowing whether I was the most blessed of the Faithful or the most damned – this confusion was further complicated by the vivid past invading the present with something hauntingly similar having happened a long time earlier –

I was lost once as a child in the woods near Stroud – it made a terrible mark on me because although I always said I wasn't afraid of anything I *was* afraid of being lost in the woods again – and I was afraid of my father –

It all flooded back when I came to my senses and realized the women who had brought me to this lonely place would not return and that I was a long way out of earshot of the mission – every detail is fixed in mind as fresh as if it were yesterday – moss on the wet rocks where I sit staring into a bubbling stream – fascinated by a sheet of light continuously rippling over hundreds of polished pebbles – engrossed – I jump when a dozen black parrots flap above me shrieking – parrots unsettle me because I still think of them as belonging in cages – I don't really *like* free parrots come to think of it – at least not in the way I like free cuckoos – a cuckoo *has* to be free if you see what I mean otherwise it cannot be understood for what it is – and I understand how delightful robins are in winter or swallows in summer – but I don't understand flocks of parrots going wherever they please – any more than they understand the poor little 'she' or what the flapping of her skirt might mean or her shooing hands now she has stood up to climb the bank of the stream –

She does not understand herself because the person *she* sees in her mind's eye is still a child – a bright vulnerable child reduced to a little bag of misery as she strays among the beech trees when no one comes to save her although I have been calling out and sobbing a long time – until I find a path and escape from the dark woods with their green grass to the back fence of a row of houses until I discover a gate which is known to me and push it open and wail for the washerwoman –

The washerwoman has yellow hair in spite of being older than anybody – she wears it in a pile instead of having a neat parting and rolled plaits – I am glad to see this pile of hair and to see her watching me across her adjustable mangle which she is proud to own because how many other washerwomen have worked hard enough to save for such a luxury?

She has an unhappy smell of yellow soap –

Her eyes are too tired for surprise though she speaks to me in the voice of a person who has never moved from her Gloucestershire hamlet asking after *your dear papa* and *your dear mama* (yet I am also this desperate 'she' scrambling over Australian rocks and still lost on the underside of the world where vines snag her clothes and fallen logs trip her as she clambers up the bank from a stream among tussocks slimy and lank – clutching at her tummy for the baby's sake) –

I wish the washerwoman could be my grandmother because when I tell her about the woods I notice her eyes are not too tired for pain and I feel like a different person who is resting her face against a moss-grown tree trunk in the forgotten world of an ancient gully –

Without quite knowing whether it is a question of escaping or returning an urgency drives her on – even as she slips and falls to her knees – which might mean she can never be a mother now (and that her mother – even if still alive – will never be a grandmother either) –

Parrots scream –

The washerwoman pushes both sleeves up to the elbow to show large arms with skin softened like chamois from a lifetime of oily soap and her hands are strong as she heaves a hefty flat-iron off the stove to bang it along the petticoat spread on her board 'You must never get your iron caught in the purfling' she explains and points out a lace trim 'if I was to tear Mrs Byrne's purfling she might send her work to some other person mightn't she?'

Yes I believe my mother might though I cannot be sure because I don't know my mother too well which is her own fault since she is always so compliant that she takes on the expression of whoever talks to her with the result that she has no expressions of her own unless she is alone and then – as I know from coming upon her at the mirror – she is a bottle full of anger –

'You had any number of caps like this when you was a tiny babe' the washerwoman assures me – picking a baby's bonnet from the pile – her ravaged but plentiful hair flops in the heat of the stove – her kitchen a shimmer of steam from a perpetual kettle on the hob mingled with the smoky vapours of starch – I decide this is my favourite place in all the world –

I will have to wait many years till my mother (grown so oppressed by the invisible bars imprisoning her that she cannot stand this extra bar being set in place by her daughter who might one day run off with a Jew or elope with a bounder) snaps at me 'Don't call her Mrs Boulton! she is your grandmama!' so I declare I – for my part – shall never be anybody's grandmama and then no one can wound me by calling me Mrs Boulton or Mrs Anything for that matter –

This is the scene in her mind's eye as the stumbling young woman clutches her tummy and talks to herself saying there are other women at the mission without a single Boulton among them so why feel ashamed? –

My grandmother's grief is already hard as a stone – I chatter while she irons underwear ready for other people to put on next to their skin – are there poisons which can penetrate the skin? I wonder – and do any of them look like starch?

I have brown hair though I do not consider it as fine as my mother's even though she is too nice to say so and in any case she cannot spare the energy to look at anyone while her husband goes on gazing into space to keep the terrible things in his mind from showing – though in my case now I am safely at home with my unhappiness again I watch him for no other reason than because I want to see what he will do next –

The young woman in the gully is not yet home –

What he does is to come out of his secrecy with a deadly quiet question 'Who let off the mousetrap in the larder?' while his nose is pinched white around the nostrils and otherwise his face goes a ghastly mauve colour 'I did' some girl defies him from behind my cup of warm milk with her unsatisfactory hair already brushed and braided ready for bed – and she remembers why it is that she ran away into the woods in the first place –

'Are you starved in this house?' he storms suddenly and comes at her fighting his way through the air to reach her – his black coat opens out like a scarecrow's coat – 'Do you need to steal the mouse's share of cheese?'

She wants to laugh which would be more dreadful than anything else and even the maid hurries out into the scullery to begin clattering dishes because he has his hand ready to strike – but this child won't say she did not eat the mouse's cheese nor will she tell of her fright when the machine (snapping shut on a knife she poked at it) might have broken her fingers – on and on he storms 'Did you not hear your mother say the mouse got into her cold cottage pie last night?'

'The mouse is God's mouse' this girl shouts to her own alarm –

And now she is in a delirium and cannot disentangle the past and the present – she is on her knees with her skirt soiled and the great trees are swimming upwards around her – she crawls and she remembers how a little old man in a Captain Cook wig pointed one toe like Carlotta Grisi expecting the paltry gewgaw of a buckle to dazzle such a father as hers.

*

Ambition is a curious urge don't you agree? being as much as to say if I do not surrender my place in life to struggle for a different place (some other person's place) then I will not quite fully live –

I am sure my parents never guessed how soon Mr Moloch would show himself as curiously ordinary considering my expectation of daily miracles and ourselves being swept along by crowds of adoring disciples – long before we set sail I believe I knew the worst though nothing could have persuaded me to admit it – then at Chipping Sodbury the oddest little mischance happened – we were lodging at the Red Lion where I woke in the dark to find my arm dead under my new husband's weight – the dead arm a terrifying object which I pulled free – but I could do nothing with it nor feel anything nor stop the thing flopping as an awful helpless weight on my chest – yet although I was silently sobbing with panic I dared not wake him (isn't this the rummest thing of all?) until by chafing kneading smacking I induced the first stab and tingle of blood to reach beyond the elbow and down into my forearm where the flesh felt wafered like leaves wrapped around bone and until finally the first cold filaments of pain crept into my fingers – only then did I bring myself to shake his shoulder to wake him and let out the sobs I had been containing 'You only dreamt it' he said –

So much for Chipping Sodbury –

The following morning we fled to Bristol (at the time I thought we flew but we fled) and those among our ladies who could truly be called disciples met us there – Mr Moloch soothed my outrage against any who chose not to come by promising that we should find infinite reserves of genteel English people on the way over – at sixteen I was not inclined to argue on an issue which went far beyond whether a mouse (or an Indian) could be said to be God's own – and he assured me the prospective disciples would include 'ladies who will not tolerate Baal or the Jesuits!'

You know he never was able to fly for me a second time – though he did try now and again if the ambition took hold of him – which is why his miracle with Louisa became such a turning-point and why he could not forgive me – but to be fair he has a heart even if he is not very clever so he never used our unhappiness to denounce me – the things that went wrong between us were never the subject of confessions – I have to say this for him.

Where was I with my story?

As I've explained – I can call every detail to mind – fresh as it was when I lived it for the first time – in fact it dogs me and won't leave me in peace – the terror of being lost – and myself as a pregnant young woman seeming quite separate from me as the observing intelligence – she in a panic and I calm – panting in the heat she is out of the gully at last! and being helped again by the native creatures who have returned to support her because they seem to know everything and welcome her again though some appear afraid to reach out or touch or offer her food while they chatter among themselves shyly covering their faces – she sees kind eyes as well as fearful eyes – indeed more kindness than any stranger has shown for a long time so she joins the laughter when they laugh – later she walks with them into the bush among the inevitable horse skeletons of progress and the panic among small furry animals – feeling confident of their companionship until cunning night begins seeping out of crannies – hollows deep in moss are already full cups of night – night lifts each scale of bark on the trees and cradles each petal with its tender darkness which stains the very air she must take into her body if she is to live – filled with dark air she suffers neither hunger nor thirst – she gives back the darkness to the night sky as a single word of discovery 'Women!' – realizing too late that this one foreign sound might be enough to frighten them away forever.

You can try doing without breath if you like and then you'll know how I felt.

She was a fool to believe she could seek a new place in life without giving up the situation she already had among her kind – a fool to believe she could deny such luxuries as the leisure for watching clouds pass or the leisure for savouring cups of tea – a fool for believing that however far one travels one can remain the same – a fool for thinking the reason why Mr Moloch had not argued against her and insisted on establishing his haven for the reborn Christ in England was that he knew what he was doing –

There among the rocks in the closing gloom she has spoken too soon and undone what she did and once again lost those whom she depended on –

She talks to herself where she has fallen on her back – she lies in great discomfort while the last dim shreds of light tear free from the high branches and she hears what ravenous interest her presence is creating among the swarms of insects that whine around her –

She asks a whole lot of questions out loud such as had Flora deceived her all this time? had dear Ann felt an anguish of her own when first learning that the nightshirts were to be burnt and accepting the commission to replace them? had Lady Edwina with her locked hip and her assurances that she believed the coming child to be God's own Son deceived her for some deeper cause than loyalty? –

'So what we have instead of life' she says aloud to herself in the language which can not belong to that place 'is mere poetry' –

Do you see that both pictures have come together Sergeant Arrell? the sad little waif who stumbled out of the Gloucestershire woods has become the sad little waif spreadeagled on foreign soil? and that she finds she feels more defiantly alive the closer the risk of death approaches in this childlike world crammed with moonlit posies of leaves on giant stems (would the forest seem so big if she were not so small?) yet she likes it here and she refuses to go on trying so hard to understand her husband because the effort diminishes her and magnifies him.

Enough of the husband –

As for her father – forget about that mouse! just remember him striking her terribly hard even when they were already out in the street which made matters worse – his glove did not cushion the bright edges of pain and she smelled a swish of leather in the air –

So she has fallen – she is alone – she dreams of walking home to Mrs Boulton's mission and revenging herself by smashing down the Hidden Stars' routines for the terrible world to flood in and do its work – yet an insurrection of contentment already seeps along her limbs – the baby kicks – setting a sweetness sweeter than honeysuckle whispering through the newly darkening and shadowy night (has she drifted into sleep or is this an hallucination?) the dream wants her to eat and drink and to tie her laces again because now she is no longer the child who failed to learn how – also to struggle up on her feet and for this purpose the dream shakes its grizzled beard at her and bows its trembling neglect of hair while listening at her chest to hear if her heart still beats and then listening separately for the baby's heart –

The women went a while ago – she is alone with the dream –

Although he smells like a wood moth he remembers his manners and only gingerly touches her face with an enquiry and his fingers test only one sample of her hair which he appears to find unsatisfactory – does he know that her mother's hair is more beautiful? – her own courage astonishes her when she finds her voice which was lost on the word 'women' and calmly explains to the dream that he is merely a dream though she must thank him for being a dream at all – while his eye buds a single tear too gummy to fall and too fluid to be withdrawn.

Well do you see her as she struggles up at last and accepts his hand? she finds the going easier for his help so she is grateful and she wants to share with him the text from Mr Moloch's last sermon 'A life for a life – an eye for an eye – a tooth for a tooth – a foot for a foot – a hand for a hand – a wound for a wound – a bruise for a bruise!' she stops in horror –

The dream stops beside her but lets go of her hand while the childlike forest blooms moonshine and night birds sing around her head inside which she is thinking that a life for a life was precisely what Mr Moloch had had of her – as well as adding together Lavinia's missing breast and Charlotte's missing ear besides her own missing toe and so forth –

With this she pushes the dream away and faces him in the full shock of coming to her senses – she recognizes him as a figure common to all those fables about men of her own race shipwrecked and marooned and so robbed of respectability that they are left with not even a rag to their name –

All the more contrary of her then that when the dream reaches out to take her hand again she allows him to do so and she actually permits some alchemy to flow between them so that their grief mingles – just as well she is not herself today! – the dream repeats the very fault in Muley Moloch she now most bitterly resents by holding on to her as if the only knowledge he has is the knowledge he has through her – he lifts a thorny vine from her path as *their* vine.

It is no use trying to hurry me into using the simple brutal words you are after – because then there is no chance of explaining the facts of the matter so that you will understand what I tell you.

A familiar resentment hints that this could be her husband's wild spirit on the loose – her husband's spirit in exile among grim black trunks where wheeling bats utter shrill screams against the approaching dawn – then her attention is arrested by a spark of light – she glimpses it ahead – sees it move – she looks to her companion for an explanation and discovers he does not know how to meet her eyes –

Up ahead the light wanders on – winks and winks out –

She is staggering under her inherited ignorance so that she cannot even say whether she is glad or terrified at the prospect of rescue – or if rescue was what she wanted or precisely what she did not want when the light winks again and creeps jerkily to the left –

Her dream mumbles a name – Mrs Somebody – but it is not her name and he stands back while she stumbles ahead – awake and unaided – she spares only a moment of the dawning light to look him over – to look at his hollow face at his battered hands at his scabbed feet while her heart jumps so painfully that the child is shocked into utter stillness – which frightens her with how far she is from safety and how much she has fallen victim to the madness of neither staying in the security of Stroud nor domesticating her prophet at the mission –

Those filthy naked feet are enough to make her shudder – and yet curiously she knows her dream person is good – in this world nothing can be in between except Purgatory itself – everything is either good or evil –

Ahead the feeble spark of light leads on into the pallid morning and this time she notices half a dozen more lanterns (all at a distance) converging around it – some of them breaking into several points – the bat population spirals above her to make the air crackle like invisible paper and she can feel the forest's greenness on her skin – yet even while she strains to make out what the lights might signify they fade and turn pinkish with fatigue – those which had moved falter to a standstill and the one remaining in the same place goes out completely – in alarm she stumbles their way and then they flutter on a dying breath when the new sky floods down around everything to douse them altogether and rob her of guidance and swamp her in brilliant loss –

She has been wandering the whole night –

Two laughing jackasses on the same branch tilt their beaks toward Heaven to let out ripples of gleeful cackling to wake the entire forest as sun rays begin slanting among the trees and a breeze thin as a finger draws cold tear-tracks down her cheeks – she puts her hands to her hair which has come loose and pins it up – the sleeves fall back to her elbows and a delicious morning caresses the tender inner side of her bare arms –

Time and again she refuses to panic because God *has* to look after the baby so she tells the baby that as long as they keep facing into the sun they must be heading east and at worst they will reach the coastal road by midday –

You see she did come to herself –

She woke from the nightmare of goodness in sordid guise – and stepped right into a situation promising immediate help because there in a culvert stood a warm horse all by itself munching some grass and paying no heed to the log it was tethered to – the fact of the rider being nowhere to be seen was neither here nor there – the animal appeared fresh and possibly its saddlebags were still full so she went up to it and spoke and rubbed its nose – this was a placid horse quite unconcerned about strangers and determined not to miss a mouthful – but whose horse was it? she heaved herself up the embankment to look out for somebody – only to find she was in the presence of evil –

A little black tent was what caught her eye – as well as three wooden legs and two human legs supporting it – renewing the unwanted pain of a scene at Cuttajo cliffs – black velvet cloth – as she now saw – with satin piping which struck her as grand enough to be a Spanish cape or a shroud for some highborn ogre with waxy eyelids and a lace collar –

She shook all over at the risk she was about to take – yet she took it – though I don't recall her saying anything more than a timid 'Excuse me' can you believe!

I beg your pardon for laughing (when will I be free of this frightful cough?) but if you could have seen how the fellow jumped! well the tent practically fell over sideways while a nice young individual struggled out blushing with guilt – I was conscious of my aloneness and the singularity of our cause as the Household of Hidden Stars – I felt proud –

'You need not worry' I assured him 'I know what this contraption is' – the morning was mounting higher so that but for the forest shade the sun might already have been uncomfortably hot – 'yours is not the first camera to be seen' – though why was he so abashed? –

He introduced himself as Charles Bailey – none other – but in those days I had never heard of Charles Bailey – cold clear blue eyes searched me with a deliciously dangerous look – then we shook hands which was how I became aware that I had left my gloves at the mission because I recoiled from contact with his skin – not that he wasn't a pleasing person but my mind jolted me back into the dream and the horny feel of another man's hand – it made me nearly faint I can tell you – so I was grateful of the diversion when he asked if I had actually looked through any of the previous cameras I had seen – and nervously lifted the hem of the tent for me –

During the first few moments the misty glass square presented a puzzle until I discovered it could be managed and that the image was entrancing because one had to create it from a jumbled pattern of light – a mere shimmer of colour you see – the glass lost its pearliness and I found myself looking straight into a living picture – a picture more like a jewel than a painting – of an upside-down place in miniature –

But how was it there in all that undergrowth?

I had noticed nothing ahead of the photographer except a dense thicket yet here I was peeping through the leaves to discover a different world – I remained under the black cloth while with appalling clarity each detail displayed for me impressed itself topsy-turvy on my mind – particle by particle – goose pimples crawled about my arms as I made sense of the scene.

I understand perfectly! you are asking about Mr Moloch but I am telling you this is not the point! because you don't even know who he is – or whether indeed he did have another accident at sea perhaps!

You are too late to save anybody so why should you be in a hurry? – if it is a question of protecting the people at risk I would point out that Miss Theuerkauf and I are defenceless ladies who perpetually live in fear of being robbed or assaulted in our beds at night – and have done so ever since Mr Moloch first left us eighteen years ago – even though in other respects we managed quite nicely without a man on the place – mainly thanks to Louisa ('You'll be trying to learn how is this?' as she says 'Well this is *so*!').

Lady Edwina? Edwina passed away only a few years ago.

You were Edwina's favourite of all our neighbours' children – I've no doubt you remember how she spoiled you when you came over from your papa's place to muck out the stables for us though your sister refused violin lessons from Charlotte for fear of what the priest would say – apparently that Father O'Shaughnessy of yours made a habit of denouncing us as lost souls – wasn't this the truth? – and we called you Tiger.

I must say it is very vexing to have Master Bailey of all people dredge up that old incident which in my opinion scarcely reflected credit on him! I have never believed he went there to photograph a miracle at all (speaking personally – as the witness who saw the prophet's shoes rise off the carpet – one has no need of a postcard to remember a miracle by!) so much for photography –

And did any of us forget how Mr Moloch raised the dead? – of course not! – even when Charlotte lost her faith and invited him to admit that Louisa's heart might never have stopped our memories were too powerfully against her so we dismissed the argument that breathing can become shallow enough to escape detection – and Charlotte got the reputation of a backslider – her doubts merely united us against her and incidentally went a good way to improving Louisa's popularity –

Louisa saw a golden light and felt free of the flesh even to being able to watch her own body tossed senseless among the waves followed by the horror of reluctantly answering Mr Moloch's call so that she resisted his power and endured agonies while he drew her back from the brink of Paradise –

But these are not things one may subject to proof without undermining the beauty of faith – surely Bailey has the intelligence to see that the very presence of his camera would have been enough to prevent a chance miracle happening at that particular moment in any case? – and just look at the effect it might have had on poor Mr Moloch who was born with a gift he could never live up to –

It's so callous –

Perhaps both men were the worse for not going to war – people do not realize what it is for a man to have no war to go to in his lifetime – I hope your generation will be more lucky –

Mr Moloch's problem is that he is not the type to impress other males which I dare say is why he was driven to surround himself with women and I certainly do not wish you to think I sit in judgement of his vulgarity when quite the contrary I am fascinated by it – in a funny sort of way I admire it – as part of his inspiration and his gift of preaching with authentic fire –

What can a mere photographer know? –

I recollect so many many sermons it is hopeless to try conveying how they enriched us – me especially – especially at times when I was brought so low by punishments I succumbed to the creeping fear that I was being turned into nothing more than a slave – some of the sermons were based on stories I told *him* from my memories of Miss Honeywood's Sunday school – like the triumph of Saint Thomas over King Gundafar.

You've never heard of King Gundafar? but you must know how Doubting Thomas at the Last Supper thrust his hand in Christ's wounded side and all that? yes well this same apostle Thomas went to India to spread the word you see and arrived at the court of King Gundafar where he was warmly received – not because the king was persuaded about Jesus Christ as saviour of the world I'm afraid but because Thomas like Jesus was a carpenter (did you know the name Thomas means 'twin'?) and by all accounts an exceptionally talented carpenter too or at least the Hindoos thought so – their King Gundafar who was much loved owing to his habit of believing what he was told (coupled with his other habit of spending rather too freely) promptly invited the apostle to build him a new palace and supported the offer with a large sum of money –

Now although Gundafar was loved by his people these people lived in such terrible poverty that Saint Thomas pledged himself to do something about it and spent the money on building shelters for them – money the king had paid for a palace – he housed and fed the sick and tended them – not to mention giving away handsome amounts to beggars and the like –

Well even the carefree Gundafar was bound to hear of it sooner or later so he called for Thomas to report on his progress with the palace and of course Thomas would never tell a lie which meant he was thrown in jail – so the apostle who had always expected the worse got what he expected –

For many years he lived as a convict in chains until the time came when the king's brother died and the whole country went into mourning because this prince had lived a pure life which of course meant he would go straight to Heaven – when he got there they showed him many marvels but none more dazzling among all the dazzling sights of Heaven than one particular unfinished palace so he asked 'Who is to live here for all eternity?' and was told 'This is the palace being built for King Gundafar by the apostle Thomas' –

As you may imagine the prince begged the Almighty to allow him to return to Earth for just long enough to whisper a message in his brother's ear – which is how Saint Thomas came to be let out of prison and King Gundafar with all his people was converted to the true faith – no doubt leading to a positive festival of mutual congratulations –

So pause before judging our humble home –

And before judging Muley Moloch for that matter – though no one sees much of him in town these days apart from his annual trip to buy grain and seed-potatoes besides his visits to the coast to fit the giants of 'Paradise' with shoes half a dozen sizes larger than the largest available in any shop – and the day he comes home he unfailingly raises his cap to me like a family servant and calls over the fence 'Good morning Miss Byrne' with eyes going grey as mist – so I feel my heart turn and remember when we first invited him back to live at the mission – he cried out in a loud voice 'Surely you cannot forgive me! and nor can she! and nor can I forgive myself!' –

What I might need to forgive him *for* is between the two of us and shall remain so – but what Louisa could possibly need to forgive is a mystery – though I suppose one ought not to forget the sight I saw in that upside-down square of light shown me by Charles Bailey's photographic camera.

Didn't I say?

Each detail had been carved with a scalpel and set in poisoned silence – showing the Stars in miniature – some with their backs to me and some facing me – each well-known back unmistakable and each face of those looking my way offering the dwindled version of a familiar expression – while between them lay a trench into which they gazed – where I saw a dishevelled Louisa perspiring and bent over – miraculously upside down you must remember – settling to a man's task – dumping a shovel load of clay on the rim of the trench – she was doing Muley Moloch's work for him –

The instant I saw her I found I could also hear her panting breath – plus the scrape of metal against stone – for the first time I was struck by the fact that she had survived untouched by the consumption afflicting most of the rest of us in one degree or another –

I could also hear the photographer right near me fretting impatiently – not daring to remove the tent and take back his camera he began knocking one boot heel against the other and letting out exasperated sighs – much I cared! – I was hypnotized at my peephole because now I had the picture clear I still could not make out what it might mean – then I saw something which had previously eluded me – a body laid to one side – and the frightful inverted slackness of it –

I must have flinched because I lost the picture for a few seconds – unable to find the correct angle to assemble it again – hearing young Bailey remove the screw caps from his chemical bottles – liquids gurgled – odours cut my breath – I could delay no longer – I knew now what he was up to –

Incensed at his indecent prying I threw off the cloth – only to find myself blinded by a shimmering mass of daylight – I believe I wavered and stumbled and fell against him even as he painted his Satanic mixture on a photographic plate ready to slide it into the machine –

I knew by report how the device worked – that an image would begin to be magically printed there – each detail of Louisa's bare arms and perspiring immodesty etched forever in silver – also the unexplained body – he had already snatched his black cloth and disappeared under it when I barged forward through the thicket screaming 'Beware beware!' and suddenly found myself grasped by Mr Moloch who stared wild-eyed at me and restrained me as if I had lost my wits –

I screamed into his face 'Beware of – beware of – !' I choked – helpless as Lavinia – the necessary word would not come – while ladies stood round the graveside stupid with alarm like statuary in a teaching studio (this one representing Horror and that one Grief) – but already Mr Moloch had begun shouting on his own account – shouting at me about the baby while I struggled against him –

I felt my own sobs yet I could find no voice for making sense of what I knew – until Ann having put her head near mine and heard me whisper that we were being pried upon led them in among the leaves (Charlotte and Hester and Martha and the exhausted Louisa) while it was I who now clung to Mr Moloch because I found myself staring down into Flora's dead face and the sight struck me dumb with guilt that perhaps this death *had* been my doing –

Once his anger swept through him – as when the demons were routed – my husband broke free from my encumbrance and bounded in among the trampled branches where the black tent had already been flung aside and the offender – though dragged to his knees by ladies – still held the precious photographic plate in one hand to keep it safe from harm –

Mr Moloch's problem was that he didn't know which way to turn –

His suspicious manner of squinting at the camera showed how little he understood – this brought me to my feet in a flash I can tell you because I realized that an empty camera was harmless

– but already in those lost moments young Bailey acted swiftly and slipped free – he charged off through the bracken still with the clean plate in his hand and the belated prophet in pursuit –

Bailey paused – he turned and struck Mr Moloch a terrible blow full in the face – sent the poor prophet stumbling about in shock and pain with a broken nose gushing blood – then doubled back to hoist his camera complete with frail legs in the crook of his elbow – and leapt down the slope to where his horse nibbled the grass –

Because the Stars had their skirts and their modesty to contend with it looked as if the miscreant might get away – taking his stolen scene of ladies sweating at a grave for a body dead of no visible cause – when a queer spindly figure stepped out from among the trees – a ginger-bearded oddity – bones bundled together and netted in ugly veins –

Well the horse shied and no wonder! –

Mr Bailey dropped the plate while he clutched the reins and tried to protect his precious camera – this gave me my chance to dart in – but do you think I could get hold of the beastly thing? not a bit of it! – the slippery stuff made me drop it so all I could do (holding my swollen body) was stamp and grind it under my heel –

When I looked up from this work the figure out of my dream was gone (yes I recognized him and my stomach turned) Mr Moloch caught hold of the photographer's ankle to dislodge him from the saddle only to be knocked over for the second time – then the photographer hitched the heavy camera on his shoulder – swung up into the saddle again – and rode away at a trot like a species of equestrian cripple – not fully in his seat and unable to right himself –

The shame of it! the trespass! the breach of privacy!

I went to Mr Moloch's assistance – only then did I enjoy relief at having found my way home.

When my husband left the mission for good and went to live in Bunda – and you might consider this perverse – he rented a shop next door to Mr Bailey's photographic studio – between Bailey and Brewster's Mercery Emporium –

But who has ever fathomed the human heart or its fears? –

Take for instance Lavinia's shrill insistence that we report the intrusion to whatever authorities might be in the area (a passion we only understood when she had been sufficiently whipped to confess her lascivious desires with catalogues of desperate wrong words – poor thing) – one felt habitually sorry for Lavinia because a single glance from those uncertain eyes was enough to give warning that even at her best her politeness might be no more than vacancy.

Before assuming the name Muley Moloch my husband was known to style himself Prince of the Hebrews –

To this day he still dreams of leading us to the Holy Land (being a thorough come-outer always did suit him) – yes he is back with us and indeed he very well might lead us there for all I know – though he declines to predict when – maybe from self-consciousness about his lack of education in arithmetic –

Hopeless as he has always been in the arithmetical department the one number Muley Moloch enshrined in every sermon with complete certainty was the thousand-year kingdom of the returned Christ – to begin with the Second Coming and to last until the Day of Judgement –

As I have said before – inspiration has nothing to do with how educated a person is – and who can say where the Holy Land is any longer? –

If you are surprised at his choice of companions in this great purpose allow me to point out that from the moment his family apprenticed him to the trade of bootmaker – on account of being lame like his father – he was thrown in among dwarfs and cripples so perhaps this was what gave him strength to cope with us – though I won't be questioned any more about the missing bits – like my toe – because in the long run that doesn't matter to me –

You say you want facts – well if you are to understand what the facts mean you must hear me out – we suffered what we suffered in order to fit ourselves for the Second Coming – Jesus being in our minds every hour of the day – and hymns on our lips keeping us in a state of ecstasy so we would not be caught napping.

Please make yourself comfortable.

Since you left me last night I have not moved from this chair – but don't mention nightmares!

You must have noticed how one's daytime shadow is only normal body size (see my hand there on the floor?) while at night by lamplight it grows monstrous? – well the past is like that too and even the sober truth seems not much more comfortable than the truth of the tannery –

Come to think of it the tannery is what most people know about – certainly the convicts did – and we deceive ourselves if we think our world of little luxuries and neat lawns does not need to be paid for or that it is we who do the paying – I include your grandfather who paid by going away to fight for Queen Victoria in the Indian Mutiny – forgive me but how wonderfully it would shock my dear parents to hear me sounding like the odious Mr Owen who Judge Honeywood's daughter always said deserved the gallows –

My life used to be a prison of obedience though I've no patience at all with that kind of thing now –

Have you thought how few pleasures the polite woman enjoys while confined to the drawing-room at her embroidery frame or at the pianoforte or simpering after eligible brutes who look her over with an eye for cattle before riding off to meet one another later (and with equal gratification) at a boxing ring where they pay to watch men's faces being pummelled until they bleed? –

A nice prospect!

The polite woman whether she's in Cheltenham or Melbourne – writes letters and does wool work – she dips into Thackeray perhaps and writes more letters – she arranges dried flowers and perhaps walks in her garden before settling down to write more letters – why does she write so many letters? because the letters go out into the world and travel where she would wish to be free to travel in person – they speak to people while she – in the loneliness of good manners – merely tittletattles with neighbours of an acceptable kind about matters from which good manners preclude any subject that might touch her heart –

But the sufferers are not necessarily anxious to change things – not at all! – they accommodate themselves to being deceived – here at the mission we faced the truth – we transcended letters having really travelled – and to the remotest place possible – we despised substitutes so we never rebelled against our squalid punishments – or our duties – even when Mr Moloch put a ban on stylish clothes and we had to wear woollen dresses intended to look ugly did we complain? – indeed I distinctly remember the first time I went to town wearing my brown horror I stepped down out of the sulky free from the squirmings I had felt at home – filled with gaiety and pride!

From a bird's-eye view the mission farm began as a cluster of four roofs almost wholly enveloped in undergrowth – three buildings enclosing a yard and the stables halfway along a track to our creek where the patch cleared for a garden was already matted with weeds – here the returning Christ would find us –

Very different from the place as it is today –

Into this neglect our party of pioneers arrived (with one about to die and one still not fully brought back to life) to hack at the choking plants and lay bare a ring of land around each hut – after the convicts left it was we women who wielded the mattocks to chip out the scrub – even in rain women wearing waterproof cloaks with hoods and carrying rakes rustled down to the garden – right through the winter months the clearing work went on – heaps of weeds being burned on dry days – and Mr Moloch in his shirtsleeves darting about doing twice as much as anybody while he taught us the practical use of tools – then in spring when the picket fences had been repaired and new ones built for protecting the lawn and garden against intruding wallabies (who learnt to become famous connoisseurs of lettuce and peach-tree leaves) we sowed the seeds purchased from Melbourne and planted dozens of cuttings sold us by various neighbours at Yandilli –

This was to be our living you see – the produce of our market garden was to pay for meat flour butter and tea despite the fact that most of us had never so much as grown a tray of mustard seed! – to our surprise Lady Edwina confessed herself quite an expert – right till her dying day she swore that even if the faith had not sustained her and the nearness of Jesus in those days she would not have missed creating our garden for worlds –

So you must imagine lots of seedlings sprouting in rows and fruit trees putting out blossom while Martha Sparrow (our only source of medical knowledge) gasped and choked to death – and you must imagine the crops being picked for delivery twice a week to Yandilli in the spring cart with Hester taking the reins and Ann for company – then so much fruit ripening at Christmas that we could scarcely keep pace with bedding our precious apricots and peaches in boxes or filling buckets with plums while Elizabeth Canning brought sandwiches from the kitchen and Mr Moloch worked a hand-pump to fill the tank from the creek – you must imagine such a joyous harvest that when we dragged our bone-weary bodies indoors at dusk – drawn home by the aromas of Elizabeth's cooking – we sang marching hymns to the rhythmic clash of tools and the whir of Mr Moloch's lawn mower as he used the last minutes of light to indulge his pet hobby of taming the native grass –

The only other time we sought help – as I have explained – was with building our chapel which took seventy-seven slabs of squared bark for the walls and twenty-three for roofing and roof caps – all clamped on to the frame and with a second frame clamped on outside to hold them flat – you may count them for yourself if you wish and see how wonderfully they have lasted –

Mind you we look after the place.

We were a closed community so there was no one but us – no teaching program for novices no converts no hospital no food-kitchen no refuge for fallen women and not much contact with the town besides the stories Ann brought back after marketing our produce (until her whiskers grew and she passed the job entirely to Hester) – a closed community with bush all round us spreading for hundreds of miles inland like a thick blanket on the ridges and choking the gullies between –

This vast tangle of vegetation assailed us with leafy smells foreign to our garden so we felt the constant seductive lure of adventure – and sometimes of a morning when walking in the forest we would come upon two men or perhaps a man and a lad seated on the ground sipping hot tea from pannikins while their campfire smouldered and the fern-trees rustled against a simple canvas tent held up by two forked stakes with a pole between – smoke always hung deliciously among the leaves – generally the man would scramble to his feet politely enough but the lad most often just pushed his cap back off his forehead and stretched his legs to show off their length in long leather gaiters reaching right up to the knee – sometimes the man would offer us hospitality and point to a billy hung over the embers on a miniature version of the tent frame but we always hurried off regretfully because the scene filled us with intolerable yearnings for the sweetness of lounging like that all night by a fire with nothing to do but watch it blaze and die down and break to ash while the encircling night widened into the clear dark and treetops spangled with brilliant stars filled the sky –

Not to mention the tales we heard of explorers finding passes through the mountains beyond which they discovered grasslands as far as the eye could see and eventually reached a desert which they promptly set out to cross by foot – earning a name for amazing courage when all they were suffering as men was what we women longed to be at liberty to attempt for the sheer pleasure of its limitless freedom –

Instead we bound ourselves to our routines and wasted our eloquence on the apples and cabbages we took to town for selling to people who stared at us and gossiped behind their hands to humiliate us – but what they did not know was that this gave us courage because we saw we were as far beyond their bondage to drudgery as the explorers were beyond ours –

Anyway who is to say precisely what humiliation is? –

Take the case of Mr Moloch where the photographer Charles Bailey was concerned – years and years before they occupied neighbouring shops – what can account for the prophet's visit to the studio (only nine weeks after the rout I described to you last night) to lay before him the most curious request the young scamp was ever likely to hear? –

What business had Mr Moloch as a man of God with such a shocker? and yet I have a suspicion my husband felt able to put the proposition because he knew he *was* putting it to a shocker – and that a more conventional man would call the police without further ado – no offence intended – so Bailey it had to be –

And when he recovered from being struck speechless he consented to think the matter over –

Meanwhile Flora had been months in her grave and I was confined to bed with the impending birth of my famous child – the expectation gripping our Household grew too intense to be described so let me simply point out the fact that everyone forgot about spying on everyone else and even Hester was touched for once with maidenly kindness –

Towards me they were angels – absolute angels!

Being confined to bed again gave me such a lot of time and energy for thinking I became obsessed by the *unfairness* of fate when I thought of poor dear Beatrice still back there in the hot stony ground on Ascension Island while I luxuriated between the sheets awaiting the arrival of a baby who would be the saviour of us all – not only had poor Beatrice lived her entire life without ever knowing the flustered elation of placing one's hands on one's tummy to feel movements under the skin but now neither she nor Elizabeth Eyre nor Flora would share in the fearful prospect of helping guide the child as he grew (for it was certain he must be a boy) to face the task of wrestling against a world gone mad on the wickedness of electrical things and steam engines – not to mention photographs I suppose! – and expecting to satisfy its greed like a rabble of Digby Barnetts picking up nuggets of gold without even the need of honest labour – a world the poorer for losing these dear ladies –

Even more surprising was the idea that fate had also been unfair to Louisa Theuerkauf – her unrequited love for my husband might well have given her reason for turning into a complainer yet she refused to complain –

Well a full week before the baby was due everything at the mission stood spotless and in perfect readiness while friends sat with me all through the day and night to await the first sign and young Charles Bailey rode up on his horse to ask if he might camp down by the stream – in case you are wondering I have to explain that I did feel terribly agitated by this arrangement and could only calm my fears with the thought that nothing mattered compared to the fact of the miracle happening in my body –

Naturally I knew how supremely significant the occasion was and that I must make sacrifices – but to have myself photographed! – to have the very moment of birth photographed! – well it violated every instinct –

Privacy a thing of the past –

I was to become the most public figure in history since the Virgin Mary and even my happiness could not be thought of as private because it must be shared by all true believers throughout the world –

Charles Bailey being so tall and strongly made was really quite handsome and a frock coat looked very well on him if you could see past his oddities (no I haven't set eyes on him for years) because in those days he had a long thick neck supporting a rather insignificant head but his *manner* left everything to be desired in that he ducked and leered – a real specimen of a primitive! – and set his big hands hovering around the equipment – even around the subject which in this case was me in my bed if you please!

I thought I should never endure the shame but I was no longer a private person and had little choice so his camera on its props faced me for many days until the glass eye began to seem scarcely more intrusive than the mirror in the corner or our own table with a bowl of water upon it –

Now and again Mr Bailey would amble in bringing his black cloth and request permission to check whether all was still in readiness – on one occasion he asked for my bed to be pushed right against the windowsill to make maximum use of the light 'What if the baby comes after dark?' the evil Hester Partington asked and we all laughed but Mr Moloch dismissed the possibility because why else had God inspired some inventor to construct a camera if not for the sake of this occasion? – he was right –

I believe Charles Bailey began to think of himself as one of the Chosen –

The camera peered straight at me from the end of the bed exactly between my feet – generally simply the eye of a box but from time to time (as happened on the morning of my worst pains) the eye of a humped black-shrouded human shape filling me with unspeakable horror particularly when the midwives – which is to say Elizabeth Canning who knew what to do but was hampered by her wheelchair and Louisa who did not know what to do – stripped back the bedding and strapped my legs in position while Hester sounded the alert which brought Hidden Stars from all quarters still fresh with the odours of interrupted duties – I caught a whiff of smoke from the boiler fire and a warm horse smell from the stables – then I was suddenly beyond noticing anything and thank Heaven the physical pain was too savage for me to care about the camera or the anguish suffered by my modesty at the first nauseating exposure.

So now perhaps you begin to suspect what class of witness you were listening to when you let Master Bailey have his say!

How many photographs he took I do not know but he left when the ladies covered me with sheets – my only memory of his departure is a brief tableau of him picking up his packed equipment and shaking my husband's hand – he said nothing to me and avoided acknowledging me at all – as he went he nodded generally to the Stars who stood back from my bed shakily singing hymns while Louisa at the washbasin turned my way too with her hands dripping soapy water and released that glorious voice to soar high above theirs in a free descant –

My baby boy was perfect –

Then and there we christened him Immanuel while the prophet Moloch recited Isaiah's famous words 'Behold a virgin shall conceive and bear a son and shall call his name Immanuel *God with us*' – you might have expected hovering angels to join in the refrain – you might at least have expected me to be filled with unspeakable joy at having found favour with God – quite the contrary – the whole event struck me as somehow rehearsed to death (do you know that?) besides being irrelevant to the precious little bundle warm in my arms – so it is no good complaining that God does not send us presentiments –

Hester asked 'Are you sure Baby isn't a dwarf?'

I felt more like a mother with the ordinary exhaustion of having delivered a new life than the Mother of God despite all the tiptoeing and the hallelujahs going on around me – not to mention old friends being too shy even to meet my eyes – the truth is that I felt overwhelmed by fear because my baby would surely be found out and exposed as nothing more extraordinary than a human child of the usual kind – yet at the same time what could be better? and this was precisely what I wished to prove so I could forget every other duty apart from relishing the simple joy of a mother – accordingly I stirred my memory again in desperation for some hint of how my pregnancy might have happened except through God – inventing wild tales of forgotten moments and farfetched transmissions – wary in case somebody might read these thoughts and report me as a heretic – let me tell you this hidden palpitation was worse than anything – meanwhile my baby began to squirm under my nightdress and to feed from my breast so that the pain of surprise came as the deepest pleasure I had ever known – filling me with pity for Lavinia especially –

Lavinia – you'll remember – had only one breast because the left side failed to grow when she was a girl – she wouldn't even have been any use as an Amazon unless she learned to fire a bow left-handed – peculiar people those Trojan women – and they say there were also other Amazons in Africa cutting off one breast – imagine the frightful great wound left there and how did the skin ever grow back? not to mention what a cut-off breast might look like by itself – let's say just forgotten on a table – still with the cut-off section of her tunic partly covering it – it makes me shiver even now – and I never felt quite at ease with Lavinia once I had marked her with this idea –

I began to feel so sorry for the legless Elizabeth (saying 'Botheration!' while she managed wonderfully) that the tears streamed from my eyes – and sorry for Ann who grumbled 'How should I know where a handkerchief is?' even while she produced one and passed it to me –

What more can I say? in any case – ssh! – here comes Louisa to offer us some luncheon.

There have been scenes of dreadful treachery hereabouts – you will certainly have heard how Mrs Atholl shot her husband in a most unnatural manner and was treated treacherously in her turn by your neighbour dear old Mr Earnshaw (still in good health I trust?) cases of secret revenge by convicts against former masters though I mention no names – and by violated girls against seducers –

Frightful things happen in this parish involving knives and poisonings not to mention the natives – such frightful things that I am surprised you can find time to visit me day after day simply for the sake of adding another gory item to the catalogue – because what has been done cannot be undone – and as for justice there are issues more important than justice all things considered!

I beg your pardon? yes of course you knew Immanuel with the two of you being near enough the same age – you must remember how adorable he was as he grew up and what a great favourite with the Household – his sunny ways cleansed us of staleness just by filling the mission with chatter – no one could doubt he was already our saviour which made it all the more urgent to decide how we should prepare him for the unthinkable responsibility he had to face –

The answer in the Bible was that God Himself revealed the

truth to Jesus saying 'Thou art my beloved son in whom I am well pleased' – admittedly this might take one problem off our hands – but before any such announcement could be made Jesus had to be raised in hiding from the wrath of Herod and taught the carpenter's craft by his father – well we decided to tell Immanuel nothing so he could grow up healthy and useful as a bootmaker's apprentice until the time came for him to be called from On High –

We recorded the passing years on his baptismal robe (because of course no one dared baptize him as a baby so Ann cut the garment a suitable size for a growing lad) – sitting round in the afternoon wearing our caps tied under the chin with ribbons and our heads wagging as we talked each of us embroidered the white cotton with a flower for his birthday – ready for when he might be washed clean of original sin – for example Ann did a white rose and Elizabeth Canning did a white iris then there was a white carnation by Charlotte and Lavinia's white and gold honeysuckle woven in with my white lily while Lady Edwina – who used the excuse of shaky hands to cover the fact that she felt the task beneath her besides being too fiddly – read out loud to us and on one occasion was quite agog at coming across a mention of Captain Cook in a new book by Thackeray especially as Mr Thackeray claimed that a great number of the descriptive passages in *Cook's Voyages* were notoriously invented by Dr Hawkesworth who 'did' the book – and we felt suitably superior since our experience was indubitably authentic – this was before Edwina shrivelled up because she turned out to be one of those women who do not so much age as desiccate.

No – Louisa never learned to embroider and she never apologized for her ignorance either.

My memory is clear today –

From the sixth year Charlotte filled the gaps with extra carnations and the honeysuckle grew seriously crooked in the ninth year (I have to say I am reaching an age when I begin to doubt that either of those ladies caught the consumption from me yet undeniably we did spend a tremendous amount of time nursing sick people) –

My recovery became an example to all – others were punished for not living up to it –

Meanwhile Immanuel grew to be a terrible scamp who delighted in tricks and dreamed all through his lessons until we despaired of teaching him anything – though never big for his age he was too strong for us to hold – he tormented the goats and laughed when they chased him through the gate where they kicked holes all over Mr Moloch's lawn – poor Immanuel caught it that time – once he crossed from end to end of the apple orchard jumping from tree to tree through a ruin of blossoms – do you think we were delighted! – he teased the ladies in awful ways causing them to spill their tea and prick their fingers – except Ann who was his favourite – yet they forgave him and only the prophet had enough confidence to punish him as if he were an ordinary boy –

When he was ten he gave us a devastating fright by going missing – then at sunset returned home very tired but cheery to tell us his adventures down at a logging camp on the Yandilli road where he had talked to some axemen and watched a great tree fall – he spoke of that tree with awe – but no matter how we scolded him we made no progress against his wildness and he enjoyed a great deal of freedom because by this time he was trapping rabbits for the cook pot and could expect to be away from the house for hours at a stretch in any case –

Immanuel turned twelve (which was the age when Jesus first preached in the temple) and yet God still did not intervene directly though we knew the boy needed to be told who he was – told soon – and shown that he had become our saviour already – loved by everyone for his freshness – that our lives had not always been so filled with joy – and that just as he had changed us without knowing so he must go forth and change the world –

If I had had a grain of sense I would have taken this on myself and spoken to him straight out in private – but did I do anything so simple or sensible? I did not –

My abiding weakness is that I have never been able to refuse anybody anything – well we devised a ceremony in which each of us could take some part – dressing him in that clean white gown and anointing his head and feet – except Louisa who would come into her own by singing 'Rejoice rejoice rejoice greatly' you know the thing – well the communion table was set up on the lawn and a new lace cloth spread on it – dazzling under the sky – I think I can say we each felt God had never been nearer at hand while the boy himself simply shone until the moment when all the Stars instinctively stepped back at his approach –

He realized we were in earnest and I have never seen a face collapse as his face collapsed – I knew we were in the wrong and I thought of *you* – yes of you – because you once came down from the hills telling us you had seen some blood spots on a slab of stone and your father told you that this was what happened when the wild folk made a boy into a man – I thought does Tiger know a way of doing it at no more cost than a couple of drops of blood? –

'Aunt Ann' he cried and reached out to catch hold of her as she quickly slipped away to hide in the chapel (have you noticed the surprising dexterity of fat women?) 'Mama' he called and I did find enough courage to clutch at his hand but in such a way I suppose that my humility hurt him all the more –

He bent down and grasped the hem of the robe to pull it up over his head – sweet lad – crumpling the flowers and struggling to free his arms from the sleeves and getting in such a state that by the time he tugged it off his face was bright as a strawberry – on the verge of tears he screwed up the lovely embroideries and trampled them underfoot in a passion of helplessness – then blundered away in pursuit of his favourite – letting the chapel door bang after him –

We followed and crowded into the blinding gloom – colliding with the boy who was already storming back to reach the prophet 'Papa' he demanded in the dark 'tell me I am all right!' –

The air was so cool –

Well from that day Ann could never muster the spirit to be grumpy again even though she grew a beard which ought to have given her more cause than ever – and if you had been in a position to witness Mr Moloch's expression (as we were *not* in that dim place) I believe you might have seen fear there when he replied 'You are all right' – certainly his voice took on so urgently serious a tone he seemed to be indicating a deeper meaning – I can tell you I have listened to him in my memory countless times hoping to recapture that exact tone –

'Then why' Immanuel demanded 'don't you smack me for spoiling my shirt?' and he defied the prophet to raise his hand – wanting it and aching for it and shrugging off my protective embrace – so Mr Moloch came close to peer at us – faceless silhouetted head turning from the boy with his pleading eyes to me with mine –

'What am I to do?' he asked – and thus the beautiful ceremony was ruined by questions –

Thin stripes of light scored our backs and shoulders while every now and again a gleam caught the brilliant tears in somebody's eye –

This was not how we had meant it to be – and from that day forward the boy became absolutely uncontrollable –

Cruel to our cats and neglectful of the pony he loved he was more often running amok in the bush than home – and when he did come in he would set about washing his hands in the most compulsive way – no sooner were they dry than he washed them again – and then again – sometimes eight or nine repetitions until I scolded him for wasting precious water – meanwhile it was no better during dinner-time – he chewed the food twenty times on one side of his mouth then chewed it twenty times on the other before swallowing – a meal could last for hours let me tell you – ending in an infatuation with counting – counting the ticks of the clock and the calls of an owl in the pepper tree – the aggravation of it nearly drove us mad – he counted the number of steps he took to carry an empty bucket to the well and a full bucket back – till eventually he began a slow daydreaming sort of count which turned out to be the number of breaths he drew if you please!

Our joy had been shattered in the most unexpected way and no amount of prayer made the least impression – do you blame me if I felt horrified and tried to shock him out of this state by the most stinging remarks I could muster though I was never given to such boldness with anybody as a rule –

Quite soon another misfortune happened to him because his face lost its character – the brightness faded to a resentful expression – and when his mouth twisted he was suddenly shown as looking like no one so much as the prophet in the days when I first saw him deliver a sermon from a pulpit in Stroud – with prominent ears and a prominent nose – except that this smaller likeness refused to utter a word and indeed appeared to have lost the power of speech altogether –

The upshot was that we returned to our old solution – we blamed each other – although with one tremendous difference in that I no longer carried the brunt of the blame – a new reign of petty terrors started with beatings and humiliations and the penance of having to go without sleep – how deeply I knew it! but I could not resist the luxury of my new status – also I am ashamed to say I did enjoy the sin of revenge against those who like Hester had persecuted me through the years –

So as tension at the mission grew to an unbearable pitch Ann began coughing blood – I suppose we knew something must break –

One morning the sun's rays sloped among the tree trunks as usual – birds chattered and the busy life of the hateful bush took on its customary inane complexity while I stood in the yard – conscious of breathing free from pain (like the alien I was) – when the sky hollowed itself so that it drew all substance from everything – sucking the substance up into empty space – leaving the dry world discarded like an empty chrysalis – this was how it felt – 'Immanuel!' I shrieked – already in panic and calling him again and again because somehow I knew he had gone –

Two of the sisters came running from the chapel – they let the door drift shut after them and stood blinking against the glare unconscious of the dusty stencilled knee marks on their skirts where they had knelt in prayer – or the scatter of cats – and suddenly the sky was full of clouds swooping down among the trees with shafts of sunlight lancing in under a turmoil of threatening vapours – you never saw anything so unexpected –

Oh I cannot bear to talk about it – you must forgive me Sergeant –

This cough is getting worse with summer.

You will judge me I am sure but when the Voice came back with its usual assurance I interpreted it as meaning that the lad had been taken to Heaven – our crisis was over – I felt ashamed of my doubts and relieved (yes) to be freed from the grand role thrust on me – 'You may depend upon it that the Lord is coming!' was what I felt I was being told – so Immanuel *would* descend in a chariot of fire after all – and I sensed God closer than ever before –

At last I must have done something right!

Others of the Stars hurried in and out of doors conferring as they passed me – vanishing round the back of sheds to return a moment later with nothing but empty hands to show – Hester even peered down the well – and Mr Moloch emerged in his heavy boots unwrapping a gun so that I knew what he intended and found myself calling out 'The boy is in his Father's keeping' –

All movement stopped while the faithful listened on every side – 'Fear not!' I added while Mr Moloch shook all over as if to rid himself of some clinging pest and ordered them to look sharp –

'Bring whatever weapons you can find' he begged 'while Hester rides to town for help' –

'Fear not' I cried out again and the Sisters glanced from one to another bewildered 'he is in his Father's hands!' I repeated because it seemed the right thing and smiles broke out –

'He has certainly gone' the crippled Elizabeth spoke up timidly to be sure I knew –

I replied 'And the Lord be praised!' to which a number of them whispered 'Amen' but my husband rewound the oilcloth around the breech of his weapon and strode towards me threateningly 'Whatever the truth of the matter' he roared without respect 'we cannot pretend to know – so we must do our duty the best we can' –

I simply smiled now I understood what power I had and explained 'The Voice tells me' –

But he fumed in an even greater fury 'What does the Voice tell you then?'

And I answered 'That he is with his Father' –

There was a desperate light in Muley Moloch's face – which if I had ever seen previously I dare say I might have recognized for love – at least this is what I believe as I look back on it – seeing his whole body twist with the pain it cost him to defy me further 'There is the danger of being lost in these wild woods – there is the danger of snakes – and there is the danger of demons' –

I smiled saying 'Shouldn't we be mindful of Saint Luke's warning and be ready to forsake even our family if the Lord so wills it?' – he flinched because he had often quoted this to us as a text applying to our forbidden letters from home – I continued 'Besides I have been among the demons myself and found them simple people whose whimsy it is to wish themselves back into the shapes of animals' I had the authority of knowing my destiny 'but they laugh as we laugh' though in fact we seldom did laugh –

'You dare put the boy at risk?' he raged –

I kept smiling and said 'Can you not hear me? he has gone to his Father's keeping' –

In the hush before the rain a whole flock of black cockatoos dipped and flapped among the branches 'I am' he uttered these words more ferociously than any curse 'his father!'

You cannot imagine the solemn shock this produced on the

ladies who lacked my strength – yet God sent no thunderbolt and when a few fat drops of rain thwacked the soil and a few splashed against our faces Louisa seized her moment 'I have been the one who is raised from the dead isn't it?' she took charge of the centre stage 'to me must even Mr Moloch tell the truth if Catherine is wrong' –

My husband passed his wrapped-up gun from one useless hand to the other as he addressed the ground 'I am the father' he repeated –

Rain fell faster –

'Then how is your wife knowing nothing?' Louisa grew to the stature of a judge –

'She did not know' he admitted vaguely (I invite you to put yourself in my place at this moment Sergeant with the earth opening under my feet and a void which I had seen briefly in the sky now happening inside me) 'Catherine did not know' he repeated as if nothing more need be said –

I shrieked '*What* did I not know?'

All around us our voices could be heard to echo faintly in the empty mission buildings and faintly in the well – while I recognized anguish in my husband's face – a face disfigured by trickles of rain 'She was too ill – ' he explained and he looked up at me with pleading eyes ' – to know' –

He was pleading for Immanuel – just as the love I glimpsed had not been for me but also for Immanuel.

I shall not say I was shaken with hatred because at that time I was too powerless to feel anything beyond my numb shell filled with loss – too blinded by the squalid shame of his confession to see anything beyond the dark spots appearing all over his clothes like a contagious disease.

I keep a diary and I spent last night reading through that very entry – eighteen years ago – you see I sometimes wonder whether Mr Moloch has any idea I loved him or how great a fool I made of myself leading us halfway round the world just to be able to live with him –

For his part I simply cannot tell if he hated me or if he was too self-conscious but he never had any sort of freedom with me despite the fact that he could share a joke with the others –

Little mouse that I was perhaps I did my destructive work at night in my dreams who knows? but the loss of my son drove me to such a state that Ann felt so disquieted on my behalf she grew preoccupied with my problems until one day on a ladder she missed her footing and broke her hip – next came poor little Lavinia whimpering as she hurried about her tasks and even though she always had been a bit cracked nothing prepared us for the stormy outbursts she suddenly let fly or her being found hiding in a cupboard when Hester drove back from town bringing a constable to have us investigated – I can never forgive Hester and at the time I could only marvel at the prophet's forbearance when he walked to the gate to let the policeman in and welcomed Hester with a ceremonial kiss on the cheek.

In Yandilli the cry had gone up that our entire mission should be burned down to cleanse it of contagion – and nothing less than the local lethargy could have saved us or our belongings – the others were ill and I was supposed to be possessed –

Yes the inquiry was carried out but it produced nothing definite despite the fact that my influence was now suspected everywhere from Adelaide to Brisbane – within a week of Oliver and Digby Barnett staking out a new farm down on the coast they were at each other's throats over the fate of their old selection and rumours that I had somehow bewitched them into leaving it – at least this is what Florence Love has told me since – and I have to admit that even at home Edwina became addicted to snuff and left hideously stained handkerchiefs in the least expected places – and Mr Moloch took to shooting bullets at a target for hours on end – not to mention reports filtering in from Yandilli such as the news that a tin of mutton was found to be blown after young Tommy McNeil died of food poisoning (though one wondered what a butcher's wife was doing feeding her family from a tin!) even the Brian Boru Inn moved to Cuttajo to put its customers at a safer distance from me and my grief –

the consequence of this was that your Father O'Shaughnessy found himself recalled in disgrace over a matter connected with Mrs Gilbert the publican's wife and the only spot of relief for the churchgoers was a surprisingly cultured Welshman who arrived to take his place with strict instructions (so we heard tell) to keep his hands off the women of the parish –

At the heart of it all was the loss of Immanuel –

That superstitious nonsense was simply gossip – I am a good Christian and a soldier of Christ – the grief which had driven me to hate everything in sight came as a cleansing fire because I was rebelling – eager for conflict against all humankind so I couldn't have cared less about who got hurt – I needed a larger field of operations than our mission with its dismal choice between creating scandal among prudes or persecuting the helpless – that's when I threw off my reticence and took over Ann's market duties which meant consorting more and more with Hester –

Once in town as a regular identity I began to care what our neighbours thought of me and accordingly soiled my clothes and loosened my hair – Louisa was the only one able to note these changes without censoring me – I used the succulent vegetables we produced as bait to lure victims my way in Yandilli high street where for every sixpence worth we sold I delivered a diatribe against the commoner sins – backed up by Hester –

We became known as the vegetable people – local gardeners envied our skill – and according to legend people surreptitiously invoked our name when planting their crops – but this was a wicked liberty –

Then strange plants were belatedly found sprouting in the region – fleshy little knobs appearing harmless enough along the roadside until some child pricked its thumb and they were diagnosed as cactuses – soon to bud extra knobs like puffy fingers on a puffy hand – a visiting botanist from Amsterdam declared them a pest and within a week was proved right because they turned out to be prickly pear – an acknowledged curse up north along the Hunter River – in next to no time they grew waist-high – so dense that they choked the pastures and surrounded farmhouses all along the valley from Yandilli to Bunda – which naturally did not include our property – we took two sulkies and drove down to view them one Saturday afternoon – speechless at the sight of paddle-shaped growths crowding by the thousand round the walls of a cottage – they clustered like the heads of a rioting mob swarming in from all sides to besiege the place and chase the owners away – the house stood silent and abandoned – we were told the starved cattle had been driven elsewhere – 'What for?' I asked querulously 'so they can spread the pest wider in their droppings?' –

This was considered both indecent and malicious as I later heard –

I suppose I ought not to be surprised that farming folk felt they needed to blame somebody (we had gone through a similar process ourselves) or that they presumed the consequences of my new outgoing routine would prove ever more noxious until I succeeded in corrupting and bankrupting the entire community – and maybe it *was* I for instance who drove the Roman Catholic congregation to ever more frenzied pagan lapses of female-worship so they paraded their idol (a thing of painted lips human hair and clattering beads) down to the wharf and back to church – who is to say? – and maybe it *was* I who lured the new outlaws to ever more clandestine plots against the young Queen Victoria's legitimate interests –

God knows I suffer enough –

Although our own confessionals were back in full operation no one dared touch me – regardless of the admissions and imprecations I called out and the penances I inflicted on myself for the failure of our hens to lay or for a pimple disfiguring Elizabeth's nose or for the hardness of the timber we split as firewood or even for a change in the wind – my crimes were so endless I insisted on all-night chronicles till I had no strength to stand and sobbed myself to exhaustion admitting it all though nobody wanted to hear me out – I begged them to forgive me because I believed the same as they believed and it never crossed my mind we might be mistaken in our faith – so while they accused each other I accused myself – but only now does it occur to me that sometimes they were lying as I was and that not so many things had gone wrong really.

No! the nonsense about me being a witch was started by superstitious children in Cuttajo – you mustn't believe a word of it – the only power I have of this kind is the eagle eye – given me by God – a chance gift beyond my control – like my knowledge of the most ancient times when Earth broke open and the first humans crawled out among the plants of Eden (Eden means 'the world of plants' according to the dead Beatrice) well this accounts for the tree-demons we found – I never told Mr Moloch but there was an occasion when a demon came my way and I used the eagle eye to stop it in its tracks long enough to get a good look – taking account of it as a leafy thing with a feathered tail and with grass growing along its shoulders – I dared it to stay though up until then the creature had not noticed me – it stopped stepping high steps and a clump of grass fell off – then without further ado began to turn into a human being – horrible!

You still have such curly hair! such capable hands! – I hope I am not keeping you?

Your horse? yes I have been thinking about your horse and so has Louisa because I see her at the well drawing a pail of water for it right now so you need have no worries on the horse's account – isn't the weather appallingly dry! the whole bush a tinderbox ready to go up at the least spark.

One way or another Louisa was a puzzle to the rest of us (a fresh cup? sugar? cream?) for a start she came from God knows what kind of family and then there was the question of why she stayed with us once she found she had to cope with a 'grisly' wife –

But I suppose I am not telling you anything really unless you understand the burden we bore in those days – the burden I've been explaining – our power to injure and destroy (though the injuries and destruction we came to be accused of were nothing to do with us) – prior to my loss and my outburst this had been a matter we devoutly begged God to lift from our shoulders – He declined in His infinite wisdom so we had to face up to our duty and submit to punishment –

Before Immanuel was born I remember hundreds of occasions when I stood before my husband's judgement while he summoned others to witness what I said and then talked quietly to me in a wheedling tone which I knew would set them going until sure enough a response came – from Elizabeth Canning in her wheelchair perhaps – in the same cajoling mode with echoes of similar references to love – assuring me of my place among the Chosen – but soon rising in pitch at the mention of a leak in the shed roof maybe or the persistence of her own headache – and by this time let me say her face would be reaching right up against mine with her eyes wide and her mouth agape for me to feel the heat of her rage on my skin before her claws raked at my hair as she tugged my head back or the jolt when she hit me while she screeched accusations that I had become host to evil spirits endangering everybody by giving the Devil house room oh yes this was my life and proof of my wicked influence because soon afterwards others would join in a chorus beating me down on to the carpet demanding nothing less than perfection – you may say all this was behind me and yet it remained vividly in memory –

So now that my turn had come I don't mind telling you I made the most of it – the fact is that people grow more vicious the worse their illness until they are little better than beasts by the time their ravaged bodies are dragged to the brink of death – the only thing holding them back is weakness –

I became the one – when the show was over – to bring cups of cocoa and digestive biscuits for the others – to help them up and stroke their hands while they drank – you have no idea – in a way it was like singing in a choir and losing yourself in the harmony – you felt so refreshed afterwards.

Mr Moloch left us in 1880 when there were still seven ladies here – Louisa Edwina Hester Ann Lavinia – who have I missed?

– did I say Edwina? – yes – Elizabeth Canning and myself – yet within a year poor dim-witted Lavinia took a turn for the worse and Elizabeth was already bedridden – sad times –

I could never accept Hester's theory that the consumption was a symptom of faith – 'Where does that leave my recovery?' I demanded to know –

When we told Mr Moloch he had to go – this tremendous thing we did – Louisa Theuerkauf took it upon herself to show us we could not only handle his machines and tools but make the decisions –

Some said that without either a boy to trap rabbits or a man to shoot kangaroos we would never manage for meat but Louisa encouraged Hester to practise until she became a better shot than Mr Moloch and eventually this saved the mission a tidy sum in wasted cartridges because she didn't need to bother keeping in practice – meanwhile the rest of us turned drudgery to our own advantage and discovered new freedoms hammering and puttying and mowing so that at night in the dormitory we began to exchange stories about our families – previously we would never have dared because this was the very stuff of our spiritual spying –

Yet still – for some reason – we left Louisa out and made her sleep in the room she had commandeered for herself when we first arrived –

Even so we allowed her to take part in the history we began to compile – beginning with Judge Honeywood and the voyage – the aerial battle – and including her own vivid account of being drowned and chasing the demons –

'Those feather masks!' I cried out with a shudder and Louisa smiled at me – yes she smiled –

In my case they have never lost their terrifying power because they come out of a man's imagination and they are very foreign to anything a woman might dream up – even when I think of the masks as masks and the demons as natives (even bringing to mind my memories of their jolly wives) I am not really reassured – they still surround me in nightmares from time to time which is curious when you think how often I am out among them these days besides having a real affection for the wives – nothing to do with any rumoured witchcraft let me say.

I have no doubt you are right and that this does make me unpopular with people in town but I have decided upon my new mission and I do what I do because at last (with Louisa's help) I have fathomed God's purpose in sending me here and putting me through all the torture of grand hopes and deception to reach a stage of wisdom where I can laugh at myself – as the legless Elizabeth used to say 'No extra dumplings for taking the solemn view!' to which Edwina had a standard response 'It is only a matter of life and death after all!'

May I freshen your cup?

I suppose I never felt my position did justice to my abilities or insight until I was told I carried the divine child – which may be why I came to believe – though I am sure I do not wish to sound the least bit complacent – before then it was a case of battling against the current simply because the current existed – more like an instinct than a policy.

Well for a start I mean against evil thoughts which resulted in being haunted by the flutter of insect wings and by something touching me after dark with feelers I imagined as long as your arm – besides by such nuisances as encroaching creepers taking over the whole mission so that hard as one fought them back by day they burgeoned in the knowledge of our abilities and grew while we slept – until any morning you might find their long shadows reaching in again to trespass on your bed –

I include the wider problem of the bush surrounding us with its infestation of little hairy legs and its plague of champing jaws and microscopic couplings especially in this parish – especially in those days – because I assure you rank fertility was rife enough then to be smelt on the breeze like sour skin –

Who was to doubt the cause while we remained a community of ladies? – what else should we expect but an invasion by these wasted teemings and swarmings in pursuit of anyone who might conceivably be thought fair game for the Devil? – but do pardon me – a man investigating murder scarcely needs reminding that the entire bush is overheated or the bounty of it! the wonder is that there are not more rapes and sonnets than there are – and that the burghers of Bunda don't come crawling up here on hands and knees to sniff round in their droves –

Mark my words – all we are doing in this place is *returning* – trying to make a journey back to the innocence we can never find again at home – don't ask me why –

I cannot explain what a struggle it is to have to sort among the thousands of words in my head for the few I need to fit the case.

Did that door creak? I suspect so though your ears should be sharper than mine but it is all we can expect considering the traditions of this house – the peeping and listening in – so I shall not care a jot – I used to be driven mad but now I refuse to bother – go ahead whoever you are! don't consider me! – mind you I know some secrets of my own though we ought not to mention them just here and now.

Maybe you have occasionally felt real demons brush past unseen with their itchy clothing and hot lewdness – you know what I'm saying? (be an angel and pass me that cushion will you?) well despite this I don't doubt that the natives here do sometimes *mean* to be taken for demons – though for a long while I could not be sure why my husband had pranced about offering to fight them – did he believe in them or not? – what of the possibility that their paint was intended to look simply festive? –

Though personally I would never be foolish enough to take any natives for granted – especially painted ones who are pretty sure to be up to no good for the very reason that they have painted themselves – let me not preach to the converted – there is nothing more interesting than art because it can be understood – whereas religion goes on baffling us –

Did he believe they were demons? –

This was the question that dogged me –

Doubts lodged in my mind since Mr Moloch was famous for

being able to recognize Satan anywhere and I had never seen him behave in such a way before – far from bouncing around with his fists up he usually froze on the spot – so for example one might be in a city street seeing him stiffen for no apparent reason – or one might be watching sailors scamper down the rigging like monkeys or a single man at Yandilli wharf stand up from where he had been seated on a bollard and Mr Moloch going rigid like a dog catching a scent – the frequency of these contacts simply demonstrated how thoroughly rotten society had grown and how close at hand the Second Coming must surely be –

So I won't let you poke fun at Mr Moloch –

I shall never forget Beatrice telling me how one morning in Stroud she saw a grey bird flutter down out of the sky to settle on his hand and leave a gold ring there which he wore as God's sign for his mission till the day he left us though I'm blessed if I know what has happened to it since – despite the festering doubts –

I have to confess that perhaps I still do believe in the prophet's message – most of what he said is confirmed in the Scriptures – you remember the man coming up out of the midst of the uttermost sea in Deuteronomy eighteen? –

One night he came rushing from his hut demanding to know how Satan had found him here – considering that as Nicodemians we followed Christ in strict secrecy – and with wild looks informed us at the time when we had set sail for Australia the only person to be told our true destination was Judge Honeywood – in days gone by an intimate of the great Joanna Southcott who believed she was pregnant with the Holy Ghost and died giving birth to nothing – though this by no means disproved her claim – so the judge could not be suspected of breathing a word to anybody – oh no! –

My husband questioned us – had he not guarded our secrecy in the chapel without windows? had he ever given way to the temptation to seek notoriety or praise for himself? – and I confess my eyes filled while I felt the old guilt rise because in my heart

I honoured him as the young man who led me through a tannery to show that I could survive even Hell with his guidance as long as I was told the truth and only the truth.

Looking back a lifetime later?

Yes he failed in what he believed he was to do – yes of course that's true – but perhaps from the greatness of his belief rather than the smallness of his spirit and one has to admit he always insisted that he of himself was nothing – which we put to the test eventually when we invited him to leave the mission and without a murmur he went back to his trade as a bootmaker –

An interesting trade because shoes do grow to be part of a person as no other article of clothing does – is it too farfetched do you think to claim that shoes wear into the shape of our character? – you will know how if you have ever worn someone else's – this was the prophet's belief which he demonstrated by inviting us to exchange shoes with each other – I defy anybody to explain the strange message of the wrong foot shape or the way it conflicts with the way one stands and what that means –

'The message of the simple shoe' my husband explained 'is like the riddle of a prophecy – the meaning must be felt because it cannot be described' – from which he would go on to another of his favourite sayings 'Those who need descriptions will never rest content until they reform the world – whereas when Jesus returns he will instantly destroy and just as instantly rebuild it – what's more we shall be privileged to witness this because we are living the last days!'

We looked forward to a future which would obliterate the past forever – there was only one thing Mr Moloch wished to rescue of the past – he was convinced he had connections with an ancient family – hence his original journey to see Judge Honeywood whose mother had been the daughter of an earl and was – so the prophet said – his own grandmother around whom he built a kind of fairy tale in which the poor boy in rags who feels himself born to more chivalrous things finds he is a prince indeed – consider Moses and Jesus being raised in secret –

by the bye now I have mentioned chivalry Mr Moloch insisted that God speaks as often to women as to men.

Precisely – the Voice.

Judge Honeywood's daughter told me the judge was an authority on Chinese calligraphy and quite famous apart from his duties on the bench – I cannot say how he took the notion of being related to my husband.

Oh the fact that Mr Moloch may well be *mad* is no more an argument against his prophecies than Joanna Southcott's imagined pregnancy was against hers – I am sure the Honeywoods would not have thought so either!

Wasn't I about to tell you how the killing itself happened?

Immanuel disappeared and Ann made efforts to comfort me because she had withdrawn the gruff person she used to be but I accused her of dishonesty because I wanted to hear nothing but disasters – having been brought to understand the full extent of the boy's danger now he was no longer a divine child assured of God's protection – you may imagine how sick at heart I felt – how soiled – how disgusted by my credulity – and beyond everything how worried for his safety – like any normal mother I pictured him being butchered by escaped convicts –

We immediately set out in the rain –

For three days that rain continued to pour down in relentless torrents creating throughout the forest a strange dim light made up of gleaming fragments mirrored by dripping leaves while we plodded deep into the wildest places to search every gully we came upon (ourselves in fear of being lost) soaked to the skin and calling the whole while – mocked by our own forlorn voices – eventually trailing home at night bedraggled and aching with bitterness until on the third day Louisa shook off her fatigue to remind us of the Scriptures and what the third day meant to the risen Christ –

This enraged my husband –

I actually feared he had lost his reason so wildly did he dash himself against the trees and punch his own head when no doubt he really wished to attack her – a profound mistake because quite apart from frightening her he let her see him for what he was – Louisa's mould of flesh set to marble while his frenzy played itself out – then having assured herself he was calm enough to understand she addressed him in a stony public voice 'Was it my own body with no life left already that you loved?'

He lost his last shred of power and lost it forever – what came to my mind was the text he often quoted with such relish 'The House of the Dead is the place of birth' and to think I always considered it meaningless!

In fact we did find the boy that third day –

We followed a stream to its source – wading knee deep in swirling water – clambering up over boulders – we reached a hidden clearing high in the jungle where the rocks were as overgrown with lichen as a Gloucestershire church – here Immanuel stood on a flat slab of stone – deep in conversation – speaking to a creature with its back to us though you may be sure such a wild thing had heard us coming and declined to turn round for its own reasons.

Forgive me – I shall be all right – in a moment –

Neither did it turn round a few seconds later when the smile faded from my son's face as he caught sight of us emerging among rain-drenched ferns – I say 'it' because the poor soul was so little like a human or in any way decent – at this point I distinctly heard Louisa say under her breath 'Shoot!' (she was right behind me) and distinctly heard this order followed by a tiny sound – a sound which made me shudder – excuse excuse me – the mechanical click of a gun being cocked – immediately a frightful bang went off leaving a stink of gunpowder –

Immanuel watched us with great dark eyes –

The wild thing still with its back to us watched Immanuel –

We watched them both –

How my heart stopped when the Voice repeated *The Lord is with you* and I remembered that John the Baptist had been a wild man –

Some fumbling went on behind me – the gun clicked again –

meanwhile silence billowed among those prehistoric trees lasting for such a terribly long-held breath I realized we were saved – the second terrible bang shattered everything – and the anger seizing me was that childish anger against the whole world – the creature dropped like a sack of bones –

I cannot explain why none of us had turned in time to prevent Mr Moloch having another try – and I accept blame being the only one left (apart from Louisa who tells me she was merely disgusted by the wild man when she made her comment '*Schutt*' meaning 'rubbish' so I believe) – there you have it – eighteen years have passed since Muley Moloch committed his crime.

That is your answer – and I suddenly saw why people thought him weaselish –

I don't know how you found out there had been a murder at all but I am glad to get it off my chest – you must promise me you will be gentle with him – he is older than his years and quite frail – I'm sure I could never live down the pain of being the one to put him in if I didn't think you would hear me out and understand how much an accident it was – although it looked like murder the poor man never intended it to be murder.

The truth is that if we are to be any use tomorrow we have to accept what happened yesterday – so you may be sure there's something amiss when one hears so much about what we will do in the future while there's never a peep about what we have already done –

But I cannot talk to you any more – I'm too choked up.

I don't doze off exactly – I simply lose little bits of time – for instance I can be busy with something and then find I am doing the same thing but facing the other way.

Ann was the last to die though in her case it was not consumption nor even cancer really – she died of humiliation – that fluff of white beard did it though for my part I assure you it was rather sweet in its way – quite a bush with a moustache to match – she felt she could never show her face in the street without being frightfully stared at so it was no wonder she stayed home and hid indoors – she said she even caught *us* staring –

Dearest of all she scolded me to cover how much she loved me –

Dying in her bed she gradually degenerated into an old man – her plump face hollowed out to the ridges and pockets of her skull – lips stretched so thin across big teeth that she got into the habit of licking them as if feeling to be sure they were still there – she had shown me so many kindnesses during my life that I could not bear the thought of living without her which is probably why I could think of nothing appropriate or comforting to say and why her distress irritated me so much I found it actually distasteful to be with her –

She wanted me to hold her hand and tell her about Heaven – instead of which I criticized her for not getting up – I chafed her wrists – I threw open the window and let the blinding sunlight in and demanded answers to my questions about how much she had improved since the day before – oh dear me.

I sometimes see myself – I am standing at a table and nothing at all is happening except that the knife in my hand has sliced an onion in two – the kitchen is rich with meanings so is the onion and so is the knife – I feel my heart will break for the joy of seeing my part in the great human tragedy while our clock makes the tremendous effort of ticking and the big hand trembles jerkily from minute to minute though the hour hand remains collected and steady –

Other times I see myself reaching out towards my young son while he shrinks – I am remembering how grief-stricken I was when he lost the power of speech although as soon as he recovered it he used it to wound me – I don't believe that that boy had any idea what I suffered or that I have suffered since because I saw him suffering – then and there in the jungle he needed nobody to tell him the man who lay dead at his feet was an Englishman – nor the reason why Mr Moloch threw away his gun and burst out with 'I am the one who wanted the world to be a good place!'

One day Sergeant Arrell you will wake to find you have grown old and this will be the day when you realize time does not pass – it accumulates – there is such a lot of it blocked up in me I can hardly move –

The point is that when my husband fired the fatal shot he couldn't have known this was a white man with the fellow so indescribably filthy and shaggy besides being completely naked and burnt by the sun –

I know we ought to have buried him but we had no tools with us – Mr Moloch took the corpse by one wrist and dragged it off among some bushes to be heaped with soggy dead leaves – then he delivered a prayer sincerely commending the fellow's soul to his Maker – after which he turned towards us and I suppose despite the rain we *had* assembled in the usual way ready to listen – he confessed that maybe this was not the only man whose soul he put in jeopardy 'So I give back the name of Muley Moloch to Muley Moloch – and pray the Lord God Almighty that no one should suffer punishment for my sins but myself alone' he said 'I shall again take the name my father gave me' –

It has to be admitted that he did not report the death when we returned – which was wrong – and so this spelt the end of the mission as it had been – the end of our decent place and the end of our great secret – though we went on living together –

Illness transformed the remaining Hidden Stars one by one – Elizabeth Canning losing her pained look of a cripple to be touched by the beauty of childhood – doubt creeping into Hester's perpetual carping to entirely take over – while Charlotte shed her familiar gentle character and emerged as a ravaged tyrant –

These precious friends took to their beds – each in turn – and died lonely deaths – mostly of the consumption as I have already explained – though in Lady Edwina's case it was a seizure which at first paralysed her down one side and then took her altogether

– until in '95 my dearest Ann's turn came – the sadness makes a mockery of our hopes really.

Mr Moloch had long since gone to re-establish himself in his trade so Louisa and I had to bury Ann's corpse unaided – being the only ones left –

We were presented with the problem of making her decent – you will recall what a large person she was and we did find her a terrible handful – experienced though we both were and efficiently as we worked on either side of the bed – first we stripped and sponged her ready for arranging her in her best ironed clothes and dressing her hair – well I had only just begun wiping one bulbous white leg when the feel of that dead flesh made me qualmy – the nerveless rubbery weight of it I suppose – I don't know – but apparently my weakness showed because I found Louisa watching me and realized that this was a Louisa who had put off her customary cold reserve like a wrap no longer needed –

Having counted a little too much on my strength I now understood that so had Louisa because her eyes were clouded with tears and it cost her an effort to hold them back – impossible tears – well – from this moment I knew she could be reached and that I was not doomed to live wholly alone and that much as I would miss Ann with her lovable grumbling God was providing somebody to remain here with me – to help with my work among the natives – I won't say I realized He was providing somebody for me to grow fond of – which came later – but company at least –

I asked her whether or not my husband had ever made love to her (you may not believe it but this is how bluntly I opened the subject) – she gave the matter some thought while attending to the corpse and gravely wiping the left leg as I wiped the right before straightening it out – 'No' she replied – unless I wished to count his miracle in bringing her back from the dead –

I caught myself imagining her there on the bed in place of the corpse – her limbs might look much like Ann's and her flesh might feel as solid and cool under my hand – I imagined her *being* the corpse until for a horrid fleeting moment I experienced a flicker of the interest Mr Moloch might have had in her –

We sponged Ann's poor feet with their bunions and dried between the toes – I glanced up at her face and I could have sworn I caught her breathing – but no – then we shook the folds from a petticoat still warm with the cupboard smell and heaved and hefted and tugged at the unwilling cloth to get it over her head – pulling it down – difficult because her skin was damp –

Miserably flushed and with our hair flopping loose we struggled at the task of restoring decency – although finally brutally we found we had to bounce the body when we came to work the dress over its hips and pull the stuff straight – by the time we came to brush her hair and coil her bun as she liked it we were wrecks –

Over a cup of tea the full awfulness of marriage seemed suddenly obvious to me – the folly of respectability and knowing one would rather *die* than be made a fool of – the revulsion I felt in that instant was against my own jealousy and against the useless pain of having lived so many years in the grip of suspicions –

After resting we worked together once more attending to the matter of plugging our friend's ears and nostrils with little balls of cloth – then we hoisted her head and shoulders on to some planks set in position to slope down from the top step into the waiting sulky – as we bent to ease her on to this slope I recalled the attitudes of stooping men scouring skins at the tannery and the way they had glanced up at me from under their brows and the vile thoughts they had obviously thought – her head thudded with a painless impact –

I was trembling from exhaustion by then and so was Louisa but we still had much to do and drove together up to the graveyard without a word while something happened between us and the mounting turbulence urgently rising to choke me was – I believe as I look back on it and despite the occasion – joy!

We buried her up there with the others – you should be able

to see the crosses – yes – all our bodies have been buried in the one patch – our Hidden Stars.

I wished Mr Moloch had been with us for the sake of his authority at funerals and to lend a helping hand because as it was we undid a lot of our good work by dirtying her dress and making a mess of her hair – yet the grave we had dug was adequate and she lay in it looking relieved while I delivered a service in my own way – then Louisa sang a strange beautiful melody to Latin words (which I hoped did not come from the Catholic mass but found so moving I dared not interrupt even for the sake of rescuing a dead friend's soul) I underwent my usual irrational anxiety in case the corpse might not truly be dead and only in a coma of apoplexy or partial suffocation – it had been the same ever since I felt we ought not to leave Beatrice among those stones on Ascension Island – afterwards we dropped flowers in and covered her with a blanket –

We would miss her – we would miss her strategic discontent –

We were too weak to unbuckle straps when we got back home so we left the pony in harness and plumped ourselves on the edge of the well with heads bowed to recover our broken breath – wheezing horribly I reached out on impulse to touch Louisa's hand as she had once reached out to touch me when I was pregnant – to my astonishment she grasped it firmly and drew me towards her – she folded me in her arms so the smell of our stale labours mingled and for a moment we clung there as survivors of a shipwreck –

I knew then that I was so free from Muley Moloch it would make no difference whether or not I saw him again – that he might even come back someday to live out his old age – I could employ Louisa as my housekeeper and let her take him in for a lodger once we partitioned the old dormitory into several rooms – suddenly I was full of plans.

More and more I find myself dreaming of England and the most common dream is a winter morning with fresh snow lodged on bare branches while a dozen rooks flap away toward a spinney of elms across the valley just beyond the farm fence – it is one of those days when everything seems old – yet I am walking hand in hand with Dora listening to the soft crunch of snow under our boots – we look back to see something of our character in the footprints as if time has hesitated to let us keep hold of actions just lost – I am wearing gloves and so is she yet I can feel the shape of her bony fingers through the wool and her warmth as well – we carry Bibles in our free hands and we are in no hurry to reach the Hall having set out early on purpose – the sky rests old gentle close and grey on a land crusted with crystal and I am tremendously happy so I pray to God never to let me forget one iota of this feeling which includes a special reverence for the little church in the village away to our left at the foot of the long hill – an extremely old church built of the same grey stone as the cottages with a square tower rising high above the surrounding roofs and we can even see little dots of snow on top of its spiked crown as well as the finest white eyebrow above each arched window – or at least I can see this and I am sorry for darling Dora because she cannot – Dora who has near-sight explains that though she *sees* the village she can't make out anything *of* it but she appreciates what I tell her because after all there is nothing new in what I describe – which brings me to stop in awe at having the first important idea of my life –

'Catherine dear!' she gasps and alarm fills her eyes 'are you ill?' –

I am not at all ill – I am simply unable to put words to my thought without destroying it altogether so I let go of her hand and place a woolly finger on my lips to keep her from speaking till I have time to get used to what being clever means (I can describe this now but oh my goodness it was difficult then) my idea is that there might be no such thing as a real village or a real anything – because while I look across the valley and see a village clearly Dora can look inward to what she knows by memory and see the same village every bit as clearly – which surely makes her idea as real as my solid stone! –

When we walk on we are no longer as happy as we were though I have the advantage of being a superior creature –

So Dora sulks and pilots us to the side of the road where she can kick at some frosty tufts of grass and trample a frozen cobweb but she is only angry because I have shut her out so her anger flatters me and by the time we reach the gate I am positively triumphant – I tell her I love the way these stone gateposts lean and the way the stone caps on them have worn (especially the one with a diagonal crack) – when some imp in my brain tempts me to make a show of opening the gate for her to put her even more at my mercy so I dart over to the latch and grasp the great wooden beam of the top bar but she sees more than I do – she sees my motive as well as my action and refuses to be humiliated –

With the energy and boyishness of a much younger girl she manages her skirts and climbs the gate to swing over and leap down on the other side before I have a chance to let myself through – so now I am the one who is cross because she won't allow me to enjoy an idea without having to tell her about it – this means I am no longer blissfully happy yet I still want to be – which must be why I clash the gate behind me and run up to her and begin dusting the snow off her clothes after her escapade – all the while scolding her for the scalliwag she has become –

Being called a scalliwag pleases her immensely and we pause a moment at the roadside on the brink of an ice-crusted ditch while a trap comes bowling along the road and the gentleman in it raises his hat though we giggle because we do not recognize him and we know he has come a long way since his horse's flanks are smoking – then when he is out of sight we gaze across at the ivy-grown wall of the gatehouse and remark on the curiosity that no snow has collected on this ivy so we decide like a committee that the wind must have come from the north-east or this wall would not be so sheltered – old bare trees tower over the gatehouse and among their net of twigs looms the Hall with its chimneys – stone chimneys having lozenge patterns carved on some and twisted candy braids on others – I point out the peacock perched at the peak of one roof with his tail dusting the snowy slates and ask Dora humbly where peacocks come from – 'China' she replies without hesitation and kisses my cold cheek –

Having crossed the road we push through a squeaky iron turnstile at the side of the gatehouse to make our way up the broad gravel drive enchanted at finding the snow has moulded the judge's garden to smooth simple forms – like an outward expression of my soul at that moment – with clipped hedges of evergreens carrying domes of snow and the sundial standing on a perfect oval carpet where the star of pathways converges – statues of heroic figures in plumes and armour lean on shields or broadswords – mature yew trees gather all the shadows of that bright place into their rich recesses and broad shallow semi-circular steps lead down to a frozen pond beyond which the grand old house stands gazing over its domain through majestic windows —

Miss Honeywood is waiting for us because there has been a scandal in the village and she intends to learn everything she can from us before the cottagers' children troop in for Sunday School – the scandal being that a notorious poacher called Giles Coney who once ravaged the woods in the eighteen-twenties until he was caught and transported to New South Wales has returned after serving his sentence and the point is that he has cut a great figure in the district by showing the welts on his back to some drinkers at the White Hart and swearing to break every bone in Judge Honeywood's body for having sentenced him – even if the luxury of this revenge costs another sentence and the rest of his life back in the colonies in chains –

We have heard my Uncle Herbert on the subject so we are able to assure her that this is indeed what the creature said –

We sit either side of her fireplace in the small wainscoted parlour watching logs crackle and the glow reflected by panelled wood – our noses and ears are pink and we sniff politely while enjoying the comfort of warmth – we feel very close and very happy because Mr Coney's threats are nothing to do with us and we have never even seen Miss Honeywood's father so how can we imagine what it might be like for him to be in danger? – then I am surprised again by the logic of my original idea concerning the village as I saw it and as Dora imagined it –

Because this logic must apply to everything in the world –

Is the real brutality suffered by a criminal more real than the ideal suffering one may imagine when hearing about it just because it is more painful – any more than the real discomfort of influenza is more serious than the evil thoughts by which somebody else may cause it to strike?

I have worried a good deal along these lines since then (especially since coming out here and eventually learning that we could no longer rely on Mr Moloch for guidance) well we should remember the pious Wesleyan preacher's estimate that every twenty years each of us is likely to commit six hundred and forty-nine million sins – any one of which would be grave enough to ensure eternal damnation – so where does that place us in respect of a man caught poaching and sent for fourteen years in chains? –

Never let it be said that coming events do not cast their shadows before them – or that our true life is not lived through memories.

Thank you Louisa you may bring the sandwiches now – we are firm believers Sergeant in the healthful properties of a sandwich taken with a glass of water.

I rejected England you see and so did the rest of the Stars who came out here to help create the New Jerusalem for one reason or another which I do not wish to go through in detail – but there is a profound difference between this and the case of a Giles Coney being spurned *by* England although I could not condone the man's lawlessness (since he belonged in Cold Dean which was a village I knew) I do claim that even in the case of crimes more serious than poaching the causes may not be as simple as they appear –

Did I mention that the man's left wrist was badly scarred or that he had certainly been a convict? no – not Mr Coney – the wild man.

What I suppose I am saying is that our worst offences are often overlooked and nothing in my life fills me with such horror as the thought of my husband stealthily using me while I was unconscious – despite the fact that he would always have been welcome when I was awake – so I cannot tell whether or not this also stood between me and Immanuel though I believe I felt the same love as any mother has for her child –

Let me confess that in order to allow my husband to disappear and start a new life we reported him lost at sea – well it was only a white lie because he very nearly had been – then just as soon as I inherited the property I cast off his surname in the same ceremonial way he had cast off Muley Moloch's name – I went back to being Catherine Byrne as I had been when I fell in love with Dora and when she fell in love with a strange man who didn't even notice her but who floated up off the floor for me –

We let the lawn go to pot –

There was never any mention of whether Giles Coney had scars on his wrist as well as his back but until we heard of his return to the district I don't believe I had given a thought to New South Wales so I suppose this is what put the idea in my head – ready for when I suggested it on my wedding day as a way out of suggesting a mission to China!

Yes I believe one day my faith will be restored to me but it cannot be hurried because there is no point in chasing after faith – faith comes or does not come and when it does it is always as a gift to the undeserving – so although one should never indulge one's wickedness it is no use imagining one can ever *earn* faith by good works – I am tremendously down on good works – and who among us can truthfully say his life is not a battle against his nature?

What else should I confess to you while I have the chance to influence the way you judge all this? I'd like to flush the whole lot out of my system in the interests of fairness to Mr Moloch – because he is the one who still needs help –

For a start I ought to clear Louisa of all responsibility – she had nothing to do with anything and she was in no position to overhear what Immanuel told me after the murder so she could never have guessed the victim was one of us – apart from which she is my employee these days – as I say – so I take responsibility for her provided she cooks and minds the cats when I am out because I spend a good deal of time in Yandilli – occasionally I drive as far as Bunda for the Sunday service – nor must you hold it against her that her saying is 'It's time for women to be led by women' because who can be sure whether she means it or not? –

You might be interested to hear that her singing voice sounds as clear as ever though I happen to know she is fifty-seven but please don't let slip the least hint that I told you or that she has the curious habit of stretching her lips to cover her teeth whenever she opens her mouth wide –

Louisa never learned the piano you know despite having a certain skill at vamping accompaniments – when there is any serious playing to be done I am dragooned into service though she is terribly critical of my abilities – she has even given me some singing lessons because of our little secret – recently I have begun learning a new piece which she was engaged to perform when she was supposed to return to Germany years ago and never went – it's a duet – and though we have no music she remembers both parts (mine was intended for a tenor so I take it up an octave) – since she has taught me this strange modern composition – I have it completely by heart – everything else begins to sound artificial by comparison *'O sink hernieder Nacht der Liebe!'* – glorious yet simple – and because we have no piano part we can sing it while working in the garden or walking through the forest down to the main road now a road has at last been put through *'Herz an Herz dir Mund an Mund'* or my little solo bit that goes *'zu täuschendem Wahn entgegengestellt'* (do you have any German?) 'Heart on heart and lip on lip we defy the delusions of the world' very sad – 'make me forget I live' so haunting – Louisa describes it as peaceful music which makes me wonder about her – though in a curious way it *is* peaceful –

Human pride is a terrible thing when you come to think about Louisa accepting a contract to tour the Antipodes simply because Mr Wagner was only going to cast her as Isolde's understudy in his new piece – but of course she adored him and she was young –

The cats? yes there are five cats and since we put the fence between our two houses they have taken to staying over there more often than living with me although they were originally mine but I do not begrudge Louisa in the light of everything she has given up – make no mistake about it to turn one's back on fame must be a tremendous sacrifice not to mention the loss of that peculiar satisfaction said to be unique to artists when they perform – really it was thinking of this that I set out to become her friend once Ann passed away – in the beginning she was thrust upon us as a disaster and yet eventually you could say Miss Theuerkauf became the one to set us free –

It makes me wonder if there might have been enlightened souls among the convicts too – I mean we simply do not know what talents have been lost – convicts must be born like anyone else with their share of native wit – some mute inglorious Milton here may rest – here – some youthful genius stifled and taught only how to die – A youth to Fortune and to Fame unknown – and so forth – do you recognize it? – Heaven did a recompense as largely send – He gave to Misery all he had (a tear) – He gained from Heaven (twas all he wished) a friend – the lovely lovely lines of dear Gray –

Incidentally if anyone was ever victorious in death that would have to be Ann Whittaker who surely flew straight to the arms of Jesus –

Did I tell you how Immanuel ran away again while we were busy covering the wild man's corpse? and that no one noticed? well the last I saw of him was his cheeks going purple as he stood goggling down at the dead man before screaming in Mr

Moloch's face 'He looked after me!' – this was why we decided to leave the boy to his own devices until we finished the job as best we could with a mound of leaf mulch – we called him when we were ready to start out on our way back down the creek but he was simply nowhere to be found – though we called and called among those mossy jungle trees there was no answer except whispers beginning all about us and continuing high above – no sound of fleeing footfalls or sign of the child who was to have saved the world and reigned in majesty for a thousand years – nothing but a multitude of whispers –

I never saw him since – but I think of him lovingly every minute of the day –

He did write to me once from the Ballarat so I dare say we can thank Digby Barnett and the habitual Barnett failures for Immanuel thinking he might pick up a fortune in the street there (though I don't mean to include young Barney who has been a great help lately) but in all justice I dare say we do the same thing in our own way while we continue to keep ourselves ready for a miraculous future –

Ten years later Immanuel sent me a letter from England which I carry next to my heart – I have it right here and I shall show it to you – just wait a tick –

Till I get – breath – 'My dear Mother, I do not have anything much to say, except a powerful wish to say that this is so! Besides, I do not wish you to waste your grief on me thinking I am dead or anything so easy. I must thank you for the tales you told me when I was a child, these are what I remember, King Gundafar in particular as well as the tale of Mr Giles Coney, but I have discovered that the judge died peacefully at home so Mr Coney must now satisfy his passion by frightening Miss Honeywood instead . . . all for a brace of pheasants and a hare or two, it makes me glad to be an Australian! The occasion of my writing today is to inform you that I have spoken to my grandfather on the subject of the Empire and the changes that may soon happen with the loosening of ties, but he offered no more than to declare himself glad to hear of you alive although he does not wish to see you, so he hopes you are going to stay in New South Wales. My great-grandmother Boulton left me her house in Stroud, a very poky little place, hardly fit to live in. I dare say I shall sell it as soon as I am able. Finally, I send my love to Aunt Ann and wish you well. Your dutiful son, Immanuel Moloch.'

Do you see what a hand he has! I taught him to write like that! but of course he was never *Moloch* he was Immanuel Heaps – oh dear! – and I have been trying my best to protect us all.

We defeat ourselves.

Truth to tell I feel horribly tired.

Now you come to mention it there *were* some alarming noises at night the Monday before last – that was Boxing Day wasn't it? – yes and when Louisa called me quite late I went outside to listen with her but for a long time nothing else happened – it was a hot still night and the mosquitoes were bad – we listened – hardly daring to breathe – then we heard what sounded like a gun shot down on the flat towards the cliffs – but of course that's a good two miles from here – a single random pop ominous enough to stop the heart – well we looked at one another across the fence – I believe we relived the same memory because Louisa's voice shook a little when she cried 'What is this?' – and it takes a lot to make her voice shake – then the very instant the question was out another shot sounded – at about ten or eleven o'clock – followed by screams from the same direction – screams swallowed in silence – sucked up into the night among the unblinking stars –

So there we were – each in our own garden – each with our piece of the divided lawn which Mr Moloch had cut that very afternoon – straining to hear what we could and afraid of believing what we knew –

Louisa hissed at me 'Was she screaming *Father*?' which made me go cold all over and shiver at the thought of little Immanuel's voice (my own too) – but we caught nothing more – not even that murmur of a million spirits which sometimes drifts down from the mountain – though we waited until the mosquitoes were beyond bearing and the cats got back into her house so they had to be put out again –

We shook our heads as I recall – and very possibly the whole thing was a prank because we were warned there was to be a dance at Cuttajo hall and the sinners would be out in force for sure so the road was most likely crowded all night with young folk on their way to perdition.

Sergeant!

Do you mean to say *this* was your murder? only the other day? but when I was telling you about everything – ? I thought you meant our – well our terrible event – excuse me – yes – and I wanted you to understand.

Immanuel Heaps as I say because his father is John Heaps the Bunda bootmaker – we often drove into Bunda on a Sunday to hear him preach privately at his house – but let me say it is quite quite impossible to suspect my poor bootmaker of violence.

How many victims? two sisters and a brother in their twenties? no no Mr Heaps is not particularly strong and we took his gun off him in any case – you say they were laid out in regulation order? how peculiar.

This is shocking! oh the poor woman! to see her children dead! there can be nothing more terrible – even the thought is a stone in the heart – can she survive such pain? – we must do something for her.

But what on earth?

Yes I *know* he left Bunda a month ago – this was because I invited him to come here and live next door as Louisa's lodger – let's not go over all that again – well perhaps because I hoped to punish her if you like! – on the night in question he was asleep in bed – you see she and I didn't go back inside for almost an hour and just when we were saying good night he appeared at the door of her place – eyes blurred – quite happily clad in nothing but his nightshirt with the weather being still so hot – he looked so little with his nose and ears bigger than ever –

I recall thinking about that nightshirt (though I knew it had to be a shop-made article and not the one sewn by Ann) and thinking these were the feet in the shoes I had once watched rising off a carpet –

When he asked what we were doing we simply waved him back to bed – no point in trying to explain to him – you see he has grown completely deaf and become a peeper – I must confess we both get a touch short on the odd occasion when we have our own worries – I wonder whether the deafness may perhaps be connected with going bald – my only objection to a bald head is the way a man's scalp wrinkles when he tilts his head back –

The oddest thing of all to a person brought up in a family believing in the absolute ugliness of evil and the absolute beauty of good is to realize that some of the ugliness was not (well not by any very serious criterion) evil at all – whereas plenty of the beauty was certainly as evil as evil – and that the way to reach this realization is through laughter –

As a matter of fact Louisa herself doesn't have much sense of humour though she is the one who puts things in such a way that others see the funny side – so she gets in quite a huff when you laugh and she can't see why – never mind –

For instance the day we buried Ann Whittaker and clung together at the well until I grew calm enough for Louisa to let me go she said 'To be fearing death we are correct – ' and added 'only an idiot is not afraid' – she thought for a long pause – 'yet each lady lying dead is like the same lady found in a different mood isn't it? – always your Ann was provincial already and a person as you say skin deep – until I help to lift up her body and feel how heavy it weighs' – despite an extremity of exhaustion this struck me as appallingly funny – though I was too polite to laugh openly –

Yet at the same time Louisa's words brought the living Ann

to mind in an unexpected way because she always *had* been provincial though I'd never seen through her until that moment –

Poor Ann – did I ever understand her or what her life meant or even what her real hopes might have been or why the prophet accepted her as a disciple? – later the idea came that with her dead a bit more of that unexplained battle we once heard out in the Atlantic Ocean died also –

A bit had died with Beatrice and another bit with Lavinia and more with Edwina so that – though I kept my share – most parts were dead and buried – unless – unless Mr Moloch's deafness is a case of the real world being shut out by the need to reassemble this lost world in its entirety –

Could it be that he has been taking it back into himself all these years – fragment by fragment – cramming the whole drama into his head (does it belong there?) to be pieced together again – who knows? – perhaps when he pads around at night and appears at the door in his pyjamas – perhaps the whole thing is exploding in there – echoes booming around his skull – the dome of his disappointed life expanding to become as vast with freedom as a whole hemisphere of sky – maybe this explains why he carries his head as if balancing the weight of it – even when he shuffles along Louisa's corridor or stands at the back door – bewildered and damp – transcending his failures to become custodian of great forces locked in a raging crescendo – while his forgotten shell is left framed at the brink of an uninterrupted night – artillery guns booming without the slightest effect on cicadas or frogs – individual soldiers' groans made negligible by the universal terror and panic heard only inwardly – the bush upright and motionless with not a leaf disturbed while milling horse hooves pound the imagined Earth – the Earth a drum – the pounding relentless and chaotic – and the recollected air rent with a clamour of cries which are really neither cowardly nor heroic because they are the voices of illusion and an escape from truth –

This might explain the tension in Mr Moloch when he taps his stiff fingers on the fence rail as he is brought up short and props there without a word to anybody – or taps the table while Louisa prepares our dinner – or taps his thighs as he ambles among mementos of his failures down by the creek –

It's my belief that his body is too full of death to be able to die on its own account – and I dare say that in among the bursting shells and screaming horses he hears phrases from his sermon 'Death does not destroy the *value* of life – whatever is precious is only precious by virtue of the fact that it can be lost – I do not give thanks to death because it will bring my troubles to an end – I give thanks to death because it will bring my joys and my faith to an end – ' that's what he used to tell us at those passionate meetings when his face lit up with knowledge of God's word and his eyes grew big and brilliant and so dark you could lose yourself in them – 'This is why we must forever fight sin and not surrender to it – because the death of sin gives meaning to sin' –

Perhaps he hopes to inherit the Hall!

If there's such a thing as wisdom it comes when you realize that life is lived altogether in the imagination – each instant as it happens is already past – there is no dividing line between the window you are looking out of right now and Judge Honeywood's tall windows giving on to his park or Mrs Boulton's window dim with steam –

At times (because the world moves on and solid objects and painful afflictions become harmless souvenirs) I feel cheated – but generally I have been so strengthened by my experiences I feel I have enjoyed too much benefit and that I am an impostor.

Shall I call Louisa for you?

This frightful cough – do please excuse me – she won't be a minute.

The photographs? those indecent photographs? – well Mrs Pringle tells us that Florence Love told *her* Charles Bailey used them not so long ago to survive the Depression – she has reason to believe he sold them in sets of six to teaching hospitals in

England (here comes Louisa) so of course any thought of my ever going back home has become utterly impossible now –

But as for the future – 'a new Earth wherein righteousness dwells?' – all I can say is that nothing is ever resolved – we are eternally caught waiting to be rescued – although with Immanuel in limbo and nearing thirty – do you see? – one can never tell – aha!

Captivity Captive

There were crows in his eyes when he came right out with it, confessing that he had been the murderer. You could see them flapping in there. And now and again the glint of a beak. You can't tell me anything about crows I don't already know at eighty. Nor about him, either.

It's no good saying, like Norah used to, that I'm the one who always let his imagination run riot. You ought to have seen the hungry fluttering in that look of his, those scavengers working away at the rotten flesh of corpses long dead and mostly forgotten.

Poor old bloke, the dill. Dismal is what you'd call him. Dismal the whole of his life. I can be sure of this because I knew him for all but the first couple of years of it.

He spoke the word *murder* in a croak. Even this came crow-sweet, what with Ireland still hanging on him, afraid to let him go, counting every one of her children (me included) and mad for numbers. *Mar*der, he said it. Then, on account of being in his deathbed, which this time was permanent enough, the wings in his coaxing eyes fluttered and folded, twitched out again, and really did fold.

He looked peaceful; the picture of a man who has confessed his soul's torment and expects eternal absolution just for the saying of it. But I knew he was raging with excitement. What he always promised himself he would do, he had done. He never thought he'd rouse enough courage. And now here he was, flat on his back, being listened to by an inspector of police. Oh yes, he had gone that high. Not just Jim, our local constable, but an inspector down from Sydney on a special visit to nobody else.

Poor coot had scored the top brass and you could see how it

set his blood spinning with grief that he hadn't made this occasion when he was younger and might have enjoyed it to the full. But there was no one else to blame, so he shut his mouth and shut his eyes and made such a good impression of being gratified that, if the whole town didn't know him for a wowser, a witness might have been pardoned for thinking he was drunk. This excitement put the colour back into his skin. He looked as if he might not die, after all. One word, *murder*, bringing him to life again. I thought: We shall be laughing over this for years to come.

Then he spoke some more, the flurry of crows now getting to his voice, muffling and rattling it.

'That was when I bashed the horse's brains in with the bludgeon-stick,' he said.

Those exact words. He said them in front of us, even knowing us the way he did. Also knowing what we knew about him. Can you believe? But I don't think he realized the inspector's question might have been several questions, in each case tricky enough. Barney was a dill.

'Why? That's what I don't understand. Why?' was what the inspector put to him.

'Why?' he bellowed, eyes still shut, the fast blood giving him strength he had no use for any longer. He was panicking. His mouth hung open with his tongue humping and writhing inside, a fat white slug working its way over the question.

Even my mother, who walked round in a cloud of the darkness she gave out, couldn't have touched Barney Barnett for resentment at that moment, though I am convinced he thought the question *Why?* simple enough, the point being that he never expected to have to answer questions. He planned to do all the talking needed. Finally he got his white slug past the boulder and grumbled: 'This is 1956, don't you know?' Then, as I understood it, his dim cross-grained mind got onto the fact that if he wanted to die famous he would have to fight for it. He gathered energy during those failing minutes and spoke out of an irritable hunger, still with his eyelids kept down so no one could see in to where the scavengers were busy. 'I'm not talking about no bloody horse, I'm talking about him. Him and his sisters!'

The bedsheet had a bit of cottage lace along the edge, worked by his grandma, more than likely, whose needlecraft had made her a local identity. Like a baby, he hooked his finger through a hole where some stitches were coming adrift.

Barney felt ashamed of his granny and grandpa, I might mention, both of them being English; they came in on his father's side and he swore he was his mother's son. So he was. She gave birth to him in Ireland, the country of his heart, and he never outgrew it. In that way of being boastful about his Irishness, there was some sympathy between him and my brother Michael, this cannot be denied. But with Barney it was a snivelling don't-put-me-off-my-stroke-or-I-might-miss-it-altogether kind of thing, whereas Michael bounced around boyish with cheerfulness and forever working things out by getting them wrong. Michael, who was one of the victims he just claimed to have killed fifty-eight years previous to hanging on by a hole in his English grandma's sheet.

Our family didn't bother speaking like Irishmen, not even Pa or Mum. We were Australians with a healthy scorn for any superstition brought out here from the old country. Unless you mean the Church. We went to mass, all but Ellen, the youngest of the murder victims.

A priest was with us at the deathbed. He was the one to keep murmuring in the inspector's direction: Don't you think he's tired? Don't you think I should take over now? Don't you think the last rites will settle his mind? Surely we should let the poor man turn his eyes to God before too late?

The old priest, Father Gwilym, would never have cut such a feeble figure. He'd have been master of the occasion, with his purple stole on, critical of the crucifix and candles already set in place by the householder, and sprinkling holy water with casual flicks.

This new man fumbled when dabbing the consecrated oil at Barnett's nostrils. Did he so deeply dread the mortal contact?

The pad then touched eyes, swollen lips, and ears burning with the sin of pride. The words of absolution escaped him in a voice little better than an apology, the same voice he found to say thank you when handed a dry specimen of lemon on which to cleanse his fingertips before accepting the towel folded in his honour. He stepped back a pace and committed a quiet sigh.

We were a great age. I looked at the others and they looked at me. Poor Barney, said our looks which we made no attempt to conceal, the fool thinks he was big enough to plan a crime so famous it is printed in encyclopedias. Sly even then, he let his eyes show only a moment, unable to resist checking if he had outwitted us. Black wings gave a twitch in there. Finding the effort too taxing, perhaps, his gaze sank to wander from one to the other of his hands as they crawled about his chest like sightless creatures.

The Sydney inspector switched an unspoken question to us, but was offered no satisfaction, so he addressed the dying man again, politely controlling any sign of how exasperated he had become.

'Look, Mr Barnett, you need to tell me something we don't already know. You're going to need to tell me something new, something only the murderer could possibly tell. I am not empowered,' he explained almost pathetically, 'to take your word on such an important matter.'

Startled crows fluttered a moment, but Barney wisely let his lids droop once more. He never could make an artifice stick. Yet he managed quite well at having it seem that they drooped under the weight of injustice which would not admit he knew whether or not he was guilty, would not allow him to sacrifice his reputation to the ultimate penalty of notoriety.

'If I could accept just anyone's word,' the inspector grumbled, 'where would we be? I suggest you cast your mind back to the night of the murders.'

By way of answer, the parasitic hands sucked at each other in a desperate effort to rise to an occasion suddenly difficult beyond all expectation.

'I need only one thing, one detail unknown till now. That may be enough to clinch the matter. You must have thought about it for years.'

Oh the poor fellow, laid out to die with his lies. And us gathered round his bed already putting him in mind of hell. We were the problem, no doubt about that. We were the ones he had not planned on seeing, the survivors, so square and blank that the gaps between us stood solid as the absent three who had been murdered, Norah, Ellen, and Michael.

Our mother had died of grief because she could not learn to weep, any more than she'd been able to learn to laugh. She set her curse to work throughout this occasion because she predicted the murderer would never be allowed to die without confessing for all the world to condemn him. She breathed out her expectancy, simple as air. We breathed it in. We knew she had come.

But the chief figure towering over us and taking up most of the available space, as rigid and dark as basalt rock, was our dead father, seated on his dead black stallion. His hands, blunt and hairy as lion paws, one crossed over another while clasping the reins loosely – I felt my own hands the same, though they only held the brim of my funeral trilby – and the apprentice corpse struggled to disengage his finger from a hole in the lace. The horse exchanged weight, left haunch to right. Father's hat rose an inch, enough to touch the ceiling, and sank again.

My good humour had the power to kill. I could see an end to the misery and complications.

Even with a ghost filling that bare room, the coward in bed braved his fate and refused to give in. He stuck to his story, eyes squeezed tight against fear, knowing as he must that absolution for his other sins would count for nothing in heaven if he died under the weight of this last lie, plus trying to steal the priest's forgiveness from the sinner who truly needed it. Meanwhile, the priest himself remonstrated against any further investigation, at least having enough wit to see the saved soul might fall into subsequent error.

'I used a bludgeon-stick to bash their heads in,' Barney's feeble voice insisted, as if this were no different from the statement he made before. 'I swung it with both me hands.'

Pa's horse arched its tail to achieve that fastidious ceremony unequalled by any other beast.

The inspector straightened up. You couldn't help being sorry for him, so disillusioned and frustrated he looked. He might have paced the room had there been space. We watched him, which is to say all except Pa, who watched only me. I knew my father's expression without checking, the dead eyes indifferent as they had been when he whipped me, indifferent as they had been when I first ploughed the fifteen-acre paddock and believed I had done well. Then I did check. Yes, exactly as I thought. He was waiting to see if I would tell what I knew.

Can you imagine how it felt to have such power over him I could keep him sitting on his stallion, hold his gaze, and refuse to say anything?

'They were my marders,' Barney's voice insisted contemptibly. 'All mine.'

Pa was a sad giant, as big as any pair of us except Jerry, Jerry having taken after him in size. When we were young men he liked to wrestle us two at a time. We could never hold him down. I don't believe he knew how much we hated him for this. I think he hoped we enjoyed the intimacy, in a life offering not much warmth you could relish. The palpable heaviness of contact, as I remember it, was made stranger still by sensuousness.

He never laughed, my father. So at one stage I considered him insane. As for us, we laughed a lot. I suppose he hated our laughter as much as we hated his wrestling matches. But this was not the worst of it. He suffered terrible attacks of rage, which Barney Barnett, incidentally, would never have known about. He'd beat you to the ground, then strap you on a bed-end and flog you for no reason he could explain through the froth filling his mouth. I do not wish to make it sound as if we thought our childhood hell; no, we accepted our parents as fairly typical and conforming to the general rule. What I say about my father applies, more or less, to my mother too, but I shall try to account for her later.

Pa said he never wanted us to leave home.

You might have thought we were a burden, all ten children having survived in those times when you could usually reckon on losing at least one in three within its first twelve months. But no, he raged against us if we tried to skip the farm. When I was nine, my eldest brother William, at twenty, asked permission to go up north and seek work on the railway line. The request alone was enough and a proof of treachery. Pa crushed him – I witnessed this – smashed his ribs and collarbone, took him by one leg and growled, 'I'll break it now if you like, or wait till you try giving me the slip and break it then.' William, being already proud as a man should be, swore and lay silent. But he gave in. That night he went for Pa with a butcher's knife, gashing his shoulder, but the old man beat him up so badly he never fully found himself again. He came round and got better. But it wasn't the Willie we knew – jaunty on horseback, a squire for the women hereabouts – who ate at our table and drudged in the fields. He emerged from that fight a different shape, flesh hung heavily on him and his spirit went a separate way. Previously Willie had been the one we turned to when we didn't turn to Norah with our troubles.

After this I used to tell myself, under the blanket at night, that I had better grow up as quick as possible and practise running. I couldn't wait to cut loose. But the way life happened, I need not have worried. It makes you laugh to think of: Pa didn't want me to be confined at home. He wanted me to learn about the world outside. Not like Danny, whom he threw out when the time came, but not like the others either. You'd think I was a reproach to him, a reminder of some person or event greater than myself. That's how it seemed to me at the time. Only for my mother wanting me to stay, I believe I might never have been around the place on 26th December 1898. If so, I would probably have died of common old age long ago, I dare say, with no punishment to sustain me.

Now you have a rough idea of Daniel Murphy, the father. But let me give you a few more facts while I'm at it. Born in Tasmania, though he never had papers to prove anything by, he stood six feet ten inches in his socks and weighed twenty-six stone of solid graceless strength, everything about him being dense and thick. His wrists! It amazes me to think of them. Nothing could hurt him. Once, the winch let fly when we were hauling logs and the heavy handle spun over, knocking him off his feet. We had hopes, I can tell you, but he got up and grabbed hold of it like a chicken farmer wringing a bird's neck. He never even showed a bruise that I can remember. We couldn't help being proud of him.

Johnnie and I used to have a joke when the first tractors went to work down our way: 'Useless bloody things,' we'd say, 'you could run over Pa with one of them and he'd get up and kick it in the arse.' That was the kind of joke we used to make, while Norah would come flying over to tell us we should be ashamed of ourselves, but immediately forget and veer off at a tangent: 'Just look at your hair, Johnnie! Have you been pulled backwards through a hedge, then? Sit down and I shall cut it for you so the girls'll all see you for the handsome lad you are. My, but you're growing,' she'd prattle affectionately. She might begin to comb his thatch right then, while he sat docile in the power of her happiness, and she'd take the shears to it till one of the younger girls limped indoors crying, so she'd have to fix that drama with a dab of perfume or some small treat kept tucked in her pinafore pocket. Back she'd come to find young Johnnie had skipped away and she'd laugh, threatening to leave him lopsided for a week with half his hair cut and half shaggy.

Our childhood was filled with happiness, with flights of swans and hailstorms at night when the clouds were lit like giant flowers overhead, heavy with honey and rooted to the soil by lightning. Life was, in its unrepeatable way, perfect. You could say it stayed like that. Even to the murders.

When Polly got married we were glad to lumber the butcher with her calamity of foolishness. Polly did not see what you or I might see. She saw only herself and her necessities. She couldn't talk but the gossip hopped out, fluttered and flopped like amphibious creatures losing their tails but almost too transparent to be seen at all. The crops will be ruined if it doesn't rain soon, you might say, at which she'd clench her hands in despair and reply: 'I suppose this is your way of telling me I shan't get my new bonnet I need!'

The butcher had to be a bible-basher himself, or he'd never have got the notion she was marriable. They had Connemara forebears in common. Our grandparents had not survived long enough for us to actually know them. Except Mum's father, who was recollected by Polly from when she was a little girl. He had white whiskers stained brown in patches, she once told me, and flabby lips he couldn't keep still from trembling. Even his voice, which was very deep, shuddered while he spoke. I dare say William would have remembered him too if he hadn't been beaten up that way and gone partly blank in his mind; I had never thought to ask him before too late. So Polly was my only link with someone I might, for all I knew, take after.

As for my parents, they could not be asked to recall simple things like names and appearances.

If they had not found each other, it is difficult to think how either Pa or Mum would ever have married. As he was a giant, so was she a giant too, with bones on a big scale overlaid by hard fat. The very day of the murders, she pushed me into a corner till I made her a promise I'd keep out of the bookmakers' clutches, and I knew, as a person does know, just the push of her weight by itself was beyond my strength to resist. So I did not try. Sometimes I enjoyed being reliable. She was only two inches shorter than Pa.

I should say I am an ordinary five feet nine inches and, at that time, weighed not much more than half what she did, though I was thought a great athlete in the district. The uniqueness of their marriage lay in more than physical bulk. More even than the sharing of inherited prejudices. They were suited in a deeper way. Since neither one felt any tenderness for us once we grew out of the baby stage (except perhaps for me as Mum's favourite), they faced no recrimination when their eyes met. They exchanged thanks for this closeness, in their daily routines, by silences chock full of accepting the rightness of Mum to be mother and Pa to be father. They believed in themselves so completely I doubt if they considered there could be any other kind of household. You may not think this possible. But they had few friends, no one visited us, and they went nowhere except to market or to mass.

I shall have more to say about the annual picnic races at Yandilli and about our Polly's marriage to the butcher, both of which were exceptions, times when they were seen out together.

I must add here that my parents' lives were upright and decent. They never coveted their neighbours' house, nor did they desire his servant, nor his handmaid, they never committed adultery (who with?) nor stole nor took the name of the Lord in vain. But when we come to the sixth commandment, murder is not so simply set aside.

My father's father had built the farmhouse and fenced the paddocks, and he was the one who hammered the name of the place on copper and screwed it to the wall beside the front door: PARADISE. He saw here the chance of a life free from the poverty of his youth.

We used to hear about our grandparents only on ritual occasions, such as the renewal of fenceposts. 'My own pa split these posts,' Pa might say, and look them over critically. 'Not a bad job,' he'd observe, 'for a clumsy bloke.' We'd sweat at digging, at lugging the new posts laid ready months before, mopping faces with our forearms, and we'd lean on the long shovels. Then he might add: 'Very particular he was, my pa, about keeping a straight line, him and his spools of thread.'

Likewise, on Mum's side it was often household work that brought Grandma to mind. 'My ma,' she'd burst out in her resentful way, 'always reckoned she rolled the flaky pastry twenty times with twenty lots of lard, if you please.' Having said this, she'd look round ferociously, challenging us kids to judge her by her mother's performance, though we'd never known the old lady. Then she'd go vague again and pound away at the dullness of what she had begun.

A famous photograph was taken at Paradise in 1880, the year our Ellie was born, who was destined to be one of the victims. This was also the year they caught the outlaw Ned Kelly, tried him, and hanged him. The trial confirmed that he had become the most famous man of his time, not just as a bushranger but as a spokesman – by his deeds – for the underdog. I was small at the time, so I remember nothing of Ned Kelly, but I remember the photograph being taken and how it terrified me. The photographer liked the look of our twenty and lobbed in one day to ask Pa's permission to set up his scene down there by the creek near where it flows into the sea. He took a fancy to the line of swamp mahoganies and that nice flat patch looking the right spot for a likely camper to choose.

Let me tell you what I recall about the occasion and then explain how the photograph came out. I have a copy, so I can describe it for you in detail.

First came a funny feeling in our house. Mum asked, while she bent over her meal, who was the fellow in the gig that came bowling across our yard? Pa stuffed his mouth full of potato and seemed like he wasn't about to give a straight answer. I sensed something special was happening, because Norah gave a swift motherbird look around the table, to be certain not one of us young ones would pipe up and put ourselves in the line of a swinging fist. We kept our eyes on our plates. I mostly found myself fascinated by the crazing of the china under its glaze, the entire plate a web of faint brown cracks that still were not cracks on the surface. Here and there, chips round the rim were the same discolour. Mum didn't ask again, as I recollect, but Pa swallowed what he had in his mouth and pushed his dish away to give room for the grand word he had chosen to share. Photography, he said, pronouncing it photo*graphy*. That out there was a photo*graphy* man come with his gig to take a picture at the bottom of our twenty, he explained. And suddenly everything was all right. 'I can't put it,' he added, 'more fine than that.'

Mum mustn't have voiced her opinion of photography, or we would certainly have known it. Later, when her Polly had a wedding portrait taken by a friend of the butcher's who was an amateur with the camera, she let fly her bottled-up fury against the sinfulness of graven images: photographs were the work of the Devil and unnatural. What happened, she wished to be informed on this later occasion, when your image went inside that little black box, because if it didn't *go* inside, how did it get there for the print to show it afterwards? Graven things, they were, she insisted. Thou shalt not make to thyself the likeness of any thing that is on earth or in heaven above, she quoted. But we just thought this was because of the many times Father O'Shaughnessy repeated the commandments in his sermons; also to remind us she, at least, was taking his instructions to heart. He was a priest whom she never tired of comparing with the new men, always to their disadvantage.

So, perhaps Mum held her feelings in, as she so often did, letting them stew away and build up a good head of pressure for when she chose to blow her top and could muster a scorching catalogue of instances where life had let her down.

Anyhow, a week later (I know a Sunday came between because she had her say to the priest and most likely put forward some unexpectedly curly theological knots for him to unravel), Michael came running over the paddock to where the rest of us were mucking around with the poddies, and just stood there, hands on hips, jack-knifing, so winded he was. When he swallowed his breath, some words got out. These were chiefly warnings about how careful we'd have to be if we wanted to be in on it at all. The end was that we crept after him along the fence going down the home paddock and in among those she-oaks at the bottom. There we could stand up and not be seen from the kitchen, so we picked our way through the clump of little paperbarks, which I loved for growing so close together you could hardly squeeze between. We came out at the swamp, of course, and pushed on a little way to the corner post. You'd never imagine what we saw.

First I noticed a fellow in a white shirt with his back to us, a fair way off, tightening the surcingle on one of his horses. I mean, how did he get his horses into our twenty for a start! There were a whole lot of them too, maybe six or seven, and all loaded with who knows what, saddles and packsaddles, weighed down they were, and standing patient, shaking flies off their faces, watching him with the lead horse and that surcingle giving him trouble. He had a new hat on, by the look of it. This was what gave him away. He didn't know a thing about those horses. He had the wrong hat. Only then did I see what else was happening. A tiny black tent stood over to the sliprails side, plus a pair of man's legs stuck out under it. And then an arm poked up from the black material and waved. I was about to pinch Danny, because we were special mates at that time, but Michael put his hand across my face before I could make a move or let out a sound. I smelt something stinky on his fingers, but I couldn't wriggle free. I think I must have turned to Norah to have me released when I saw what Norah was looking at. Over where those paperbarks cut in along the fence at the bit we always had to check because that was the wire the cattle generally had a go at, also being the weakest stretch by bad luck, as Pa said while Mum put in her two-bob's-worth about Satan, some Aborigines were creeping up quiet as cats. Most of them had nothing on that I could see. One must have been wearing trousers, though, because later he took a stone out of his pocket.

Creeping up like somebody on springs. We watched from the side. Their spears were sticking out a long way in front of them, each spear maybe twice as long as the hunter who held it. And all aimed at that white shirt. The points wobbled like snakes ready to strike. Any minute they would whisk through the air and bury themselves in a man's back. Hat or no hat, and despite his horses being on our place when they shouldn't have come past the first gate, I couldn't help it but I had to yell out.

Mike got me and nearly strangled me. Norah had to fight him off. But too late. I'd already yelled *Watch out!* in that kind of a scream a kid can give which carries a mile on a windless day.

One of the horses played up and jumped sideways against the fence, the little black tent went mad with some fellow inside struggling to get out, while the chap in the hat knocked it off his own head and the Aborigines just sat down where they were and laughed around their broken teeth. I never saw an Aborigine laugh before. But they laughed so much they gave themselves bellyache. And then, of course, came Pa thundering over the rise from where he'd been watching, already struggling to unbuckle his belt and pull it out from the loops on his trousers. We were for it! And I was the guilty one who had opened my big mouth.

But something even more amazing happened. The fellow from under the tent tried to catch Pa by the arm, a thing no sensible man ever did, and Pa swung round to fell him, but changed his mind just in time. The fellow shouted out to the hunters, who gathered their spears and shuffled up, then wandered back in a lazy way among the trees. He called to Pa, who was already on his way towards us again: 'No harm done.' I shall always remember those words. It became one of my own sayings from that day on. No harm done. Pa, ready to kill us, stormed over. If you watch, he roared and choked, you'll see a real live photo-*graphy* took.

The picture was put up in the photographer's shop down in Bunda. I saw it there many years afterwards, still the same shot, and that's when I bought my copy. It was called *Caught Unawares 1880. From the studio of Charles Bailey.* Bailey had painted across his shop window: NEVER-FADING PORTRAITS, A MOST APPROPRIATE WEDDING PRESENT.

Sure enough, the print shows black men with spears poised, only a few steps behind their unsuspecting victim, who is not doing up a surcingle at all but unloading a tent and gold-fossicking tools. The horses are too fresh to fool anybody but a rookie. Even the gold pans and sieve, even the shovels, don't look as if they'd ever seen dirt till that moment of being propped artfully against a heap of tentpoles.

So the picture was the kind of thing you purchased in those days for sending home to Ireland, to show what pioneers you were, and snakes not the worst of it by any means. The hat, incidentally, comes out quite all right in the print and doesn't look too new. But what I can't get over is how scrubby our twenty is made out to be. I never would have credited this unless I'd unearthed the very picture for you.

I think of the paddock as spiky grass with lots of cowpats, hoof holes, and scattered dead wood gone white and hollow as bone. The usual. But here it's a mess of fallen branches and ragged trees. And now I realize something awful. This could not be our twenty, not with that big spotted-gum just to the right. No spotted-gums were left there at all. Ironbark, yes, and a couple of wollybutts, but no spotted-gums, because Grandpa had laid down the rule that they were treacherous, being so tall and straight with so few branches and small roots. You don't want them blowing down in a storm on top of your good beasts, the saying went. No, this was not our property. After me letting out that yelp, they must have gone elsewhere to try again for some atmosphere. I don't remember this. I remember the photography being at our place.

I put the print away, but I wasn't satisfied.

That spotted-gum was the clue. It haunted me. I felt I knew the tree from somewhere. Then I had it: the base of this tree was where they found Norah's body. *Caught Unawares* had been taken eighteen years before the real murder, acted out by native people with no harm left in them, to show us what we might make of the affair when it struck at the same spot. Mum went to the Deaseys' for her lying-in with Ellie when the photographer called by to show us his work. I don't know why she went. She gave birth to all the rest of us at home. But Ellen was born over at Mrs Deasey's.

What a commotion she made when she did eventually see the photograph, though. This was in Bunda and a long time later when Ellie was already walking. As a treat, we'd gone all the way there for the big Boxing Day races, instead of just to Yandilli. Mum was doubly outraged when she discovered they could make copies, as many as anyone wanted from a single negative. This seemed more wonderful to us than anything you could imagine. But she told Pa: 'Those savages are going to get ideas from this, mark my words, they'll come round here spearing your own daughters for twopence, you and your photography man giving them ideas best left unthought.'

They were, of course, the blacks meant in Blacks Creek. I always thought it was for a person called Mr Black when I was young. I'd supposed Mr Black might have been here before Grandpa chose the creek bank for our house site. Not till I went to classes with the nuns after I got my job did I ask about history. The answer turned my world on its head for a moment, because I had never known any other place and I suddenly got the impression I didn't know this place either.

Before going further, something ought to be said on the subject of our church at Cuttajo. The priest, Father Gwilym, was Mum's pet complaint. First because he wasn't a patch on her Father O'Shaughnessy, and second because he wasn't Irish. Father Gwilym was a foreigner from Wales whose passion and ambition was to have music in his church good enough to serve God and glorify the Holy Virgin. Accordingly, he taught the boys to sing and the girls to play the violoncello and the organ. Every mass, we had music on some scale. One service in particular left me with the feeling the sulky floated all the way home. Aged about fifteen, I suppose, because my voice had long since broken, I felt heaven all around me. The harmonies showed me the bush as I had never seen it before: full of light. Our sulky rolled through the glare, smooth and silent. I wanted to sing, but felt embarrassed by my croaking voice and those blurting deep notes which sounded like someone unknown to me, or more like some thing, perhaps, escaping my mouth.

We were all afraid of provoking Pa to violence. Years before, I had sung in the choir and served at the altar. Now I was a renegade who secretly scorned religion. But I thought these harmonies, on strings and organ, sublime. 'Did you see,' said Mum, spitting dust, 'the church had more Judies sawing away than god-fearing worshippers?' I heard this with shock. 'Like a pub on Bedlam night,' she added, while I flicked the horse with the reins.

Some years later that same sulky was given to Bill McNeil as a wedding gift for taking Polly off our hands. It was the one, patched up and kept going, which he habitually brought to our place when they visited (though we knew full well they owned a new model for deliveries) and which he lent to Michael on the fateful night for driving the girls to the Cuttajo dance.

This much was true, those same church players played our waltzes and our Dashing White Sergeant at the Cuttajo Hall of a dance night. Older though they had grown, and no matter how many children they gave birth to, they always hung together and never gave up their love of the thing. They were the ones who had gone home from the hall when Michael and Norah and Ellen arrived late, to be met by a locked door and not a chink of light anywhere but from the houses in that part of town.

Pa was afraid of hell. Hell was the one thing he was afraid of. But he hated mass. So he went only as often as he thought he must to keep in favour with heaven. Mum used it as a weapon against him. She had two weapons: her mulish ability to obstruct events by doing nothing; and the everlasting punishment that awaited almost all of us almost all the time, but never her. This is not to say she felt safe, far from it; she simply took good care not to overstep the mark. In fact she was obsessed, I suppose you'd have to say, with the threat of evil. There were times when I looked at her big solid face hoping it would show some expression and all I saw were the eyes flying wide with a lust for fear, which she would burst rather than show us. Even her acceptance of the inevitable drudgery of a cocky's wife, expressed in that flat voice, those large simple gestures of not caring, were outward signs of the purgatory she created in her head for us all.

When my mother came into a room she soaked up the light. It wasn't just her shadow. She exhausted everything alive and sunny.

This was how Polly came to be her favourite daughter and Norah the one she mistrusted. She loved us all at some time or another, of course, though she had a clumsy way of showing it. But Norah, as her warmth grew too strong to be stifled, saw the milder side of her less and less.

Yet, perversely, I was Mum's pet among the boys; and what this did to my father I shall never know, but he made special efforts to correct any false impression I might have got by treating me with particular strictness – not the same bashing William had come in for, but steely reminders that my transgressions against his rule of law were never to be forgotten and, though to voice any such threat would have been beneath him, would eventually catch up with me, thanks to his memory and unswerving justice. Only much later in life did I realize he respected me as the clever child.

In a family of twelve you have to look after yourself pretty much without expecting too close an interest from a parent who is out working the farm from dawn to twilight. I believe he saw in me the one among his offspring who would later sum him up and possibly weigh him in the balance. This counted. He wasn't going to give me any quarter and he felt my mother's marginal indulgences should be rectified, but he nonetheless granted me some power of the future which he did not see in the others.

I suppose it was Jerry who drove me to music and intellectual attainments. Jerry, the next brother below and two years my junior, had our father's build. At Cuttajo agricultural show in 1892, when he went in for the contest of strength against grown men, local farmers and fishermen from the fleet, he took out the cabbages which were the third prize. He was just fourteen, that's how I remember the date. Long before then he had outgrown me. So I was more or less driven, you could say, to be the intellectual. I did my share of work and reckoned on being pretty healthy. But you know how brothers are, forever competing; they grow by beating each other down. And Daniel, a year older than me, always disdained young Jeremiah's company. Go and pester Pat, he'd say. Always Pat. Danny was generally safe from me too because, although we're much the same build, that year difference gave him the edge. He saw himself as having a destiny outside the family, Danny did. And though he didn't want to go just yet, when Pa sent him out into the world, he told me later he was never happy before he succeeded in getting away. That's how he saw it.

Michael still had the marks on his wrists at the time of the murder. Our policeman said this was where the killer had strapped them behind his back, as they were when his body was found. But I knew chain marks when I saw them. Pa had chained him to the bed-end the day before, to stop him playing up, drunk on Christmas cheer. Michael sometimes got chained without being drunk, just to keep him from behaving wildly. If you ask me, Pa felt good about being able to pin his twenty-nine-year-old son and get the locks on him though he lashed and punched and struggled to break free.

I meant to find out from Michael why he never tried escaping this humiliation. He was so cheerful and full of life, you see, besides being the most handsome man in the shire and all the girls crazy for him. Something held him. Something stronger than the disgrace of beatings long after he had grown beyond boyhood.

The time has come to introduce the third victim.

I think of Ellie standing on one leg at the stove, the free foot rubbing the back of her supporting knee while she stirred our breakfast porridge to keep it from burning, this being one of her jobs. We all took an interest because there's nothing so foul as burnt porridge; milk porridge, that is. We enjoyed the luxury of milk, thanks to our house cows. Ellie was independent. She thought for herself, she spoke up, she risked beatings (which she rarely got, in fact). She was the only person I ever met in all my life who could not tell the difference between good and evil.

I had already begun work at the convent while Ellen still attended classes there. 'You look after your sister now, Mr Murphy,' Sister Veronica would say to me when I came with the trap to take the young ones home. 'She's as good as an angel.' But Sister did not mean Katie, who *was* good as an angel, she meant Ellie.

I knew the truth. So did we all, Ellen included. Nothing was hidden from her. She wasn't in the slightest degree ashamed.

These three set out for the Boxing Day dance at Cuttajo: Michael still in the spring of life at twenty-nine; the eighteen-year-old Ellen, whom Sister Veronica mistook for an angel; and the most loving, most understanding, most beautiful of women, Norah, who never lived to celebrate her twenty-eighth birthday. They were the ones who did not come home by one o'clock in the morning, when Mum grew tired and lugged her duty into the bedroom where Pa snored, drunk on the store of liquor he had confiscated from Michael during the preceding weeks. They were the ones Billy McNeil the butcher went in search of at eight o'clock the next morning, 27th December 1898. Strange how persistent the number 8 becomes in all this: symbol of the knot and of the infinite.

The crown magistrate asked how McNeil knew where to go to find the bodies, since – in the words of one witness – they 'lay a good mile off the road in their blood, hands strapped behind backs and the leaves above them sighing,' also – by his own account – in 'such a quiet spot a couple of tree trunks rubbing together in the wind gave me a shock, because the eerie moan seemed to come from the horse sprawled nearby with its legs out of kilter.' McNeil replied that he had harnessed a gelding (one of ours, because the one he had brought to our house was by now the grieving carcase) and ridden towards Cuttajo, looking in every direction as he went. A bushman knows to watch for signs, even when he's just on his way somewhere to buy seed or woo a lady. Well, he did see a sign. Eight miles from Paradise he spotted wheel tracks heading off through the sliprail gate to the east, down towards the sea through that big paddock the Earnshaw family leave fallow every third year. He knew what he had found because one wheel was wobbly. From this he recognized his own sulky, the one Pa gave him at the wedding for taking Polly and her gossip off our hands.

Let me tell you, there's something in us we don't put a name to. We feel it, right enough, but can't say exactly what it is. Norah claimed to know that this was God, waiting for us to be worthy of Him who is already in us, hoping to shine out from what we do. Many's the time we talked it over. But I couldn't be brought to see life that way. If I could, I'd have taken up the offer to study for a priest. With Mum, she wore this mystery outside, enveloping her thick as a cape. With me, it has been a sensation of greatness; not a greatness belonging to God, but some power in my own body waiting for the chance to show.

With Michael it was a little thing, simply calling him home. He told me, because he was another one you could ask. Ellie laughed like rusty iron when I put the question to her. Young as she was and with her throat so slim and tender, she sounded older than the rest of us put together. 'Is it what William lost?' she taunted me. 'Is that what Pa knocked out of him?' To which Norah replied, 'I want you to keep a respectful tongue in your head when you speak of your brother.' But Ellie laughed more wildly, till we all ended up laughing.

Michael could never seem to really like her; Ellie, that is. As he was such an easygoing bloke, this surprised me. In certain ways they were alike, forever prancing around. And look at how soon he could recover from the beatings he suffered. She hardly ever got beaten, but if she had I don't think she would have cared. Just the opposite of Norah. Norah had feelings. Even the decision to go to the dance in the first place was a case of Norah thinking of others. There had been quite a stir earlier in the afternoon.

The whole family including Polly and her Bill drove down for the Yandilli Races seven miles south on a pretty rough road. Two sulkies went (one being McNeil's, which developed that wobble on the way in spite of the butcher saying he had fixed it for good) plus some of us riding: William, Michael, Jerry, and me. We planned a bit of a race along the straight. For the fun of the thing we swapped horses. Then the nag Jerry was on (mine) got a painful stone in her hoof. She might have gone lame, so he had to walk her till a cart came along, and beg a ride, tying the horse on behind; by his good luck this turned out to be Father Meaghan, a new priest in the district who was still falling over himself to win us locals over, though he never would succeed, being, as Pa said, wetter than a dish rag. Already he had put himself in bad with most folks by criticizing Father Gwilym's violin band. He had no time for godless entertainments, he declared in an accent freshly starched and ironed in Kilkenny. Did we have a gutful of Kilkenny before he had been among us a month! Anyhow, I'm wandering from the point. He it was who took Jeremiah along, Jerry sitting up there, bouncing gloomily because he was a habitual misery, and the mare he had been riding hopping now and again to nurse her tender foot. He must have been imagining what chance there was that Pa might come belting along in our big trap, full of fire, a silent reproachful Mum beside him, bearing down on this evidence of folly and the chance of losing a sound beast he could ill afford.

We three did not stick around to see.

William wouldn't even stop. He took one look at Jeremiah and dug his ankles in, hustling the little bay to get a safe distance ahead. I'd hung back as Michael offered to wait with him. But Jerry said in that fatalistic way: 'What the hell, there's plenty of folks on the road today.' We knew he wouldn't wait for long because we had already passed half a dozen parties which were not far behind. It was just a question of who happened by first. This was the end of our fooling. But of course, when we got there, Michael entered the races themselves. You could never hold him back. A bit of a liar, Michael. He swept his hat off to this one and that and smiled for all the ladies whether he knew them or not, while young Johnnie and his mates killed themselves laughing at him. Though what with the times Michael had been to Yandilli and to the bigger town of Bunda beyond, these females mostly did know him, at least by sight.

But I was telling you about Ellie, wasn't I? Yes, and how

Michael never seemed to like her. This day at the races, while we were eating our picnic, just our family minus Polly who went to her Billy's family picnic (and for half an hour she and Billy and Billy's old folks came visiting us), Ellie asked who was going to the Cuttajo dance, because we'd all been discussing it for a fortnight at least but nobody could seem to arrive at a decision. 'Michael?' she said straight off as if he was the one she had most in mind, 'are you on my side?' And he shied off. So cheerful he had been till then. He grew suddenly glum as Jeremiah and wanted to know why him? Well, Norah came right out and ticked him off for trying to cool the girl's enthusiasm and treating her like a child still.

I don't remember when he changed his mind and started saying he was definitely going. I suspect I was the one who began it anyhow by whingeing about being expected at work when I'd far rather have a pretty sister invite me to the dance than an ugly Sister boss me around at the convent, plus having to clear the rubbish out of the scullery, which was always my first job and the one I hated most. Pa rumbled and swung a punch at my head from where he sat on the grass, a halfhearted effort which missed. He said he wouldn't hear indecencies from whelps. Mum leaned over to push me against a nearby tree. That awful hot deadweight of her. But she kept her face turned away and stirred the dark around her with mutterings about blasphemy, not to mention honouring thy father and thy mother. I slipped out and ran off, laughing at them, mortified, yet confident I could get away with just about anything on Boxing Day, when so many neighbours gathered, all trying to outdo one another in respectability. Sure enough, the Willoughbys from Burnt Ridge Road called across to us: 'You've got a bright prospect there, Mrs Murphy!' Mum looked out at Belle Willoughby through her cloud and nodded like the end of the world. They thought this was meant to be a great joke and everybody laughed successfully. Maybe it was. With our mother you couldn't tell what she might intend. While I was doing the rounds of people I knew, so as not to have to go back to my place, Michael must have come good with his promise to take Ellen dancing. But later when we stopped on the road – I was going straight through to work but I waited with the others while Johnnie opened the gate to Paradise – and they confirmed their plan to have a bite to eat before setting out for the evening's fun, Norah did let slip an expression which took me by surprise. She said to Ellie: 'I shall be there to look after you.'

As she said this, Jeremiah coughed loudly like the stupid kid he was at heart, though only two days off twenty. I have everything particularly clear in my memory. 'Hark at the frogs,' Katie said. And truly, frogs were singing out so loud you could think yourself deaf, which wouldn't have been surprising if it was about to rain, but it wasn't. Maybe they were singing in protest against the driest Christmas on record. We always expected rain at that time of year. The races were usually run in hot muddy conditions.

I don't doubt it was this dusty weather which put everyone in such a wild mood, laughing like desperadoes because what else could you do but go mad, seeing the grass parch and get kicked to powder while your beasts lost condition? Apart from growing wheat, we ran steers at the time, before William – with the farsightedness of the simple – converted the place to dairy cattle.

That Christmas night when Norah was dressing Michael's wound she let slip her indignation at Pa's cruelty. Jerry, who was there with us, spoke up harshly. 'Cruel is not a word for Pa,' he explained, 'Pa has to be one step ahead. Look over there.' He pointed to the open paddock in moonlight. 'That was filled with enemies: trees, men, women, kangaroos. They had to be chopped down one by one to make room for us. The fences keep nothing out, they are just a sign that beyond this point any intruder has him to deal with.' Norah asked: 'Even death itself?' Jerry nodded and went on: 'When Pa whips Mike, it's because he sees the enemy in him. His job is to keep us up to the mark. And if he thought you were against him, he just would not understand.' I could see Norah's astonishment when, at this point, Michael agreed. Though perhaps he only did so because he was drunk, or perhaps for the sake of Christmas.

Anyway, the next night he was dead. Both he and Norah were dead. And Jeremiah knew he had said dangerous things in front of me, like Pa seeing the enemy in Michael, like Pa not understanding those of us who were against him, and this could only mean Norah our comforter. Or Ellie, the one neither like him (as Jerry was) nor afraid of him.

Our house had never been painted. The wood grew silver-grey, decorated with swirls of weatherworn grain. I think it never truly had an outside. The verandah all round (the style you still see in Queensland) made it like a house whose walls had been taken down, if you know what I mean. You looked straight in to the skeleton, among rooms and open doors, with, often enough, the family sprawled or squatting on the verandah in the spaces between the posts which held up its flimsy iron roof.

The house sat low. The soil lay flat around it, just two steps down, deep in dead dust for the dry half of the year and green during the wet. Of a morning in those half-seasons between, mist would drift indoors from the verandah, right to the most private rooms, and Mum's gloom would come sailing out, tearing this mist to frayed stuff as it clung round her; just the way sister Ellen might rush by in a swirl of white; or the frothy milk pinging into a pail, warmed by its own steaminess, would be almost invisible while damp air clung to the underside of our house cows.

That was my job, milking the cows before breakfast, with my hands chapped and unwilling and my mind too quilted by sleep for taking in the world of paddock and pens, the big spongy tufts of grass, or long slim branches of swamp mahoganies reaching up to catch handfuls of leaves from the sky.

I put things this way, let me confess, because I have had many more years for seeing what I used to miss. I am the one who still lives in the house. I am the chief one, at least. Jeremiah in his wheelchair shares it, also William. Willie's job is pulling down the holland blinds at night. Now we have a main road passing not a hundred yards from our door, we never can tell who might be snooping. He also catapults the blinds up again in the morning. If they won't snap quickly enough, he raises them twice. Their edges are cracked and torn along the sides from being worked too fast and crooked. He does the whole house, letting our warmth and darkness escape to run out all over the soil. The house is sometimes floating on water when the January rains are heavy and we old men, William and I and Mack, as we call Bill McNeil, who lives in the kennel at the back, have to paddle through it with trousers rolled up above the knee. Not Jerry, though. It would never do for his wheelchair to rust. He trundles round the place, wheels grinding and thundering over bare floorboards. At least he can never sneak up on you. But William is always doing that.

Willie knows he is simple. And because of this, I question whether he *can* be. He even knows how he first became simple, remembers the bashing Pa gave him, Pa who never laughed. He remembers because he is forever telling us the same tale in his droopy way: I was heading up north to find work on the railway, that's why he bashed the daylights out of me, he busted my ribs and my head. Other times Willie tries the alternative opening: Pa put these wasps in my head.

And he will thump one ear as if we might expect to see a buzzing swarm of anger come flying out the other.

We four are the ones who dare not die. Those murders keep us alive, William, Jeremiah, Mack, and me. We are strengthened by the knowledge that one of us has blood on his hands. Such is the true gold of the conscience: we are not kidding ourselves with little household slip-ups, nor petty confessions worth only a couple of Hail Marys.

And then there's Pa. He stays in the house with us too. Only you cannot rightly say he lives there, being dead this last forty-three years. He sits at the head of the table. It must be the anger that preserves him. He doesn't need to talk. Well, he seldom did talk much at the best of times. At least he keeps the flies off. They won't come near the place with him here. Something in nature, I dare say.

The women never understood silence, except Mum. And all

that is left of her is a shadow which moves from one corner to another to another, under the table, behind the sideboard. She is always moving, though you might never catch her at it. Even if you look as hard as you please, she seems to stay stock-still, lying doggo, but an hour later, when you think of her again, she has gone, lurking now behind the door or at the side of her famous wood stove. She doesn't mind the heat. She doesn't mind the cold either. All she is shy of is light. So when Willie does his rounds, and he's pretty slow, being ninety-one, snapping up those blinds, he is not just letting the warmth out, he is shooting the house full of light, driving our mother frantic, so she vanishes from where she filled whole rooms and choked us with her solid old weight, to pop up here and there underneath lumps of furniture she once took such pride in. I cannot say I pity her; she has some answering to do, and the Good Lord will not be mocked.

Did I tell you that we all look alike? Not just the three brothers and father at present in our house being invaded by mist, but Mum and the other seven brothers and sisters as well. Our parents could have been identical twins, their likeness was so remarkable many people commented on it – sometimes, I suspect, to hint that there might be untold secrets. The real puzzle was this: though Norah was the most beautiful woman you could imagine, the youngest sister, Katie the clown, looked so ugly she made you laugh. They had the same nose, same mouth, same eyes and forehead, but the spaces were different. Where in Norah this added up to a face beautiful as an angel in the holy pictures Father Gwilym gave us for good behaviour, in Katie they seemed about to fall apart, constantly having to be screwed and twisted to keep them together; she knew she could not allow them to rest idle or her face might collapse. Now, why did I use a word like *collapse*? I don't know, but I can't think of any other way to give an impression of how sad her jokes were, how desperate she was to stay alive in spite of our mother and father. Mum would appear in a drift of mist, steering her darkness before her, ready to stifle the least sign of joy in the family short of godlessness or cruelty; Pa, just behind her, knew nothing other than cruelty in his powerful ignorance. Some of us ducked for cover or rushed off to our chores, William cringing into his stupid state of a blank mind; others like Michael, who never learnt, habitually greeted them openly; and the two little ones, Johnnie and Kate, were just as likely to begin horsing around and getting in everyone's way. Strange, that. Only Jerry stayed late in bed. In Jerry they found their match, a giant like themselves. If it comes to the point, I suppose you could say he was the one they had waited for.

We don't know exactly when Pa died. He was getting old. He always sat in that carver chair, and one day in 1913 we realized we had not seen him out of it for about a month. He could have chosen any moment during this period to go. But his rage lived on in the way he sat. People had come in and gone out – including a policeman checking on a chicken theft – nodded and greeted him, and left without noticing any change. I think he felt cheated by those murders, that was it. Michael he despised, and only the day before the tragedy, after eating Christmas dinner, Pa had wrestled him to the floor and chained him on a bed-end; Norah he hated because she kept us human, undoing all the work he and Mum put in to have us beasts for life (obedient for life, as they would term it); but I think he was a little unnerved by Ellen, she didn't react against him like the younger ones who clowned and joked their way out of the nightmare, she didn't care; she was the only one apart from Jeremiah not afraid of him. But she was more of a puzzle than Jerry, who, at least in temperament, sided with him. She never considered Pa cruel, accepting the way he showed himself to be. He couldn't fathom that, if you ask me, and wasn't comfortable with it either. So – since I do not believe he felt any particular shock or bereavement, nor even outrage at the crime – I can only explain it as the idea that somebody had stolen from him what he didn't expect ever to have stolen: his power. By these three, more than any others among us, he set the boundaries of his power. In all he thought of them when they were alive, he never once guarded against seeing them dead. His rage prejudiced the opinion of at least some members of the police commission at the magisterial enquiry. Yes, there was an enquiry, conducted by Mr A. H. Warner Shand, Acting Police Magistrate at Nowra, plus the Commissioner of Police, an inspector and two sub-inspectors. The enquiry lasted thirteen sitting days, during which forty-five witnesses were examined. None of the others suffered such persistent hounding as Pa. Plainly the magistrate thought he might uncover enough evidence to commit Pa for trial. The deposition clerk wrote eight hundred and thirty-five pages of depositions. It came to nothing.

I ought to tell you about Billy McNeil, the butcher Polly married in one of her fits of silliness. Mack, as we call him, is one of those fellows who thinks it is okay to repeat to you what you have already said to him. 'This rain is set in for a week,' you might offer as a greeting. To which he'd reply, after taking a few moments' silence: 'Set in for about a week, I shouldn't be surprised.' He was the one to nearly drive the magistrate mad. You may imagine: 'If your memory is so accurate, Mr McNeil, concerning how you first found the victims' bodies, might you, perhaps, care to explain how it was that you forgot your own brother-in-law's name a moment ago and referred to him as Patrick and not Michael?' 'Well,' he answered solemn and important, 'I forgot and called him Patrick and not Michael. When,' he added apologetically, 'it was Michael.'

Young Johnnie, waiting his turn in the public gallery, as we called the bench at the back of our courthouse, laughed loud as a goat gone crazy. The town was scandalized.

The paddock where they lay violated and shot, two of them together and Norah separate at the foot of a spotted-gum, stood quiet with that buzzing muffled hush of something you will never forget . . . thick from the horror that had been there, frogs dumb for a whole day after the shock of a lifetime. Imagine it as if the boulder had been rolled from the mouth of Nicodemus's cave to show, instead of the Living Dead offering words of comfort, the dead alive with a million flies, faces and wounds seething black wings and legs. Blowflies crawled and clustered up the girls' skirts and fought for the best portion of their thighs.

Mack found the victims at 8.30 a.m. According to him he rode straight to Cuttajo and made enquiries for Sergeant Arrell at the Brian Boru Hotel, where they directed him down the street to the fishing wharf. There he told the sergeant his story at 9.15 a.m. It was 27th December. Christmas dinner had weighed on the stomach for only a day and a half, and our winnings from the Yandilli races still jingled in our pockets. You may be sure we did win too. Luck of the Irish. We won every year. Maybe only a few shillings, but we always came out in front. Clem Brewster, who acted as bookmaker once he'd closed his mercery store for the holiday, used to smack his forehead and groan: 'Here come the bloody Murphys to clean me out of my honest earnings!'

Sergeant Arrell remained a decent-enough cove, as police drunks go, till he got scared of growing old and turned vicious. At the time I'm speaking of he was still only about thirty-five, though. He rode back with NcNeil and reported what he saw:

> I found the bodies of Michael Murphy and Ellen Murphy lying back to back, quite close one to the other. Twelve feet from the man's head lay a heavy bludgeon-stick. I observed blood and brains stuck to the thick end of this weapon. The brains I surmised to come from Ellen, whose head was seriously smashed and the brains falling out of the back of the skull. Michael's skull was also smashed on the right-hand side. The body of the woman Norah Murphy lay somewhat apart. Also her head had been smashed, presumably with the identical weapon, this time on the left side of the skull. Signs of dishevelment suggested they had been violated and had struggled for their honour as well as their lives. Both also had their hands and feet tied. Norah, the one laying apart from the others, also had a leather hame strap fastened tight around her neck. The sulky stood a few yards off with a dead horse still in the shafts, its reins had been carried forward and looped

over the bit. The beast lay on the right-hand shaft, which had not broken, there was a bullet hole in its head, point-blank.

Note: The post-mortem examination confirmed that the women had indeed been violated, besides discovering that Michael Murphy was shot in addition to being battered, a bullet lodged in his brain.

When we came to see the bodies and knelt down to check that they were dead, flies arose as a swarm. The most awful thing was to see how beautiful the flies appeared at this moment – no longer black but luminous in the tilting light.

We stood back to allow Mum her rights as principal mourner. Even Pa recognized that death, like birth, is women's business and shows the men's business of labour and war as shallow by comparison. But our mother, pushing her fate across rough turf and finding it heavy to move as a barrow full of dirt, stood back still. When the flies settled again, the loudest noise was Mum's breathing. At last she spoke, without any show of surprise or tears: 'Now I have got only seven.' And there we all were, though she did not check. Pa never went near, he took root like another old tree and let the breeze sort among the hairs of his beard, bringing out the white ones more clearly than they had ever seemed before. You wouldn't catch white hairs on Mum; not till her dying day did she have one – black was her colour, and so she stayed. She didn't need to change clothes for mourning, she already wore mourning as her everyday. She didn't even need to change expression. She made no move towards death, and when it came rushing at her she was not a bit surprised.

Mum died only four months later, at the age of fifty-five. The smell of our house changed once she was gone, so that we knew then for the first time that it was a smell Mum created. I have only caught a whiff of anything like it a few times in the years since; and each time I have found myself carried straight back to the way things were, the dim pictures of our grandparents reflecting her walking past as a dusking of wind across water, the floorboards and wall studs creaking an accompaniment to every move, big body stirring her special brew of air. I suppose this brew consisted of lingering aromas from the food she cooked, wild herbs she dried to slip among the linen, goanna oil which she massaged into her scalp to prevent her hair going thin, miscellaneous odours of our coming and goings (including even accidents) – all were breathed in by her, mixed and breathed out in immense lungfuls of her own unique blend. She only ever went outdoors to go to the privy or mass, or to do the washing and hang it up, yet she breathed a tender air of bread and old clover. As a result the place became unlike anyone else's house. To me, the word *home* calls to mind this smell more than anything else.

During our last half century it has been lost.

Danny's wife screamed. Did I tell you she was staying with us over Christmas too? Yes, Danny's wife and Polly's husband. They were the only two to be married into the family at that stage. Although our young ones, Kate and Johnnie, got spliced later on, four out of ten isn't many. And curiously, not one of them had a child survive. It was said that Johnnie risked damnation with his contraceptives, but I don't know. Polly gave birth to twins, both stillborn. Kate herself died in labour and her son Paul, who was the only living nephew I ever knew, lasted till he was three. So the line will die out when my brothers and I finally earn our release.

Well, as I say, Danny's wife screamed. Remember, we were still at the site of the murders. The sound of it went nowhere, the bush just gulped it in and she was left, mouth open, appearing foolish. Beryl, her name was, which Mum declared couldn't be Christian at all. The explanation had to rest with the fact that Beryl was bred a Protestant and converted only when she came to marry Dan. Perhaps this was to prove how much she loved him, though by then he'd already become a policeman and it's a specimen of freakishness in a woman to love a policeman. Poor lass was probably on edge anyway, Mum having given notice that she would not stand for any hanky-panky in her house at night.

When Danny's wife or Polly's husband came to visit they bunked in with us, put to bed in the boys' rooms or the girls' room, as the case might be. Also, this Beryl claimed she had had inklings. You see, on that Boxing Day, policeman Danny got up first in the morning (usually it was me for my milking stint, but I felt dog-tired) and realized the sulky had not been put back in the yard. He went to the room which Beryl shared with Norah and Ellen. He found his wife alone. The other beds hadn't been slept in. Then they woke Mack McNeil because the sulky was his now, and at this stage the worst thing likely would have been a breakdown or else that one wheel finally come adrift.

If you ask me, Beryl looked like a pig when she screamed, nostrils wide and square face all chops and chaps. She stayed this way. Right till her end in 1938, the scream stuck on her face.

Barney Barnett had not been invited for Christmas because he wasn't one of the family. Since he was only a fiancé and destined never to get any closer, our parents were unlikely to clutter their house with the likes of him when it was already so crowded we fell over one another and cursing could more often be heard than celebrating. He did join our picnic at the race meeting, however. Also he challenged Michael in the fifth event, the eight furlongs, run immediately after lunch. He never liked Michael, to express it mildly, and took any opportunity of trying to put him down or make him appear stupid. Come to think of it, he behaved as if Michael was a rival for Ellie's admiration: little did he know they avoided one another at home. Or perhaps he was truly infatuated and had the insight of love. The family did not bother to include Barney among the mourners. Pa said the fellow could read all he needed to know in the newspaper.

The Bunda *Advocate* made a meal of it on 29th December. The editor recognized the only chance of glory ever likely to fall into his lap.

MURDER.

At Cuttajo on Boxing Night

One of the murders of the Century

The Worst in Australia

Two Sisters Ravished and Murdered

Their Brother Also Killed

A Fiendish Crime

A Terrible Story

Full Details

When we were dressed for the funeral, Barney Barnett came riding up to the house. He simply slung the reins over the piebald's head and left her there to graze on a patch of cloud. We had never seen such a thing. He came wading through the prohibitions, up our two steps, among unmade beds on the verandah, and into the big room with Pa sitting where he is now in a carver chair at the head of the table. Here Barney lifted his rifle and fired a single shot, apparently aimed to kill. The statement of a man who passes his own judgment. He came and he acted: nothing like the sly coquettish confession he later offered the police inspector from Sydney. But the joke was that he missed. Even at point-blank range he couldn't hit a giant like Pa. You'd wonder how he ever shot any game or caught a feed for his table. You certainly wondered how he expected to support our sister. Pa never moved, but he did speak. He said: 'If you come in reach of these hands, son, I'll choke the life out of you, and that's a promise.'

So Barney fled. He rode away without shutting any gates. Danny's opinion at the time was that if he had killed Pa this would have been the first life he had taken, barring our pig . . . It was the opinion he repeated, as a police constable on oath, in the courthouse. Ellen, he said, had escaped marrying a cove yellower than his teeth.

When I think of Barney lying in bed, no more than four miles from our place, hanging on by a single finger, crows fluttering in his scavenger eyes, I want to choke him myself. Him! Where did he get the idea he could just pick and choose his time or that he was big enough for fame? Dismal all his life. What price had he paid to expect anything more than a dismal death? Drunk with pride that he scored an inspector instead of Jimmy, our local cop, he was too flushed from hopes of a second chance at life to notice a twist in the police inspector's question: 'Why did you do that, Mr Barnett?'

What was the meaning: Why did he bash the horse's brains out, or why did he use the bludgeon-stick, or why did he concoct a confession? He had probably rehearsed this scene a thousand times, over the years, till the lines came to be the most real thing in his life, a reality all by themselves and nothing to do with what happened. The priest gave him absolution and he reckoned he would make it into the annals of notorious crime, his name to live forever, glorified by the murder of the century.

But this inspector knew that a murderer wasn't one to forget what he had done, wasn't one to say he bashed the horse's brains out with a bludgeon-stick (Sergeant Arrell's word, anyway) when the horse was shot. Also, both those shots in the head, the one in the horse's and the other in Michael's, were perfect shots. Whereas the bullet Barney aimed at my father, sitting in all his broadness and never flinching, is bedded in our wall at home a good arm's length wide of where Pa still sits as a witness.

I am beyond that age when a man's mind occasionally tumbles headlong down shafts of memory, glimpsing some small moment among humble objects and feeling his heart contract with grief for a life he once led: I have reached the point where this is my *normal* condition. Now and then the reverse happens and I am swept up level with the present, dumped in my shell somewhere I'd rather not be, longing only to sink back to a region offering room for hope, time for seeing every least thing as completely as human eyes can see.

This is why I found Barney Barnett so hard to get along with. He saw the past just the way he had when fifty, or thirty-five, or twenty-eight. He didn't acquire the gift of wisdom, having never made the past his own. He still lived it among strangers, kidding himself till the end that he had a choice open to him.

The confession killed him. He suffered a seizure right there, with us watching. The priest mumbled devout sentiments, Pa's stallion let drop a couple of extra globes, and the inspector snapped his briefcase shut, not troubling to disguise his irritation.

Hateful as Barnett was, I couldn't leave his finger caught like a baby's. I pulled it out from where he had hooked it through his grandma's lace border. The priest poked at the dead eyelids with a shrinking gesture, needing several attempts to close the eyes. Afterwards, two little rimples of skin smoothed themselves, settling to the shape of the eyeball so you would swear, for an instant, that he was cheating us still.

Good luck to you, Barney! I thought. You took the plunge in the end, you rat. Even though it failed, this was better than nothing.

Outside in the yard the inspector's car door shut. After a pause the motor roared to life, gunning away through the gate. We said nothing: Willie, Jeremiah, Mack, and me. Pa's horse shifted its weight from one haunch to the other: his hat rose an inch to touch the ceiling and then sank again.

Moments later, a fine pall of dust drifted in through the open window to settle over the bed and the face of the poor failure in it.

*

My mother's one fancy was a bead curtain. This hung across the doorway between the livingroom and a small workroom where she sewed and knitted and slammed flat-irons along yards of bulky skirts, breathing a tart stench of hot cloth and raw soap and giving it out, even this, as her musty-green smell of home. The workroom had better light than any other part of the house. In the middle of the inner wall, fringes of this light hung as drops, trapped by the beads – red light, sapphire light, and drops of clear water.

Norah, learning the finer points of housekeeping from her, often worked there too. At these times, I would stand long minutes in the livingroom looking out through that glittering waterfall at the younger woman's bent head, at tender stray hairs on her nape as she stitched some cloth deftly and sang to herself, not at all suppressed by any mushrooming resentful secrecy. Mum, knowing the load of mending still waited in her basket, would let the job manage itself while she withdrew further into an obscurity of intentions.

Perhaps what the old lady liked about that bead curtain was the warning it gave when anyone came through, clittering and shivering jewelled light. Sometimes she might sense me there and shoot a hot look into the gloom, straining to see past her own bright innovation. Once or twice she caught me and called: Is there no work left round the farm? Or: Idle hands are the Devil's holiday. Or she'd thrust a handful of repaired socks towards me and say: Put these in Willie's cupboard on your way to the paddock.

She knew why I was there. And I knew she knew. Part of her fate was the slow plan shaping; she had changed her mind. To save me, she needed to get me out of the house and keep me out of it. The chief obstacle was that I had always been her favourite. She knew I had to be expelled, but she wanted me to stay. And her heart prevailed. She bullied me and crushed me and rolled her scorn over any small thing I did, in order to stifle my spirit. She refused to treat me as a man and called me Boy right till she died. All because I was the one she longed to keep, I know it. She hungered for me to remain a child and dependent. Just like Pa beat Willie into an idiot because he couldn't bear the idea of living without him, so she loved me and called me Boy. There we were, Willie and I . . . the two they loved.

They respected Jeremiah for being one of their kind and an equal, but this is not to imply any actual warmth towards him. Each male child was welcomed as an investment, a free labourer. They never loved the girls at all, as a general rule. Despite the way Mum made a bit of an exception of Polly, Pa couldn't see the back of the goose fast enough; also they got rid of Danny, though he hung about and trailed after Pa with worship in his cow eyes. That was the way they rewarded the ones they chose as breeding stock for the family's future. But how were they to see any value in generosity, as such, the quality both Norah and Michael had? Quite separate was the indifference with which they treated young John and Kate, whom they ignored as they might ignore a couple of boisterous puppies our blue-heeler bitch had unfortunately whelped. The only one they were afraid of was Ellen, because they knew she thought them no different from other people. Oh yes, her look would say while Pa dragged Michael lashing and kicking into his bedroom, throwing him bodily against the walls and chaining him up for a night, the victim bellowing and swearing, oh yes, well, this is one of the ways the human animal is in the habit of behaving.

So when Pa stormed back to finish dinner and struck out with his huge paw to knock Michael's rum bottle on the floor where Norah would have to clean up the shattered glass, still glorying in his mastery, growing more a giant than ever and Mum a giantess because of him, the only eyes he would not meet were Ellen's. Ellen gazing cool and, you might say, scientific. That was it: she examined our parents as specimens she might one day find a use for. Her hands were transparent from churning butter, this being her job as mine was milking. She skimmed the cream and poured it into the churn's tray, turning the handle and watching a whole series of ribbed wooden rollers thresh the cream. Unlike me, she loved her job. Having slapped the pats between oblong oak spatulas to shape them ready for storing in the drip-cooler, she pressed a carved seal on the top, printing a four-leaf clover, which was the family sign. All our lives butter would be stamped with that four-leaf clover, ever more steadily once Ellie was old enough to take charge of this refinement. Her transparent hands stayed clenched in death, as we saw when we arrived at the scene of murder – the opposite of Norah's, which spread open and helpless under swooning flies.

Another reason for Pa not making any move to crush Ellen like he crushed the older ones among us was that he saw she made his litter more complete. She gave him something to marvel at. Because she made no distinction between right and wrong, he could not guess how he figured in her judgment. When he laid Willie out at a blow, or Michael or me for that matter, he could tell we hated him, and accepted our hating as a measure of his strength. This made him feel good, if anything ever did. He knew too that, as he stood over the fallen body, Norah would be waiting her chance to move in with a cool clean cloth and gentle fingers, with healing words whose calm grew deeper the more barbaric his outburst; this was a measure of himself as well. Even with the young ones when they learned to laugh, transforming pain and fear to clowning, he could see through their antics and discover himself clear behind them. But Ellen had him baffled. I think he believed that given long enough he would come to see into her too, and that then he could draw forth a new treasure for his collection of beasts.

All this while, you could say, we grew closer. Except three: Jerry single as an alien, Willie too far gone to be any use in the survival game, and Polly, whose refuge of silliness was entirely selfish. The rest among us found our world complete. I suppose we loved one another.

I once tried to get Norah a husband. A mate of mine I'd known from school had a brother Norah's age. I was seventeen at the time and this bloke Artie Earnshaw was twenty-three, just right, a year older than Norah. He was a local champion, you could say. He swam and chopped wood faster than any man his age in the shire; though a bit heavy for riding, he stood undefeated in the Bunda agricultural show boxing carnival. And I knew him. I went out to get him for Norah. I put myself in his way. I borrowed his tools (but not his axe, which he would never lend) and returned them unused, cleaner than ever, plus a bag of mushrooms picked one morning and taken up to the gate when I knew he'd be passing on his way to work the day the forestry teams felled a patch of timber between us and Cuttajo. I risked being skinned alive by Pa, wasting a whole half hour waiting for him to come by, and then I was almost too shocked to speak. What could I say? It looked wrong for me to pick mushrooms for him. He might take it amiss and beat me up on the spot, so I came to the point and lied. I told him they were a present (what inspiration) from my sister Norah. So the lie hovered between us.

Artie Earnshaw paid her a visit and, from what I saw and overheard, was fascinated by her. The fascination deepened when she insisted she had sent him nothing. Probably he disbelieved her, recognizing this as a symptom of modesty. They might have gone on to make a couple, except that I suddenly realized what he meant by his attentions, that he looked on her as flesh to be possessed, that she could become wholly his, and I had behaved like a complete idiot in not facing the fact. I wanted to kill Artie as he stood easy on the verandah, leaning back on his hips, broad hands making simple gestures of being pleased, his worn boots of an active man, and his throaty musical laugh. She fancied him. This wound now worked its pain so deeply in me I could not remember how I had felt before. He said he might call again. But I swore he would not win her off me so easily, because my claims on her had been precious long before we ever heard of him.

I strolled out of my room and through the kitchen to the top of the two steps. We were close enough for us to have shaken hands. I saw then that our family had a destiny and would be truly doomed if we fought against it. I heard my voice break free from shyness (we were all shy except Ellen): 'I've got to own up,' my voice said, so that it became the voice of the space still between them, that space ripe with afternoon sunshine, polished to the roundness of full golden fruit. 'It was a joke, Artie.' I glanced at Norah and then away, horrified by the instant flame of hatred in her eyes, fearing this far more than any violence he could do to me. I hung my head and confessed: 'I didn't mean it, Norah, I didn't think anything would happen. They were good mushrooms,' I added lamely, already throbbing with triumph at having reached her deeply.

Artie Earnshaw stared at me, stared as a man will who is caught on a razor-edge and undecided whether to hit out to restore his pride or draw the clown by the shoulder, holding him close as much as to say: Look, what you thought of as a prank is something we shall all live to thank you for throughout the rest of our lives. And Norah was keeping him on that razor-edge. By her silence, by the stricken whiteness of her anger and the flush of blood following it, she held him back, forbade him either action, and demolished his pride as anything worth restoring in this case. I know, because I mustered the courage to turn my appeal to her again.

Norah's wonderful slow smile gathered and blossomed. This was not a smile for Artie, generous enough for me also to find forgiveness in it, but the other way round. She kept him in suspense as she spoke exclusively to me: 'Then, Pat, you have put your sister in an unpardonable position with Mr Earnshaw,' she said.

He knew this cut him out altogether. He wasn't even to be permitted the right to thump me as I deserved. He was not permitted feelings at all. He was to become, solely, the person to whom she offered her gift of gratitude. Gratitude was what he must make do with. Nothing of the flesh, nor anything of the spirit would be his now. He had given her . . . me.

I saw him often since. He lived to a good age, being happy with the wife he did marry and his six children. It was in Earnshaw's paddock, about a mile and a half from his house, which was still his father's house then, that Norah was murdered. Artie, as one of the witnesses at the magisterial enquiry, said he could not understand why we Murphys appeared so unmoved by the crime. At the time, his father had sent him on their best roan gelding to carry the news from Mack and Sergeant Arrell to our place. He set off, by then a young married man, just twenty-eight and with two fine daughters, filled with the shock of what he had seen. And filled with dread at having to break such news to a family he had once been as friendly towards as any man could claim.

I remember him riding up, face bright red with hectic news and the wild gallop, strong hands clenching on air as he greeted me, asking whether my ma and pa were home because he wished to have a private word with them. As he later told the court, once indoors he found himself facing both parents, the mother towering over even him (he was a man six foot tall) and the father sitting at a table, both dark in the dim room. The kindest thing he could think of was to tell them bluntly that there had been a murder, or three murders. By this time, I should mention, I was an unseen witness and I heard him, in his manly way, bring it all out – clear, simple, yet made gentle by his feelings on their behalf. I stayed on the other side of that bead curtain in Mum's workroom.

Silence.

'I know this is a terrible shock,' he added. 'Will you come back with me now?'

'No. We'll finish the chores and then we'll come,' Pa said.

Artie knew his duty and wasn't the type to back down.

'The police sergeant is waiting; nothing can be done till you show up.'

'Do you hear me?' Pa thundered quietly. 'We'll come when we're ready. All dead you say?' he asked a moment later as Artie reached the door.

'Yes.' And you could hear from his tone he thought this was a breakthrough to a more natural turn.

But Pa simply left it at that; and Mum wheeled her weight of air around, droving it out into the scullery without a single word, without a cry or a tear, without even seeming interested.

Speaking personally, I have a notion that Artie Earnshaw still felt a soft spot for our Norah. He was more shaken by seeing her corpse than he'd admit.

Mum's task was to bully the youngsters. They, of course, though supposed to be washing the dishes, hung suspended in a stone-cold hush, striving to suppress the blood's clamour and overhear what our handsome neighbour came to say. This is what I surmise because, from where I stood in the workroom, I heard a sudden banging of pots, scuffles, and a stifled shriek. At that moment a thought arrived in my mind which has never left it since: Mum behaves like a woman who is barren.

True; her ample body, her outsized breasts and hips were more for armoured padding than child-succouring or child-bearing. Then I was visited by the further idea of Pa being much the same, giant though he was. His potency had never been of a giving kind. Yet they were fertile, as the ten of us attested. They must be victims: this was the conclusion I reached. They must be victims of an unwanted, unnatural fertility, hating us for coming. I imagined their coupling as stubborn and sullen. Often enough we heard the mountainous shudders of it throughout the night, but I recognized it now, not as consummation or joy, but as a despairing admission that the flesh is doomed.

In fairness, I ought to explain that I myself have only ever once made love to a woman. The power in me then was beyond anything I thought possible of the human body – and her fierceness, for a gentle woman, so . . . ravenous, I have never brought myself to the test again. Or, put it this way, as we lay burning together, I thought of my parents, fearing maybe they too had felt this divine fury the first time, lost in each other just that once and never finding their way out of the labyrinth again (Father Gwilym had told me the story of Orpheus and Eurydice) – certainly past the need of talking as they trod through hell. Might it be that they looked back, though forbidden to live the same experience twice, and sank into an underworld of failure each time they were within reach of rising to a new and saving moment? And the failures swelling her womb, hard as knotted rope? I recognized, in myself and my brothers and sisters, the mockery of their fumbled attempts to find freedom once more. I saw their fertility as something separate, malignant, and coarse.

The larder and scullery retained the same coolness. They shared a single doorway. They had been built from stone as a separate structure linked to the kitchen. The only other solid parts of our house were two brick chimneys: one stood outside the kitchen wall to carry smoke from the stove recess, while the other, the taller one, leaned against the front of the house, a verandah roof wrapping around it, for the fire in our main room. Mum lived in her larder because she liked its raw air in all weathers, plus the smell of grain, the cold sweet meat under wire covers, and aromatic stores like tea. Back in the scullery she could slap my sisters with her open hand and then in the larder be alone with her satisfaction afterwards, because no one but her was ever allowed there. Unless it was the Polly of old, helping bring out ingredients for our Christmas puddings and dumping them on the kitchen table ready to be mixed.

When Artie Earnshaw left, Mum, having said not a word to her husband, stood long minutes in the cold larder surrounded by shelves of dead meat, dried fruit, and crushed seeds.

One thing more than anything else persuades me I was right. Jeremiah. They were always at peace with Jeremiah. My idea is that he had the proper gloom, the same shape and ponderousness as their own failure. He did not behave as a child of fertility, he never laughed or ran amok. He offered them a mirror for the lumps of unwilling flesh they had become. When I was attending special lessons with the priest and being taught to enter the world of Raphael and Swift, Father Gwilym once placed his cool hand on my knee and said: 'I believe I shall never break through the boy's shell.' I knew who he meant. And a moment later, when he had withdrawn his hand, leaving a colder impression of it still there, he added: 'It is as if all his growing up were done before he had the chance to be a child.'

My guess is that Jerry has remained virgin to this day. Now he is seventy-eight and crippled, he doesn't have much time for cutting loose, either.

It is possible our parents had the idea that if we could only fight back we might drive them out of their morbid tomb and, vulnerably, into each other's arms again with a young passion. Likewise, Ellen's perversity, as I think about it, possibly gave them promise of challenges they had not foreseen. Did her lack of morality, her inability to judge them cruel, set lust flickering, warning symptoms of a terrible eruption doomed to growl down and hibernate under the shelter of violence or indifference? So Willie's idiocy, Polly's silliness, Michael's gaiety, Norah's warmth, Daniel's earnestness, and the young ones' clowning . . . all were monstrous growths of their search to find again that Eden of the sexual act stumbled upon in innocence.

They went to mass because they had it in for God.

I want to show you what we were like in the light of love. You could easily imagine us (in love) as a family of pigs, thick with bristly skin and hard round meat, bouncing off each other if we collided, our short thick legs and knobbly knees, our eyes of the captured always on the lookout for a hole in the fence, a way out of the world. We all went to mass, except Ellie.

Even Michael's free-and-easy style, which brought him adventures with many girls and older women, was only a rebellion against his true nature. If not, why did he come home and drink himself rotten till Pa bashed him senseless, chained him to the bedstead, hand and neck, and left him there to sober up in the cramps of next morning?

Nothing less than love could have led to the climax of

Earnshaws' paddock, those strapped, lacerated corpses sprawled for anybody to witness the shame of their ignorance.

In the world of our sty, in among the real pigs which we were, ran the squealing squabbling piglets we gave birth to: butting greedy little appetites, the clatter of jealousies on trotters that might one day be chopped off, stewed, and set cold in gelatine for a polite picnic lunch at the races, tiny clenched brains and pumping hearts to be grilled for breakfast or stuffed and baked on festival days. Even while we bowed our heads at the big table for Pa to say grace, the floor squirmed with lascivious snufflings and nips, the brush of a sprung flesh tail against your bare leg, the odour of insatiability and the wild confusion of an equality in squalor. The respectable silence of beasts devouring a beast above the board floated thick as oil on the pandemonium of what was being stifled below.

Why should we need anyone outside the family? We had a full-time job playing the games we did. Pigs are well known as cannibals if they get the chance. The outsiders we did meet seemed pale and too simple. They said yes if they meant yes, they said please, and when they expected you to say thank you they also expected that you intended thanking them. They teased us with tentative sex, the passes of men wearing boxing gloves, of women who will blush if their fish-eyes so much as slip to notice your body. With their mechanisms of work and play, unearned loyalty and fatuous opinions, how could they imagine we would have patience to suffer their childish advances twice, let alone with enjoyment? While we waited, marooned on the gaunt rock of such contact, for a single dry sign of what they intended, the tempest at home raged without us: Mum loomed from the depths of the larder, heavy with accusations that would be exacted in blood; Pa out there, abandoning the horses to their own company, swung the whip on his own sons for having fouled up the job of gentling a new stallion; the healing attentions of the girls worked their erotic balm on wounded flesh; and our taciturn speech was offered merely as punctuations in the flood of what could never be spoken because it was too intense, too complex, too intelligent for anyone to talk their way out of if once they got into it.

Such was nature's punishment on Mum and Pa. They knew. They never put this into words, nor did we. But they felt the little piglets butting round them, caught thick complications in the air, they smelled the stench all right. They knew we could never find anywhere interesting after this. They knew we would never let them be free of us.

So, when Artie Earnshaw strode in with his innocence of a young father, his concern at being the bringer of evil tidings, our parents put up the shutters against him, barricaded their privacy, and manned the loopholes with loaded firearms. They knew this was no release. They knew it would not be a question of three burdens, three reminders, the less; but that the murders raised our power over them far enough beyond control for their paradise to go under and never be recovered.

They had hung on to the shreds of innocence, the possibility that one day they might chance back into the magic circle. But now, I'm sure they knew, no innocence could survive. So why should they be in any hurry to set eyes on their disaster? God had aimed this at them.

Sitting round the oil-lamps of a winter's night, Pa read *Lives of the Saints* at the rate of about one sentence an hour. Mum read even more dreadful things in the darkness beyond her own familiar dark. And we played a card game called Happy Families.

When the wind blew from the north-east, which it often did, we could hear a distant crash of waves down at the cliffs below the twenty. And when we had gone to bed – as we preyed on each other, breathing each other's snores, turning together in our separate sleep so our bedsprings made harmony or screamed in someone else's nightmare – the cracks between the planks of the rough walls gaped wider and hair-fine glints of a silver sheet turned its wave to our drowning eyes; our bodyheat went sleep-walking till the dogs grew restless and put up their pointed noses and the horses, musing as they stood round in mockery of sleep, bent to stir the fog with caressing tongues and shook magnificent necks in the moonlight of a mare's eye. While the ocean, that relentless heart, beat beat beat away at the rocks.

Like me, Norah chose a bed next to the wall. And in the morning I would pick splinters from the palms of my hands.

Michael and Willie slept in my room. Michael forever climbing out of the window, thrashing about in the greenery over by the chookyard, sneaking back panting and slicked with dew, forever arcing and humping under his blanket, gasping, grunting, letting slip eels of satisfaction, smelling and damp with his strong body turned to the wall, swinging back to catch me awake, and groaning: Oh Pat if you only knew, if you only knew! and then going off in a spasm that threw him almost out on the floor, while Willie sank silently into the pool of his wondering, diving without a ripple to dredge up some single simple waterlogged version of knowledge – a singlet, a sock – and wake from the very posture he fell asleep in the night before. He'd open his eyes as blank as the morning sky and shake his clubbed brains till he got a basic pattern clear: obedience. He'd put his ugly white feet out and let them scout around like a couple of blindmen for his boots.

Then I knew it was time for me to go and milk the cows.

The Earnshaws' bottom paddock was eight and a half miles from Paradise – eight from our gate to theirs, plus another half down the old rutted track seaward to where that photograph of a faked ambush by blacks and the dread of a real murder of family happened.

We let Artie set off well ahead of us, for the sake of form. When we were ready, our tyrant gathered up the flags and tatters of his victories, clamped his hat tight like a helmet, and mounted to lead us on a retreat into village impertinences. He turned his back on the territory where he, having transformed his father's subsistence scratching, produced meat and honey for the slaves who kept him imprisoned there among his splendours. Mum was already seated passive and ruthless as an idol in our new sulky, which I was to drive. Hers was the magnetism that held us; while he dragged the whole lot along in his train, his customary knives and axes lustrous as he urged us on with the war-weary gesture of impatience, once he had begun, to see this duty done. Black flames tore at his sleeve. He whipped up a wind, with his heels dug into the stallion's startled flanks, an old scent of danger marshalling his body to heroic massiveness. I was proud of him. And proud of driving my mother, who sat secret as the Ark of the Covenant, gold glimmers among her resting fingers, her hair black with energy and her eyes black from glimpsing the face of the God who had turned away.

So we came, beggarly and majestic as the Middle Ages in our patched motley, the longbow of our pride strained tight and ready to let fly at the first fool to oppose our grandeur with the triviality of public tears. We rode through the sliprail gate at Earnshaws', golden dust nestling in creases and brushed on our horses' coats, the slowness of our approach storing its own power – Mum, Polly, and me in the sulky, plus the others on horseback – a sable king and his giants come among those whose small lives were set at a sensation by other folks' deaths. Clear as a curse, our slowness said: this is not your grieving, leave us to understand the knotted wrists behind their backs, the hame strap round the neck, the rubric of a scratched thigh, the clenched fist and the open hand, the mortuary of fœtid secrets which ought never to be shown. Our slowness said, as we approached in a squadron: these are twists of an agony we know but ought never to see lie still and permanent, made obscene in the formaldehyde of your amazement. As the sulky jolted over turf, the scene jolted too – those dead bodies jumping closer, flat on their backs and bouncing our way as the dead horse with his nose set for hell plunged into a gagged scream of gory anguish. You want to know how I felt? I felt like a burst of trumpets!

Even our Danny put on his constable's uniform for the ceremony.

Mack (who had fetched Sergeant Arrell) was waiting there to help his wife Polly down from my sulky. Also Barney Barnett, who had broken his oath by getting drunk with the sergeant at the Brian Boru the previous night, stepping forward to freeze his hand in Mum's reclusiveness, fumbling for her arm as if she couldn't crush him by her scorn for his presumption, let alone with her weight. The Earnshaws, senior and junior, stood at a respectful disapproval, judged to a nicety. Beyond them the riff-raff of Cuttajo sightseers already shuffled with impatience at our delay, having come from six miles closer, besides being winged by a craving for novelty into the bargain, while beyond *them* the shadows of the ancient Koorie people, men who had collapsed in laughter once because a child called out to warn the white man of their ambush, flitted and fragmented while standing still amid the margin of trees they belonged among.

At last I looked across at Ellen's corpse, back to back with Michael, shimmering fly-wings and humming loud as a harmonium from the wounds of Barney's crow-pecking for the scraps of notoriety as nearly heaven as anything he'd ever find within his reach. Mum pushed him aside with her shadow of air; and this was a sign for us all to dismount. Except Pa, the king, in his remote high tower, who took off his helmet and let the wind ruffle plumes on his natural head. His stallion opened blood-red nostrils and stamped its hooves at the invasion of death. Down below the cliff obscured by trees, seagulls set up a sudden screeching, wild, angry, and mournful.

My mother looked straight at me. You drove me here, her look said. And I was more afraid of this than of the police investigations.

Barney Barnett went among the townsfolk introducing one of the corpses as his fiancée, while Artie Earnshaw stood aside, deep in mysteries. Old Mr Earnshaw, good neighbour and generous heart that he was, approached to offer what support his family could, without intruding. Mum faced him as one colonel to a rival, equal in nobility. Neither bowed, though both accepted the fatal field as an end to such alliance as they had known before: 'Thank you, Jack,' she said and dug her heels into the sod, driving her cortège forward to the brink of disaster. She looked first at Michael. She had often seen him laid out before – defeated, smashed about the head – confident he would wake to a fresh gallantry of childishness. Then her pondering mind led her to Norah, whom she had loaded with her tasks of a mother, the mother she herself had no wish to be. Back she came. Slowly she stared into Ellen's staring eyes, Ellen who had at last seen evil and, therefore, ceased to be of any use. The dead eyes no longer flinched at what they opened on, and if the living eyes still could not take in the present, they knew the future clearly enough, in my opinion. Johnnie and Kate hid their nausea against each other's neck. But the rest of us looked. Jerry was the one to speak: 'Can you shut their eyes?' he asked Father Gwilym, who shook off his centuries-old decorum and flamed with anger. For a moment the priest appeared insane, cheeks stuck with thorns. He picked on me as the one among our barbarians who might be softened to love of the Lord. 'Pat,' he said, 'come with me.'

We walked aside, observing our feet press down and crush the grass. We might have been two men in a conspiracy of condolences. Perhaps the others guessed he wished to instruct me in our duty to the dead. But I began to know something I had never suspected of having happened through the years, which added up to just this moment on just this clear midday: 'Give me your hand,' he asked when we were a safe distance away. We shook hands . . . mine closing on a disc or coin in his palm. 'Take it,' he explained, 'it is yours.' And I saw the flames were not anger but shame. I thrust my fists deep in my trouser pockets as we strolled on, just as I often did when I had nothing to hide.

I served at the altar for years without knowing who I served. If I'd asked him at the time, he would undoubtedly have answered in his beautiful foreign voice: Why, boy, the good Lord, our Heavenly Father! And I might have been deceived into accepting this. I loved those winter mornings when the little church floated out of the dark and my pony put on an act of being blown as I let her wander round the verge of the graveyard to browse while I ran in at the last minute to where Father fretted, already waving impatiently at me to be ready to help with the alb, while he took the amice, kissing it and placing it a moment on his head before doubling it back to the collar of his cassock with practised dexterity, crossed the cords, right over left, and tied them, giving off an odour of cleanness which was not quite the right smell for a man. He thrust one arm into the alb, then the other, as I danced round like Norah did when she fitted sister Polly's wedding gown, teasing the cloth so it fell evenly, two finger-widths from the floor. Next came the moment I knew he always found fresh. He interrupted the vesting prayers he had been reciting under his breath – and turned to look at me in that longing manner of a person given over to the freedoms of piety: 'The cincture, Patrick?' So I'd pass him the girdle. Sometimes his hands were damp as he took and tied that symbol of the bonds of Christ fiercely tight. Finally, he would present himself for my inspection, resplendent in his red chasuble, if this was Pentecost, with its whiskers of frayed gilt thread.

Then we would be out in the open church, surprisingly large, timber creaking like a ship at sea, arched ribs above us, and still the lovely sickening candle fumes and spent incense. Opening the missal, he escaped my gaze (as I reconstruct the scene), his voice, magnified, coming back from the roof as words fit for God: *Introibo ad altare Dei*. And my own shy piping, because I knew I could never do justice to his gold and jewelled ritual: *Ad Deum qui laetificat juventutem meam* . . . while out there in the scrub kangaroos went crashing through undergrowth and some fellow's dog barked big excited dwindling barks. Then the first two worshippers arrived, wrapped against the cold, and knelt, choosing places widely separate, bowing their heads darkly. All this came back to me when we paced the inquisition of our return to my family, bearing what we knew and could never tell. Father Gwilym and I, linked now not just by the laws of man but in the judgment of heaven.

As we drew close I saw Jeremiah, to my amazement, wiping away tears. So the least likely among us had been able to show grief.

On special days we took a picnic to the beach, which was only a quarter of an hour's walk from our house. We sat there on the sand to eat, when we were small, and ran away to play in the caves, chasing bats out, or we went shooting rabbits along the cliff line. We never took our clothes off. Not one of us could swim. As we grew up we came to think of sand as a nuisance. Till we only went because the ocean was a thing to be seen.

Ellen once jumped from some rocks into a pool. She came up coughing and laughing, her pinafore and petticoats stuck to her body in a way I could never get out of my mind. She was fifteen then and well shaped, though never to be beautiful like Norah. Michael went mad with fury, he said he should whip her if he had brought Pa's whip. Mum looked on from her recess out of the sun, with never a word. And Pa appeared more interested by Michael's sudden temper than by the dripping, hiccupping girl, who declared it tasted like blood, a big swill of nothing but blood.

Most of us looked at Norah to see how she would take this. We felt she had to be protected because time was slipping through her fingers. Outsiders had begun referring to her as our spinster, a taunt Polly instigated in some flash of spite, because of her own apparent barrenness, no doubt.

On Christmas night (I'm talking about 1898 again now), when Michael hung chained to the bed, dribbling and dozing with his nightmare strung up to dry, Jerry came to sleep where Michael belonged because Mack had taken *his* bed. Jerry had not been in our room for six years. He was twenty, as I've reported previously. So when he did walk in, he filled it. Willie already snored from that corner, and the lamp on my table burned. I had just settled. He said he did not want to come. But now he was there, he stood in full view and stripped. The night, hot as usual at Christmas, crowded in. He wore only a waistcoat and shirt. He flung the waistcoat aside, then tugged the shirt, one of Norah's professional linen shirts, over his head and dropped it out of sight on my floor in the shadow of the table edge. His braces hung down in loops either side, I remember. He kicked off his boots, sending them flying under my bed to thud against the wall and raise a little cry of alarm from Norah awake on the far side. Then he looked at me to be sure I watched, and undid his fly. The thick soft trousers fell in a sudden heap. My younger brother stepped free of them and, at the same time, one pace nearer me. I should explain quite honestly, that I was envious. Since he had become a man, I had seen no more than his arms and his neck. Now he filled our room with the tranquil forms of giant strength. This was the Hercules that Father Gwilym showed me in his book of world art, except Jerry was much younger in the face. The heat of his calm choked our small privacy to suffocation. His carved form, heavy as marble, glimmered in lamplight. He could overpower me with one hand, and insisted I should know it. But he didn't even need that one hand: he didn't need to move. His genitals hung, turning slightly on an axis, the balls shifting against one another in their firm bag. Jeremiah, who had never laughed, any more than Pa, began to smile. By this I knew he knew what I was thinking. He stood a long time with nothing happening apart from his smile and that slight but terrible business setting his limp parts shifting ever so gently. I could not prevent myself thinking it was as thick round as Norah's wrist. Then I prayed she did not have her eye to the crack, as I sometimes did from my side. I dared not stop looking, because his silence forced me to what he wanted, forced me to study everything, from the huge shapely feet to a mop of curly hair flopping round his ears. Maybe quarter of an hour he stood in the hot night, maybe an hour, while he watched me lose every confidence I had in myself; he watched the questions of my virgin anticipation and courage rise and subside, my hairy Irish limbs stiffen and sag. He stood in my room till he was sure he had driven me back into adolescence by crushing my self-respect. Then he turned his back on me, the back, if anything, more massively plain, more matchlessly ideal than the front, and stepped over Michael's bed; he threw off the sheets as much as to say he would not soil his beautiful body by contact with them, and lay on the bare mattress, despite its deeper stains of longing. Lay, face up, aware he still had me mesmerized, but not looking at me now, the smile fixed where it had grown. It was the strangest performance I ever witnessed, and ruthlessly brotherly. To be such a man, he had left me nothing but my boyhood and the sweet gravelly escapades of a boy's despair at making anything add up. That was Jeremiah for you. Next morning, when I awoke, only his heavy hollows remained in Michael's mattress, and Michael, discarded it seemed, with that sordid little dump of sheets kicked into one corner as the victor strode back to his own world.

After I brought the milk pail to the kitchen and set it down for Norah, who cooked our breakfast, she would not meet my eyes. I knew then that she had been watching. Jeremiah's smile might not have been directed just at me. This smile came to mean more than I had feared.

When we swung off home, leaving the murdered bodies behind, we had grown smaller. I no longer felt the jubilation in our strangeness. Success had diminished us. Jeremiah, as the new master, stayed behind to oversee the police enquiries and the bodies being covered. Our Danny joined him, Constable Daniel Murphy, appropriately in uniform and suddenly on duty, though no one asked him in.

Pa as a high stone tower grated on his iron seating, still with the hat in his hand like a weapon, his stallion's haunches shuddering from an encounter with knowledge.

A sudden sheet of fish-scale clouds sliced the sky off high above us, dimming our gold-dust and blurring the fringes of pennants and favours. How ugly we were with our inaccessibility intact, our finery dirty from yesterday's race meeting, the trail of something shabbier than grief being tugged through the air behind us like a net drawn briefly sparkling from the lake only to be seen fouled with weeds and the saturated jetsam of human occasions. I suspect Danny was glad to see the back of us. Mack (yes, even those devoid of moral stature felt their ascendancy at hand) showed how our behaviour shocked and gratified him by sending Polly home the way she had come, with me and Mum, claiming to have some business in town before he could join us. 'Business at the Brian Boru, I dare say,' I muttered as he baggaged his wife in a frill of silly snivels.

I looked back once, to see flies spread their pearly veil above the sergeant's head while he resumed cross-examining the corpses. What could be done? Wind drummed about us. 'A murdered body is the possession of the Crown,' Sergeant Arrell had said, 'so it is my duty to take the deceased in charge.' More drums. He squinted up at the chinks in Pa's craggy face. No response. 'I shall have them taken,' he announced further, 'to the pub and locked up safely.'

It was while we were riding away amid dust gone rusty that our neighbour Artie (so I was to hear later from Daniel) brought the sergeant a valuable exhibit, a hefty lump of hardwood, four feet long and four inches thick. On the end of this weapon he displayed splats of blood and a trace of brains. Together the men fitted this club to each crushed skull and found it perfect. Arrell observed that an ordinary man could wield the weapon only by using both hands, and tried it through the air. Jeremiah offered to disprove this theory. Apparently he took hold of it with one hand, and gave a mighty swipe, which just missed the sergeant's own head. The crowd, it seems, moved closer for a better look at what had done the damage. But I only have this on hearsay. What I remember was our hunched forms of plague-victims, the wind at our backs showing our clothes as the tatters of a discredited rabble, and Jeremiah riding up behind, manoeuvring his horse alongside the sulky, his face wearing an appearance of anguish or perhaps illicit satisfaction. Then he presented me with a contemptuous smile, his smile of two nights ago. I have never felt so helpless to be myself. This was worse than anything. He smiled as a man smiles at a child with whom he shares a secret so damning it cannot be spoken without the man demeaning his manhood or the child surrendering the immunity from punishment afforded him by ignorance.

Once back at home, we installed Mum indoors, where she belonged. The horses whinnied the stench of death out of their nostrils. The creek slid past, as it had for aeons before our place was built; she-oaks growing in white sand on the banks whispered murder. This was where I took my horses, in among agitated accusations, to let them drink their fill, to watch them raise dripping velvet muzzles and shake their manes now and again, before returning them to the home paddock ready for saddling later in the afternoon.

By the time I stamped up the two steps and passed through those invisible walls of our public privacy, Mum had dressed herself in a terrific grief of betrayal. Lightnings flashed from her moodiness. Her hands clubbed at her own unyielding flesh, which was too thickly packed to show any sign of distress. Tears spurted from her eyes in surprised bursts. Did she, for the first time, truly see herself as alone? How shall I describe such forlornness? Previously she had moved in the gloomy halo of a person shut out from herself and patiently knocking at a private door to be admitted again, avoiding distractions by keeping her back to the world. But now, you could see straightaway, when she had turned round and no longer knocked, the secret door swung open and some inner woman dragged her outer self right in, shooting the bolts behind her; so she had appeared at a window to weep and rage against injustice. She had, at the same time, become more shut away and yet able more openly to see us. Clearly we came in range of her fury. She began shouting between the sobs and thunders of an autocrat despite her husband: 'I suppose I shall have to do all the mending myself!'

I had arrived in time to watch her turn her frenzy against poor Polly: 'How did that butcher of yours know where to find them?' she demanded with all that this might mean, and sent Polly staggering from the house, screaming down to the creek till the horses cantered in wild circles round the rails, their great eyes rolling, soft mouths hardening to blackened brass fanfares.

Pa contributed only one thing, but not about the butcher: 'He thinks he has taken over.'

So I had not been the only one to see what I saw in Jeremiah.

Mum, finding she was no longer just part of Pa, shot him this discovered look of hers.

'Wasn't it enough,' she asked, 'for Michael to be chained all night to our bed and myself kept from sleeping by his moans?'

Reliving it, she added something more.

'And the feel of his flesh going heavy?'

Then we knew the home at Paradise had broken for good and all. Pa, fossilized in his chair at the head of the table, never moved. He sits there to this day, anchoring our house, preventing it from being blown away in a southerly gale.

Sergeant Arrell fired a question at me the moment I put my head in the door of the Brian Boru later that afternoon: 'And when did you last see your sisters and your brother alive?'

The bar had been screened off into a partly private cubicle. Sunlight bounced off the bay outside. These tall stained screens shed a dull mirrored light into the true mirrors of a great sideboard behind the bar. Here the world fitted into neat recesses backed with smaller square mirrors, in each of which passers-by outside the window flickered through the distorting bubble of a near-empty spirits bottle. The sea's repetitions slid down bevelled glass edges through filaments of red-orange, green-indigo. Great beer taps jutted above the bar, forsaken for the present. Disgruntled regulars were directed round the back to the illegal door they normally used only after closing time. A voice was heard to repeat at intervals: 'There's bodies in here, mate. Yeah, bodies. Round the back you'll be able to get a drink. Well, there's been murders.'

Sergeant Arrell sat on the kitchen chair they must have brought him specially for his rank. He waited. I answered.

'I met them on the road.'

He said (and I watched the back of his head in the mirror beyond): 'After they had been to the dance?'

'Before.'

He said (the back of his head appearing to belong to a different man altogether and one not at all clever): 'Were you travelling in the same direction or going the other way?'

'After the races they went home. But I didn't. I had promised Sister Veronica to shift her holiday garbage. And I'd promised to check the lamps for her before too late. So I rode straight on to Cuttajo, instead of stopping at home on the way. I was at the convent by five-and-twenty past seven. It took me about an hour to put things right for the Sisters. I did look in at the hall to check how they were going with the dance, but the girls told me only three people had turned up so far. All men.'

The sergeant nodded (and the mirror grew lighter, then darker, then lighter, with the coloured edges of a white sea framing him). He didn't need to ask who I meant by the girls. He had been in our community a long time. He knew that Father Gwilym's little band of fiddlers played for our amusements as well as in church.

'I decided not to stay, even if the others did, so I rode back home. About two miles down the track I met them coming the other way. They were singing, and this meant Michael was half-drunk on something, though where he got it I couldn't say. His rum was taken off him the night before, you see. We stopped and had a yarn. And I went on my way. Except for my horse going lame, I would have been home in another half hour.'

Sergeant Arrell thought a moment, perhaps about the lame horse, then pursued his line of questioning: 'I understand they arrived at the hall at ten minutes past nine to find it shut and the dance cancelled?'

'That I don't know.'

A door opened behind me (in the mirror it looked like a door opening in his head).

He told me in the voice of a judge: 'I shall want to question you further, Patrick.'

In came the doctor, who had travelled all the way from Bunda as soon as he got news on the telegraph. Dr Heinrich von Lossberg, his name was, government medical officer, plus a high speaker for German science and modern knowledge of all kinds. His shadow hopped from one mirror to another as he went straight to the corpses. Then I turned to watch him, aware that it would look unnatural not to be able to face what he was doing. He lifted the raincoat put to cover their battered heads. He dropped it straight back again.

'Sergeant Arrell,' he reported in a military manner, yet with soft corners of melancholy, 'I came as fast as possible.'

Arrell handed him an empty .38 cartridge. The doctor took it and turned slightly away from me to examine what he had taken. The big mirror showed his heavy, pale, concerned but unmoved expression. His mouth shaped itself for the beginnings of some intelligence, but he held back. Then he glanced up. And we were, without warning, eye to eye in the glass.

Once, during my special lessons, Father Gwilym had guided my hand with his cold fingers, to read for myself (he treated me as a blind person) the answer to my question. I had put it to him that butchers speak of themselves as set above other trades and I could see no justification for this. He consulted his shelves of books, more crowded than the School of Arts Library, going filmy like a bad eye and reading the spines with his fingers. Once he made his decision, the place grew calm as a monastery. He announced that I would have to search back to times before Christ to find an answer to what I wished to know.

In the first book he laid open on my lap was a lithograph of a pagan priest holding a long knife over a lamb tied to an altar. Then, some pages later, another sacrifice – this time, if I remember aright, in the Americas, where the victim was human. His finger wiped a few specks of dust from the page so I could see more clearly the healthy man chained to a grid, much as Michael had been chained in sight of us all on his rowdy occasions. This priest brandished a cleaver.

Father Gwilym's voice came feverish as his hand was cold: 'In pagan times, priest and butcher were one and the same man.'

He stole the book back, though I had not seen enough, and put another in its place. This was a bulky volume of annotations concerning the Jewish faith. He explained, voice boiling and bubbling from the excitement of knowing such matters: 'Even to this day the kosher butcher is charged with draining the blood from all meat because an Orthodox Jew must not take blood into his body and has to be confident the butcher is trained in the rituals and understands the articles of faith, so his meat will be properly prepared and fit to eat. Here you will find,' he flipped some pages, 'a list of the religious knowledge a kosher butcher must learn,' he snapped the volume shut in a sudden hurry. 'Our modern butchers,' he smiled remotely, 'remember to claim special respect for their trade but forget what they ought to know to earn it.'

The thought of Mack sitting through a course of theological studies made me laugh out loud.

He asked: 'Do you recall how you used to intone the responses to the litany for me? You were shy. No one else gave them out half so beautifully. Whenever I came to *Dominus vobiscum* you always hesitated. Did you worry that you wouldn't get it right? Whatever the reason,' his cold fingers flew onto mine and perched there, 'your *Et cum spiritu tuo*, addressed to me as priest of course, sounded specially for me as a person. As if you hoped . . . '

He sighed and his eyes grew old. I noticed the worn cuffs of his cassock. I am cursed with sentimentality. His voice faded, so faint and so suggestive you could believe it was compounded of imperfect echoes whispering back original words which still remained, somehow, unspoken.

He confessed regretfully: 'My own sin was vanity.'

There were still other things I needed to know about the butcher.

Wherever you looked, McNeil had been there first; he was the one to offer his horse and sulky for the expedition to the dance, he was the one who volunteered to search for the missing revellers next morning, and he found them in that out-of-the-way spot without a moment wasted on indecision.

Was it that the butcher saw the dignity of the tragedy? Did he, because of his trade, recognize that these were no longer family bodies but sacrificial offerings to some public hunger? Whatever the reason, he did not ride back to Paradise to allow the kin of those who'd died to be the first with the grief of it – he went straightaway to seek out the figures of authority, policeman and priest. And when the squadron of our dark closeness drifted home on a clutter of horse hooves, stirred as trees are stirred, who was it brushed an eager Barney Barnett aside and undertook to cart the cadavers to Cuttajo and lay them out but this man whose every working day refined his expertise in handling dead flesh, hefting the hollow carcases he would dismember with ceremonial precision, fastidious (yes, I allow him this at least) as a priest dabbing fingertips on a cloth after having anointed the orifices of living senses.

What were those two women to him, even without his leather cap of office? Why just the women? He left the male corpse to others, so I gathered in the illegal bar at the Brian Boru that afternoon. And wasn't it the butcher who stopped his mouth when I entered, though he did not yet know I had been asked to leave the front bar while Dr von Lossberg flew in on his travelling cape, togged up for an Alpine crossing though our holiday weather was stifling as usual. Milky heat from the Pacific broke white and tumultuous around the little hotel, swirling dirt aloft and lashing windows with a storm of dead bird-cries. High above my back, that flat skin of fish-scale cloud spread from horizon to horizon. These minutes were the inner pulsing and fury of a great creature swimming across the sky, digesting us as it went, our agony a mere symptom of well-being for that irresistible headlong rush away from all we had known.

The butcher's hands, upraised, spoke for him the words he now held back. I hardly recognized my brother-in-law filled thus with the power of office, his face moulded to a celebrant's fierce impartiality. I had seen this look before, when Father Gwilym escaped the small bother of following me with his eyes as I corrected his alb and he emerged into the church, past the bleeding heart of Jesus, glancing once, always, at the Virgin and then loosing his voice to soar on the mystery of *Introibo ad altare Dei* . . . even the mild Father and his bloodless hands mighty with that cry, becoming part of a universal invocation uttered without cease all round God's earth, his voice simply joining what was already there, the thin tone natural to him swelling to ring vigorously with some power he called from our imprisoned longings. So the silence and upraised arms, shocking as the blow of a great bell, deafened us.

'I'd ask you,' the butcher spoke again at last, 'to observe a minute's silence in respect for the dead ones under this roof.'

I stood there at the back doorway, restrained by ritual, while he escaped from what he might have been saying. Now it has been explained to me I see it all. Now I have been reminded of my lesson so many years before in the heritage of butchery, the time I laughed. Here, with my sisters and brother murdered, that immemorial tradition revived.

In spring, when bats wheeled round the house at night whistling, and in the morning dry gum leaves fell from the trees as dead wings, Willie came running down to where I worked repairing the fence in the south-east corner of the twenty. I scarcely knew him for the singing birds in his lightness.

He always kept weasels. He bred them in cages at one side of the stables. We took them rabbiting. Ever since I was a boy he had had them. After his beating and the loss of his wits he clung to their dependence on him; weasels were the ones he talked to in his mumble of a big dry tongue and broken teeth. They fought and clamoured for him just as if nothing had happened, and whatever else his brain no longer knew, he knew the sense of this – he was still their master and provider, still the one to risk his bare hands among those needle teeth, the one to choose which should mate with which in the piss-damp straw. He was the one to watch them do it in their miniature Eden and be satisfied by the squirm of litters. He knew how it was done. He knew the responsibility of guiding their lives to his purpose. He had that lordly impassiveness of deciding this *meant* nothing.

Mum, who drew the family about her sombre magnetism to have us at mass with her, took to leaving Willie at home since she noticed him unexpectedly living his private life during the service, deaf to the littleness of anything unnecessary to his inner order of holding chaos in check. He grunted during the preparation of the host, he appeared not to notice how beautifully her favourite served at the altar (Pat), he spoke simple horse noises through the Benedictus and jumped the claim of the Dies Irae by pushing his way free of suffocation among men and women, stumbling, falling, scrambling up and charging towards the open portal and out to liberty with a bellow of suppressed pain. The lopsided wreckage of his damaged brain lived it all, the inward hypnotism as a fixed focus behind his wandering eye. But this spring morning on the crackling leaves of that little copse in the gully where I was cranking some new wire tight, he called out to me in a voice resurrected from earlier times: 'Patrick, Patrick!' and his bright tragedy fixed on me so powerfully I felt I must wrestle against his shadow, that his bottled-up strength would make even Jeremiah tremble for the family's fate. His young voice called me to account: 'Patrick, come home straightaway, Mum's dead!'

I suppose I must have looked up in unmasked amazement, because he recollected himself and his fate of never knowing. The dull toad settled in his cheeks, his excited hands grew to lumps and weighed him off balance till that limber running of youth-regained tripped him and he crashed sidelong against the harp of my morning's work. Lurching off the wire, he blurted a horse-grunt in my face, hot nostrils spread wide and yellow with fear. But I was not fooled. The wild fellow who had once needed beating senseless to slow him down had escaped control in those moments, had shown himself and could not be taken back. A lifted blind revealed the Willie I remembered, proud as a man should be, the one we took our troubles to when we didn't go to Norah. I'd almost forgotten, because I was only nine when Pa crushed his ribs for daring to say he would walk away and live his own life . . . and then being woken in bed to see my lamp flare at the passage of rushing bodies, Willie gripping a knife and the flash of blood across Pa's shoulder, as he was in the act of delivering that terrible blow to silence us all and shut our heads in the muffling of Willie's idiocy, so even when we walked straight we knew it was by the grace of Pa that we didn't totter like our elder brother. I had forgotten in the intervening years, but this reminded me.

For the first time since the murders, I wondered what Willie was capable of, what might be woken in him at any moment, pent with the superhuman energy of all he had to stifle to live as our household idiot, what fury of cunning might thrust up under the lid of the simple tasks he confined himself to.

Only now do I begin to understand my father's anger. He had arranged a world for us where we could be free of the usual creeping lassitude, free of rudderless bewilderment on a sea of possibilities, free from the corruption of choice – a world in which each of us had a secure place. Australia was going soft, he saw that, and he kept us hard. We raised our own beef, we made cheese and stored it, bred chickens, and grew the fruit and vegetables we ate. Even Willie the simpleton knew the feel of this vision, had taken it in his hands once, used it as a weapon, and failed. Pa let Polly escape the boundaries of his contempt because she could never be brought to understand. She thought Paradise was just a little farm where she happened to have been born, and grew to hang round on the verandah mooning for some oaf to carry her off to parties so she might tittle-tattle and envy other females' frills. Polly was a waste of time. That's why he let her go and even came good with an old sulky to seal the bargain.

On the other hand, what if, instead, Pa had wanted to lure the butcher in? What if Polly's vamping was exactly what his kingdom required, sunlight catching the skin of her caged young body and momentarily dazzling her lover. Had any words been said when the butcher arrived in his Sunday suit – with a collar tight round his neck as a hame strap, new braces sandpapering against the starch of his shirt, all studs and strained seams, his square head heavy with the arcane calligraphy of veins his knife must follow – about how to split skulls in a manner pleasing to God?

As for William, the fact is that each child is born into a different situation even if all are born in the same household. The youngest are inheritors of rights won by those who came before. The eldest has the task of teaching his parents. Through his rebellions and illnesses, and more than anything else through his trust, he takes the raw dominance of father and mother (not even yet accustomed to the single skin they have come to inhabit as a pair) and defines their greatness for them, taking upon himself the punishment this entails. They rage against captivity and he must accept the blame, they turn violent with inadequacy and he is the scapegoat, because he is the master. Any wonder then that after twenty years of following where Willie led and facing all the trials he posed, Pa finally took rebellion into his own hands and set the question of mastery where he intended it should remain. We all learnt a lesson we never forgot. Without needing to think this out, we made Willie our special care. We looked after him and saw to his comfort in small ways. From that day on, he never lacked the harvest of his brief doomed period as the Pretender. Michael's turn came next; then Norah's, in a different way; then Daniel's, though something about Daniel warned our parents he was a cuckoo's child and not to be trusted or mistaken for one of their own, because right from the start he wore Pa's name all wrong; then mine.

But, of course, Michael still held out. Thanks to Michael, none of the rest of us had to take the full brunt. There began to be support for the task of civilizing Mum and Pa. Also, something else intervened before the succession could come down to me. Jeremiah outgrew me. But I am wandering from the point. The question now became: Could Willie have wanted to strike back at those who gained from his young lifetime of striving and loss?

Pa made for us an infamy, without which we would have been in rags. We were the tribe of the savage Paradise. Boys at school had feared us long before they met us. What other family in the district was spoken of in an undertone? The priest's housekeeper warned him no good would come of having me as altar boy; I overheard her and then walked into that room boldly. Where had I learned to be bold? I knew it in my blood. Afraid and ashamed as I was, by the very fact no good was to come of me, I had to live up to my name. A light grew in Father Gwilym's eye. As of that moment, he fancied me; whereas he had merely been willing to give me a try before, because the other fellows proved unreliable. He had his own pride of office, and at that instant we were in league against the housekeeper and her respectability. But, more remarkable, we were equals in this compact. My family's reputation obliged me to perform the rites as perfectly as could be – then I was sure to keep the gossips guessing, then they would watch me closely, following every least action, not to miss the moment of my breaking out. They never grew weary of this. Isn't that remarkable? In their conformity they could not change their minds. And if any were tempted to do so out of charity, Mum's weekly appearance at mass put a stop to that. Black hair tied in a strict bun and her strict black eyes black with what she saw of the respectable society which shunned her, she moved a tabernacle of funereal pride wherever she went, and blossomed nobly with a spirit so challenged.

You have nothing, her look spoke clearer than words, but trinkets!

The entire town speculated on what she might say in the confessional. So did we children. Pa, if he ever went, would have a good deal to own up to, including rages, whippings, and triumphs, glorying in the power he had taken, blasphemy, and boundless pride. But our mother, what did she ever do that she could put a name to and ask penance? Was the thickness of the air around her an offence? Was her rank seething fertility to be laid to her own charge? Had she invented the simple words of the English language she used? Mum clouted us, including the girls from time to time, but never in the fury of recognition; she did it absently, a reflex of the arm to some meaningless stimulus, because she would not allow us to interrupt her, she would not even be distracted into interrupting herself. Her whole concentration was on something neither good nor evil and therefore no matter for confession. How many Hail Marys, how many Novenas would need to be paid for having ceased to observe that evil was an option? What penance could she do for forgetting she had ever had a life before she married Pa? Her uprightness being in no way doctrinaire, it was without moral value. Mum remained as she was because she had no imagination. Even when she barged past the butcher's helping hand as she trod heavily down from the trap, the vehicle dipping to that side and springing back level once she was safely adrift on the soil, I think she hadn't the imagination to believe her daughters and her son were dead. She could see the corpses, yes, the wounds, a blanket spread under Michael and Ellen with patches of their blood soaked into it and ants feeding: but she saw it as the ants saw it, she could not imagine it into any reality of being obscene.

She would not have them come to her again, nor hear their voices, of course she knew this. But now life had left them, she couldn't work her reflexes round to the fact that they were ever anything different. Events had simply caught up with some intuition she might have felt, so Mum recognized the corpses with a frankness she could not spare them while they were alive and making demands on her to know what she could not ever know without pushing past the frontier of things one can grasp in one's hand. Her limit of pain was this. Also her limit of contentment. She could not catch hold of sympathy, so she had none. Ought she to have been punished for it? Mum had had uses for those three; she needed to think how to reorganize the house duties as soon as she could get home. Her role in Pa's kingdom was as its unquestioning heart. Four months later, she astonished us at supper. Suddenly she said: 'When the first of them was killed the other two must have watched, so one poor soul watched it twice.' Her darkness quivered and a bright film fled across her eyes.

She was dead, herself, next morning.

The disgraceful scene in the illegal bar at the Brian Boru Hotel erupted out of the bare branches of a dream plumtree suddenly flowering such multitudes of white anger the dangerous bees worked crazily to stuff their trouser pockets full of pollen before it all flew away in a final explosion of deathly perfume. If the tree had still been alive, it ought to have carried loads of fruit at that time of year. But stuck beside the back fence, where everyone pissed and threw up their surfeit of alcoholic poisoning, it had died. I was gazing at it when suddenly I found myself looking *through* it, between branches where the blossoms popped into focus as men's eyes gleaming with resentments which went deeper than the inconvenience of being shut out of the front bar. The sea's milky heat flecked their hungers. The butcher, with arms upraised to still a storm of grit lashing windows and walls, called for a minute's silence to save his own skin, because he knew I knew he had been talking about our family disrespectfully.

The eyes were not on him. The eyes were, every one, on me. And this was how I knew. Eyes which had nothing to hide or fear, all together as they were in that swarm, weighed down by the honey of belonging. This promised to be a real Donnybrook.

I took my glass of ale when the minute was up and would have drunk it quietly while their suspicions raged round them and stung them with the lust to know. Simply as brother of the victims, I enjoyed a stature their quelled passions envied. They would have stuck needles into me and sucked my blood if that might slake their thirst for what they knew they would never know. But from a secret corner of the squalid room, Artie Earnshaw's cousin spoke up: 'You shouldn't have left it all to us,' he said . . . meaning, as every man understood, the carting of the bodies into town.

'Is that you, Barney?' I replied, squinting at the muck of what little light pushed that far in. 'I thought you had intentions of carrying my sister off, in any case!' I said this because all the way back home in our cavalcade one thing jolted and jostled before my mind's eye – the sight of Barney Barnett rushing to be first to get at Ellen's corpse, putting his arms round her stiff resistant body to heave her away from Michael, making an awkward job of it, his boots scuffing the dirt and his face cooked in a fire of lewdness. He had not waited for permission. Being her fiancé, he took it as his right, though Artie and the butcher, in the end, did the work.

Barney jumped at me and I put him on his back with a single punch. I knew I had to leave and not return because those words, which had slipped out before I could imagine how they might sound, were not just in heathen bad taste but victorious.

I stood over him, Murphy that I was and a fully paid-up member of the Old King's black vanguard, to make certain he could not accuse me of running away. He knew he was beaten. I'm only surprised he ever tried it on me.

'You've been left with nothing, mate,' I told him. Again, once spoken, the words sounded wrong. I found I had already set my glass down. So I left it, half-full, where it was. 'And you can finish my beer if you like,' I added as I went out, hating him because I hated them all.

I tell you one thing: whatever I may have expected to see in my life, never once did this include Barney Barnett as a lonely ruin in his bed, hooking a finger through a hole in his grandma's sheet to keep a grip on life while he skited to the police about how he had been the murderer, urgent in his plea of guilty, anxious to have the purple stole of some grand office authenticate his importance and guide him to eternal life in the annals of infamy.

The Barnetts' farm was the only working property between our place and Earnshaws'. The house stood closer to the paddock where the murders happened than the Earnshaws' own house did. But it was still a good way out of sight. During the enquiry, Barney was asked how he came to be first on the scene after the butcher William McNeil.

'I took that way because my dogs would give me no peace.'

'And the dogs led you across the field to your own boundary fence, did they?' the magistrate asked and, when this had been answered in the affirmative, observed that they were singular dogs to scent dead bodies half a mile away when they could not, apparently, hear the screams and shots the previous night at the same distance.

This had Barney sweating to get off the hook, just the way we saw him sweat to get back on it before he pegged out altogether.

Pa nor Mum could bring themselves to answer much more than yes or no to the questions aimed at them, such was their scorn for the shallow life out there in society, including its law courts. The enquiry itself proved they were right to keep us separate from the ruck; even if this had had to be achieved through violence.

Of great interest to the case were some reported scratches on Pa's arms. He was required to lay them bare in evidence, though the marks had entirely healed in the interim. He did so with the dignity of a man who has no option but show his power, though vanity would never seduce him into doing so. The scratches, he explained when pressed, happened on Christmas Eve while clearing a new paddock down along the creek at the far south corner of our place.

It was impossible to imagine how we might have felt if we believed Pa would be put on trial: perhaps excited by something close to recognition. But I don't think so. As I recall, the moment we set foot off Paradise in a bunch, we felt we had risen to our inheritance, the exclusive, marauding clannishness of us. They never bothered interrogating him or me or my brothers on the work we did together, so they missed the whole essence of the family. Without work we were a simple tyranny and fit for pity.

The great project of clearing a new paddock had begun months before. We'd hoped to finish by the beginning of December, but one thing or another delayed the last few acres. 'Christmas!' Danny jeered before he left for work in Bunda, 'it'll be Christmas before you lot get through that patch of scrub.' He was correct, though it cost him a swipe from Pa for saying so and he had to have Norah clean up his uniform again. 'Christmas!' said Michael, always cheerful, 'we'll swear to have it done by Christmas.'

So on Christmas Eve we were down to the very last patch and hell-bent on seeing it through. We got up long before dawn, lamps lit, our shadows clubbing each other in the opposed indignities of sticking arms into unwashed shirts and thrusting our hands out for mugs of steaming tea from Mum's cavernous duty. The beds, behind us now, eased themselves free of our shapes, blankets disordered and thrown back, pillows grey as cold muttongrease. Drifting woodsmoke mingled with an intrusion of the humid outdoors to burrow in our boots waiting on the step for when we had filled our bellies with porridge and tea and shuffled from the kitchen, barefoot and already hot, to tie on our work for the day. Right by Mum's hand, the open firebox of her black stove licked its scavenger's chops, the red raw ribbing inside huffing mouth-warm against her skirt and casting a glow on the cupboard door across the room where dark fugitive legs flickered past. Standing round the cook pot like soldiers on guard duty and feeding without bothering to sit, we ate in our sleep. Far off, the ocean roared in towards land, bringing dawn on its back. A lone wakeful dingo, somewhere down beyond the blacks' camp, crowed tragically once; and minutes later, once again.

Then the day marched in to get us, suddenly brisk and ceremonial. Light chimed against the windows and tramped across the verandah, and threw a gold bar in on the kitchen floor. The fire grew pale. Mum's great shadow shrank, heavy and tricky as mercury. 'It's five o'clock,' Willie said in the voice of a clock. And Ellen, who was to do my milking chore while I went with the others, picked up two buckets. First down the steps, she was struck by a halo, a flood of sun-rays at eye-level. Lifting one bucket, she shielded her dazzlement with a forearm. Michael galloped in pursuit, scooping his boots off the step on the way and feathering his ankles with a rainbow of assaulted dew. He went a few paces past her and swung round, walking backwards so he could face her while he said whatever it was those flustered pale moths carried up with them into the trees. Then he laughed, probably because he knew Pa would be staring across at him, censorious as a judge, and that Mum must by now have slammed the iron door shut on her dancing fire and dragged the kettle into place with water for scalding the pig still snoring in its pen beyond the scullery door. And I remembered I had to be back home by noon to lend Mack a hand, because he had promised to do the job professionally when he brought Polly to join the girls in decorating our house, in laying out clean linen for the festival, and baking pastries plus an extra batch of bread.

We armed ourselves with axes and saws, and slung the winch in an old trap Pa used my school pony to pull (this was the pony's only job now, in old age). Michael led the big horses up from the creek to meet us at the ford, the shaggy hairs stuck to their fetlocks with clean water. We turned to watch him: Pa and Willie on the job, Jeremiah, young John (then sixteen), and me.

We worked together like a single machine, felling trees, lopping branches, using the stripped trunks to roll the scrub aside, shoulders swelling at the weight, soil on our hands, breaking holes in the sky and filling them with the smoke of demolition. Whipbirds darted about ahead of this progress, clinging low down on unfallen trees, snicking us with the late-coiling thongs of their cry.

It was just such bush that Pa's father first broke into, a forest so thick you worked in it by intuition, hearing a multitude of sounds but seeing little, frogs calling from high among the leaves and the ground alive with animals, furred and scaley tails disappearing beneath the mould just in front of your boots, each axe blow echoing (I thought of a match struck in a maze of mirrors). And beginning with a single tree, his first victim, picked at random, he broke a space for the sun to reach, a space where he and his wife could dig with wooden spades, plant their handfuls of wheat, and then go home in a buoyancy of exhaustion, with the idea of naming the humpy they had built of stacked bark Paradise.

Relentless as a cancer, our grandparents ate into the surrounding scrub, the sunny patch growing large enough for a whole field of wheat. In forty years of slavery, hair falling thick over their shoulders, eyes sparkling alive and ambitious, they cleared a hundred and eighty acres, adding pasture for sheep to their crops; then Pa took over with his grand plan of beef. He bought a block of timbered country to the north, which everybody said was good for nothing, till the pit-sawyers arrived and cut us planks to enlarge the house by a verandah. The gap they felled led straight to the fence between us and the Barnetts. Pa had his eye on a creek out that way, Burnt Bridge Creek, as it was called to commemorate some forgotten mishap maybe higher upstream. The water was good, though not so plentiful as our Blacks Creek, but he chiefly wanted the land for the way it lay. Pa could look at a dense heap of scrub where you'd barely make out what was fifty yards ahead and see it as a place for, say, potatoes.

So, while Barnetts lost hold of their pride and failed by a small margin each year, we Murphys were ready to make an offer on that potato patch along the precious creek. Once we got it, we went in to clear it, singing and slashing, steel blades and winches at work, Pa in the middle, still respectable in his sweat-soaked shirt and waistcoat, heaving trees aside with a silent surly ferocity, now and again checking on his sons as we routed the wildlife to smash forward yard by yard, attacking virgin undergrowth and leaving behind a widening band of mangled leaves, split branches, and raw black soil.

By Christmas Eve the fires had almost died away in huge stumps and hollow charcoal shells of fallen trunks. We were down to raking and piling smaller rubble when Oliver Barnett and his son Barney called over to see what we had done that they had not been able to do. They smoked a pipe with Daniel Junior (the only one among us to have the habit), while he explained that he was home on a couple of days' furlough, just for the festivities.

'Nice job you've made of this, Dan,' old man Barnett said to Pa, and I thought how handsomely he rose to the occasion, seeing what he had lost.

'We'll fence her in the new year,' Pa agreed, and this was a lot of talking from him. But he spoke it like he once said to the beaten Willie: Shall I break your leg as well, or leave that till some other time?

Ruin was slow coming to the Barnetts, but it didn't let up. Their folks had arrived with plenty of cash, which they lost on an early venture and then, after a spell at gold fossicking, lost again, till it came down to Barney lying on the family bed with his granny's sheet up round his neck, adam's apple a shrivelled fruit long past the time for picking, and his mouth falling open over to one side, showing the white slug inside which the priest would have to dab with chrism while a cracked bell went ringing the alarm: I'm not talking about no bloody horse, I'm talking about him and his sisters!

We didn't invite them over.

Then I said: 'Time for me to go. Mack'll be up home.' I waited for Pa's permission, and once he had given it some thought he nodded. I dropped my tools in the trap for Willie to drive home that night and set off up the hill. I heard Barney yell: 'Hang on.' But I never thought he meant me. Next thing, he's panting alongside. 'Is it the pig?' he asked. 'It's the pig,' I replied. He said: 'I never killed a pig.' I said: 'Mack's the butcher.' He said: 'Can I lend a hand?'

The whipbirds, having nowhere better to go, now we had cleared their corner of bush, whistled frantic whippings around us. He came.

'Dad won't care,' he explained, and this was what seemed the most astonishing thing to me.

'We're only having a turkey,' he whinged as we reached the road and jogged along, not to be late.

'Are you coming to the races?' he asked, sounding blown.

'I won fifteen bob last year,' he laughed boastfully, weakening.

'Ellen promised we'll go in together with the profits,' he almost sobbed.

'Listen,' Barney Barnett begged as we approached the rise where that stony gully cuts across the road, the spot Michael drove the sulky at too fast the time he busted the weak wheel which Mack fixed once it was given to him for taking Polly's gossip out of hearing.

'Shall we walk awhile?' he gasped.

I prided myself on being like iron. I could run home and back to Cuttajo without taking a break, even after a morning's labour. I liked the way I felt. I had him beaten. No one asked for his company. I kept on running while he dropped behind. I didn't once look back. No need. He had been ground into the dust, and I enjoyed the thought of that. I ran on in my work boots, shirt-tail hanging out of my pants and my collar stud missing so the wind ran big warm hands over my chest. I was sweating and I wished somebody would drive along to see me, some wagonette carrying a crowd of females to see my plastered hair and disreputable loose shirt, watch me steam past in a whiff of male smell and later think of me again when they came upon poor broken-winded Barney, hopelessly outclassed back there, probably bent forward, one hand on each thigh like an auxiliary piston, driving his legs straight to help heave himself up the slope. I beat him by a quarter of an hour.

When he arrived through the gate, doing his best to make light of his defeat and glancing round to find out from the ladies' expressions whether I had mentioned him at all, Mack and I were just dragging the pig to where we had set up a frame to bleed him on. Barney's flat voice (whining: 'Goodday, Mrs Murphy; goodday, ladies, Mack . . .') brought on the afternoon and hunger. Though I'd promised myself a bite of bread, I had not stopped to have it, and couldn't now. Mack said: 'Are you helping too?'

'Too right I am, if I'm let,' Barney offered.

'You can do it all by yourself if you're so keen,' Mack told him.

'That's our one pig for Christmas,' Mum warned from the scullery door. 'Don't you boys go spoiling him.'

I had worked with Mack before, and we made a quick job of lugging the beast out and lashing it down with the ropes put ready. It had been done this way for centuries in Ireland, using the Kilkenny frame.

Hunger suddenly seized hold of me; my gut raging with emptiness, I saw scarlet lights I mistook for a glimpse of something our ancestors on the far side of the world had handed down to us. Warlike monks in monasteries holding off the Viking marauders, Saint Brigid – buried at Downpatrick beside her dear friend Saint Patrick, and Saint Columba on the other side – Mary the Gael, as Father Gwilym called her, his voice clouding as it did when he was teaching Edith Earnshaw the violoncello. Mack walked round the victim, inspecting it, his pouch of knives, worn like a sporran slipped sideways onto his hip, clattering, and the steel swung by a cord. He selected one long, pointed blade. The pig watched him hone it, then watched him thinking as he stropped, then screamed at the top of its lungs.

Norah, I knew, hid her head indoors. She could never bear the slaughter. Mum rumbled back to the stove to be sure her great iron kettle kept on the boil. Young Kate in the peartree peeped through a Venetian lattice of fingers, trying to laugh. But of all the women, it was Ellen who caught my attention. From the scullery door she looked at this pig, absorbed in watching it. Even though Barney put on a tough act to make her notice him, she had eyes only for the pig.

'I'll do it this year if you like,' I offered, and the hunger in me was a kind of speed, a kind of concentration.

Far away a wakeful dingo answered the howling pig with a howl of its own: the one a desperate betrayed outrage, the other a timeless longing. Ellen's expression changed at that instant from curiosity to what I can only call recognition.

Why he did so, I don't know. But Mack, who was in charge of the job, ignored my claim and handed the knife to Barney, whose pleading, irritable anxiety of a beaten person fell away from him to reveal a champion. He brandished the knife admiringly, though Ellen still refused to notice. Eager to snatch glory from a life of defeats, he drew his arm back to drive the blade home.

'No!' Mack ordered. 'We just puncture the vein. There.'

Barney trembled. I watched his pants quivering. Was this rage or cowardice? Mack, shouting over the rumpus made by the sacrificial beast, which he alone knew the authentic way to kill, explained the art.

'If he doesn't bleed slow, the meat won't be white. And then you'll have Mrs Murphy herself to deal with.'

'Don't mess about with my pig,' Mum's voice warned from the kitchen.

Barney stepped forward and let the point in through the skin. At first it wouldn't go. Then suddenly the resistance gave. Blood squirted out all down his trousers and onto his boots. He jumped back, letting the blade fall. Mack took a swipe at him but missed, and retrieved his precious knife, which he then wiped clean between finger and thumb, checking if it had suffered any damage. I rushed forward to do Ellen's job, now she was no longer needed, positioning the milk pail to catch the blood. The pig knew what was happening. He wriggled and clenched, thumping the frame the way Michael thumped his body against the bed when he had misbehaved. But the pig did not have words to curse our house of a tyrant like my brother did, nor the lovely fire of alcohol to brace him or muffle his pain in warmth.

Down along the creek, the blacks came walking, feet sprung like tall birds, till they could see the house and what was going on. I thought they must be too far off to get any clear idea, but they stayed interested, so perhaps their eyes were better than mine. Each year they heard our pig cry, but it was still new to them. Perhaps they couldn't work out why we seemed unable to kill it outright, why it had to go on crying, moaning and sobbing for ten minutes or quarter of an hour. Perhaps they couldn't even see such a simple thing as why we needed to tie the animal on a frame to do the job properly.

Barney apologized to Mack. And again I was reminded of Father Gwilym, but this time of how his voice could change in the middle of my lesson and I knew next minute his white hand would perch on my working boy's scarred brown one. Barney said it was just his clothes and the shock of spoiling them, not the blood that made him jump, no, nor, he shouted over a renewed wail from the beast facing a certainty of death, the pig yelling. 'I suppose it'll wash out,' he added a bit stupidly, ashamed now Ellie began to laugh at him. And even more ashamed when he found she was, more likely, laughing at the pig for making so much fuss too late to be saved.

Mum brought boiling water. She heaved the great weight of the kettle and carried it herself, out down the steps, squinting in the sunshine and steam, to set it on the bench placed ready; and then carried back the bucket of blood for cooking. This was so full that the contents tilted and some streamed down the side, landing with a soft slap in the dust, which instantly soaked it up. Mum glanced back a moment and went on her way.

The pig's cries had guttered out to a hoarse panting, and now we heard again the remote gunfire from the ocean. An eagle's shadow rippled over grass, onto the dirt, up across the pig-frame, fitting itself to the lovable plumpness of dead flesh, then away, rising the full height of a stone chimney, flickering on smoke from Mum's fire, to vanish in the blue heat of the day before the day we must all celebrate. Next time we looked across towards the creek, the Aborigines had gone. There was just a flat plate of water turning silver on its axis at the bend where one bank had collapsed in the previous year's wet.

'Look at the horses!' Kate shrieked, leaping down, prancing

round the orchard and climbing an apricot tree full of Christmas apricots.

We hooted at the miserable cluster of them in the farthest corner of their yard, tails swishing the fence posts. Barney, under Mack's direction, had already begun the scalding and scraping.

'See this?' the butcher called to Ellen still at the door like a Sunday. 'When you get him for a husband you ought to have him apprenticed as a butcher. He's got the feel of it, when he doesn't go throwing a man's good knives around in the dirt.'

Ellen laughed. And I laughed also, at the insulting notion of a twenty-two-year-old man going for an apprentice.

As the scalding and scraping progressed, the pig's skin gave out a rasping whistle under the blade, a persistent ghost of the sound the beast's lungs made when it was dying.

The idea had never come to me before that other animals are covered with fur, feathers, or scales but pigs go naked like ourselves. So the screams which I'd heard once a year now made me feel cold. Each Christmas past I had listened to them without realizing why our neighbours looked in during that quarter of an hour of bedlam. This particular year they included Mr and Mrs Earnshaw enjoying a drive, who waved, and the O'Donovans, cantering through the gate and far enough down the track to get a close view while young Clarrie yelled out that they'd come to check, in case you was murderin' someone! I couldn't be sure what he said at the time, but I saluted on behalf of the family, needing a part to play now Barney had cut me out of my job.

Kate in the apricot tree heard, being that much closer, and she told me a few days later, when I returned home from punching Barney in the Brian Boru, my memory hot with the loathing I saw in the eyes of men I'd known all my life, men who would not, they said, lay a finger on me if I got out right away.

I ought to say something here about my patron saint. When Pa first sent me to lessons with the nuns at the Sacred Heart Convent, he had to pay two shillings a week for my education. Though this came as a great surprise to my elder brothers, William, Michael, and Daniel, the point was not so obscure: to celebrate our little world, the family needed a historian, a lawman, a clerk, an accountant. Norah was clever enough, but because she was a girl they didn't even consider her. When I came along, I was to be it, all these things rolled into one for the sake of thrift. I had a talent for learning and for politeness, which was another reason why the priest chose me to serve at the altar and why he began taking the trouble to give me extra tuition, gratis. 'Shall I tell you about your very own saint?' he asked me one day when I was still persuaded I'd become indispensable to him. Naturally I wanted to hear everything.

First he shook my faith in religion itself by explaining that Saint Patrick was an Englishman, born at Bannavem Taberniae, thought to have been near the river Severn. Such monstrous news made our world seem no more substantial than a dangling medallion, something beautiful, round and complete but too compact, too deceitfully perfect to be lifelike. When I reported this crime of Saint Patrick's to Mum, she muttered against letting that foreigner into our church in the first place. As a consequence, I found I had to fight for the right to go back to Father Gwilym the following week. I learnt a lesson from this: though Pa and Mum wanted me to have knowledge, it did not follow that I was to be at liberty to spread the muck around. My job, like a librarian's, must be to store it away so we would have it safely in the family. This knowledge might never be used, but our pride was incomplete without it. So Saint Patrick came from

Britain and his parents were Christian citizens of the Roman Empire.

Accepting his word gave rise to a change in my relationship with the priest; our meetings acquired a hint of the illicit, an exciting aspect of conspiracy. The story went that the young saint was captured by Irish marauders and carried off to Ireland as their slave. You may imagine the stained-glass window of this scene in my mind: dense lines of lead, a matted confusion of ships' masts, ropes lashing the boy's hands behind his back (a boy with my own features and colouring) and his new masters dragging him off to work as a herdsman on the slope of Slemish. Even though I was not yet fourteen, I was a herdsman myself. Since the time I began to walk, I helped with our cattle and did my share of farm work.

I began to see that Patrick *had* to be an Englishman, he had to be an outsider. Nothing ever gets done if everybody is an insider. So this was the true reason why my parents insisted I go to school; I was to be made the outsider. When he was twenty-two, my saint heard a voice promising him a mission, but he must free himself first, he must face the fact of his bondage and take action. (I myself was twenty-two in 1898, when the murders made our old life impossible to go on with and broke my father's power.)

Saint Patrick – so Father Ellis Gwilym told me in his tapestry voice of metallic glints with frayed edges round its stiff innocent pattern of words woven together as a design of facts in which each detail came forward equally with the others and nothing was relegated to background – escaped to France. There he received the call to return to the country of his enslavement and convert the Irish people to Christianity. He was consecrated as the second missionary bishop to be sent to Ireland, following the death of Saint Palladius. 'The second!' I cried out, betrayed in my dream again. 'Yes,' Father Gwilym confirmed mildly. 'There was only one who tried before him.' I wondered then if Saint Palladius was an idiot like my elder brother Willie, but I didn't know how to ask such a thing. Anyway, the church portals began banging in the change of wind and I found it was almost evening, so I faced the dangers of riding the last miles home after dark, my mind filled with demons and punishments, not least of which were the actual whips of my oppressors. 'It is probable,' Father Gwilym had said as I left, 'that Patrick, armed only with faith and knowledge, was the greatest and most successful missionary in history; foreigner though he was, within his lifetime all Ireland was his.'

These were the words I said which so shocked the women; while the pig's carcase glittered with sheets of steam and the knife rasped through tough bristles and the butcher whipped thin blades along his steel and whipbirds mocked his ceremony from the surrounding bush and Mum carried the afternoon sun in a bucket of blood, I said without preamble or explanation: 'Before Saint Patrick died, all Ireland was his.'

Mum put down the bucket, letting its handle clunk against the metal. She withdrew into the doorway. Norah, who had come to the workroom window when the pig's cries ceased, slowly raised a hand to her throat and held it there. Ellen, on her way to soothe the terrified horses, paused to look at me questioningly, in her calm and curious way interested. Polly gave a silly shriek from indoors at the sight of blood blazing on the threshold. And Kate fell out of her apricot tree while she acted the fool, spraining her wrist which had to be bandaged, and that's how it remained (she felt an idiot, as she put it) right to the day of the funeral when not only the residents of Cuttajo and district came but, thanks to sensational items in the city newspapers, hundreds of idlers who travelled from up and down the coast and even by Cobb & Co. from Goulburn and Sydney. A few came from Melbourne, over four hundred and sixty miles away. That was how famous we became.

Cuttajo parish used to be very proud of our church in those days. Now people couldn't care less, and the paint has been rubbed off by sea winds. St Brigid's was built only eight years before the murdered bodies were put in it, yet the outside and inside had already been repainted twice. This will give you some idea. During the building, Pa had helped with timber, allowing volunteer pit-sawyers into a patch of our forest to cut the joists and rafters out of the straight logs he offered them. I remember it going up. I was fourteen.

The light, never too good in there, suited a funeral. Once we were all seated and the simple coffins set regimentally at the foot of the steps before the altar, Father Gwilym made his appearance. He looked deflated, as if he had mistaken his way, as if seeing no flowers on the coffins caused him to doubt there was anybody inside them, so much so that he might knock on each in turn and not be satisfied unless he heard answers from within. An altar boy finished setting the cruets on the credence table for the requiem mass and knelt exactly as Father Gwilym rose from kneeling. How many times I had done this myself I could not count. I was thinking: Soon the kid's knees will begin to ache and his whole mind will be taken up begging the old fellow to finish fussing with that chalice. When it came to the funeral service, this was the boy who carried the jug while another held the priest's cope open so he could incense the coffins and splash holy water on them. The aromatic smoke drifted in the air, so heady it might have been a leftover from some far more ancient fertility rite.

St Brigid's was packed.

Outside, a solemn crowd of Protestants waited for their share of the pickings. At the graveyard the problem was to keep these people back. They felt they had rights and pushed close round the cortège, with their hot prickly clothes smelling of lust, hats in hand and combed heads bowed. Under their brows, cruel squids' eyes flashed and bodies dangled from their heads, feet drifting along while the firm shoulders wedged them in the best vantage point obtainable. I must have counted three hundred horses tethered to the fences on the paddock side, plus at least a hundred and fifty carriages, traps, and wagonettes. Even the bishop's landau was there. He had brought it with him when he arrived on the steampacket that morning (coincidentally with his provincial tour), though the matched grey horses belonged to the publican. His Lordship had to travel in style, I suppose, for the sake of his high office. Maybe the reason our priest shrank so badly, and the O'Donovan child clattered the sprinkling-wand in its brass jug, was simply that they knew a bishop sat, masquerading as humble, in the front pew.

At the graveside our family stood up front, hulking and immovable. Father Gwilym gave me several signs I could not interpret. He repeated them despairingly as the bishop stared at Mum, while gravediggers rescued the dead from ignominy, shovelling black soil over them, blanking them out from the impertinence of moral scavengers. I have studied fish oaring toward each other and stopping a respectful distance apart, apparently locked in some convention which will neither let them approach closer nor swim away. I felt the same, the priest's signals completely mystifying: a warning, a displeasure, a bewilderment, and an accusation. Eventually Father Gwilym produced a handkerchief and blew his nose discreetly, catching my eye above the exclamation of snowy linen. No one in our family was weeping. That was it. Only Polly, the ninny, standing apart in her lace-up boots and leaning on her husband's arm, spouting tears from a face so crinkled she looked as if she was at a music-hall and laughing fit to burst her stays. She was a McNeil now.

I found it impossible to believe the three victims would fail to turn up and join the rest of us in our amazement at the scene, the indescribable excitement, the sense of *life* all around. People half-dead a week previously were out and about and vivacious with opinions and gossip.

While the funeral proceeded, public investigators were busy boiling the dead horse's head, and this very afternoon ordered the Post Office to be opened specially for them to send a telegram to Sydney headquarters conveying the information that a bullet had been extracted corresponding exactly with the cartridge case found, and adding that two good horses had been reported stolen from a farm ten miles away. EXTRAORDINARY MYSTERY ABOUT THE WHOLE CASE, the telegram concluded. So there was.

And this mystery, even more than the evidence of common bloodlust, was what enlivened the public mind.

To give you a summary: The events looked simple. The sulky had been heading back home (south) when it turned off to the left a mile and a half from Cuttajo and was driven a further half mile till it stopped at the scene. Eight witnesses saw the party on the road, seven of them also saw the other brother, Patrick (myself), on horseback at the specified times. Everyone exchanged greetings because it was a fine, clear moonlight night. There was a lot of good cheer, owing to these neighbours having been with each other at the Yandilli Races earlier in the day. Of the witnesses who saw Michael and our sisters, some also observed an unidentified man of heavy build leaning against a tree where the sliprail was. When, with her son and a friend, Mrs Carroll of the Cuttajo greengrocery met the Murphys on their way to the dance, it was just at this point. Mrs Carroll saw the man watch Michael drive the sulky past (heading north towards Cuttajo) and then walk out into the road straight for her own cart. He passed just behind, so she and her party saw him closely, but not his face, owing to his having a dark felt hat pulled down over his eyes. Her thirteen-year-old son thought it might be the new fellow employed by the butcher. Five of the eight witnesses who passed along that road during the hours 7.45 p.m. to 10 p.m. saw the stranger. Yet Sergeant Arrell, himself returning from Yandilli with a friend (whether they were drunk, as suggested, or not), had no such encounter. But not only did Miss Florence Love (who also met the sergeant on the road) see the unknown man, he approached her, passing within ten feet and muttering something she could not quite hear. Thomas Drew was quite definite that he had seen him too; and Gordon Pringle (eighteen), who passed the sliprail at 7.45 p.m., described the intruder's strong build and hat. Later that evening, others met the Murphys behaving like revellers on their return journey home. Two witnesses claimed to have heard screams in the night and shots also. Louisa Theuerkauf, at her employer's house a mile or so from the sliprail on the other side of the road, having gone to bed at 9 p.m., was woken by the cats still in the kitchen at 10 p.m. (the clock struck), so she got up to put them out the back door – this door faces Earnshaws' paddock – and heard two shots, one long after the other, and two screams from the same direction repeating the word *Father, Father.* But she didn't like to wake anyone else in the house. Catherine Byrne, another resident on that western side of the road, heard screams loud at first but fading away, from the direction of Earnshaws' paddock. Such was the main evidence. The witnesses were in substantial agreement, but the facts were slight.

The overriding question in the public mind was still the one put by a reporter in the paper: How could a strong man and two healthy women be persuaded to leave the road and submit to being bound and tortured without the least sign of struggle? The tracks of the sulky with its giveaway wobbly wheel showed quite clearly that the driver did not suddenly diverge; they sloped off at an even, shallow angle, denoting a clear intention from some distance back to turn through the sliprail. Once in the paddock, all tracks were lost, while at the murder site such crowds had gathered on the hysterical advice of William McNeil and Barney Barnett, both there early, both sounding the alarm and urging witnesses down off the road, they obliterated any original footprints which the black trackers could possibly distinguish.

Had the victims, the newspapers conjectured, been killed first and then driven there to be laid out, all parallel with feet pointing west (in which case, why no blood in the vehicle?), or had they gone willingly (in which case for what purpose?), or had they been hailed and guided perhaps to rescue a hypothetical injured man (in which case, why no sign of the sulky being pulled up on the road and changing direction?), or, taking account of the fact that the killer was certainly armed, were they already being held at gunpoint while in the sulky (in which case, why were they seen so cheerful on the road minutes before the calculated time of their leaving it?)? The question remained: How could a single attacker, supposing the man in the hat were the murderer, overpower and bind three people, especially as he would need to put down his weapon to do up the bonds? Did that leave us with a gang theory? And if so, where were the other members of the gang, why had no one seen them come or go on an open road busier than any other night of the calendar? Why was Michael's skull smashed to make it look as if he had been murdered the same way as the girls when, in fact, after he was exhumed seven days later, a bullet was found, a bullet lodged in his brain, that the medical officer Dr von Lossberg had overlooked? Could the blows of the bludgeon, delivered with equal force to the right side of Michael's head and the left side of each of the girls', have been delivered by the one person? Was he ambidextrous, changing hands for these several attacks (the angle of the fractures betrayed the exact direction of the blows, which could then be quite accurately reconstructed)? The puzzle had many aspects. And finally, why was the Murphy family so reluctant to give evidence at the inquest, or even to see the bodies and bury them; why did they (we) behave in a manner so markedly unorthodox as to provoke the presiding magistrate to observe that it was as if they (we) were holding something back?

The magistrate asked Louisa Theuerkauf if the word *Father!* which she had heard screamed might not possibly have been *Arthur!*? Yes, she admitted, it could certainly have been Arthur, though she had not thought of such a thing until this moment. And Catherine Byrne also conceded the voice might have screamed *Arthur!* This witness added, with some shrewdness: But whether the screams named the person attacking or the person who might best come to her defence against the attacker, she, Miss Byrne, could not say, having often deliberated on the subject of fear and prowlers, on her house being broken into and herself assaulted.

These were puzzles. Altogether, over one hundred possible suspects were questioned by the police, and some of them detained. The ramifications welled even wider. Timber workers and shepherds reported wild men howling round their campsites wielding knives and clubs. The ironmonger did exceptional trade in new bolts and locks, also cleaning out his entire stock of ammunition. Crosses were painted on doorposts. I saw them myself and heard of cockerels secretly slaughtered for a kind of prayer dredged up from the distant superstitions of Europe and the Islands. The publican at the Brian Boru – Mr Gilbert, his name was – made a fortune out of visitors as Cuttajo earned a place on every New South Wales map printed from 1899 onwards. Our murders began to be called The Mystery. They were never solved. They still have not been solved. None of the explanations could be made to stick, not the one accusing Pa, at the upper end of the scale, nor the one accusing Sergeant Arrell at the bottom.

Yet the reason The Mystery was so widely accepted as a name had to do with more than just who might have committed the crime and how; in a religious sense, as well, it chimed with our deepest fear of life's meaning. As to the reported black magic, I'm sure I scarcely need remind you that while we speak of Australia, we also speak of Britain and the Continent. Certainly in those days most Australians had not much notion of a separate nationality, merely a separate opportunity.

In 1898 the grand imperial powers, for all the palaces in their capital cities, the boulevards and galleries, for all their glitter and aristocratic scepticism, were a spent force. They lived resplendently, but the decay had eaten too deep to be cured. The ideas going about at the time (I mean, by this, the high ideas) quite commonly involved a doctrine of pure blood-lines, a polite name for witchhunts against any intermarriage with aliens. The leaders in this debate were nearly always weedy little chaps, having narrow chests and an asthmatic delivery, who undertook lecture tours, during which they worked themselves into a fever on the subject of Orientals, or Slavs, Negroids, Jews, or even Irishmen. Father Gwilym had warned me about this. But I did not just rely on his word. I went to the lectures and subscribed to a Travelling Library. By 1914 I was in Europe and saw for myself, being among the first and oldest to volunteer for the

Army – the AIF, as it was called in those days. Incidentally, Artie Earnshaw joined the same platoon. He lied about his age; he wouldn't see forty again, that's for sure. We struck up a new friendship and remained mates right through till his death in 1938. We saw it all in Vienna at the end of the war. One look at the place was enough.

But during the years leading up to this, we had no real understanding of how we had been used, no notion that our governments were old-boys' clubs; we only knew that here in New South Wales people had the good sense to resent and resist all forms of authority. That's the one reason we escaped a full share of blame for the worst follies in the war. If we had a virtue, this was it.

The Germans and the British had turned on each other, the Bulgarians and Russians, cousin against cousin, clan against clan, using weapons which included fear and rape as well as bullets; nothing to do with their declared motives, but all with the ferocity of a closed family for whom there is no future, no self-expression beyond carnage. When you look back on it, you say to yourself: How did it happen? such madness? such murder? the lies so senseless, so impossible to unravel, the blame so hard to assign to pardonable causes?

Is it any surprise that, in the years when these atrocities were brewing, a nation like ours thrilled to the news of a mystery at Cuttajo? No wonder people cared more for this murder and felt it reached their souls more hauntingly than any case of kindness could, or any case of heroism. The horror spoke with a million tongues. The names Cuttajo and Yandilli became instantly famous. And even Paradise was heard of in the city.

Now, after the welter of theories, none of which fitted the case convincingly, in 1956, here was that dill Barney Barnett, one-time suitor for Ellen's hand, killer of the pig, whose bloodstained trousers caused immense excitement among the investigators, hanging on to his life long enough to call an inspector of police from Sydney and make his confession.

You should have seen his face when *we* walked in as well, me and Willie and Mack followed by Jeremiah in his wheelchair and Pa on horseback. He had just begun his tale when he saw us being let through the door by the nurse. I swear it is a tribute to his strength that his heart didn't give out that moment. But he had no time to lose, intruders or not. The priest finished his preparations, mucking about with a couple of candles, setting his stole ready to put on, fussing with the tiny phial of chrism, and dropping his bottle of holy water, luckily on the bed, where the inspector himself saved it.

I watched crows flap in his eyes and points of ivory show. Poor dismal old bloke forcing out the word *marder*, as he pronounced it, and currying enough nerve to defy us, the family.

'And then I bashed the horse's brains out with the bludgeon-stick, you see.'

Willie, I might mention, showed no sign of understanding, but he knew Barney well and kept giving him a poke on the foot to be recognized.

'Why?' Barney bellowed, emptily repeating the inspector's question, which might have been any number of questions and all tricky.

'This is 1956, don't you know?' he went on after a bit of dying. 'I'm not talking about no bloody horse, I'm talking about him and his sisters!'

He shot a look at me, the crows flapping in there a moment to let the vision through before the priest went dabbing the lids with oil, dabbing his nostrils and his ears and mouth, and uttered the words of absolution in such a voice that you'd swear it was him about to kick the bucket.

The inspector listened, calm and polite. Mack and Willie and I stood round with the nurse hovering behind us and the priest ready to pack his box of tricks.

'Aren't you going to write it down?' Barney whispered. 'In my words?' he pleaded from lips gleaming with the blob of oil, knowing now that there was no escape from hell.

'Thank you, Mr Barnett,' the inspector replied as he put his silver-trimmed cap on. 'I think I have heard enough. The horse,' he observed as he paused at the door, stern yet regretful, 'was not bludgeoned. It was shot.'

And left the fellow helpless there among us, suffering a seizure, his little nurse, daughter of Father Gwilym's best violin player, pushing us around and begging us to give him room to breathe even if we were old friends. Pa's stallion swished its clean tail and stamped one hoof. It was then, as I think I have mentioned, that the car door slammed and, a moment later, a fine pall of dust came drifting in to settle on Barney's claim to fame.

We had had the revenge we wanted.

How was an important fellow like the inspector to know that Barney's mistake did not necessarily prove he was lying? When you're humble enough, you realize the big things in life are the ones we do get wrong. They are the things which give us no rest until the brain can put its own pearly coating on them and make them bearable to live with.

After the priest, with a shrinking gesture, drew the sticky, dead lids over those subsiding wings I had seen in there, Jeremiah grumbled: 'Is he finished?' being unable to manoeuvre his wheelchair close enough to be sure.

I shook my head, though he was. Then I looked at Willie, trying to guess his feelings. But he remained mesmerized by the judgment before us. Mack nodded off to sleep on his feet – you might have guessed he wouldn't last long, having no fury to keep young.

Pa had gone. He would be at home when we got back, and there he would stay, because the rest of the business concerned nobody outside the fences we had put around Paradise.

*

As I look back on Barney Barnett's funeral I question whether anyone can guess what love costs. Undoubtedly the cost begins in that remote babyhood pre-dating our conscious recollections: naked mounds of warmth, a delicious skin smell, pink growths, webbed fingers (destined one day to reach adulthood perhaps by clutching the handle of some steel implement being forced into flesh), intimacies of damp hair and saliva. But isn't the cost also to be found later: while being lifted and held by some parent – the big dry warmth – who has the arrangement of the world at his or her mercy? Surely it does not just begin with that adolescent discovery of how startlingly lips move when pressed against other lips no longer quietly murmuring an anticipated lullaby; nor just with some girl called McCheyne who threw you off when you tried finding out what you were ashamed not to know; nor just with Artie's mother hoeing her kitchen garden, presenting firm smooth forearms, capable, tender, a knob of bone at each wrist and fine grey veins; not just with the rutting violence of powers within yet beyond yourself, hurling your body out of kilter, helpless to resist a monster known only by its appetite? Who else is competent to say what love costs a young lout unlearning, through the appeasement of blood, the reticence and primitive rage of childhood – exultantly feeling bones crack under his hand? Who is to gainsay the bat-wheeling pandemonium in the brain, or put a limit to it, or claim to know when it started or stopped? Whom am I to say I loved Ellen, or that I did not love Norah?

This much I can tell you for certain. The sort of person the authorities put in a magistrate's chair is he who imagines a plain man may copulate with someone tied up and helpless, and asks what sort of hell that would be.

The answer might be heaven, of course; as you will know if you have ever dared refuse to be woken from the enchantment of your free mind, from the sublime superiority of your solid body achieving flight, from capitulating to a new harmony nobody dreamed about before . . . taking fresh gulps of it, gazing in at irises wide open as the body's orifices to receive you, measuring your finest minutes by her breath spurting hot against your shoulder; while down there, in an ocean's upheaval, profounder secrets lip you with hunger – hunger for the defeat you bring by your self-sacrifice, the ultimate victory of the victim, the arousal of a yearning for cruelties which are beyond the human body's capacity to perform, until you come to understand that the deepest insecurity lurks in our physiological ability to receive more than we can give . . . what then is left to do but kill? And kill for the reason of love's ambition? Kill because of the very power of beauty, the knowledge that to repeat such a defeat-in-victory would make any other solution each time less possible? Pride aches to cry out, I have crushed your strength with my strength; I have dominated you with such excess that the time is past when I can make do with your fainting desire, your anger or loathing, delicious though they are. By then love has become as desperate as art, which must have a conclusion if it is to bring spirit and flesh together. Pride accepts nothing less than this. Human imagination, as I have found it, returns to the one image of heaven it knows. The murderer does not cast his victims away, he takes their lives into his own. Each victim becomes wholly his. The candle gutters and dims, and the void of helplessness has begun. For what can you do with the body dead, the mere doll of your dominion? Imagine, only, the virtuosity (the virtue, even) of holding off this fate, of committing your crime three times over.

In such a case, surely only a coward would count the compounding, the multiplication of misery to follow? Isn't the knowledge of such hell-impending the very mark and measure of a momentary elysium? What man who is a man will deny his virility at the moment of discharging it, by warning himself that he will be filled with regret once it's over? And what woman would not suffer fury and insult at sensing such cowardice, such narcissism in the moment of his self-loss to her victory?

How gross, you may say, but is it more gross than accepting squalid butchery as the sole logic? Doesn't this at least allow for a fearful joy, austere in its being stripped of trivia, perfected out of the fires of doubt, simplified beyond deception? Soul to soul, flesh to flesh, pure energy? The public must sense this, or why else have they been fascinated for sixty years, savouring the horror? In relation to such an act, mere notions of right and wrong are as tuneless and as fragile as cracked plates.

Let me speak on behalf of my family. It was for this speaking that Mum sent me off to Father Ellis Gwilym during those years of study, and Pa bought a special oil-lamp (which dimmed on the night he rushed past, pursuing Willie) for me to study by. What are we old men still waiting for? I'd put it this way: the longer we (my brothers, my brother-in-law, and I) defy death, the more the guilt and the glory of those murders becomes equally shared, belongs almost impersonally to our collective clan. So you see, we do still grow! Most people will feel cheated if they are not shown a culprit – the reason being their appetite for comfort. 'Not us!' they say. 'So *he* was the one!' they say, fooled into believing life's tangle has been neatly unravelled for their inspection. 'That's what I thought,' they say, 'that's human nature for you!'

Now let me make another admission. Above all, I long to come face to face with the lovely erratic call of simply being a man who was a boy and who, after threescore years and ten, might have expected to be ready to confront his end with a philosophy of having lived as a man should through his abilities, his intelligence, his body, and his place (given or made) among his fellows. This, and not my parents' long-term foresight that the family would one day need a historian, is the reason I put my name to the present document.

I have come to see that one purpose behind our training in good and evil is so the land, this unimaginable and largely uninhabited continent, can show itself as beyond such littleness. If, like Ellen, we throw over our infantile desire to be told we are right, we're the poorer in this one respect at least, that we lose the scale of our insignificance compared to the vast country we have the preposterous nerve to call ours.

There is, do you see it, a new heroism: waiting. The old heroes went out and did battle, but our twentieth-century heroes are sufferers – the bombed, not the bombers. In my modest way I too have waited. I was a young man when the murders happened and I had a great deal to suffer before attaining strength to face what I knew, or even to see how much I did in fact know. I was still in that vanity of being at the centre of the world.

The most exciting thing in life is to be a new adult. Just that. It is making a person for oneself. Taking who you thought you were and creating someone as close as possible to a person you would like to be. This risk (whether failing or succeeding) is surely the climax of what we know. There's no need to look further than the realization that we can amaze our old school friends and even our parents into having to take a decision as to whether they like us or not. I don't believe Michael ever achieved this. Young Johnnie at sixteen had made more of a surprise of himself than Michael at twenty-nine. 'Hold on, John,' we'd say, 'what the hell do you think you are doing?' But we were never surprised by Michael. I know what you're thinking, that because I was seven years his junior, this would have happened before I knew about it. Granted, I might not have been attentive enough as a boy to notice, but the process also shows in the way we are treated by others. Even Mum sometimes spoke to Johnnie with respect. Never to Michael. I would ask you to keep in mind his childlike quality, contemptible as well as charming, throughout this last phase of my story.

If I must name a motive for each crime, then let it be love, for the first murder, love for the second, and – though more enigmatically – love again for the third. As to an explanation of how no guilty party was ever discovered and how the investigators made assumptions which led them to connect the wrong things and so not see the truth, I must take you back to Christmas Day in that year 1898.

After lunch Ellen proposed a ramble up Blacks Creek and into the hills, where we had seldom ventured even as kids. Mack and Polly said that after so much pork crackling, such quantities of plum pudding and fresh cream, they needed a snooze; Jeremiah could never be tempted, any more than our parents; Daniel had his uniform to think of, plus his wife's sulky mood not to be bruised; and the young ones were already off on ponies to visit their mates the O'Donovans, bearing a parcel of Norah's mince pies as a gift between families. Willie said he'd come, but then changed his mind without a reason. And Willie was the one who stood on the verandah watching our departure so suspiciously.

Had we planned it this way? I don't know. It's not just that I cannot remember. I believe I didn't know at the time either. But we could not have been better pleased by our party, just the closest, the most affectionate: Norah, Michael, Ellen, and myself. Yes, affectionate is right for the tone of our general feelings, but I mean it also to cover the fact that I guessed by this time I was in love with Norah. Of course I did. And once admitted, I recognized the knowledge went back a long way, even to a dream from before puberty, a dream in which we two lay among hay-stooks, me lolling on her naked breast. By various other factors I can estimate my age as no more than eight or nine. She had no idea, of course. That would have been unthinkable. And as we set off in pairs I took care, out of a delicacy which was becoming habitual, to walk with Ellen.

Once we crossed the last of our property, the oldest paddock (called the fifteen, though I don't think it was more than twelve acres in fact), laughing as we dodged cowpats and set the flies dreaming, laughing as Michael tipped his cap at an anthill taller than himself and wished it good afternoon, laughing as he and I tramped the wire down and stretched the top wire up to let the girls through.

That had been the first paddock I ever ploughed by myself as a lad; and made the mistake of looking to Pa for a word of praise. The wound still aches through my bones, the lack of a simple gesture, even a smile. Well, once we had put Pa's kingdom behind us, we were in uncharted territory.

The bush closed round us. There were no tracks here unless they were shortcuts to a wombat hole. High trees leaned over the water and we had to fight our way through dense growths of fern along banks thick with fallen debris which floods had thatched and stacked treacherously among the roots. Already we overreached the rule of law. When I stopped to look back, I could not see Norah our comforter . . . only a woman making a delicate gesture of alarm at how her skirts might suffer among so many snags. I turned to face my companion and share a younger person's patronizing acceptance of the slowness of those beyond the twenty-five-year limit . . . to find, not Ellie the way I had known her, but a mature creature with unpredictable eyes, bosom already heaving inside her bodice.

We loitered on a flat bank beside the creek which, though it still flowed, showed signs of how deep the drought had grown. We were in the middle of a patch of dead reeds, the frail canes snapping as we brushed a passage through them, animal tracks impressed plainly at the water's edge, the deep sharp claw marks of kangaroos.

At the time I was struck by so slight a thing, I hesitate to mention it for fear of cluttering this account with unnecessary detail: the women held hands briefly. Though I cannot say for sure if this was done as a greeting or a parting, it certainly planted the idea in my mind that they had a compact, that even if Michael and I did not know what we were venturing into, they did.

The further we followed the creek, the further we escaped the cruel heat of that day. Deep in delicious groves of shade we picked our way. The sandy bottom with its clear ripples of glinting fish gave place to mud. Mossy rocks cluttered the banks, and logs jutted from the water among lances of light. We stood and listened to bellbirds, the marvellous density of their sound compounded of thousands of single short piercing notes, a shimmering forest of harmonics every bit as untamed as their habitat.

Trees now shut us away from the land beyond, the curtains of it drawing close on all sides. When we spoke, our voices echoed faintly. Echoes slipped off among the tattered trunks, busy as betrayers. Our laughter, though we laughed less and less frequently, took on the clucking non-expression of sounds belonging there. We came to a huge fallen tree trunk spanning the creek, solid as a bridge. A new and terrible possibility became quite clear when Michael almost rested one arm across Ellen's shoulders but withdrew the gesture as premature. Instead, he leapt up to join me on the bridge, breathing lightly and easily. He took hold of my arm and I had a memory of the girls clasping hands so little time before: just as I loved Norah, he had fallen victim to Ellie. His grip tightened, confirming that he knew I knew. Michael, famous for impulsiveness, had to keep his balance.

Till now, danger offered us a game – I had been the sole outcast among four, also the least among us if judged from the standpoint of personality. But with my brother lost to the same madness (my brother who survived his repeated defiance of Pa, my brother who would act first then think afterwards, and who had already earned a name for local amours) I recognized the thrill of our being hunters. The bush itself trembled: intense, vigilant, inhuman, swallowing us, confounding our sense of direction, teasing our ears with whispered invitations.

I thought back to a previous Christmas at the beach, when Ellen jumped into a rockpool fully clothed. How furious Michael was. I could picture Mum looking out from a cave she made of air simply by sitting wherever she sat with darkness cupped about her, watching Ellie taste salt water for the first time since she was a child, and what Ellie said about it.

Everything would be different if Jeremiah had come with us. Had he been our parents' proxy, there could be no magic, no risk. He might well cast aside his clothes, dive off the fallen tree, and plunge in the pool, throwing a chain of bright drops from his hair as he surfaced, his serious face of an animal intent on survival tilted up to reap the victory due to daring – for like the rest of us, he could not swim – water sheathing those bullish shoulders with steel.

I was glad, whatever might have been let loose, to be with Michael. Perpetually cheerful as he remained, he was the realist who wore permanent marks of an altogether different chain round his wrists, old discoloured welts. The only one not to believe in ghosts.

We reached down to help the ladies climb beside us – Norah flushed and uneasy, but Ellen thoroughly delighted, pointing where dragonflies skimmed the surface among weeds and dipped to glints of water which showed as an oily blue sheen amid the rattling stems. We listened while a frog wound up its watch during one of those unaccountable lulls in the collective glitter of bellbirds.

Children these days have so much time for play they could not imagine how any bushland as close as this remained unexplored. But then, in Queen Victoria's reign, before Federation, when New South Wales was still a colony, we worked from the moment we could sit a horse or lift a shovel. School was our leisure. We were a generation envied by our elders for having a school to go to and for learning to read. A lad with an intellectual bent was thought specially pampered if he had been allowed to put it to any use. So there we were, the four of us, excited by the unknown. We could see no sign of a home fence, no glimpse of a safe paddock beyond. We were in hostile territory. Any rules which might apply here were so alien we would scarcely have recognized them as rules at all.

At every clearing the sun blazed down, stuck at one angle. The creek bed rose steeply. Instead of broad pools of becalmed water pinned to the bottom by reed stems, here Blacks Creek fled past us through narrows, now and then presenting little basins of bubbles, spouting through fissures, flurrying among clustered stones, or twisted to coils like diagrams of human muscle. Ferns on the bank thinned as the great trees thickened and the canopy met overhead. I do not know at what stage the first change came about, but I recall hesitating, my boots skidding on wet rock, to glance back for the others (I could see the tops of their heads, the ladies with hair parted identically down the middle, giving the appearance of the same person seen twice, and Michael gallantly offering them an arm each), then scanning the forest. This was when I noticed how the land, instead of being shut away from us by riotous growth, surrounded us and swallowed us. The continent lay behind as well as ahead and on either side.

The others looked up to where I stood, their expressions instantly clouded by the same knowledge, eyes darkling violet, and their skin a wonderful texture of frail silkiness. Stubble began to show on Michael's chin; so he had not even made the effort to shave for Christmas. When I thought of the house back there, less than an hour's walk away, I could not believe anyone would recognize us again. You know how it is at those moments when you take your life in hand and steer a new course; not only do you hope your familiars will cease to recognize you, you dare not believe you will recognize them either – at least, not in anything but the unliving facsimile of a nose, a brow, and impersonal generalities such as height or hair colour. That appalling house, weighed close to the soil by Mum's unforgiving quest for release from her reiterated losses, Pa's savage fiefdom in the panoply of ground he had made productive, ground he had scourged of the spirit of those who inhabited it while our folk were paddling coracles at the outer fringes of some bog, cogitating an idea that if the mud could be dried it might be made to catch fire and burn with however surly a heat, folk domesticated in the service of some sickle-wielding dumbshow paganism we had risen to after we saw no future in human sacrifice, or at least after we grew sceptical of butchering selected victims one at a time, and chose the more democratic and wasteful system known as war.

That appalling house held shades scarcely more credible than Mum and Pa: Willie haunting the windows, casting fearful, slow, cunning glances round the verandah, hands clenching and unclenching like valves necessary to the operation of his thinking mechanisms; Jeremiah enthroned in flesh sufficient to be its own warrant, biding its time and content to remain apprentice for some years longer to a trade of tyranny about which he still had much to learn; Polly and her butcher snoring porky satisfactions in neighbouring rooms, a perfect match in subtlety of mind. The Christmas heat pressed in as sky; the wall-less house taken over and subdued.

We had trespassed outside our fence, yet the continent took us to its cool recesses as holiday adventurers. We men rolled up our sleeves. The women gathered skirts clear of undergrowth. In an obsession to reach somewhere unknown, we had lost the power of speech. This was the odd thing: we were now in a hurry. Scrambling and leaping, pressing ahead through the gully's dense vegetation. Some powerful urgency drove us, or rather drew us, until we shed all sense of effort and, instead of pushing on higher, seemed to be standing still while the land itself slid towards us complete with timbers and thickets, the creek foaming free at twice its speed, birds gathering close in deafening excitement over our intrusion. The foliage fluttered with eyes and fingers, a flicker of white feathers, a dash of ochre paint, whole trees gliding by and ridges of veined rock gliding too. A columned ravine opened ahead, swinging wide and already painfully bright; its rugged line of cliffs etched harsh repetitions of pulsing light in the eye. Behind our heads leaves dangled sharp as knives, honed blades chiming faintly and multitudinously. A foreign odour lingered as a tidemark in the atmosphere, an odour so foreign it roused ancient memories of numberless forebears, a collective awe, an inherited taboo, moveless as ourselves while that hinterland swept to engulf us in so vast, so unsoilable an innocence no name would do for it. We stood in a drifting grove of macrozamia palms which had most probably been alive when Captain James Cook first sighted the land, and even a hundred years earlier, when Dutch traders quit these shores as unlikely to offer any treasure worth taking; alive when King Henry VIII outraged all credulity by naming himself head of the Church for a whole nation despite every article of believable faith – yes, that is how ancient these stumpy tufted trees were, these same individuals, being among the longest-living things on earth, elders of all plant life and animal life, now alert as a committee around us, passing in review, fans of leaf sprouting elegant headdresses, a convocation of weirds, hiving their huge phallic seedcases which would break apart on ripening raw red, rot and collapse in the hope of tempting flocks of pterodactyls to feast at them, to come gliding on leather wings beneath the spotted-gum canopy, wheeling, settling, crocodile jaws busy and ponderous lizard bodies shuffling over bark-mulch, feasting right to the foot of two tall rocks which stopped the heart, rocks solid like our parents yet a hundred times bigger, brooding moss-grown judgements, heavy as the moon, knowing as the heart. So unexpectedly they loomed over us, all courage drained from my body. At the foot of these rocks a broad flat stone was disfigured by smears of blood where patterns had been painted in yellow and orange clay.

The blood lay, as still as our amazement, drying around the edges but quite fresh, each fleck isolated, anguished like a marine creature in some killing element, cast up by a vanished sea and left to die of air and warmth. The whole idea of sacrifice has always been that the killers may live longer and more prosperously under a malign despotism of powers whose vastness necessarily sets them beyond comprehension, beyond such errors of scale as virtue and vice.

The bellbirds had fallen silent. Rushing leaves now hovered, still and deadly; the creek carried jagged shards of sky down into the gully out of sight, witnessing the way we had come. The beating of air, still thudding on the inner ear, became an answer to our hearts. We were surrounded. The whole bush alive with mouths and hands, with flowers and twigs stuck on to living shadows in patterns dictated by ancestors, dead long ages ago, but gathered perpetually at that arena to oversee the ritual and assuage their innate fury of the disembodied.

Under our boots the lichened stone lay long and flat as a tongue. This was the estranged world, the world we call grotesque because, though we may have forgotten its forms, we have not outgrown our fear of it. The ravine's emptiness was what gave that spilled blood its peculiar power.

Astonishing to think our peaceful creek, from which we drew water for ourselves and our cattle, rose in such wild springs.

I had reached my province. As altar boy, school dux, special pupil of the learned Father Ellis Gwilym, assistant to the Sisters at the Sacred Heart Convent, and the only one beloved of our mother, my training led me to this moment: Michael was in my power, Norah too, and even Ellen (if only for reasons of inquisitiveness). Clearing the new paddock, burning trees, defeating Barney, and watching the pig slaughtered . . . all fell into place as the prelude to a revelation flicking round me in spears of light, the cliff line bonily gauzy as an insect wing, earth heaving its segmented body, hundred-celled eyes turning upon us as we stood where human blood had already been spilled.

The Holy Spirit spoke in whispered syllables so protracted and dreamlike I could not tell what they said, though I knew their meaning. I was shown the vanity of those destined to die with a mission; the vanity, in other words, of being one among the damned, the supreme opportunity for making my claim on God's personal wrath. Think of that, a sublime glory second only to the glory of claiming His personal love, which is the exclusive lot of the saints in paradise.

Norah had already rushed back the way we came, panic betrayed in the loose flutter of her sash, the wide-flung despair of those pale handsome arms, and Michael leaping after her.

They were gone. The Holy Spirit whispered. Heartbeats of Its malignancy or benevolence (who is to dare judge?) throbbed closer. Ellen watched me, maybe expecting me to speak, and then stooped down. I could not have guessed what she was about to do. Gathering her skirt in one hand, she reached out with the other, this girl who was not even afraid of Pa and had yet to be taught the imperative of morality, and placed a finger in the congealing blood. She shot me a challenging look, paused a moment for my reaction, and then studied her finger. We were joined by our listening to the sound of Norah's flight and Michael's pursuit: we heard a branch crack, we heard her utter a stifled shriek, we heard his voice soothe her with words as impossible to interpret as the pulse of air. Then, like a naughty child, Ellen licked the finger clean. She even held it up to show me: See? All gone! . . . that finger, shiny with saliva, such a slender girl's finger, held the way we tested the direction of the wind. The hot afternoon gushed about us, woken again to a swirl of birdcries, a cacophony of screeching and tinkling.

'No harm done' was all I could think to say.

If I then took hold of Ellen, took her in my arms, wasn't it to save her by my own sacrifice? Wasn't it with full knowledge of ambush? Hadn't I watched the whole scenario of *Caught Unawares*? Trees tossed wild heads above us while the undergrowth flashed and flickered. I shielded my sister from the consequences of her sacrilege. I understood that I could never, now, go home to Paradise.

In those days, you see, we had no books to tell us what was expected of a man. All we knew, from Pa's readings, was how the saints behaved. There was no cinema to show us the body's language of love, however falsified a version it might be. We had never seen a man and woman kiss, except as a greeting or a farewell, and then rarely – because who went away? My doubts concerning myself were absolute. We knew a terrible lot about God's program for punishing us if we did begin to sin seriously, but nothing at all about how to incur this punishment. Those of us who went to school had heard plenty in the playground, and believed most of it. Yet some deep sense of self-preservation warned me that this was not the authentic evil, this was hysteria, this was nothing more than the salaciousness of those who were too young to know. So, in our ignorance, Ellen and I held each other.

'In England,' Father Gwilym once told me, 'Saint Brigid is known as Saint Bride.'

Far below, where the creek reappeared to glide from one placid sandy pool, already violated by our footprints, to another, sunshine rippling over its clean gravel bed, Michael and Norah emerged. They had dwindled to tiny figures in ridiculously white clothing, with ridiculously pale doll-limbs. They paused to see if they could make out what we were doing. They stood gazing back up to where we vacillated at the high lip of the ravine. They shaded their eyes as they stared straight into the sun to look for us.

I do not know why Michael got so drunk that night. He filled the house with laughter. While Pa was trying to beat some decorum into him, he laughed. Once or twice during the night, even, chained to the foot of the master bed, he rattled the frame that held them (Mum and Pa) together, and let slip a further chuckle. I was awake to hear, being held to account by Jeremiah, the only one still true to the faith of the house, dropping his rough clothes on my bedroom floor, displaying himself to rob me, with the sure instinct of an inquisitor, of such power as I had found in myself that Christmas Day.

You see, I did go home, after all.

The one thing I cannot explain is why I carried my revolver on Boxing Day. I understand my brothers and sisters perfectly well. The puzzle is myself. Willie's suspicions were obvious, even though I had not then glimpsed the possibility of his subterfuge, the complexity of his revenge against authority. Just as clear were Barney Barnett's reasons for jealousy. We had no idea either of them might be present, of course, any more than they suspected one another. But my own fatal whim to carry the .38 is simply beyond divination, an inspired stupidity, a genuine touch of providential will, perhaps. (Again, the vanity of the damned!)

Well, having come to the day of the crime, let me repeat that while we were still at the Yandilli Races, Ellen asked who would escort her to Cuttajo for the traditional dance: 'Michael?' she suggested straight off, as if he were on her mind. And she looked past me to make clear that our moment of closeness the previous afternoon gave me no special rights. As for him, he didn't take to having it put like that. He was still sore, I suppose. His wrists and neck rubbed raw, so I don't imagine he relished wearing a collar. But Norah put him in his place: 'You make too much of your own feelings.' And instructed him not to treat Ellen as a child still: 'She is a woman and we ought not to forget it.'

Norah's strictness with him reminded me of a youthful dream . . . the virgin in a walled garden had Norah's face, just as the pale naked unicorn she nursed in her lap had mine. *Paradise* began life as a Persian word for *garden*. In this tapestry the walls were high and the enclosure crowded with flowers and the knowledge of prohibitions itself went to our heads like perfume.

1898 was among the driest years on record, as I remember. We felt the drought even in our damp corner of the country.

Grass, having been parched brown by the sun, was then nibbled to its roots. Bleached earth crumbled under the hoof. That track we had cleared to the new creek helped our animals, but they were still desperately short of feed and in dire condition. The whole district lived on edge with worry. Yet at Christmas the weather played strange tricks. Night showers lasting twenty seconds shed enough moisture to rest on the dusty ground, lighter than insect eggs, through the cool snap of dawn, to rise again and float up in a mist as fugitive and sterile as a mirage.

When we four parted that evening, I on my way homewards and they on their way to the dance, I expected the sulky to return soon. Naturally I did. Hadn't I looked in at the hall, spoken to the violin band, and seen failure already stamped across the occasion? Either they declined to believe me when I reported this or Michael had planned an excuse for getting the girls home late. As a fallback we arranged to meet in Earnshaws' bottom paddock, because the stock had been moved only a week before and the place stood empty. We said we might conduct our own private dance, just two couples, a celebration as exclusive as it was illicit, a climax to the previous day's disturbing events. And when would another opportunity arise for discussing the urgent things we needed to say? I think I might reasonably claim that the others (Norah and Michael, if not Ellie, never Ellie) felt as confused and guilty as I did myself, as lost in the labyrinth, as anxious to be comforted. I only question whether they would have stayed in town had the dance been on. I'm doubtful.

Don't you see how it always is? Once we reach the very boundary of our known world and its morals, when we look, as our Lord once did, over a vast plain filled with possibilities of life and riches, *then* the Devil tempts us. If you think that my first surrender on a ceremonial rock high above a native gully (innocent enough in the light of what followed) would have shaken me to my senses, sounding such alarms the whole of Christendom might hear and condemn, then you know nothing of such matters. Up till the moment I reached this forbidden border, I could find strength to endure the part-life I had come to accommodate comfortably enough. Yet from the moment I turned my gaze outward, nothing would satisfy me but total ruin.

The moon being bright we went for a walk by the sea, Norah and I. Earnshaws' fence in those days ran right along the cliff top. We stood witnessing the rise and collapse of dazzling waves as meaningless, as unlimited, as restless and spiritual as the land we had ventured into the previous afternoon. I wanted it this way: my mind a clear space in a safe cavity. At last I realized why I had brought the gun. Truly the plan had been subconscious and struck me as inspired.

If I took the lead, this was thanks to my liturgical education and being the one schooled in how irrevocably we were damned. The last remnant possibility of purity would be judged by the coinage in which we might pay at the end of this horror. I determined to seize the opportunity of having the matter out in the open between us and visualized myself, not just with Norah, but with Michael and Ellie too, calming their distress and solving the enigma: we should put an end to each other's lives, cleanly, quickly and, yes, lovingly. But as it fell out, I could not wait until we got back to where we had spread a blanket for us all to sit down together. I became possessed by a mad desire to shine in Norah's eyes.

'I am going to shoot myself,' I told her.

That was how I proposed we should make love. Suicide was the wound she must save me from. She must save me also from hollow impotence, from the inadequacies I suffered as a consequence of Jeremiah's claims on power the previous night. Only she, she as a woman, could restore me.

Doubtless you will say that, had Norah not been willing to do it anyway, no threat on earth would have persuaded her. But I don't believe this does justice to her dedication to healing. Afterwards, of course, the gun presented quite different possibilities. We did not have to speak of our intense joy, or of the certain fate we had invited into our lives. I repeated the same thing in its new context.

'I am going to shoot myself, Norah.'

My feeling at the time was certainty, an inspired certainty that she would beg me to release her and shoot her first. She just nodded slowly. But not for me, I sensed, for herself somehow. Slight as it was, that exclusion of my feelings, of my love for her which burned more horribly than ever, shocked me into reconsidering. It was as clear as this: Did she, to put it vulgarly, want me out of the way? We had not spoken about love. We had not spoken about anything yet, this was the strange part. Norah, adopting her entrenched protective role, simply put out her hand for the weapon. What was I to do? The old craven Patrick, Mum's favourite, succumbed. Almost as unaccountable as my having brought it in the first place, I delivered the revolver into her keeping.

'It's warm!' she objected with surprise (surely not distaste?).

'I put two cartridges in,' I explained and let my explanation hang, because a suicide who means business does not need two. Also because I then knew I had never intended to include Michael or Ellen.

Suddenly she was running. That's all I know. Taking me completely by surprise, Norah ran and stumbled. My heart leapt into my mouth; I thought she might fall and the weapon go off, the cliff being pocked with a warren of rabbit holes. She almost went down, but the force driving her would not permit it. This must certainly have been the same force holding me in check. Aware that I ought to give chase, I made no move. The sensation came close to being the most profoundly gratifying I have attained, that lassitude in the face of disaster. Once she was out of sight I was released from the charm. I ran after her, dodging among shrubs and wattles till I came out at the corner of the open paddock.

The flash of the revolver gave a dull angry gleam to what was already perfectly clear. My horse trotted off toward the gate, the other horse whinnied and stamped and shook itself still. The sulky's shafts creaked.

Michael and Ellen, still clothed, had been so engrossed in one another they neither saw nor heard anyone approach. Let me repeat: there was a saintly patience and precision about Norah, even in this act of holding herself in check till she stood right over them before squeezing the trigger. We all knew how to use a shotgun, which goes without saying to anyone brought up in the bush, but I don't suppose she had ever handled a revolver before. Her flesh felt chilled when I took the .38 from her. She offered little resistance. There had been no shout, no scream, not a word exchanged that I could hear; the echo of the shot drowned any noise my brother's body might have uttered in shock. Suddenly I knew the Spirit was still with us, the watching beast of our expedition the previous day, a presence now akin to a mountain of stilled air.

I put the revolver in the sulky for safety and then returned to where my sisters knelt on the blanket, redressing Michael's clothes, using the hems of their skirts to wipe him clean, and fastening his buttons. They rolled him on his side with the wound upwards as being, perhaps, the most neutral, the most natural position in this wholly unnatural circumstance. He looked pale as putty. His head lagged and lolled horribly. The task became a matter of efficiency, a familiar challenge to achieve results beyond criticism, beyond punishment, in which we had been professionals since childhood.

Still no one spoke, but I drew closer to Ellie. She and I must protect our Norah. Michael, having died the instant the bullet pierced his brain, was beyond help. As yet we hadn't room for grief. Shock simply wiped out whole areas of the mind, to isolate the immediate scene and clear the issue of any clutter which might reduce our efficiency at securing Norah's safety from the law. Norah herself felt it; she took a modest part in the work, accepting the station of an assistant, prompt in her anticipation of what might be needful, always following, always humble. Right from the decisive moment when she relinquished my weapon she acted with gratitude for our quietness of duty.

In the looks we exchanged by moonlight we acknowledged that no simple comfort could be sought. Everyone at home would still be up: Mack, Danny, and Jeremiah playing cards, the women preparing supper, Pa reading a sentence an hour from *Lives of the Saints* . . . no, we could not return without Michael or the blanket, hoping Norah and Ellie might talk their way (or even mine) out of a murder charge. They had to be armed with an alibi so convincing not even a court of law would question it.

Once the decision had been taken and I had tied them up, using a sash and handkerchiefs, I had the idea that I ought to drive them closer to the road and leave them at a spot from which they would never have been able to witness the murder. Too late to untie them, I'd have to hoist them into the sulky. But they did not seem to mind this idea when I put the new plan in that hasty, hushed voice of a conspiracy. They lay on the soil, mute with terror and guilt. I cannot tell you what delusions of masterfulness surged through me at this time as I turned on my heel to go to bring the sulky closer. Beside the horse stood Willie. His hand caressed its neck, gentling, wooing the beast not to give him away.

Willie, solid and arrogant in one of Pa's hats (the hat identified by the old man at the inquest as his), was not the Willie we had come to expect. He aimed my revolver at me. That was what I saw in the clear moonlight on the night of the cancelled dance, when already I was expected home from work. Willie, like a child, transformed by importance in the moment he chose.

How shall I put it, the way he stood? His gesture became crucial. There was, in the standing, a certain triumph which could have no other cause than that he had seen, and therefore was judge of, our crimes. His tilted hips, the squared shoulders, the head cocked for listening to a private catalogue of what he now held in memory to empower him to ride over our superiorities, made clear he knew Michael and Ellen had broken the law, human as well as divine. Neither was it impossible that he knew about Norah and me. Certainly he had seen my darling Norah shoot the brother she was closest to (yes, this is the bitter truth it has taken me a lifetime to face). He knew the three of us planned to conceal the murder. Behind that steady barrel, aimed unflinchingly at me, stood a suppressed fury we none of us had taken seriously. This stocky man already approaching middle age was the one who paid the price of partial liberty for us all; only to see us end up in the clutches of vice. You knew how little he had to look forward to. For some years now, William had been going bald. He took shelter in a mortified slyness from such evidence of his life having already been laid waste. He became more like a retarded uncle than one of our generation. We could not forget that he had done nothing to earn this partial death except wish to leave home. And now Willie knew, by whatever intuitive faculty, that so long as he kept silent about the crime, he could exact the same payment from our freedom as Pa had claimed from his. Somewhere in those dim disoriented relics of a brave mind he claimed us as his creatures. He saw this and – guilt being an especially swift and acute aspect of the intelligence – so did we.

Some terrible alarm began ringing in my brain: Michael is dead. But I could not rise to the consciousness of it.

'This is a matter for Pa,' I said in a tone of reassurance. And they were the only words spoken since the tender things I'd offered Norah, including a proposal of dying together.

I began to walk towards William, my hand held out for the .38, eyes fixed on the brim-shadow where his were hidden. Slow as a snake I moved, not even sparing a glance for the girls. This new Willie, if he was capable of lying in wait and storing his evidence without once crying out in horror or compassion or even jealousy, might also be capable of firing at me. Nor was I free from the hope that he might, because then he could not shoot Norah. He made no move as I went gliding closer. Calm as the big spotted-gum trunk he stood beside, that tree with a rotten socket about twenty feet up where a branch had once broken off and fallen, long since decayed to mould underfoot and powdered to dust in the drought we were suffering, Willie waited.

The appalling scream from behind me, followed by other, longer-drawn and more despairing screams, locked me in mid-step. Surely the revolver had not gone off? I saw no flash. William never flinched or changed aim. Pa's hat sat as a solid block against the dry silvered backdrop. The horse whinnied again and again, rearing up as far as the sulky would allow, lashing his hooves.

To this day, I marvel at it: not only did my brother find the resourcefulness to catch us out and keep hidden from sight till he could be certain we were his captives, but he must also have seen, past my advancing hand, past my shoulder, past the dead body on the blanket, past Norah and Ellen (who had now stood, leaning together for sheer human survival, wrists and ankles bound by satin and linen, invested with helplessness as a plea before the full fury of the law, tottering poles of women bedecked for some pagan festivity), the wild appearance of Ellen's fiancé wielding a length of timber.

Abandoning myself to William's mercy, I spun round to find Barney Barnett victorious above a huddle of Ellen's clothes. Norah, still drawing out her scream to a length of shining silk from as far back in human history as treachery was known, a slender banner more hideous than any parasite, turned the gape of her shock to me. She had become unrecognizable.

'Now,' said Barney, who sounded a bit shaken, reaching to grasp Norah's bound arm but addressing us men, 'it's her and it's me as well. You have to keep the secret for both our sakes.'

Norah's loathing as she realized what he meant knotted her body in a spasm of nausea and wrenched her free of his grip. How shall I convey that pitiful sight, her attempt to edge her way towards the cover of the nearest tree? You must remember her feet were clamped tightly together by the binding I myself had tied. She worked her dancing pumps sideways, miraculous in her balance as she was tragic, tall as she was vulnerable, her objective transparent as it was useless. Simply put, Norah's instinct drove her, I suppose, to do something, however inadequate; the very effortfulness of her escape being a blaze of defiance against that calm elation said to be felt by victims of tradition, whose cultural role in a ritual greater than the sum total of its celebrants may represent the triumph over self.

William held still, a judge-figure and revenger before whom any squalor of human passions and fallibilities was destined to be played out beyond all compromise or mercy. He did not fire when I sprang at Barnett. He must have watched me (was it with a family satisfaction?) as I caught the club swung at my head, wrested it from the murderer's hands, threw it aside, and began punishing him. I did not want to knock him out, as I was fated to on the following day at the Brian Boru, because I intended to hurt him. But I had not long been working on him, standing over his doubled-up form, smacking at the side of his head with my fist (as much as to say: Chin up, man) while forcing his arm to tortured angles, when he let out the wild howl of a trapped scavenger.

The horse, already moon-eyed and scared out of its wits, reared in the shafts. I looked back to see it high and dangerous above Pa's hat. William shot the animal on the spot, peremptory as his dignity of office required, and no further disturbance to be tolerated. Bang . . . order had been restored. Night poured into its night shape. Yet it was Norah's whispered words rather than the shot which paralyzed me so I let my victim go.

'I can't stand any more of this.'

I don't believe Willie heard, although the frogs and crickets had been shocked dumb and even the ocean confined itself to hushing among rocks. Still, he let Barney creep away, which proved to be the cleverest tactic of all. That cowardly form diminishing through undergrowth beyond the fence, as I have thought about it since, allowed free, kept open the possibility of our family surviving. Willie may not have heard, no, but he himself did speak.

'You better be careful, Pat, or you're in trouble.'

This was when Norah turned on me, her manner almost as brutal as scorn. Of all the consequences which might have arisen from the maze we blundered into the previous afternoon (memories of dead reeds snapping, the deeply incised claw marks in sand, of blood spilt and outraged invisible presences, the beast unfurling its stony gauze wings, earth shifting as a segmented body, of Ellen's wild heat nestled against my own wildness, of Jeremiah naked, of our casual charade at the picnic races and my horse going lame on the way), one thing I had never imagined possible was Norah's hatred.

I set my back to Willie now, for I knew what he could not know: that he had no more cartridges left. He went on aiming at me, I presume. I had no fear of him unarmed. Nothing but pity. And for the moment, this pity was overriden by the pain Norah's words caused me.

'Him?' she cried in a fury as she stood wavering, still bound hand and foot according to our rescue plan to save her paying for Michael's murder. '*He's* got no trouble, no, except that he raped me, William. Raped me! Do you hear?'

I have referred before to the curious action of shock in protecting an emergency part of the brain from unwanted information. I, as a man able to defend myself against Barnett armed with his club, against my elder brother regardless of what he might be doing behind my back, stood helpless under these few words, unmanned by a feeling of futility. They severed me utterly from everything I treasured, the simple fantasies and security of a world experienced freshly as *the* world. Unmanned also by a philosophical exhaustion, by so grand a panorama of the ideas which have shaped history that neither one nor another can claim more than to have been, and to have been noted. The power of what was being played out in this tragedy went so far beyond me that I had acted as a mere instrument in the conflict without waking up to the fact that I was never my own master in any sense. I don't mean this phrase *in any sense* for an excuse or to claim the rights of either helplessness or irresponsibility. I mean that, strongly as I fought, agonizingly as I felt, vainly as I believed I was appointed to civilize my family, in those moments I came face to face with my insignificance. What had I done, after all, but commit a mortal sin, knowingly defied the millennia of warnings, dressed my surrender in the motley of free will, even of justifiable revenge against oppression . . . as if there were not a whole world of possibilities beyond the Paradise fences, or means enough to escape for a person who already travelled nine and a half miles a day to work at the convent and nine and a half miles home. Shame robbed me of strength. I could not oppose her. Much later I came to wonder whether this might have been the exact opposite of the effect Norah hoped her accusation would provoke. But if so, any shortfall in my fury when exposed and denounced was adequately taken up by William.

I have noticed that once we are off our stroke, blow after blow may be struck, and we seem unable to do more than stagger back to our feet and wait, only capable of gathering wits enough to be aware we are once again too late to ward off a well-aimed attack; only capable of lurching from some absurd mishap to a second and a third. Barney armed with a bludgeon was one thing; Willie, similarly armed, quite another, witless as he was.

Fatally, as I saw him rush at us, I presumed *I* was to be my brother's victim. And who would not find excuses for him, driven to the madness of nemesis, dedicated wholly to destroying the destroyer of whatever honour our family might have salvaged from this crime? It was not vanity that flung me aside to dodge the anticipated blow, far from it – nor even a symptom of self-importance – it was the instinct for survival. But by doing so, I lost the chance of regaining my balance once I saw my mistake. Willie's victim was not me at all. He was after Norah. Ankles tied to prevent her running and wrists bound behind her back, her submission rendered extraordinarily touching, this was a Norah transformed anew: just as fury against me had shocked her out of any semblance of generosity, now her peace appeared to be instantly restored. Of course she, also, must have expected I was the one Willie would attack. Only at the last fragment of her suffering did she recognize the relief she craved. The look she turned on him as he swung his club in one hand (the left, because he was left-handed), and brought it down on her skull with crushing impact, was what I had hoped for myself: love.

At Barney's own funeral there was no visiting bishop, nor a senior police officer with silver laurels on his cap, and not even Pa. Pa had finished with him. But I sat in the church thinking things over.

This was not the old church Pa helped build, but a cold brick box with Byzantine pretensions. The new generation of O'Donovans had faithfully produced yet another altar boy. An electric organ bleated and the priest bleated too. Then I noticed to my astonishment that the child, so clumsily rattling the wand in the brass jug, appeared to be crying. There was an explanation. Barney's daughter, who died the previous year in a car crash, had married Gary O'Donovan, and this was their son. What would the boy think, I wondered, if he knew his grandpa had murdered my sister Ellen and claimed to have committed two other murders as well? How ruthless the dying are in their thwarted ambitions. Suppose Barney's bid for notoriety did convince the inspector – wouldn't this little chap be hiding at home now and facing a life of ostracism, real or imagined?

Our Cuttajo congregation muttered responses. A wind from the sea smelled of loss and damp rope. The salty autumn daylight crept in at the open portal. Blots of muddied sunshine splashed across the aisle from sightless orange windows.

Maybe Barney was more cunning than we gave him credit for. It's not impossible that he thought he would trap us into a giveaway objection when he claimed sole credit for baffling everyone. This way, in the act of escaping by natural death, he'd have enjoyed the satisfaction of knowing we must face ruin.

Was it possible, on the other hand, that the scavenger intended his deathbed confession as a kindness? With Willie and me both present, his taking the entire blame on himself might have let us off; might have been to acknowledge that, but for him, Ellen and Norah would in all probability still be alive. Did he also suspect that if Ellie were betrothed to any suitor other than himself, she mayn't have yielded to Michael's lust? Whatever the case, I'm glad I was too old to be called on as a pallbearer.

Mack, kneeling beside me, suddenly leaned nearer.

'It's for God to strike the blow!' he hissed in his deaf man's whisper; then he leaned the other way to Jeremiah's wheelchair and added, grunting as he stood up long after the rest of us: 'Before they stick him underground.'

Even though I'd had my revenge now that Barney, terrified of hell, had failed in his plan to be absolved of this sin of murder, I was infuriated at the least possibility that he might have been trying to take it upon himself to save us, to gain power over us, and defeat us by presuming to be our protector. I swore then that I would begin writing this history as soon as I returned home.

It remains only for me to explain that when I smashed Michael's head in, I used both hands on the haft of the weapon, as Barney had done, to strike an identical wound. How could I have brought myself to do it, you ask, even though he was dead? Well, I did not think of the plan right away. First I got Willie, who had been drained of wrath and left more lumpish, more witless after his brief mastery than before, to help give me a leg up the tree. Having reached the hole about twenty feet above, I found, as experience of timber had taught me to expect, the trunk was piped and at least partly hollow. I dropped the revolver in and heard it clunk down safely inside. With my free hand I sorted about in my pocket for the empty cartridge shell I had picked up from where Norah fired at Michael. I cursed myself for not having carried it in my teeth, and retrieved it only by turning the complete pocket inside out. I dropped the cartridge in the hole, to be lost forever with the weapon, then jumped down and asked Willie to fetch my horse – which had strayed to the far fence, such an impassive creature it was, at the shots and screams. He seemed grateful to have someone else take on the burden of thinking. In this nightmare of lost bearings, I could only cling to small practical things, all else threatened me with formless horror as a wild hinterland of violence and meaninglessness.

Ellen had fallen near Michael. Whether from some trivial motive or a devious foresight, I lifted her and placed her body beside his on the blanket. My reasons are beyond me to reconstruct. But yielding to squeamishness, I positioned them back to back. I remember doing that and thinking of what I was doing too. The good side of her head looked familiar still.

Willie brought my horse and stood with it near the dead one, his whole demeanour begging to be told what this was about. How could I hand him over to the law? The less so as he certainly knew the secret of my crime of tenderness. But to save him meant saving Barney too, which explained the expression enlivening Barney's face as I let him go – the artless smirk of a player who holds the joker in his hand while others must calculate each move with their utmost (futile) skill.

The torn edges of Michael's wound, that hole blasted in his temple, bright even by the ruthless moonlight, gave me an idea: what if our best alibi were already in existence, already active in the public mind? I will explain in a moment.

I instructed Willie to pick up Pa's hat, which had fallen unheeded at some stage, and dust it so Pa wouldn't know. Then sent him off home by his own way. He possessed whatever cunning was needed for this completion of his plan, whether he intended the carnage he caused or not. As he went, my horse snuffled closer to where the corpses lay, groping for grass though Earnshaws' cattle had bitten it down to the roots. I noticed she had gone lame again in the same leg she hurt when Jeremiah raced her that morning on our way to Yandilli. By the time I set out for work at the convent the injury had looked better. But here she was, favouring the foot. While her main attention remained on the chance of feed, her hoof felt for the ground as tenderly as a lesser creature with a shrinking mind of its own. Well, now I had an alibi! Plus a reason for walking home and avoiding, as far as practical, the stony road.

Piece by piece, the horror shaped itself in my mind to something absolutely unforeseen: crime. The word *alibi* switched on a light. This was a crime. A crime big enough to have the whole shire fascinated. Yes. The fascination would reach deeper than horror.

I aligned each corpse, head towards the rising sun.

Calm, like an aspect of the weather, I viewed the scene. I have never thought more clearly, or felt more intensely necessary to Pa's kingdom. This was to be my expiation for those I loved who lay dead. They would be made famous by the same stroke that would save Willie and the rest of us. One adjustment to the facts (I sensed this rather than asserting it) – one, or two at most – might raise the crude brutality of evidence to the realm of the inexplicable.

Michael was the key, there could be no doubt, Michael, who had not been bound as the girls had, but who bore the weals of his humiliation on Christmas night. All I needed to do was supply the missing bonds. I recalled one handrail on the old sulky having worked loose even before the wheel was knocked awry, and that I had stopped the rattling by a temporary measure, warping it and tying it with some cord left over from Mum's clothesline. The cord was still there. So this is what I used, fitted to the fresh welts. Essentially The Mystery was set up. By making all three of them helpless as victims, it would be implicit that they had suffered at the hands of the same killer or band of killers. Nobody would think of accusing any one of *them* of murdering another. And, perhaps even more importantly, nobody would suspect the girls' deaths had begun with love. Without doubt it would be construed as rape in both cases: most likely by the same assailant. And mightn't such an assumption be reinforced when it was found that the identical lump of wood had been used to kill them? There was no doubt in my mind: the use of this weapon would be taken for the murderer's signature. So I disguised my brother's fatal bullet wound – as I have already explained – with a similar blow.

You must understand something else about my state of mind, as I now think back on it. At the instant I had seized my chance to surrender to the supreme pleasure (what a word for the stringency of love!), I accepted that its brief release could never be repeated. Norah, incapable of consciously sinning, would not fall twice; I believe I knew this, though I had no way of foreseeing the means by which she might seek to elude temptation. I have come to accept that what made it so complete a fulfillment was my rashness, the fact that I wittingly sacrificed the remainder of my life in return for a momentary escape. Well, nothing could be precious to me again, you see. Somewhere in the back of my mind I felt I had a right to punishment. It was my inheritance. And I needed to live in order to suffer it as fully as could be. For the sake of this suffering, I must avoid the immediate danger of being convicted for what I had not done (the murders), so that I might be truly convicted for what I had done.

I worked at fever pitch, as if rehearsed in each detail. To answer the question: How did I bring myself to do it? I shall reply: Inspiration.

Mind you, this was a very different matter from the nausea I felt when, just as I had checked everything, smoothed such footprints as were visible at night, attended to the details of leaving nothing incriminating, nothing to connect the crime with William or Barney, I thought to provide the girls too with a second death such as Michael had. Quite like a surgeon, I removed the hame strap from the dead horse and slipped it round Norah's neck. Why Norah first? I bent above her, suddenly overwhelmed with the intimacy of what I was doing. I became dreadfully ill as I jerked the strap tight. Sweating with fear and not able to look at her, I felt the leather thong bite in.

My body shuddered, appalled. There was no way I could find some similar device for Ellen. Composure shot to pieces, I staggered across to my horse and leaned on its warm breathing flank, the smell of it being indescribably wholesome.

The truth hit me, as I fitted the strap round her neck, that Norah never loved me in any way except with the maternal love of a sister for a younger brother. Really, I'd known since the previous day when I caught sight of them emerging from that ravine as a couple. Just the way they turned together, as one, and raised their arms to shade their eyes against the lowering light, I knew, and possibly Ellen in my arms for protection against spears knew also, that they were not trying to pick us out for our sake. They were simply and completely doing something together. They were celebrating their escape, not just from whatever sinister rite we interrupted where little puddles of blood still lay wet on the stone, not just from the rule of law at home,

Pa's violence and Mum's resentment, but from us . . . from, when you come down to it, me.

To a Murphy, you see, no matter how sordid our lives may appear on the outside, Paradise contained the full variety of human richness. Not its fullest possible extent, of course, no single life can offer that; but whatever one may conceive as valuable and contributing to the majesty of mankind's unique opportunity in the world had its expression in some or other particular within our family. However small, the glints of enlightenment seemed precious to us. Kindness which could defy Pa's wrath had a heroic cast difficult to match in any situation since the days of convict labour. Virtues and sins were known to us, often in intensified form, as that surrender of personal expression so close to the heart of the monastic ages when dedicated martyrs achieved an ecstasy envied by laxer eras.

The brutalities of our life at Paradise, the blind rules and desperate suppression were all in their own way moral. Yes, and most moral where most wrong. You will think me perverse for saying so, but the grimmest peaks of suffering, those feelings of being most hopelessly trapped, are the times I hold precious as I look back on them. Whatever else, they were not tainted with the contemptible blandness, the utterly grey indifference and suffocating comfort now fallen like a blanket on the whole country. I accept what this, ultimately, means. I have no wish to throw it in anyone's face, but my view of life has been cast on a huge scale by the sin I committed against my own blood. If hell exists and I am damned for what I did, I accept the price.

I wonder, did it occur to you, too, that I might have smashed Michael's skull partly from anger? You see, Norah may, just may, have shot him for what *I* had done to her, shot him because this would not simply be justice (as shooting *me* would be) but an act glorifying her revenge with outrage adequate to the crime already committed against her body. If so, it might account for the look in Ellen's eyes: Ellen, who had at last and only then come face to face with a recognition of evil.

I rode the lame horse for some of the way to confirm this God-given lameness. Also to get clear as quickly as I was able, because someone must have heard the screams. I could not risk any further time checking details. As events transpired, I made only one mistake. I lost a small, an unimportant object: a Saint Christopher medal Father Gwilym had once given me in a moment of enthusiasm for my progress at managing to recite the Dies Irae complete and without pause. As this was the first gift I had ever received from any person outside Paradise, I treasured the medal far beyond its actual worth as an object, or apparently its symbolic worth as a protection against accidents! By habit I kept it in my pocket.

Late that night when I undressed in my room, in the respectable captivity I had thought to escape, with Willie – having arrived well before me to face the hostilities of a turbulent household – snoring against the wall, docile as ever, I did not think to put it under my pillow. I was too agitated to pick up the threads of normality. I did not miss it. Not even next morning. Not even by the time Arthur Earnshaw galloped in at our gate, flinging himself off his big gelding and rushing headlong, deferential but unstoppable, into the main room to confront Pa the giant and his giant consort with news that their offspring had been murdered in his dad's bottom paddock, and stood there confounded by their lack of anything to respond with, outraged by their failure to be moved, nor knowing (as how could he know?) that life had not taught them anything with which they might make sense either of such an intrusion or of such loss.

They were homespun giants, my mother and father. There was a time when I thought them filled with a wisdom they had no ability to pass on. There was also a time when I thought them completely successful in imposing their own laws, however these might contravene the laws outside our boundary fence. But now I see them as people so reclusive as to have been almost in hiding.

Maisie O'Donovan (one of the violin girls through all the years from church to the hall dances) told me much later that the photographer Charles Bailey of Bunda had proposed to her parents, who were shorter people than average, that for a consideration of ten shillings, which he would pay them, he would be pleased to have them agree to a joint portrait with Mr and Mrs Daniel Murphy at Paradise. Just a photograph of good neighbours, Bailey said. So his coming and using our twenty for that first try at *Caught Unawares* might not have been as innocent as it seemed. Did he hope by this contact and by making one corner of our property famous enough to sell in public, he could smooth his way to propose the real treasure of his imagination, a further essay into the bizarre life of the district entitled *Ogres and Gnomes*, perhaps? Was my mother's time at church, at the rare fête or race meeting, wholly taken up in an agony of self-consciousness about her colossal size? Every pleasure poisoned by needing to assess how freakish the most ordinary behaviour must appear on such a scale? Not until she had been dead some years did it occur to me that the answer to Mum's riddle might be shyness – shy about her six feet eight inches, for all its grace, shy about her lack of education, about our family reputation, also wishing to keep private from the world for fear of Pa breaking out into violence? Perhaps she was, in this way at least, a benefactor to the community.

Sheer bulk could hardly have been such an embarrassment for a man. Had Pa, then, surrendered his liberty to be with her? Did he prove she was normal by not seeming any more eager than herself to mix with other parishioners? Now I think back, I remember, behind the refreshment tent at the Yandilli racetrack, children's peeping heads spying on the monsters at their picnic; I see their gasping faces, their pink excitement, the star of an open hand being clapped across its owner's face as a gesture beyond words. In much the same spirit, Mum had prevented Willie going out, after his brains had been rattled loose. If she let him be seen, even on the road, folk might treat him as an idiot or investigate how he came to change. So, though he grew to be almost unknown among our neighbours for most of his adult life, she may not have asked any more of him than of herself.

The judgments we make depend largely on the way we view things in the first place. I used to think Mum's choice of a bead curtain, as expressing her ideal for our home, was some kind of lapse from native austerity. I now see it as an image of the essential woman: light-catching and frail.

Another fact which must be told in this history concerns Pa. After his name was cleared by the magisterial enquiry, and when scores of other suspects had all disproved allegations of guilt against them, an ugly determination arose in Cuttajo to find a scapegoat. I have already spoken of the Aboriginal tribe still haunting the hills hereabouts. Well, the rumour went that they had been interrupted in the middle of a heathen ceremony the previous day and had taken revenge. It was said that these people still initiated their young into savage practices they ought to have outgrown long years before, that they speared the occasional (always valuable) sheep for feasts culminating in weird cries and chants which they sent winding down the ravine toward civilization such as we knew it, unsettling our dogs to a frenzy of barking.

One autumn morning, mist stirring around the horse's hocks, Pa rode out on hearing that justice would at last be seen to be done. I followed him, as ever. He – whom these blacks had watched year after year setting up the Kilkenny frame for crucifying a Christmas pig – might now (had the news arrived in time for them to come down and stand invisible among the trees as only they know how) see him ride out on his kingly black stallion, towering above that rabble and their heat of justice – he who never spoke of the tribe his own father dispossessed unless to dismiss them as shiftless, made a speech fine enough to have belonged in *Lives of the Saints*. He (whom this journal might release from his vigil, while also granting his wife's shade the peace she vainly seeks behind cupboards, under tables, even on the far side of people's faces) floated on cloud through our gate, where PARADISE had been burnt in wood by young Daniel before joining the constabulary. His coat winged out on either side, the fortress of his great sadness thrown open to marauders, and the way to his soul stood for once unguarded.

'I am the one who bears the wound,' he asserted as he rode up out of the mist to block their furtherance with his determination. 'The wound is not yours but mine to bear. Though not an easy man to know, there is strength in my heart and my blood. My heart is strong. Harsh I have been, but never false. I can face the fact that you are doing this for me. I can face the insult of it and the kindness. We are not a thinking breed. But when we have nothing more than habit to support us, then the habit of peace is a treasure. I do not say we are bound to put some curb on ourselves when we feel we are doing what is right, I only say that a curb is something we understand, but knowing what is right is better left to God.'

His horse sidled a few steps and presented the other flank. His hand lay huge and reassuring on its neck as he faced them again, offering the left cheek.

'Are we to climb into hills,' he continued, 'where we have never set foot? Hasn't one Mystery been enough?'

He took off his tall hat and set it on the pommel between his thighs. The horse felt then, as animals will, what the moment of grace required, and stood steady as the dead, sensing the humiliator humiliated.

On that autumn morning, when Pa spoke of the wounds as his and claimed strength for his heart at the very moment of exposing its weakness; when he, our absolute dictator of what was right, surrendered this privilege to God, I knew how we had come to the pass we had. My throat betrayal-clogged, fury welled painfully through me.

I looked from one face to another, all complacent in stupidity, some from the stupidity of kindliness and some callous. How had they gathered, these fourteen riders riding here to assemble fourteen incompatible pasts, bringing fourteen lost boys scolded by fatuous wheedling forthright mothers, fourteen memories of fathers whom they might once have supposed rivalled mine in his special standing with the universe, two of whom I knew as active Federalists, six as Christians of our own ilk, the rest as Protestants, except one Jew who had no religion the way we understood religion, which is to say something separate from the rest of his humdrum life. I put the age of the youngest at nineteen and the oldest at sixty, so it was neither headstrong ambition nor world-bitterness that lured them. Their horses shuffled in a shifting clump, some passing behind others, some tugging at reins to investigate the road for fodder, some whisking flies or opening their lids to show each other dangerous sickles of their intentions, stamping, anxious to be off; the milder beasts meanwhile – hoping this inaction might promise a companionable walk back home to the fixed social priorities of a paddock properly fenced, and time for philosophy beyond the taint of usefulness – sagged on their fetlocks. What had brought such riders out in their horrifying ignorance? To look into their eyes was to see only contemptibly domestic issues, small worries, and capability cramped by lack of challenge. The men did not move, drifting among one another, their concentration never deflected from Pa. Only the horses moved, muffled drums trembling through haunches, manes shaking and the sky gauzed across their glossy vision.

Pa, with his iron grief, held the party of their retribution magnetized. Wrong as they were, they should have gone on; their self-esteem demanded that at least, none being man enough to actually think a matter through. I could not have conceived such timidity: this one a hoary freckled lad and famous still for pranks; this one, who became adult at twelve to fend for a family, and lost his high heart in the thicket of habitual bullying; this one, keeping to the rear, blank yet watchful under a broad-brimmed hat; this one smirking, already on his treadmill of excuses; the fellow with a pottery nose and cured leather cheeks, wire beard, sleeves pushed up from thick ropey forearms and from the curse of hands, thighs hardening and outsized genitals bagged in loose trousers, who must have felt all pleasure drain from expectation while his neighbours' resolve began to fail; this other, who went to Athens competing as a jumper in the first Olympic games for sixteen centuries, now facing a future of local adulation he need never do another thing to earn; this one charmed with lack of bloodlust, despair of his generations; this fat whiskered elder extracting pipe and tobacco pouch which, in itself, signalled that the business of arms had become a business of the intellect; this tough and handsome timber cutter scratching at his skull as if he might dig out an idea of his own; this clan of worriers, escapees from the routines they'd chained themselves to. Their lives hung round them, sloppy as old garments worn soft by work and threadbare, faded, and clotted with the muddy enterprise. Their little eyes shrank in caves, sly night creatures when it came to talk or thinking what was said; even their shuffling being done for them by horses knocking nerveless hooves together on the desolate ground. They had brought along the odours of shoddy shelters where they'd left anxious wives, the thinkers of the household, in doubt, and fiercely partisan youngsters; where the baby, silent at last after a night of squalling, sat agog at the event, storing impressions that would later fruit for harvesting in childhood as a crisis from which its sire might emerge heroic, and an ancient dusty waistcoat famous. Were these the very men who volunteered to hunt down the outlawed Ned Kelly, poachers on the estate of an indulgent judiciary, sniggering oafs who'd turn and fire the other way out of anarchist abandon for any whim, but never for an arguable reason well thought through? With their mixture of self-importance and cruelty, their lust for the hunt and the illegality of it, their salacious indulgence of collective irresponsibility, they watched Pa. Despite those tireless bodies you could see exhausted souls laid open – finning, suckling, soft mouthparts groping for some comfort to fasten on to, souls as fleshy nodules, primordial organisms in damp places. The parliament of horses nodded and took a step forward, sidled, or exchanged position, rumps brushing, warm nostrils scenting loss of action.

The men had eyes for no one but Pa. They did not understand

a word he said. He might as well have addressed them in Arabic. Their fine-tuned measure of power and its fluctuations buzzing alive as an electric charge, they waited only long enough to gauge which way the intuitions of chance would lead them, whether this meant more or less fun or none at all, and already casting in empty hollows of mind for the best tone – how far to contract the eyebrows for indicating decisiveness, an appropriate seat in the saddle for presenting themselves to their wives though unscathed and still untried – plus acknowledging that the future would in all probability grant few such chances. The fellow with the pottery nose, having watched Pa's mouth give out words, was first to look away, contemplating his own grainy forearms hard as logs, even the huge but sinking genitals: he saw only disappointment and thwarted plans, admitting there was nobody he could rely on. Thanks to their holier consciences, their scruples, their spouses, their respectability, their gutlessness (all these being obstacles won over in the festival of setting out from Cuttajo), they would turn back. He signalled his mount to move. And when he moved, so did they, their collective bullish bellicose intention fated to trot home to its stud paddock, too thickly encased in compact flesh to recognize such a backdown as craven.

Pa reviewed his victory. But I flamed at the disgrace, at his furling our standard and bundling away the pennants and favours of so many campaigns in order to plead with that rabble. How could he renounce the pride of our elite by showing his heart to cattle, offering them words he never offered us in all our faithful years – these locals whose tame superstitions had baffled even Father Gwilym's efforts to civilize them? Pa jammed his crown back on his head and faced me, perhaps for confirmation that he was in the right. I might have wept. This was worse than the rest. My disenchantment beyond concealing, he saw what he saw.

We rode home side by side, together and apart in our isolation.

Being drawn towards the shore by a force as invisible as willpower, Artie Earnshaw and I stood on deck among other diggers returning home via Sydney on the coastal steamer. We watched well-known headlands loom in their nether aspect of a seaman's view, and beyond them the radiant fields of wheat, the sunlit flocks of sheep. Engines beneath us thumping and pulsing, twin funnels spouted plumes to hang in the air above our laboured progress. A mat of soot sank, from time to time, to choke us, and then lifted its frayed feathers, hovering, a giant bird slightly beyond the steamer but always in reach. We watched Cuttajo wharf appear as a finger of civilization pointing out into Cuttajo Bay, and the closer we drew, the more inevitable the crowd of miniature colours clustered on its top and bottom tiers, sunlight streaming down to break as a surf of tiny white handkerchiefs waving. Beyond our powers of resistance, like some appallingly logical conclusion to the wildnerness of nightmare called France and Flanders, we had earned our homecoming – a lesson in the truth that one cannot escape one's origins, or even outgrow them. I nearly spoke of this to Artie, but caught his shining expression of a true victor in reach of laurels and a future full of luminous hopes.

'Home, eh?' I said.

He included me in the loving breadth of his smile, but could not find the voice to speak.

I hung over the side and watched the last fatal chasm of deep water slip harmlessly beneath us, our shadow forcing its cold blunt passage across submerged rocks, driving schools of fish before it, arriving like the carcase of some blind force washed in towards marvelling watchers, as incapable of not arriving as they were of fending it off, gliding, bumping, and swinging broadside to the wharf. Timbers yelped and groaned too late and a chuckle of water escaped among the pylons, wagging beards of weed. Only then did I look up, because I supposed I had to face my welcome.

On the top tier, just above head level, my reception party hovered over me in the full blaze of afternoon, all but Jeremiah leaning out from the rail, orifices gaping, dentures gnashing to chop the separate words of greeting into bleeding parts, hands open eager to acquire my head, to grasp the hair and drag me up among them or push me under. Voices tempting me in the laconic vernacular of Paradise, celebrating my survival even while I shrank from contact.

Then Artie slapped me on the shoulder and my vision jumped to the shaded lower tier, where his five youngsters (the eldest boy, who went to Melbourne to enlist, just as the war ended, had stayed there) and that nice placid wife watched him with adoring eyes already clouded by concern at what the closer focus showed them of the world he brought from places where they had been told our history was made. They were the ones I called hullo to. And, briefly, they were distracted from the shock of knowledge to wonder who I was.

The blind beast, lashed firmly fore and aft, strained against its bonds. That was the moment when, still gazing into dim recesses of the lower tier, with its slashes of brilliance slicing from between the decking above, I thought of Danny – Daniel junior, still back there, festering in a mass grave called duty, buried in trench-mud, mute and inglorious indeed, and I knew his death was meaningless. He had died so that the whole carnage itself might *remain* meaningless, he died to oblige the rich, to persuade all who knew him that the war had been personal. In this conspiracy, the gamblers did careful sums, no question about that, they multiplied our Danny by eight million dead and multiplied that by at least five relatives close enough to be persuaded. Forty million acceptances, they reckoned, ought to buffer them sufficiently from any irresponsible backlash, at least till next time. You could not argue with it. My brother's death alone made argument obscene. Only at that moment, already too late, I glanced up again towards the welcomers who had come to fetch me, finding myself channelled ashore by comrades and pushed straight into the clutches of Katie, who repelled me with kisses as if nothing had happened in my world which had not also happened in hers, and to Johnnie, clowning to hide his chagrin at not having had the guts to make it to the front before the whole adventure squealed to a halt. Unable to account for why I had returned at all, I took refuge in shaking hands with Jeremiah, already in his wheelchair and grown smaller, lighter – even his bones wasting away and soon to be not much thicker than my own.

'How are you, old son?' I said, and these were my first words to the family. The stroke, I saw immediately, had taught Jerry not to presume anything. Now we had at least this much understanding in common.

Polly was too busy with her Mack, also returning on that steamer, to spare me more than a passing fragment of her world as it flew apart:

'And what's more, I said to Mrs Halligan – you wouldn't know her, Patrick, she's new to the district, I hope your wounds are healed Pat, that's the spirit – the whole point is a question of the jam judge, I said, the jam has to be judged above suspicion, our good name depends upon it, but Mack it does, or we shall see the annual show go down the drain with so many others and this we must never . . .'

The blind beast had been unbound to sigh and sag away from the firm structure of our arrival, to drift bereft and used; so soon after rocking us in its care, so soon after being the extent and confinement of this life, so soon after delivering us to fate, it was seen to dwindle, to sail beyond reach, repelled with disturbing swiftness, reduced and vulnerable, an ugly little craft, unsafe, an impertinent object, an intruder on that glittering expanse – even its smoke smudge cleared away quickly and was lost. We were left with a blank of missing years. We would never retrieve what we had missed, or shed the burden of what we had done.

Between us and our youth yawned a ravine. (When I look again at the view from the high tip of that other ravine, far away beyond Michael and Norah's doll-like figures, hadn't there been another person also shading his eyes against the sun to watch me embrace Ellen, a dour witness scuffing among broken reeds lower down the creek, leaving unmistakable footprints? And yet, on second thought, mightn't the dourness itself be my habitual error in seeing only what I accepted as explicable? Mightn't he have turned to climb back through the fence, heavy with power, exultant that his plot worked so perfectly with only the slightest prod from himself in the timely refusal to accompany us? Even as he had leaned on the verandah rail, wearing an expression of hostile suspicion, making certain we saw him, had he been busy behind the mask, suppressing anxieties that we might prove fallible as usual and break, scattering like idiotic sheep to frustrate even the cleverest and most patient of shepherds?) I did, at length, face William.

To my surprise I knew, in that instant of acknowledging my eldest brother, what it felt like to confront the faceless men. All through the Great War we had sworn vengeance against them. Once we hid before the artillery onslaught and knew the enemy hid before ours in a stalemate none but a hero could fight free of, and then only in flashes of suicidal abandon, the whole conspiracy slotted into place. While German soldiers and Allied soldiers remained locked in helpless combat, brokers on both sides were free to go about their importances of angling, slipping into evening suits and complaining that the oysters tasted two days old, minds clear of distractions and exultant in this clarity, composing symphonies of pure mathematics.

Poor pathetic Willie did not appear to recognize me with any certainty, yet his eyes were surprised to a silver ripple of closing steel and glass.

How had I never recognized him as the new man, in tranquil offices, signing yet another promise with his executive pen, speaking by telephone or buzzing secretaries? I had been too much a creature of last century to guess that dominion was gone from such simplicities as clearing scrub and planting potatoes, from an empire of defeating sons, or even chaining them to the bed. Our worn-out heraldries had mouldered to a dumbshow of tatters; even the sewers of the defeated civilization were walled up – and price-tags dangled from sacred images. The new man did not go underground with silly Corporal Daniel Murphy, who would never be promoted and was lost as soon as mud clutched his knees and refused to let him stagger out lest whole communities might get the idea they could question why so many lives needed to be put to the bullet. The new man created a modern order out of nothing more than his lameness.

As for us, we never ceased to recall the recent past of slugging away with our rifles. Our ears were still clubbed numb, and our shoulders jolted. We never ceased to recall our jubilation when scoring a bull's-eye and watching a man fall, to know ours was the bullet that brought him down – do you think there was any difference between this jubilation and nausea?

Now the steamer had vanished, dragging its hot oil smell and the lingering throb of its heart. For a brief spell the shore-bound boots' surprised clatter also stilled. In this clearing air, a violin band could at last be heard on the fourth repeat of 'Land of Hope and Glory,' while surviving heroes clasped lovers and children in their arms. Barney hadn't gone to war, of course, so he made himself as scarce as he could – in those days he worked for Immanuel Moloch who became our first millionaire with an ice and refrigeration works – he only drove to the wharf to bring the old witch in her trap. So Catherine Byrne was there in all her glory to praise us for saving her from the Hun (even while she explained that her friend Miss Theuerkauf had suffered terribly, what with people being so suspicious, afraid they might lock her away in an internment camp), also to prophesy a new life about to begin for everyone in the district. 'Isn't that our dream?' she cried, 'A new life? Isn't that the future we have been hoping for? And it's thanks to you boys.' Yes, now and for a whole month, we could expect to be treated as heroes, till people lost the energy to pretend they knew what we had done.

Willie was the one who mattered. He took that terrible blow from Pa, which I saw as my oil-lamp flared in the wind of their passage, to teach the old man he should never completely lose himself in violence again. Without Willie, the rest of us may not have walked straight either. I accepted his hand and understood that this was why I chose to stay. This was the Ireland of my youthful captivity, which I, like Saint Patrick, must embrace again with the faith I had learned in France. I must at the same time love and defeat him. Pride gave me no choice.

Historical Note

In the cemetery at Gatton, in southern Queensland,
stands a monument:

IN MEMORY
OF
MICHAEL, Aged 29 Years.
NORAH, Aged 27 Years.
ELLEN, Aged 18 Years.
The dearly beloved children of
DANIEL and MARY MURPHY,
of Tenthill,
who were the victims of a horrible
tragedy perpetrated near Gatton
on December 26th, 1898.
REQUIESCANT IN PACE.
This Monument has been erected by public
subscription to the memory of the
above innocent victims.

The unsolved mystery of the Gatton murders has been carefully researched and written about in a book by James and Desmond Gibney, *The Gatton Mystery* (Angus & Robertson, 1977). For the purposes of my novel, I have used the actual names of the victims and their family; William McNeil, the butcher and husband of Polly Murphy; Sergeant Arrell; the government medical officer Dr von Lossberg; and the Brian Boru Hotel. The distances from the farm to the race meeting in one direction, and to the township in the other, are the same, as are the times involved in the crime, plus the testimony of witnesses who passed the victims' sulky on the road and heard screams in the night.

Details of the condition of the murdered bodies, where and how they were found, with feet pointing west, is as described on pages 3 and 5 of *The Gatton Mystery*; the account of the stranger at the sliprail is on page 70; the screams heard by Louisa Theuerkauf and Catherine Byrne on pages 77 and 78; and the newspaper headlines from the *Toowoomba Chronicle* of 29th December 1898 on page 2.

All else is my invention. The action has been transferred to a hypothetical farming district in New South Wales. The character of the persons involved, their physical appearance, the settings, conversations, motives, and confessions are fictitious.

Both *The Second Bridegroom* and *The Grisly Wife* are fictitious in their entirety.

R. H.

Barragga Bay, December 1993